# BOUGAINVILLEA EXILE

*Davies McGinnis*

*To Marlene, Eric + family with much love + thanks*

*Lyn*

*New Year 2017    Albuquerque.*

Copyright © 2016 Lynda M. McGinnis
All Rights Reserved

ISBN: 1539499294
ISBN 13: 9781539499299
Library of Congress Control Number: 2016917223
CreateSpace Independent Publishing Platform
North Charleston, South Carolina

# COLORS

Vancouver, 2004:

Greg might have painted the scene in front of her; the scene she saw from the long front window of the white wooden slat gallery situated in a remote corner of the marina. A touch of muted golden ochre would capture the sun's rays on the tips of the dark green evergreens. Indigo would be fine for the islands that just were emerging from the heavy veils of grey sea mist. One could almost smell the pine-scented breezes pushing those heavy mists out to sea. Greg had loved the onset of autumn. He had called the tossing leaves, 'Glazenov gay', and the first white snowflakes, 'Glazenov's harbingers', the deeper blue-black tones of on-coming winter.

Laura, arms wrapped around her to keep warm, and to stop her nerves getting the better of her, relived a 'memage', as Greg would have called it, of him perched on his swivel chair, bent over his slanted canvas, the air redolent of turpentine, as he put the finishing touches to creamy-grey swirls of clouds in the translucent sky. He'd bite his lower lip in concentration; his light brown hair tousled; the sky a reflection, in oils, of his blue-grey eyes.

She wished she were home, standing in his now empty studio out in the woods, sensing him there. She conjured up in her mind's eye, her memage, her younger self:

"Chai Wallah."

He'd swivel around, long fingers splayed out on his bony, olive-green corduroy-trousered knees; cheery in his red and brown check flannel shirt:

"That's my lovely girl-slave! Come kiss your master with those honeyed lips..."

They'd kissed, Vivaldi playing on the old gramophone in the background, and had forgotten the tea. The pale golden light of day had given way to scarlet and purple dusk, creating a surreal glow in the studio, a glow that had been mirrored in Greg's paintings.

"I love you my harem Lulabelle; my dark haired beauty with long, upturned, nut brown, laughing eyes," and he'd kissed each eyelid, "and perky, retroussé nose," and he'd kissed her nose - "retroussé," he'd murmured, kissing her neck, nuzzling on down..."

"Laura!" – the jolt of coming back to the present reality hurt – really hurt.

"Laura, are you alright?"

"Just wool-gathering, Wilby. You cut in on a rather tender memory there you know."

"Sorry dear, but it is time." Lord, hadn't he said that as the long black hearse bearing Greg's coffin had pulled up at the door? She'd been wool-gathering then too, to escape the finality of it all.

Wilby minced off, Ellen and Dora in flustered pursuit, papers cascading from nervous hands, eyeglasses askew.

"Open the doors, Ellen dear, do please do. Laura, don't worry. All will be well. Greg had a devoted following." Wilby paused, lowered his crinkly grey haired head, wrinkly blue eyes closed, as if in prayer. He took a deep breath and raised his head again, eyes open, and spread out his short, chubby arms to encompass all around him. He didn't say anything. He didn't have to. The paintings said it all. She smiled, suddenly recalling how Greg had called them 'painthings', when he'd struggled with a work.

"First exhibition without him, but you'll see, it will be fine. Look around you. Greg is with us. His poster art – it reflects almost a cult of escapism and joyful, vibrant color in a time of darkness and depression for so many. Such vivid portrayals of a better carefree world gave us hope in those hard times, and here in the inner gallery, Greg's real genius – brilliantly sensitive – reflecting his deep love for our rugged, beautiful country, where nature runs riot in all her faces and moods. No one could capture those faces and moods as intuitively as Greg.

Come, come now, let's get our notes together. All in the greeting you know – warm and welcoming, no condescension, no unwanted invasiveness. Let them be introspective. Let the paintings weave their magic on their imaginations…"

Wilby's practicality took an emotional stumble, his voice cracked, his eyes filled with tears. He shook himself, and bracing his rounded shoulders…

"Let Greg weave his spells. God bless him!"

The day had been very successful. They had sold many works, sold many parts of Greg's being, like a body and blood of Christ thing! When asked, she had given little verbal essays on his life that had related to the work in question:

"Yes, Greg did capture snowstorms so well that you feel the biting cold, the danger of becoming suffocated by the texture of a blizzard. Well, you see he had a special relationship with snow. Greg and I had been trapped in snowstorms in the Rockies many times. He always had known what to do." Laura let a secret smile hover over her lips for a moment, reliving those sensual moments, making love under blankets, honoring life in defiance of, or possibly in concert with, the storms that raged outside.

"Greg had loved horses, all animals. They had helped him so much in his life, with their hard work and devotion and courage.

Look at this one of a horse up to his knees in this weed-covered pond in the woods. The sun's light is muted by the evergreens. It is such a tranquil scene: the animal's fine head, soft black mane, strong muscled neck, lifted in silent appreciation of the pale green-tinted peace. See how the moisture in the deep brown eyes sparkles, making them seem so real.… and then this one of four bears, the berry juice dripping off their muzzles, congealed in their fur, the fur done in such detail, with hidden colors, not just shades of brown and black, but hidden blues, gold, reflected by that golden sunbeam that penetrates the stormy sky and forms a perfect rainbow through the branches of the evergreens, and all those colors of the forest and sky are in the color of the bears' fur - animals and habitat as one. You can sense the motion, strength and freedom"… and so on, and so on, until the blessed release of sunset over the darkening sound. This, a mixed blessing, for she had relived Greg's art and their life together in all those paintings, which had reflected his love of nature; no humans in those works. In his commissioned poster art, done to keep them housed and fed, and done so that he could afford to go out into the wilderness of the Rockies to capture his soul, he'd had to include humans: sunny, laughing, carefree humans out to savor nature for themselves, out for adventure and the chance to escape their mundane, often hard lives.

Wilby turned on the overhead strip lighting, much to Laura's chagrin. The crowd had dwindled to three or four people murmuring softly as they reflected on Greg's intentions, moving from painting to painting to prove their points.

We did it! You did it! You captured their imaginations again, made them see your Canada, you wizard of the paintbrush, you, Laura thought to herself. Now she was free to go home, back to their world, and re-run their old movie of a life. She'd make a mug of hot chocolate, add a tipple of rum, put out a plate of hot buttered scones, get the log fire going. Maudey would put her head on her lap, Catsby would curl up on the rug in front of the fire, and she'd sit and wait for the rum to kick in, to feel the warmth, and then… in he'd burst, smelling of turps, oil paints and pine, singing some aria or other at the top of his voice.

"Hey, Lally, tipple-time! C'mon gal, cosset your old man."

Before they'd stretch out on the soft old brown leather couch, wrapped around each other, the only light that of the dancing flames, Rory's books scattered over the low coffee table, he'd put on a record of Drax's nocturnes and, as she'd do that evening, they'd drift away… It hurt, this world without him, without all the old gang, talking, being so creative and exciting…

"Excuse me!" The young strident voice was like glass shattering in Laura's head. Reluctantly she returned to the here and now, and tried to replace angry resentment with charming interest. She turned to face a young woman, possibly early twenties, or late teens, baggy olive green slacks and jacket, hood up, scruffy backpack on her shoulder, figure hidden as well as if she were wearing a bourkha – a covering she'd no doubt sneer at on her Islamic sisters. She was short, about five feet two, pointed face, longish nose, tight mouth, demanding expression in her nondescript darkish eyes – no bright color anywhere – just olive drab. What was she doing here amid vibrant poster art of the late thirties and fifties? Escapism? Kids like her didn't need escapism. They wallowed in realism, confrontation and angst.

"How may I help you?" My, how old her voice sounded!

"You are the black haired girl in the posters, right – the artist's wife…er…?" she glanced down at Greg's biographical notes, "Laura?"

Laura sighed to herself, but smiled.

"I'm amazed you could tell. I was in my twenties then. I don't look anything like that now, and I'm not saying that to get any kind of response. It's just a fact… of life."

The girl smiled kindly, sympathetically, and her face suddenly took on a semblance of color – pale pink, some freckles, nose and mouth softened to prettiness and her eyes livened to green-grey.

"You seem happy with your age."

"Happy doesn't come near – let's say at peace with my age."

"And appearance?"

"Yep."

"That's great!" she replied, smiling broadly now – nice neat teeth. "You should be. You're okay for…" she glanced at her notes again, "eighty five?"

"Are you an artist?"

"No. I'm doing my doctorate in political science at the University of California, San Francisco."

"American?"

She nodded.

"Do you mind if I ask you who the blonde is with you in some of the travel posters? She seems to be the same blonde in that poster of a girl in a white dress, short blonde hair blown back off incredible cheekbones, sitting on a balustrade around the porch of a white cabin covered in red and purple bougainvillea, liver-spotted dog at her side, large marmalade colored cat sitting on the rail with her; mid-ground - brown earth, rows and rows of green vegetables; background - distant blue mountains, looks like the San Fernando Valley circa the thirties or forties. The reason I ask is, it looks like the setting in which my heroine, the subject of my thesis, was born, looks like her too. When you are together in the posters, you look like good friends. Wasn't a ménage a trois was it?" she smiled teasingly. Cheeky brat! Laura couldn't decide whether to smile suggestively, even wink conspiratorially, tease back, but keep tantalizingly mum. She decided to be truthful:

"No, not a ménage a trois, I'm afraid. We were good friends. Nessa was a wonderful girl."

The girl froze:

"This is amazing! So incredibly amazing! I thought she looked like her, but I didn't think she could be. I mean - all I've read about her – this travel poster model stuff is so out of character that I had to be mistaken. I thought that maybe Greg Macklin was trying to make the girl look like Marilyn Monroe or Lana Turner, Mandy Travis, you know, implying that, if one were to travel to Southern California, glamorous film stars were a dime a dozen, seen sitting on fences anywhere and everywhere, but she is her. Wow! How mind blowing!"

Laura's mind was blown away. What could this child of the new millennium know of Nessa?

"She is Nessa as in Nessa Eiles right?" the girl asked tentatively, yet with a soupçon of suppressed eagerness. "The Nessa Eiles who wrote those wonderful witty, pithy scripts for stars such as Fiona Kyrke, Sigi Andrus, even the sex goddesses, Mandy Travis and Alisyn Kendale? Wow! She gave them depth, layers, great insightful analyses of different sorts of women – almost analyses of the actresses themselves, that we have to wonder how much was make-believe, the role they had to play, and how much was based on their real lives?"

"Well, they were good friends, Nessa, Sigi, Fiona, Mandy, Alisyn and Lorna Trevelayan."

"God! Yes! Lorna Trevelayan too! Incredible scripts, when scripts and characters carried the movie, not special effects." - Laura saw shimmering silver. "Her women brought enlightenment to what it is to care." - Laura saw lavender. "They showed what mothers, lovers, wives could achieve, and should achieve.

Then there was the way Nessa took on the controllers like McCarthy and the god-awful ultra Right that smothered all enlightenment with their paranoia and parochialism, and continue to do so, taking America backwards not forward." - Laura saw a suffocating black.

"Are you a communist?"

"Hell no! You?"

Laura smiled.

"I don't have to be a communist to have a social conscience. I am a Canadian. We have a social conscience. We pull together to help all. You Americans run a welfare state for the wealthy only. Your rich guys have you whipped but good – but I bet you're wearing a Che Guevara T shirt under all that olive drab."

The girl laughed.

"No, but I have one at home." They shared a smile. "I can't be excited by something so paranoid and rigidly mind-dead as Communism, or selfish Capitalism. Oh God! How I long for something new and creative. Something just plain enlightened. We're trapped in a stale old world as far as ideas go." - Laura saw the color of stodgy pastry.

"Free spirit of the new technological age then?" - (white gold)

"Not quite that naïve. How did you and your husband become close with Nessa Eiles?"

Laura felt a laugh bubble up from deep inside – sheer joy for all the wonderful ways life creeps up on you. No matter how old or chilled the passage of time can make you, life was still full of surprises – feelings stirred by suddenly discovering something new in Greg's paintings, or Rory's words, or Drax's music and Nessa's plain-speaking wisdom. This girl here today, so out of time and place and character, or so it had seemed, and then so apt, so very apt, it hurt. The joy of being remembered, appreciated by the young, of having generational significance. It hurt like an ache of longing suddenly released, fulfilled, that brought tears to the eyes and a lump in the throat. It hurt like Drax's nocturnes, full of yearning, longing, pensive, ethereal, indigo. The music had such nuance of feeling that couldn't be felt in the chaotic, hectic light of day. It was like love blossoming under the caressing light of moonbeams, the gentle embrace of darkness that revealed pinpoint stars, which beckoned to lovers and adventurers alike, to all those nursing hopes of something beyond the present reality. It suggested a whole new cosmos of possibilities, in which dead and alive come together again in dreams and imaginings. They'd had to believe in such things as young lovers on the brink of war.

They'd had to believe that whatever happened, the moment of love could transcend it all and be somehow eternal. Such music Drax had composed for Nessa, the Nessa Eiles only he had known. The wonderfully sad compositions of love felt and lost in those complex webs of their times; webs woven to cruelly deceive and ensnare. Drax had become hopelessly, tragically entangled by that same web of honor/glory Nessa had warned about years ago in her high school valedictorian speech, before it had all started, before they all had to succumb to an evilly contrived reality's control - black lines tinged with blood red, filling up a pale green background of youth, and blanching it to white bone and grey ash nothingness.

Laura was taking her trip down memory lane that night, but not as she had planned. Instead, she found herself seated in a window booth of the crab shack with Gilly Toms, for that was the girl's name. Night had fallen over the cove. There was the regular tinkling of the boat and buoy bells, stirred by the breeze, and the waves foamed with a gentle whoosh, and ebbed quickly and quietly away. There they were, framed by the red and white check curtain that fringed the window: two women, one young, eagerly taking notes; the other of advanced years doing most of the talking; their eager faces aglow with candlelight from the little round jar on the table in front of them. The black wooden shack restaurant was busy that night, but the others were visible just as glowing pinpoints in the background, like stars in galaxies, each self-involved, yet also aware of one another across time and space.

# INFLUENCES

San Fernando Valley, Southern California, 1935:

Three white wooden cabins stood on the side of the long dirt road that cut its way through mile after mile, acre after acre, of neat rows of leafy green vegetables. There were two cabins on one side, and one on the other side of the road. The one that stood alone was shaded on one side by a big oak tree, and in the small fenced front yard stood a beautiful apple tree, heavy with fruit in the summer, laden with pinky white flowers in the spring and golden-red leaves in the fall. There was a porch on the front side of the cabin that faced north.

If you drove down the highway to the Los Angeles city limits at dawn, when the distant mountains were a paling indigo, and the far horizon was a vivid lime and blue line at the edge of navy blue night, in which the morning star hung like a diamond, you might catch a glimpse of a girl sitting on the wooden balustrade of the porch. You'd be going by too fast, even in those days – mid thirties – to be able to fully appreciate her beauty, but you'd get an inkling of it, and you'd smile and think to yourself, Wow, she was quite a looker! She might even occupy your thoughts for several seconds, maybe hours, maybe for the rest of your life – the what if, if only, parts of your life – for just one glimpse of Nessa Eiles could fill men's dreams for an eternity.

Before the tractors could stir up the brown dusty soil into the air, smudging the virgin blue with orange; before the smell of fertilizer and insecticide became too cloying, masking the subtle scents of lemons and orange blossom, Vanessa Eiles liked to sit on the porch rail, among the entwining purple and red bougainvillea, and watch the sun come up; Randy, the liver-spotted gun dog at her feet; Riley, the large marmalade cat, licking his paws on the rail beside her. This was Nessa's dreamtime and place, when her mind was in communion with that rapidly fading star.

The steady waves of immigration had changed Southern California to suit the notions of homelands left behind. Accompanying this influx of settlers, were the usual rabid bankers and businessmen, who grabbed up the available resources, and established their control through bully boys and the 'police', the law courts and newspapers.

So what is real democracy, other than the right to cheat and boss around one's fellow man? Nessa thought to herself by 'the dawn's early light'. FDR was changing things for the better, chipping away bit by bit at the heavy black miasma of the Depression and Drought that had descended on them all six years ago. It seemed like they had deserved it. People had spent frivolously, exploited the land ruthlessly. The Twenties had been a time of wild gaiety and laissez-faire economics, with no check or accountability, but then who could blame them after the horrendous abattoir that had been called, euphemistically, The Great War of 1914-1918? The Great Insanity would have been far more appropriate.

When many other girls of seventeen were dreaming of becoming famous movie stars, or of setting up home with boyfriends, or crushes, transformed in their imaginations into husbands, why was our Nessa, who truly had the potential to become a movie star and trophy wife, worrying so much about society's mores and mayhems?

Well – Nessa's grandfather, Magnus Eiles, had been driven off his land in the Owens River Valley by the big Los Angeles tycoons seeking water for the poorly irrigated lands in the San Fernando Valley, lands they had bought up at ridiculously low prices. They had cheated the farmers of Owens Valley into thinking their lands were being reclaimed to help out the water shortage in the city of Los Angeles, a shortage deliberately created by dumping water from the reservoirs. The business sponsors built an aqueduct that brought water only as far as their lands in the San Fernando Valley, and once these holdings were well irrigated, they sold off the land, for which they'd paid a pittance, at an amazingly high profit.

The Owens Valley farmers had not objected to giving up their lands for the city of Los Angeles, but they had protested angrily at being cheated out of their livelihoods to make the rich richer.

Resistors had blown up sections of the aqueduct in 1924, and Magnus Eiles had been one of them. They were arrested and indicted, and Magnus and the other resistors were sent to San Quentin prison. Thus their resistance movement was broken.

Nessa's father, Jeb, had been a young lad of eighteen when his family had been forced out of Owens Valley in 1910. Magnus, Jeb, Jeb's mother, Dagmar, and his sister, Lotte, had become farm hands for the wealthy landowners. This had put an end to Jeb's hopes of becoming a geologist. He'd have loved to have spent his days out there in the desert, studying the secrets of the harsh land in which Jeb saw only beauty, wild rugged beauty that needed to be understood, not exploited ruthlessly and selfishly. If Jeb were a vengeful sort, which he wasn't, he could have taken consolation in the fact that this was land that could fight back every now and again with a devastating ruthlessness of its own.

Sam Pritchard and Jeb Eiles had grown up together. They shared a deep love for Southern California, and wanted to maintain its natural resources, fauna and flora. This was a never-ending battle, as promoters, who wanted to attract more people to California, sold it as a sort of tropical paradise. One flowering plant introduced to achieve this effect was bougainvillea, which flourished, and quickly came to be associated with the beauty and charm of life in Southern California. In fact, it was bougainvillea, that the local librarian, one Loretta Pritchard Jones, cousin to Sam Pritchard, wanted to grow all over the mission-style building that housed the local library. This whim of hers brought Nessa into being so to speak.

Sam told Jeb what his cousin intended, and Jeb hastened over to the library to give the girl a piece of his mind. As he strode along the road, going over his point of view in his mind, and stirring up clouds of dust in his anger, he wrangled with the fact that Sam had held this cousin in high esteem. Jeb had never met her, but Sam had sung her praises non-stop. She was a beauty with a brain. She had returned from a school back east with all kinds of credentials. She spoke French and German, as well as her native Welsh. She had taught herself Spanish to help teach the farm hands' children. She had ideas for improving education, and bringing all sorts of political notions to the workers to help them get their just desserts. Her father, the fiery Welsh minister, Iorwerth Jones, was no doubt the influence behind all these notions. Iorwerth had taken on the tycoons many times. He'd been evident in all the labor disputes, arguing for workers' rights. Sam's editorials ran along similar lines. Both Iorwerth and Sam had been "visited" by the wealthy moguls' bully boys, but they'd had the workers to back them up. Jeb supported Iorwerth and Sam, but he was worried. It wouldn't be long before the "police" would follow up, and there was no way the workers could beat the "System". Given her family, what kind of modern female troublemaker was he on his way to combat now? Why couldn't she use native California flowers and plants?

The challenge never took place. Jeb, then twenty two, opened the door to the library, and there, sitting in a golden beam of afternoon light that was reflected in her strawberry blonde hair and her warm, welcoming smile, was the only girl to knock Jeb Eiles off his feet, and make him lose his heart in an instant.

The attraction was mutual, but the timing was not good. Loretta intended to complete her studies back east at the end of the summer, and Sam got Jeb all fired up about the war that had broken out in Europe. Iorwerth and Sam hoped that the war, instigated by the ruling classes, would backfire on them this time, and herald in much needed social reform. Sam was determined to join in the fray. He couldn't be a bystander. He had to be in on the chance to fight for freedom for the ordinary man. Sam convinced Jeb that, whether the men fighting were German, Russian, French or British, the ordinary men were united in their aim to change the old outdated social systems. In the case of the colonial peoples, forced into fighting for their European overlords, this war might help them re-gain their independence. The two champions of freedom and workers' rights packed up their kit bags and headed for Europe, a full three years before America entered the war.

They fought with the Canadians and British Expeditionary Forces, and experienced the horrors of trench warfare. Both young men witnessed the ruthless ineptitude of those directing the battle plans, the colossal waste of life just for the principle of the thing, just to maintain the wealth and power of the ruling classes, who were outdated in an industrial age that depended on workers. There would be no going back to those old unjust ways after such carnage. The weapons of the industrial age cut men down, nay minced them to bloody shreds, before they had a chance to fight. This should have been the war to end all wars.

The days of the Tsar and the Kaiser were doomed. British royalty had made the necessary adjustment by identifying with their people, and, as such, had garnered more love and trust, though their survival too would depend on recognizing workers' rights to a fairer deal.

One year after they had joined up, Sam and Jeb were at the bloodbath that was Ypres. They had the ill-fated distinction of being present on 22$^{nd}$ of April, 1915, when the Germans first employed chlorine and phosgene gases. These gases were colorless and odorless at first, so they went undetected until their effects had become lethal. The Allied forces had no protection from such weapons at that initial encounter. Sam almost died. He made a miraculous recovery, but his lungs were ruined. Jeb had his hip and leg shot to smithereens, but he thereby had avoided the gas attack. Both young men were invalided home by Christmas, 1915.

They refused to talk about their experiences, and so ravaged were they in body and spirit, that their families and friends did not press them.

"Just one look at them when they got off the train," said Iorwerth, "Was enough for us to see that they had suffered hell, and had witnessed first hand that man was no superior being, but capable of incredibly mindless evil."

Loretta had returned from her studies back east, and was teaching in the local school. She spent her free time sitting with Sam and Jeb on the porch of Sam's home. The men would just sit there, gazing off into the blue distance. She could tell they were re-living their experiences, and trying to come to terms with the horrors they had gone through. There were times when Sam could not breathe, and had to be hospitalized. The doctors marveled that he could breathe at all, but Sam was determined to live. He had articles he had to write. Loretta had the strong faith of her Welsh parents, but both she and her father, Iorwerth, did not press these young men to turn to God.

Agnes Pritchard Jones, Loretta's mother, had a beautiful alto singing voice. She had started a choir made up of workers from all backgrounds and creeds, and their families and children included. They sang their songs of hope and love every Sunday, gathered under the pepper trees, after their various religious services were over, or after mid-morning siesta, for those not religiously inclined. Jeb and Sam didn't go to chapel, but the sound of the singing that rose up into the piercingly blue sky reached deep into their ravaged souls.

It had been Easter Sunday that finally had done the trick. After all the church and chapel services had ended, Agnes had the people gather to sing the Hallelujah Chorus from Handel's Messiah. These were by no means professional singers, but the soul-deep bass of the older men provided the strength of will, the deep alto section of the women provided the loving support and resilience, the tenors and baritones had the tentative hint of hope, but it was the soaring heights reached by the voices of the young sopranos that pierced the clouds of earthly existence to break into realms of hopes realized, mysteries revealed. Then all voices were united in attaining a glimpse of those heavenly heights, the joy and wonder evident on all their faces. Sam and Jeb looked at each other, tears in their battle-worn eyes. There was hope for them. Not all men were evil. There was hope for a better life, and it lay in the hearts of ordinary folk the world over. It was in the hearts of people who understood and accepted the wonderfully unpredictable forces of this thing called life.

Loretta and Iorwerth saw the change in the two men when they returned from the singing, or Cymanfa Ganu, as the Welsh called it. It wasn't that they had found God or faith, but rather they had their faith in themselves, in their fellow beings, and in the beauty of life, restored.

"And that is more than enough," sighed Iorwerth, secretly giving thanks in his heart.

Loretta and Jeb were married by Iorwerth a month later. All the farmhands were in attendance. Vanessa Bronwen Eiles was born the following March 21st, 1917. Her brother, Robert (Bobby) Iorwerth Magnus Eiles was born June 24th, 1919.

Magnus had been a proud, independent pioneer of Norwegian (and some Scottish) stock. Dagmar, his wife, was of German heritage. The family had spoken these languages at home, while the grandparent generation had been alive, as well as their new language, English. Loretta's family language, spoken in their home, amongst themselves, was Welsh. Nessa and Bobby acquired these languages and many more, growing up with the children of the newly arrived immigrant workers from all over the world. Their grandmother, Agnes, told them to listen carefully to the music people made when they talked.

"Look at, and listen to, all these things around you," she'd added. "This music of communication is present also in the trees, plants, animals, rocks, clouds, breezes, movements of the waters and the stars, for we are connected by these rhythms, we are of them."

Jeb and Loretta had potluck evenings every Saturday night, when families got together, each wife bringing a pot of something or other. They'd all sit on Jeb's porch, by the light of Chinese lanterns, and sing to the strum of guitars, and talk, mainly about crops, about starting up their own farm on the slopes of the Sierra Madres. They would make the "System" work for them. They had adjusted and adapted, jumped through all the hoops. They had worked hard to realize the American Dream, and why shouldn't hard work be rewarded, not just corruption, greed and violence? They could make America a land of which to be proud.

Being a slave to the rich landowners had not sat well with Magnus. It had broken Jeb's heart to see his father in jail. Many had protested Magnus's incarceration, but to no avail. When Magnus was released, Jeb helped him overcome his feelings of helplessness by getting him to see that it was possible for them to get their own land again, not in Owens Valley, but in the foothills of the Sierra Madres.

Magnus Eiles became fired up with the idea of growing avocadoes, planting fruit trees and olive trees. He wanted to talk over the plan with his old friend, Mario Cipriani, who lived in the low-rent district in the flood path of the St Francis Dam in the Santa Clara Valley, where most of the families of the citrus workers lived.

The same profiteers, who had cheated Magnus out his holdings in the Owens Valley, were involved in the construction of the dam. They were well aware that there were structural weaknesses, but did nothing to remedy the situation. The dam gave, March 12, 1928, while Magnus was staying over with Mario and his family, and they, and many others were killed in the raging flood waters.

Two weeks later, Nessa's other grandfather, Iowerth Jones, was beaten to a pulp for attacking the negligent city bosses from his pulpit, and in Sam's newspaper. Sam was beaten up too. He survived by some lucky chance, but Iowerth was not so lucky. Every local farm hand and citrus worker attended his funeral, and even workers who had returned to Mexico came back to pay their respects to a man who had stood up for their rights. Afterwards, Agnes and Loretta took Iorwerth's's ashes back home to his beloved Cymru (Wales), to scatter over the craggy green hills that overlooked the ravaged mining valleys; ravaged to help create Britain's massive empire. Twelve years later, Loretta and Nessa would risk U-Boat infested seas to take Agnes's ashes back 'home' to the South Wales valleys, to be scattered over those same hills.

Nessa had loved her grandfathers, and these tragic experiences had a huge effect on the young girl's developing character and goals. Her Welsh grandfather would provide her powerful rhetoric and, along with her Norwegian grandfather, had handed on to her the determination to stand firm against all kinds of chicanery and corruption. From her Welsh grandmother, Agnes Pritchard-Jones,

Nessa had inherited her melodic, moving, strong contralto singing voice and her love of music, and from her German grandmother, Dagmar, she had inherited her looks: the prominent cheekbones, the tall, lithe physique, the blonde hair and blue-green eyes, that could be friendly, and could be daunting too, as cold and challenging as the Eiger. Her love of words came without a doubt from her mother and her Welsh side. Her ability to control her emotions and find a rational, adaptable solution came from her father.

Nessa's dawn reveries ended with Pop slamming the screen door behind him as he came out to lean against one of the verandah posts, coffee mug in one hand, the thumb of his free hand hooked in the pocket of his denim overalls, dusty slouch hat pushed back on his graying blond hair, coffee stains on his shaggy moustache. He scanned the far horizon, his blue eyes narrowed, lined, hardened by sun and wind, ruddy face burned into weathered crevices. He called back to Loretta, frying ham and eggs in the big old iron skillet,

"Flapjacks, if you have the time, hon."

Every morning Loretta found the time. There'd be a pot of honey on the large wooden table, honey taken from her beehive under the apple tree.

"Nessa baby, you up?"

Nessa exchanged a smile with her father,

"I'm up, Ma, and out here already."

Every morning the same, Ma just liked to perpetuate the idea of waking her, as she'd done when Nessa had been a child...and the working day would begin.

Jeb watched as the owner, W.L. O'Ruark, and his bankers disappeared in a cloud of brown dust. They sped off in O'Ruark's red and silver roadster, up the neat road that ran between the rows and rows of lettuce on one side and the lemon groves on the other. Long white fences separated the fields, groves and pastures from the road, with its trimmed grass border. Jeb stood, slouch hat in hand, in the grit and dust driveway to the brilliant white-painted stables. The main stable building was topped by a clock tower with brass racehorse weather vane, and behind the buildings were the verdant green pastures where O'Ruark's thoroughbreds took their ease, along with the ducks that enjoyed the pond under the giant oak tree.

Jeb slapped his hat against his thigh and turned back along the pepper tree shaded driveway to the wooden shack that served as his office. It was well concealed by trees, unlike the shiny glass and wood extravaganza that was the stable manager's, Jason Tremayne's, office, with its terracotta tiled floors, black leather couches, glass-topped desks and oak paneled walls. Jason emerged, three glamorous secretaries in tow, as Jeb approached.

"Ah Jeb," Jason scanned Jeb from dusty head to dusty foot. "I hope you understand Mr. O'Ruark's instructions."

"Yes, Jace, I do." Hick that I am, Jeb thought. He understood them better than Jace realized.

"Good man. See to it then." Off he went, a vision in shiny brown riding boots, tan jodhpurs, tweed jacket, brown polo neck cashmere sweater, thick chestnut brown hair shining in the sun, the reek of aftershave in his wake. Jeb smiled to himself, as if Jace worked that hard that he had to hide the smell of sweat. The girls, long-legged fillies, shiny long manes to cover all tastes, blonde, red and black, pranced along behind, nylons, high heels, tight skirts and form hugging sweaters in country colors. Hired for their brains, no doubt, Jeb smiled cynically to himself.

Did he understand O'Ruark's instructions? What a nerve! Oh, he understood them just fine. Get rid of the excess produce, create a shortage, raise the prices, same old, same old. He'd asked, not expecting permission, but he'd asked anyway, if he could give the excess to the farm hands. The produce was too good to throw into ditches to rot. There had been a resoundingly emphatic response in the negative.

"No, Jeb. You are missing the point."

No he hadn't. The farm hands could pay for the produce they had brought to fruition at the new hiked prices along with everyone else. No concessions would be made. After all, O'Ruark and his bankers had to make sizable profits to add to their already bulging coffers, didn't they? Where would the farm hands be if the owners weren't rich enough to create jobs for them? Where would the rich guys be if they didn't have workers to do the work for them? Well, thought Jeb to himself, we'll just have to keep putting a little something aside to buy our own small plot of land; form a little cooperative: him, Sam, Pedro, Tom Yellowhorse, Abe, Kurt and Jim Chang.

Jason Tremayne and his coterie of girls had passed Nessa as they'd sped up the country road in his shiny roadster. God! thought Jace to himself; Nessa put the others, including O'Ruark's daughters, with all their haute couture outfits, to shame. Nessa strode along on legs that didn't quit, towering over the other girls, high cheekbones tanned by the sun, short blonde hair tossed in the breeze, intelligent blue eyes, proud bearing, straight, slender build, walking as if she owned the place. She was seventeen, almost eighteen, but she had a look that ranged anywhere between eighteen and mid-thirties. She was so confident, so sophisticated, in white linen dress, white bobby sox and shoes, legs brown, arms brown, lips naturally pink, full lips. Every classy inch screamed breeding, wealth and privilege, and yet she was the farm manager's daughter, not that old Jeb and his still lovely Loretta weren't a class act, they were, annoyingly so. They were far more imposing in stature and appearance than old O'Ruark. They were more impressive in all ways than the O'Ruarks of this world. Sadly, Nessa had shown Jason that she had no time for him. She had looked at him as if she'd had a bad smell under her beautiful pert nose, as if he'd been a homeless bum, when he'd asked her for a date. In fact, and this was galling, she'd been far more friendly and kind to a homeless bum, when Jason had happened to see her talking to one some days after her rejection of him. Nessa had dismissed Jason and the girls with a curt wave of recognition. Her mind had been on a rather difficult calculus problem she'd been given for homework.

Dr. Steven Etchberry liked to give Nessa tough problems to solve. He loved the way her brain worked, so clear, so insightful. She was even brighter than Scott Freeman, the other student Etchberry liked to try to fox with difficult mathematical problems. Scott and Nessa were close friends, even dated, and they were vying that year for the title of class valedictorian. They both had outstanding grades in all subjects. They made teaching such a joy. Every student who worked hard to improve his or her knowledge was a joy, but with these two, who were often a step ahead of even him, Etchberry felt he'd been given a rare gift. Scott would be off to Caltech to study quantum physics. Caltech was not taking women, a great shame! Nessa had other plans in any case, not exactly ones of which Steven approved. Nessa wanted to be a writer, a screenwriter for Hollywood for goodness sake! What a waste of a fine brain! Nessa had plans to push her liberal views through the medium of movies. It would certainly bring them to the attention of more people of all kinds of backgrounds, but Steven felt that she'd be lucky if she would be allowed to express herself so freely, or if she'd be allowed to express her ideas at all. Hollywood was not exactly as liberal as Nessa liked to think it was.

Movies, like religions, were used to brainwash the people into thinking they were being cared for, that they were the heroes in life - pabulum really, to allay the people, not support them. The people could watch their favorite stars take on the system in their stead, a sort of substitute, so they didn't have to act to redress their wrongs. Movies and religions cared for them, God cared for them, so they didn't have to worry; so they had hardships, life was unfair, unjust, they were being bilked and abused, but in the long run they'd get their just desserts, either in Heaven, or like the heroes in the happy endings of the movies. Nessa hoped to wake up the people, make them think. Well, she had her job cut out for her there. Many of the ones she hoped to reach were too ill informed, too badly educated to think effectively. The powers that be saw to that. Steven already felt the sadness, the emptiness, of losing such a fine mind as Nessa Eiles', but he'd join Jeb, Loretta, Sam and the others in eagerly following her progress through life, for as long as life was granted to him.

When Jeb arrived home, Loretta told him that Nessa had Debating Society, and she'd be home later, so he could wait for dinner and have it with Ness, or he could have it then. Jeb said he'd wait. Bobby worked after school with the duster pilots, learning how to repair their planes. He stayed and ate with them, and sometimes bunked down with his precious planes as well.

"Only time we have altogether, Loretta. Let's not waste it. Each moment is precious now. Once Nessa goes to Occidental, it'll be the four of us, you, me, old Randy and Riley."

"That a bad thing, Jeb – being left with the dog, the cat and me?"

"No, Loretta. Lord, no! Looking forward to it." He grabbed her around her thin waist, nuzzled her lovely neck.

"Now you stop that, Jeb. It isn't decent this time of day."

Jeb leered,

"You didn't mind before the kids came along, as I recall."

Loretta smacked his arm and laughed, blushing to the roots of her blush blonde hair.

"Well, not now, Jeb. Ness may finish early."

He let her go, giving her a gentle tap on her backside.

"Ah, go on with you, woman. I'm too hungry in any case, waiting on all you women."

"All two of us?"

"Yep, you both keep me in my place right well."

She grabbed his tawny head and kissed him full on his lips.

"We love you, Jeb Eiles, so very, very much."

"Well, it is returned in full, my love."

Loretta returned to her cooking – beef chippings, potatoes topped with chives and butter, and a salad.

"How did the meeting with O'Ruark and the bankers go?"

Jeb grunted,

"Usual scams I feared they'd pull, Loretta. I may just risk it, and give the excess produce to the guys. Well, what I can get away with that is."

"Have they got guards?"

"Oh sure, but we're a pretty sly, light fingered lot, Tom, Pedro, Jim, Abe, Kurt and me. We'll get some by them okay."

"You'll lose your jobs if you're caught. They've all got young kids to feed and get started in life, except for Pedro and Abe."

"So what! O'Ruark will never find the secrets we guys got for getting the best out of those old lettuce plants and fruit trees."

"You've got magic hands, Jeb."

Jeb lowered his specs and leered at her.

"Now you cut that out, Jeb Eiles, or I may think you're not the gentleman I took you for when I married you…"

"Almost twenty years ago! My how time does fly by?"

They shared a quiet smile.

"Besides," Jeb said, shuffling the pages of Sam's newspaper, "I think we've got enough laid by to buy our own few acres up on the slopes of the Sierra Madres. Get it up and going."

"Sounds great, Jeb – you guys go ahead and do it. Nessa's education is covered. She's earned a bit from her writings for the Atlantic Monthly and for Sam. If you think the time is right to make a go of it, you do it."

Jeb went out to check on his green beans, while she made her salad dressing. Old Sol Matthews was going by along the road. He stopped and leaned over the fence. They talked about the state of things for a few minutes, then Sol asked,

"What old Ness plan to do then, Jeb? Man, she can go far, looks, brains like she got – Doctor? Lawyer? What you reckon?"

"Movie writer."

"Ah no! C'mon, Jeb. She's way better than that!"

"I told her," Jeb replied, shaking his head. "She'll just be a puppet for those rich movie guys. They'll never value her mind – let her use her brains, but she thinks she can pick her own work, maybe even direct her own stuff. They won't let a woman do that, and a lefty at that."

"Where'd she get those lefty notions, Jeb?"

"Well she reads a lot, reads this stuff to Loretta and me. She agrees with it all, and I guess Loretta and I do too. Times are okay now, but those rich guys still work us into our graves, and the owners and their slick city lawyers and bankers, well, they just pile on the problems. They certainly don't try to ease them much."

"Nessa'll convince them otherwise?"

Old Sol pulled off his dusty hat, slapped it against his leg, scratched his balding white-haired head, grey eyes reddened by wind-borne insecticide,

"Well good luck to her, more power to her I say. Yep, God bless the little filly. She's got her work cut out for her. Night, Jeb."

"Night, Sol."

Sol sauntered on down the dusty road, legs bowed, feet in his old weathered cowboy boots turned on their outer sides. Jeb was just about to turn back to the house, when he heard a truck approaching, horn blaring away. He was blinded by the bright headlights as it ground and shuddered to a stop by the gate.

"Hey, Pops!"

Nessa jumped out of the cab of the truck, Scott smiling at the wheel, the bed of the truck full of high school seniors, who yelled and waved as Scott tugged at the gears and zoomed off in a cloud of dust, grit and yells of goodnight. Nessa waved them off, and made her way over the gravel tracks to slip her hand into her father's. She nestled her blonde hair into the side of his neck.

"Watcha, Pops, how's it going?"

"Bah," he said, tousling her curls with his gnarled fingers. "Good day?"

"So, so."

They opened the screen door. Randy pushed them aside to enter first, tail wagging fit to bust.

"Yah mad dog! Where you bin hiding?" Jeb growled. Ness knelt to rub the dog's ears. The dog drooled and licked her face.

"Where have you been? Dinner's getting cold," Loretta served up the baked potatoes. "Come and get it!"

Nessa and Jeb pulled up the rickety chairs, more than a hundred years old, brought from Wales by Loretta's parents. Loretta nudged Randy aside to take her seat. The dog laid his head on the table, nose and tongue level with the food. Loretta pushed his head away, then ruffled his ears and slipped him some meat chippings she'd hidden in her hand.

"Worst spoiled dog there is", grumbled Jeb, lovingly.

"Here you 'ol lazy hound," and Nessa slipped him some meat off her plate.

"Don't know his place."

"Sure he does, Jeb. He's family, and he knows it," laughed Loretta. "Know it, don't ya boy?"

"Swear he's smiling, Ma."

"Sure he is, honey – aren't you Randy? Big 'ol smile."

"Everything okay, Pops?"

Grunt, "Guess."

"City guys bug you?"

"Nope, no different from how they always are."

"I get it, same old, same old."

Grunt, "These are better times though, Ness – much better, except for those damn Japanese and that nutcase, Hitler, stirring up the pot of war again, and Bobby raring to go."

"War, if it comes, will level the playing field some more, Pops, it has to."

"Yeah? Well, we'll see. War heaps on the problems, especially afterwards, when the boys come home hurt in body, mind and soul. War doesn't solve anything. It is a sad and evil solution to the world's problems."

Loretta had gone quiet. She gathered up the dishes and popped them in the hot soapy water in the kitchen sink. She stood there, holding her hands over her eyes. Jeb and Nessa exchanged guilty glances. Nessa scraped back her chair and got up and put her arms around her mother.

"Sorry, Ma. Maybe there'll be no war for us this time. There is the League of Nations and the Kellogg-Briand Pact that has outlawed war. Bobby'll be okay. Now stop your fretting."

Jeb got up and turned Loretta into his arms. Loretta sobbed, her shoulders heaving. Nessa picked up her coffee mug, sat back at the table, and kept her thoughts to herself.

Bobby wanted to be a flyer, but so far all he could manage was to be volunteer help for the ground maintenance crew of the "Dusters". He loved planes, God, did he ever? He couldn't afford lessons, but he'd learned a lot from those Duster boys, and he had all the technical, mechanical know-how down pat – knew planes inside out, upside down and straight on. His chance to become a pilot would come if war did break out. Bobby longed to be a pilot on aircraft carriers. He loved the challenge that offered.

"Now, Ma, don't worry. They'll keep Bobby States side to fix planes." Nessa stood up and took her empty mug to the sink, washed it and grabbed a dishtowel to dry it, as Pops was doing already with the dinner dishes. Loretta sniffed, her hands plunged into the soapy water, sleeves of her navy frock with white polka dots rolled up, white apron wet with spill over. She raised her beautiful watery green blue eyes to look at Nessa, and gave her a weak smile.

"Sure, honey – let's look on the sunny side." She raised a soapy red hand to tidy a stray lock of her hair, pushing it back behind her ear.

"Need to pen up the chickens."

"I'll do it, Ma."

"Thanks, honey. Put on the radio Jeb. Let's hear the news."

Loretta and Jeb sat in their deep cracked leather armchairs around the small potbelly stove. Jeb lit his pipe and reached for the newspaper – Sam's newspaper - for real news, not the corrupt versions put out in newspapers owned by those profiteers. Loretta reached for her knitting – green sweater for Bobby, which would go well with his red hair and green eyes - and turned on the radio. Nessa smiled to herself as, with Randy in tow, she closed up the chickens in their pen for the night, and then sat on the porch steps, stargazing. She draped an arm over the dog's back. The bougainvillea rustled, and out came Riley to rub against her leg. She tickled his ears and stroked him from head to tail. He arched his back in ecstasy and took up his place on the step, licking his paws.

"Look at those stars fellas. My oh my!" No, whatever the force was that created existence, it wasn't for man alone, and it was man who created his god in his image and not vice versa. She looked at Randy and Riley in turn.

"Sure hope you guys have a better notion of what's what."

Randy licked her hand. Riley watched her with half shut inscrutable eyes that held a hint of a deeper wisdom.

"I've got to put the finishing touches to my speech, just in case I'm Valedictorian, but I sure hope Scott gets it."

Lord above, how many of her senior class, like Scott, may be off to war? What a rotten waste, generation after generation! Poor old Pops still suffered pain from his hip injury in the last one. Sam's lungs were corroded, and his and Jeb's dreams more often than not, nightmares. The strong men they saw by day belied the men too terrified to fall asleep at night.

She thought of the guys she'd dated, Scott being her main date, going off to war. She'd enjoyed the romance, holding hands in the movies, strolling home afterwards, kissing under the oak tree. She had preferred to date casually though, finding more excitement and fulfillment in her books, being home listening to the radio with Ma and Pops, taking part in their "pot luck" get-togethers with their friends, listening to their views on life, and especially those of Sam. Mr Etchberry had insightful ideas too. He'd joined them for a few soirees - good teacher, good man, Mr. Etchberry. Yep, those evenings had been fun. She'd miss them all.

---

Graduation Day: 1935:
Jeb looked around. All the families were bristling with pride. They were all dressed in their best bib and tucker, happy smiles on their faces. This was a big day for them. Some of them had worked hard to give their children this step up in life. It's what unselfish parents did, as had their parents before them, unto countless generations. The youngsters graduating today stood on the shoulders and backs of all those who had come before them, one layer more up towards the sun. Many youngsters had to do it alone. There was young Pete Hall, father and mother alcoholics, but he'd been made of stronger stuff, and Mary Watson, father dead, mother sick, she'd done it for them, working hard to support her mother and herself while going through school. Many had social stigmas, racial bigotry and class prejudices to overcome, and they had. God bless them! Yep, Jeb had got quite choked up already, and the youngsters had yet to march in, their faces aglow, wreathed in wide smiles, shoulders braced, heads held up with the pride of achievement. They wouldn't be able to resist the - I did it-I did it-we did it - grins and waves at their families, who, eyes full of tears of love and pride, waved wildly

back. Oh dear God, here they come, all stand. God, where was his handkerchief? Loretta had tears in her wonderful eyes already. The orchestra began those stately grand old plodding notes that pulled at the heartstrings. Oh my goodness, there they are, all in black gowns over smart suits, summer dresses, black caps with silver and navy tassels…and there she was, tall, taller than most of the others, golden and straight, smiling at them, waving at them, and all he could do was choke on tears of pride and love so deep. He smiled back shyly. Loretta waved, but was choking on her tears too. Nessa looked at them, smiled softly, and he saw her eyes tear up. Well darn it, all the folks were in tears, their graduating kids too. He put his hand on Sam's shoulder. Sam was there for Pete Hall, and he'd managed to get Pete's parents sobered up for the event, and right proud they looked, and so did Pete; and Mary's mom, in her wheelchair, with a nurse at her side, and Mary too, looking very pretty.

The ceremony went well. Then it was time for the Valedictorian's speech. The Principal, Ed McGowan, explained that they had two excellent students with perfect grade scores. He had asked them both to speak: Scott Freeman went first. Scott spoke well, about the promising careers in science and technology, and how scientific and technological advancements would make for a better world for everyone, make the world a smaller place, make communications easier, and that these developments in our knowledge of our society and other societies world wide might make wars obsolete. Science might even warn us ahead of time of deadly earthquakes, such as the one on March 10, 1933, that destroyed much of downtown Los Angeles. He hoped that with the fine education they had received, all the graduating class would be assets to their communities and their country, and would be sources of enlightenment and hope for a better world.

It was Nessa's turn. She approached the podium, her height and demeanor impressive. Silence fell. She took a moment to scan the crowd, fix them with a look of determination, with even a hint of a challenge. Jeb felt a momentary qualm, and Loretta also glanced anxiously at him.

Nessa began by thanking all the people who helped to run the school so well. She thanked all the teachers, especially Mr. Etchberry. She thanked all the families and friends who supported the students, including her own, and then:

"To my graduating class, I want to say thank you for making school fun, for letting me learn from you all, share your youth, your troubles, your laughter and achievements, your wisdom and kindness and understanding. You are a special breed, and as you go out into the world, I can only feel reassurance and increased hope for humanity and all life.

There is, however, a source of danger that has faced generations before ours, and will no doubt be facing us soon. I speak of an entity called Honor Glory. For some it is a male entity, for others, a female temptress, whichever it is, it takes lives. It destroys our values, replacing loved ones and a sense of morality and ethics with a folded flag. We love the flag, but before we die, or give up our peace of mind for it, we need to make the distinction between the flag, our love for our country and the feelings we have for our leaders. Our governments are not synonymous with our flag and love for country. Some countries have great difficulty separating the two, and this leads to people committing horrible crimes against life for evil men who happen to form their governments. It takes a brave soul to stand up to such men, for he or she faces the stigma of being a traitor, but it is better to betray evil, than work for it and betray one's own soul, one's own humanity in so doing. We are fortunate to have good men leading us at this present time. I like to think they reflect the goodness in us, like cream rising to the top, but we must be ever vigilant, for some wealthy people fear ideas that suggest that wealth should be shared, and they fear us, as well. These men fear communism more than fascism, but I do not think we, as a people, would like either of these controlling ideologies.

We value our individual liberties. It is the greatest crime a government can commit, to not trust in its people, but to try to think for them, control them, keep them down.

I know that war is looming, but it is not provoked by us, but by mad men for whom life has little value, and for whom ideas, twisted ideas, their ideas, take precedence over the lives of others, even their own people. When politicians and religious leaders go this route, bloodshed is the result, and Honor Glory is their rallying cry.

Before you parents, like countless generations of parents before you, offer up your young for a nation, a flag, you need to be absolutely sure we fight and sacrifice for a government that has our welfare at heart, that trusts in us. We must not be exploited through our patriotism. We must be sure that we are not being hypnotized, blinded by Honor Glory, but that we are sacrificing ourselves, our youth, our loved ones, for a better world for all people, all life, not just our own.

I just want to say in closing that my friends here, and our families and our school, have helped us to make these important distinctions, and hopefully instilled in us the courage, wisdom and know-how to act on them. Thank you all from the depth of my being. Go and live a good life. Realize your dreams and goals, and retain a social conscience for others, that they may realize their dreams too. Do not fear one another, but trust in one another. We must not be afraid. We must have personal goals that fulfill us in body, mind and soul, and not be driven by goals based wholly and totally on money and power over others. We should not assert our will, but reach a compromise and cooperate with others. We can all live comfortably and attain our dreams, even those of becoming the President of this country, without the need to acquire vast, outrageous fortunes. Money should not drive our elections or determine our political candidates. We should all have an equal chance in all things. God bless our President, and help him in the difficult years ahead, and God bless you all as you set out on the often treacherous and confusing road that is life.

Nessa's speech was followed by a long silence as people waited to see how others would react. The principal, staff and board members sitting on the dais shifted uneasily. Then Jeb, Loretta, Bobbie, Sam and Steven Etchberry, who was the only one on the dais to do so, stood as one and began to applaud. Pedro, Abe, Jim, Tom and Kurt stood only a second later and joined in, followed seconds later by their children and grandchildren, who were graduating that day, and a little later by the rest of their families. Scott Freeman, among the graduating students, had been the only one to stand and applaud the same time as Jeb, Loretta, Bobby, Sam and Steven. The rest of the crowd stood and applauded, smiles on their faces, and then the Principal and staff joined in. A small group sat with serious expressions on their faces, and did not applaud. Yep, they were those of the rich establishment, who detested FDR and all his social programs. Some military families remained seated, certainly not all of them. Maybe those who remained seated were the realists in the crowd that day, but they offered no hope for enlightenment. They personified the fear we had to fear. Nessa had resumed her seat, her head held high. It hadn't mattered to her one bit how her speech had gone over. To her way of thinking, it had to be said.

Unbeknownst to Nessa, she was being watched intently by three men standing far back from the proceedings, in the shadows of the trees. The oldest of the three was a tall gentleman, late sixties, scholarly stoop; white curling hair hidden by a dove grey fedora with a black band. He wore a light grey suit with waistcoat, white shirt and dark grey tie. He was expensively attired, but wore his clothes in the relaxed way of academics. Behind his wire-rimmed glasses, his blue eyes held a smile, a kind smile. His companions were much younger, in their mid-to-late twenties. They wore navy blue summer blazers, tan slacks, shirts open at the collar, no ties.

One of the young men had black hair, wide angular face, deep brown eyes, and a more intense expression than either of his companions. The other young man had a light and affable expression, a friendlier, more relaxed face altogether. He had light brown curly hair, cut close to his head and clear blue eyes. They had come at the request of a friend of theirs. He had suggested that they might find someone of interest to their concern, a promising new recruit for their nascent intelligence service, still only in the discussion phase, and in no way realized, but which would be of crucial importance if war did break out.

The elderly gentleman was a doctor of medicine, a wealthy philanthropist, both in the States and in his native land of Germany. He was a Jew, who had escaped the Nazi Reich, and had come to America with his beautiful wife, an accomplished pianist and artist of some renown. They were connected with the German Anti-Nazi resistance movement, and helped refugees fleeing Europe to get settled in the States. Their names were Emil and Magda Franz.

The two young men worked with Emil to set up spy rings in Europe and the Far East before war erupted in those areas, though the friendly-faced Kerr Toddy had been involved already in the fight against the Japanese in Manchuria. His engineering skills had been put to use to help the Chinese build up their defenses. The other young man had studied medicine, neurology, at Harvard, and now was a colleague of Emil's in Los Angeles. He was going to Europe to work with Emil's friends in the anti-Nazi underground; see the lay of the land, so to speak, should there be a war. His name was Dr. Ben Robie.

As they watched the closing ceremony, another tall rangy fellow walked across the lawn towards them. He had a long, craggy face, broad smile, narrow brown eyes, kind and intelligent eyes. He had a difficult task ahead of him. He was to monitor potential supporters of the Nazis within the States, especially certain armaments dealers and their political stooges, who got rich off war, who did not have the nation's interest at heart; in fact no nation's interest at heart. They didn't have nations, only customers. It would take a brave man, who would have to make extreme sacrifices to maintain his hidden agenda, to take on this cabal of war mongers, with networks made up of the more evil wealthy and powerful throughout the world. This brave man with Emil, Ben and Kerr that day was one Biff Chatsle from the Pacific Northwest. Their fifth man, who had invited them there, was none other than Professor Steven Etchberry, British by descent, with strong ties to British Secret Intelligence Services through their Government Code & Cypher School.

———

Hollywood: 1939:
Nessa's four years at Occidental passed quickly. She'd maintained straight A's and had been, again, Student Representative of her graduating class, this time she didn't have any really close contenders for the position. Nessa had developed a writing style which was pithy, concise, her own. She avoided the dead pan, cynical delivery, then so popular among leftist writers, and tried a more challengingly optimistic approach.

Europe was at war, despite "Peace Weeks", "Peace Movements". The Nazi-Soviet Pact had fired up the extreme Right in America again, and a witch-hunt was on for those who were card-carrying communists, and those with leftist tendencies. This showed a distinct lack of trust in the American people and their ability to think for themselves, or were the extreme Right afraid of Americans thinking things out for themselves? The people certainly had a lot of proof in their history of the abuse and chicanery on the part of certain among the wealthy and powerful to think on.

FDR had endorsed unions and guilds, and had government programs that supported the arts in these difficult times, but violent conflicts still arose between workers and some companies that resisted workers having any kind of rights and representation. It was such unenlightened management and owners who resorted to violence first. In 1937, Chicago police attacked workers and their families holding a peaceful picnic protest outside the Republic Steel Mills. Twelve protesters were killed. Senate hearings did little to punish the police actions.

On the other hand, even though the union movements were created to support the workingman, and were achieving much needed reforms in certain areas, gangster elements sensed new prey to be exploited, and ill-gotten gains to be made. They infiltrated the unions, not to bully the bosses, but to bully the workers into adopting the union line, and forcing them to pay for the gangster brand of 'protection'. The ordinary hard-working Joe was beset, as usual, with taking hits from both ends of the social spectrum: from wealthy exploiters and their private bully boys and 'police', and the ever-circling predators of the criminal element, ready to exploit any and every opportunity that arose for their own nefarious purposes. It was not an unusual occurrence either, for some amongst the wealthy and the gangsters to join forces, seeing that their goals were similar – to get rich, and stay rich, off the backs of others.

Nessa had not felt betrayed by Stalin's pact with Hitler. She saw them as evil twins, brutal dictators who were hell and gone from the socialism they purported to uphold. In fact, with their iron-fisted control, they resembled the systems they had replaced.

Nessa and Scott had kept up a sort of romance, but before he went off to join the navy, he confessed to Nessa that there was a girl, a fellow mathematician, herself in naval intelligence, who had taken a shine to him, and if Nessa was not interested in him in the long term, that is if she wouldn't marry him, then he'd like to date this girl. Nessa had hugged him, and told him that she would have a special love for him always, but she did not want to marry him. She was not sure that she ever wanted to marry. She couldn't put her own ambitions on the back burner for anyone. They had parted amicably enough, wishing each other much happiness and fulfillment in life. Nessa had felt a dull ache in her heart as she'd watched Scott walk away from her life that night. She hoped that, if America did go to war, he'd stay safe.

The studio security officer watched the tall, stunning blonde stride down the sidewalk towards the big gate. Here comes another hopeful, he thought, although this one certainly had potential, but she wasn't getting by him unless she had a pass. He'd stood firm and turned away lots of wannabes who'd taken the chance to turn up on spec, portfolios under their arms, full of cheeky hauteur and pizzazz, like this one coming along now, but then again, she wasn't putting on any of that kind of an act. She looked like she had a genuine reason to be there. Still, he wasn't going to be fooled.

She approached and smiled. Lovely white teeth, suntanned face, drop dead gorgeous looks, natural blonde, he bet; deep blue eyes, nice and friendly, and boy, was she tall, could look him straight in the eye, and he was a six footer. He scanned the male stars quickly through his mind's eye, and she didn't stand a chance, she'd be taller than all of them, except Mr. Cooper, maybe.

"You're too tall, girlie. Scram."

She smiled, shook her head and handed him a pass. She grinned, raised her eyebrows in victory, and sauntered on by. Could you beat that? He shook his head, smiling the while. Well good luck to her, he thought. She had all the other girls beat in the looks department. Maybe they'd make the guys stand on boxes, unseen by the cameras of course. He sniggered. All's fair and possible in fantasyland.

Nessa was directed by a passing 'gofer' lad to a white stucco building with a red tile roof. The paintwork had seen better days. The offices, hidden behind brown shuttered windows, formed a horseshoe shape around a dried up fountain full of dead leaves and bougainvillea blossoms. She looked at the numbers on the solid brown doors, and realized that the room she wanted was on the upper level. Nessa climbed the worn wooden stairs. A few straggly bougainvillea vines encircled the covered balcony. She stopped outside room 21, and smoothed her white linen dress with her white gloved hands, straightened her pert white beret, checked the seams of her nylons were straight, and that there was no grass on the heels of her white high-heeled sandals. She opened her small strapless handbag, checked her face in the mirror on the over flap, took out her pink lipstick and applied a fresh coat to her lips, rubbed them together, and rolled her tongue over her teeth, then checked that there was no residual lipstick on them. She braced her shoulders and knocked firmly at the door. She wrinkled her nose at the smell of stale cat urine and decayed vegetation. She waited a few moments, then knocked sharply again. This time a chorus of male voices shouted,

"Go away!"

Nessa smiled and opened the door. Three faces looked up at her through heavy cigarette haze, cigarettes dangling from their opened mouths. They soon recovered from the surprise of seeing such a vision on their doorstep.

"You hard of hearing? We said scram!"

She saw before her three men in their late forties, maybe early fifties, grey-haired, bespectacled, shirt sleeves rolled up to the elbow, baggy grey trousers, ties stained and pulled down and loosened, fingers stained with typing ribbon ink. The air in the cramped room smelt of cigarette smoke mixed with the aroma of strong coffee and greasy spaghetti and meat sauce.

"What have we here?" said a craggy, long-faced guy, with close cropped grey hair, who would have been good-looking in his youth; in fact, he had a strange sort of run-down intellectual charm about him even now, tall, long legs up on his paper strewn desk top.

"I am your three o'clock appointment, Miss Vanessa Eiles? Here about the assistant screenwriter position?" She looked hopeful, pushing bells!

"Nope, don't recall no Miss Eiles."

"You, Mr. Henderson?"

He scratched his long sun burnt neck, grimaced and pointed to a chubby fellow, dark curly hair streaked with grey, small rounded cherubic facial features, dark eyes. This man, supposedly Mr. Henderson, stared at her, mouth open,

"Oh Lord! You're that college kid, who wrote that great piece in the Atlantic Monthly. I thought it struck just the right note for what we're writing now for Capra." He explained for the benefit of the other two. "I asked you to come for an interview didn't I? Well, here's the deal. I thought we needed an assistant, but there are no funds, so sorry. Still draw up a chair. I'd like to pick your brains on that piece you wrote. I've got it here somewhere in this pile."

"No you don't Harry. You gave it to me to read the other day," said the tall, craggily handsome one. "It's pretty good, Miss... er, Eiles?" She nodded her thanks.

"Well join us then, Pete. Let's all get in on this. Duff, you too, come on."

"What if Buckley comes back?" asked a nervous little man, bald, rim of blond hair, pugnacious little face, thin lips, almost pink eyes, skinny, high voice."

"Well damn well let him," drawled rangy Pete. He looked at Nessa. "Buckley Brentwood is a tight-assed Republican, as far right as they come, complete with velvet waistcoat and bow tie, if you'll pardon my explicit description. I thought you might, as your own writing is quite plain speaking, honestly open, no holds barred kind of stuff. Call it as you see it kind of writing. I had to check who wrote it, cos I saw a woman's name, but it wasn't a woman's style. Heck, it was out there, even for a guy."

"Did you approve?" asked Nessa archly. Pete, lips puckered, mouth pulled down at the corners.

"Of course I did," he emphasized the "I", and so did Harry here, obviously, but I don't know what Harry was thinking when he asked you here to interview for an assistant post. As he says, we don't have the cash to pay you, and even if we did, Buckley Brentwood never would cotton to the idea of hiring you if he read your piece. What you say is anathema to his rich paranoid soul. Duff here would never go against Buckley, would you, Duff?"

Duff frowned,

"And neither will you, Pete Gardener, if you want to have a job. Buckley would see to it that you and Harry never got a job writing for movies again."

"Ah, Duff, my lad," smiled Harry affably. "It ain't much, but we got a screenwriters' guild now. We've bargaining power, and a way to redress wrongs done us, so stuff the old hierarchy of the rich and vengeful like Brentwood and his ilk. They're dinosaurs, Duff. Wake up and smell the freedom." Duff shook his head doubtfully. With that the door burst open, and in walked a bustling pompous man, full of his own importance – thin brown hair slicked down, full red face, hooded brown eyes, five ten or so in height, portly build, tweed sports jacket, cream colored shirt, wine colored waistcoat, grey slacks, neatly pressed and a wine-red bow tie under his double chins.

"God help us, those people over in casting haven't a clue! They've messed with the script to suit the actors for crying out loud! Since when do those dressed up puppets know how to write? They've massacred it - all arguing for changes that enhance their parts, their egos. It's a travesty, I tell you! I can't deal with this. We need someone to go over there and show them what they are supposed to do: which is follow our script, our ideas. Who the hell is this? You're in the wrong place Miss Whatever. Casting is way over the other side of this moronic place they call a studio."

"I am not here to audition, Mr. Brentwood. I am a writer. I am here because Mr Henderson asked me to interview for the position of screenwriter's assistant after reading a piece I wrote for the Atlantic Monthly."

"He did, did he? Well given his radical tastes in literature and politics, I am sorry, but you are not suitable." Buckley sneered at Harry, who shared a smile with Pete.

"Perhaps you should read what I have written," said Nessa coolly.

"It's a waste of my time. Even if you wrote as I should wish, we'd never keep you once those lecherous studio heads and agents out there saw you. You know that you are quite beautiful, in fact much too beautiful. Those men out there will see the bounty your looks will bring in for them, whether you can act or not, and clearly you are intelligent, and with rather a fine look of class and breeding, so I expect you'll be able to act quite well, or at least follow the instructions those philistines will give you that passes for acting in their book."

"Please, Mr. Brentwood, I should be grateful to hear what you think of my writing. I would value your opinion, your finely crafted insights."

Pete and Harry were somewhat puzzled. Buckley would detest her writing. Then they noticed that Nessa had handed him another piece, not the one they had on their desk. She must have had it concealed in her handbag.

Buckley, somewhat fussily, yet also somewhat mollified, took the piece, raised his trousers a little to protect the crease, and sat back in his antique rocking chair at his huge finely carved mahogany desk, that took up most of the room – the other writers having miniscule desk space in cluttered corners. Nessa kept her eyes on Buckley as he read. She resisted the temptation to exchange glances with Harry and Pete, who waited for the explosion that didn't come. Buckley finished reading. Put the piece down on his desk. Put his hands together, as if in prayer, and rested his ample chins thoughtfully on his fingertips. He rocked back and forth for a few moments. Then…

"You write well…Miss…"

"Eiles, Vanessa Eiles."

"Miss Eiles. Yes, a very well thought out, well informed, clever piece of writing. You would make an ideal assistant, but I still fear that once seen, you would be sucked up in the mill that churns out inane glamour, and be devoured by the media circus of this industry, that will exploit every atom of your perfect form and being, and turn you into a celluloid doll, a creature of their greed and lust. They will not value your brain, your mind, forget all that."

"No, Mr. Brentwood, you underestimate my strength of purpose. I intend with every fiber of my being to be a writer." Buckley flapped his hand in dismissal. Nessa smiled. He looked at her for a moment or two, assessing her resolve.

"Alright, you can start tomorrow at the crack of dawn. That is when I start work. These leftist loafers don't appear until the day is half gone. You will hand on what we write faithfully. You will not include anything of your own, do you understand me? Your opinions will be asked for, but you will not write yourself." Nessa nodded enthusiastically, and thanked him for the job. She shook hands all the way around, and secretly winked at Harry and Pete. They were totally confused.

Later that evening, after Buckley had left to attend some function or other that enhanced his standing in the film community, Harry and Pete grabbed the piece that Nessa had handed Buckley from his desk. They read it avidly, and whistled in amazement. Nessa had written a carefully crafted piece that described the corruption and organized crime in the labor unions. She showed how rich, successful men can sometimes forget their humble origins, but that is their only fault. They need to be reminded that the wealthy and successful must maintain a peaceful society through paternalism. That all the people want is to be loved and trusted, and made to pull themselves up by their bootstraps, not rely on handouts from people who have had the ability to fend for themselves and succeed by their own resourcefulness. They need the wealthy, powerful benefactors to protect them from an often misguided trust in those preaching share the wealth, which would only dilute a society's ability to be strong, and not blown about by erratic winds of change, that as often as not drive society onto the rocks of chaos. The wealthy do need to be reminded, however, of that creed of all successful kings– the wisdom of the policy of noblesse oblige, if they are going to think for the people, which is what the people want them to do. God bless them! They cannot think for themselves. They are just not capable of so doing. They cannot understand all the complicated parameters involved in matters of state, and they shouldn't be so informed. It would only result in chaos as aforementioned. Those who can should think for them.

"God damn!" exclaimed Pete. "The two-faced little hussy!" Harry just laughed and laughed, and so did Pete finally.

"I don't know about you, Nessa Eiles, you're a force to be reckoned with."

"You got that right, Pete. Think we'll take in the stray, but let's nickname her, Wiles. She sure is a wily little cat!"

# INTRIGUES

Santa Barbara foothills: Mid-Summer, 1941:

The house, low ranch-style, was a Don Blanding's dream house realized. Set back from the cliff, amongst the oaks, rocky gullies and rolling golden hills, green in the spring months, the house still had a commanding view of the ocean. A stream rushed and gurgled over its boulder-strewn bed through a shady grove of oak trees to the right of the house. The house itself was made out of rocks and timber, with long windows all around. The roof was fluted reddish brown tile, shaded by blossom trees of all kinds. A huge monkey-puzzle tree dominated the top of the dusty gravel driveway that wended its way up through the hills and trees from the main road. The covered porch at the front was a tangled mass of scarlet and purple bougainvillea, honeysuckle and jasmine. A winding flagstone path led from the porch to the driveway that curved on reaching the crest around the monkey-puzzle tree. The air was heady with the scent of flowers, pine and the more stringent sea breezes. There was a round swimming pool set among the boulders on the left side, and behind the house a wide lawn that gave way to the scrub brush of the hillside. Lilac trees and tall feathery evergreens surrounded the pool and raised flagstone area, where deckchairs and low glass-top tables were set. Ivy, lily-of-the valley, with their fluted dark green leaves made up the ground cover around the house and driveway. It was an artist's haven, and an artist lived there, but she favored cold misty sand dunes and grey-green North Sea coastlines in her art over these bright Mediterranean colors. Her work reflected her longing for a return to her beloved Hamburg and the flat northern German coast. Her studio, with its large glass windows, was built high into the hillside, and very early each morning, she would climb the rocky steps to the studio to catch the early morning sea mists and fog, before the bright sun of day drove them away. How she loved the rare cold grey days, when sea and cloud merged! She was almost seventy years old, and had been living in exile amongst the bougainvillea for the last seven years or so with her husband, who was already in his seventies. Her grand piano was set up in her studio, and as the light faded, she could be heard every evening, playing those ethereal airs of Debussy or Fauré, piano sonatas and nocturnes. Her husband, baggy cord trousers, old woolen cardigan over frayed shirt, tall stooped form, white crinkly hair, would shuffle in his leather-slippers up the steps to join her, a tray of cold cuts, cheeses and crackers and two glasses of peppermint schnapps held firmly in his fine doctor's hands. After they had partaken of the food and drinks, he'd stay looking out over the sea, while she played some magical air or other on the piano, and he'd sit, hands held as if in prayer, his lips on his joined finger tips, and he'd think…deep and important thoughts of how to combat the evil in this world, not just from foreign enemies, but from deep within this, his new homeland. He'd worry about her too, and if he had ruined her chance of happiness in this life.

    The elderly gentleman emerged from the large oak front door. The sea mist hadn't cleared yet. It hung like veils in the tall trees.

He watched as the large black sedan circled the center island and monkey-puzzle tree, crunching the gravel into clouds of dust. He took out his handkerchief, and removing his rimless spectacles, wiped them and then replaced them, just as a young soldier jumped out of the driver's seat, and opened the back door for a man in a business suit. Another, an American army officer, emerged from the opposite front side, while another in a business suit emerged from the other back door, followed by a high ranking officer in British army uniform. The young soldier resumed his seat at the wheel, while the other four walked up the flagstone path:

"Dr. Franz, how good to meet you again."

"Kerr, good to see you too," and Emil glanced from the fresh-faced young army officer of engineers to the civilians and British officer.

"May I introduce Professor Alex Tanner, confidential business advisor to the President?"

"Pleased to make your acquaintance, Dr. Franz. I have heard a great deal about you and your brave work from intelligence sources here and in England." Emil modestly shook his head and smiled at the other man in a business suit, who introduced himself as Carson Shaw.

"Colonel Macklin, I know. Hello, Harold, pleased to see you again. How are you?"

"Fine, Doctor Franz, and yourself?'

"Please, won't you come in? Marisol has gone to the market, and my wife is in her studio, you see, up there on the hill. We shall be able to talk without interruption." They followed him into the house, and through to a large sunny room; terracotta tiled floor, over which beautiful cream, brown and rust red rugs were scattered. A deep café au lait leather couch and chairs were set in front of a large rock fireplace, where a log fire was prepared, but not lit. A ledge ran from the fireplace around the room, save for gaps for doors. Under the large windows, large cushions in earth tones were placed on the ledge, creating pleasant and comfortable window seats. The men noticed that most of the remaining ledge space around the room was covered by stacks of papers and books. Emil led them on through to the kitchen; bright sunshine yellow, with long windows that looked onto the back grape arbor, evergreen trees and red barn-like garage. A large blue plate of freshly baked strudel had been left on the bar counter, forks and napkins to the side. An enticing aroma of freshly brewed coffee hung in the air. The men smiled appreciatively, and sat at the round glass-top breakfast table. Kerr took a cup of coffee and two strudels out to the young driver in the car, and then returned.

"This is very kind of you, Dr. Franz. I didn't realize how hungry I was until I smelled that strudel and coffee." Kerr Toddy and Dr. Franz exchanged knowing smiles.

"I know how you like Marisol's strudel, Kerr. She made it especially for you."

Small talk ensued: the progress in the war, the Lend-Lease program to Britain, and settling on a route to send Lend-Lease weapons, food, fuel etc., to the Russians, allies since Hitler had done an about-face and attacked them in June of that year. They finished their coffee with political gossip closer to home. Replete and feeling more at ease with one another, Emil cleared away the plates and mugs, and suggested they return to the living room. They sat around the fireplace, pulling papers from their respective briefcases, and placing them on the long low coffee table, made from driftwood found on the local beach. Professor Tanner began:

"The new intelligence coordinating agency seems to be progressing at a pace, but a very careless one. Donovan inspires his people to take risks, but he also recruits some very dubious and criminal characters along with the high-minded academics, writers and actors …who have a rather melodramatic zeal. They are heroes and heroines of what are adventures on the big screen, or in works of fiction, now being given the chance to do it for real.

Donovan gives them carte blanche, which allows for the infiltration of real spies and double agents. The possibilities make the mind spin. It's an absolute circus. FDR gives Donovan a lot of leeway, but the military intelligence services and Mr. Hoover at the FBI do not feel so inclined. Hoover is responsible for ferreting out fifth columnists at home and in Latin America, and he won't let Donovan onto his turf. Donovan and Hoover have spies within each other's camps. It's a competitive field, and we're not working effectively to gather information. FDR seems to foster this. It's as if he wants us to compete, wants us to be unaware of what each of our branches is doing, possibly so that he, and he alone, holds all the strings. Donovan must report only to the President. This angers the others, who want to know what Donovan's lot is up to, and whether what they are doing will compromise military espionage ops and FBI ops. Hoover and General Marshall are furious."

"It does seem that way, Professor Tanner, but the President has told me often how the military intelligence groups and Hoover do not keep him up to date on what they are planning. The OSS was formed to be FDR's source of consolidated intelligence. It's Donovan's job to nettle the Joint Chiefs, make them aware that they are not in sole charge of this war."

"We have enough disagreement between the army and the navy now. Do we also have to take into account politicians who wish to dabble in espionage, and develop their own strategies arising there from? We are at war, which means politicians have failed. They are responsible for diplomacy and negotiation. Surely our military and security services are responsible for waging the war."

"Surely we should never give up on diplomacy, Professor?"

"Please, Doctor Franz, call me Alex."

"Politicians, our leaders, should always be on the look out for restoring peace. They should leap at every chance, no matter how feeble or tenuous, that might end the destruction and suffering. To keep on top of such opportunities, our President needs to be accurately and fully informed. He is an ex-navy man. He understands military intelligence and strategy, but he also understands the predicament of the innocents caught up in war. If he has been a little lax in this regard, due to leaders with the old-school tie and fraternity way of thinking of the principle of the thing being more important than the innocent lives involved," Emil glanced at Harold as he said this, "I am sure that his good wife would take him to task in no uncertain terms."

"Yes, well, Mr. Hoover and some of our more extreme conservatives have their doubts about Mrs. Roosevelt's actual agenda." Tanner said, reaching for a letter with FBI letterhead.

Emil smiled and shook his head.

"Just as megalomaniacs, with their delusions of grandeur, manage to infect ordinary folks with their illness, so those with paranoid psychoses, who, under the illusion they are fighting the danger by taking excessive precautions, are actually an offshoot of it, and so prevent an effective social cure – a return to normalcy. I assure you gentlemen that neither megalomaniacs, the leaders of this world, nor those with paranoid psychoses, their watchdogs, desire normalcy. If only the ordinary folk knew the real agendas behind these wars, and were not deliberately distracted and confused by the headless chicken press at the behest of its masters."

They all laughed.

"This war has definite villains, namely Hitler and his thugs, and maybe Tojo and his thugs down the road. They have very obvious agendas, so what do you mean by the chaos spread about to confuse the people?"

Emil got up and walked to the window. He stood there a moment, his hands deep in his trouser pockets, as he gazed up at his wife's studio on the hill. The others watched him, waiting, not able to anticipate what he might say.

"Strange events bring cruel people to power. They cannot achieve this alone. Oh, some say it is fate, it is written in their stars, that the Cosmos has plans of its own, but I do not take any of these explanations seriously. We love resorting to fairy tales. An organization of very wealthy people has controlled events down through history. Each generation adds to the web formed by their forefathers in previous generations, and people are admitted as they acquire wealth and power. Good leaders eschew this organization, often at the risk of their lives and the lives of those who love and support them. It is a brave man, with no personal ties, who must take them on, and these are few and far between. These evil men get rich off war. They will supply the resources of war, but rarely become leaders of countries themselves. They prefer to be the power behind the throne. Whenever the ordinary people have the time and courage to start making demands for a fair deal, a share of the profits earned off their sweat and tears, which is usually when greedy, inept economic policies increase their hardships, then the wealthy who do not want to share, will engineer war, with all its swirling accusations and innuendoes that confuse good citizens. Traps such as honor, glory, patriotism and duty, sacrifice for the good of the whole, are notions oft used and abused by evil men. Sacrifice and death and suffering are never good things. We may kill or die to protect our loved ones, as animals do, but believe me, when governments or religions ask this of their people it is never such a simple thing. Agendas underlie such requests: agendas involving sacrifice and violence, so some self-serving ideology can be maintained and spread like a plague of the mind."

Kerr Toddy smiled. "Where have I heard this before?"

Emil turned to look at him, a smile on his face.

"Yes, Kerr, in that young girl's graduation speech - she hit the nail on the head. I think we need to talk to her. I may remind you also that Shakespeare covered such ideas, but in pithy wit, through the voice of his Sir John Falstaff, but, yes, this young woman has just the abilities we need for our organization."

"So who is controlling these wars - our leaders, our rich, who?"

"The organization worldwide that creates wars, fuels war. Our governments are dupes, puppets. They don't even know what has brought war to pass. They think as you do, Alex, that it is a deranged, delusional fool, but such idiots, such madmen, are put out for public consumption. We rarely look below the surface of things to find out who is working the gears, pulling the ropes."

"What are we doing here today, Dr. Franz?"

"Call me, Emil, please. We are going to form a group with extraordinary abilities, Alex. A group of persons in whom we can trust implicitly to look for the strings, the gears moving the theater of the macabre that is this war. Our work will never be acknowledged, for the perpetrators of mayhem are on all sides."

"How do we find these people we can trust?"

"You are here already. Kerr has lined up some more exceptional people, and I am going to give a party to recruit some more."

"We've done this at Bletchley for the last three to four years or so. We have some thousand brilliant minds at work to crack enemy codes. Some of these clever folks have been preparing for this conflict ever since the last awful tragedy."

"God, Harold, are you Europeans always planning for war?'

"Proximity breeds contempt, old boy, and caution. Old Baden Powell's scouts' motto, 'Be Prepared', covers the whole modi operandi for survival in this life."

"I gather that my son has been put forward by you, Kerr, as a possible recruit. He espouses some ideas that you have put forward today Dr. Franz."

"Your writings, Carson, plus your astute observations of certain business types you have encountered, have been extremely useful. Does your son know of your work for us?

"No, he doesn't, but he has such contempt for business and finance that I am sure he will be suitable. I don't want him to know of my role in all this yet. I realize that, by joining Kerr in his work for you, Drax may have to put himself in harm's way. There is a war going on. Lots of young men and women are putting their lives on the line every day. I know, from my own observations, that there is an element here in the U.S. who has supported the German businessmen who put Hitler in power to control the communists. FDR is aware of them, hence his need for our, shall I say, even more covert intelligence services? His use of several sources of information is just a way of muddying the waters to hide our work. My son's work with your group is his way, our way if you will, of making sure that our side is staying honest, and that these shady guys do not steer victory, which I am sure will be an Allied one, into any more wars to feather their nests."

Alex Tanner gave a brief sardonic laugh.

"Interesting how old FDR put a Republican, Donovan, who is also a staunch catholic conservative, in charge of forming the OSS. Donovan had the utmost contempt for Roosevelt when they were in university together. He thought him a rich dilettante and fop."

They all smiled.

"I am sure Donovan now knows better, ever since FDR took on Tammany Hall. No one muddies the waters like FDR."

"All the better to keep tabs on folks," said Kerr Toddy.

They prepared to leave. Colonel Macklin took the chance for a quick word with Emil and Kerr.

"I have a fellow from the Royal Canadian Air Force to keep a sort of unbiased eye on things. I'll send him to your recruitment party, Emil, along with the undercover man, of whom I have spoken with you before."

"That young man and his wife are very brave, and they are making an incredible sacrifice to do this undercover work for you, as of course is our dear Biff Chatsle, but the Canadian, is he reliable?"

"My nephew, old boy."

Emil and Kerr shook their heads and smiled.

Emil watched the car disappear in clouds of dust and gravel. He closed the heavy oak door. He sensed a presence behind him and turned.

"What do you think?"

"Brilliantly done, Emil, as usual."

"Are you sure we are right?"

"We won't be very effective, but men such as these you have met today, and the others we've recruited, usually flush out a few baddies. It helps a little. They may be able to pinpoint whom we must work against in the future. Who knows, maybe one day, far distant, we may get a small victory against these self-serving manipulators."

"Ah, Utopia! Have you seen Magda?"

"No. You know I won't do that. That story in my life is over."

"I do not think that Magda is so resigned. I think she dreams of the possibility of your renewed love."

"It is over, Emil. Please believe me. I need you to trust me now more than ever. Magda and I are old, but do not think that I find her any the less beautiful or alluring. You and I have been blessed to have the love of such an amazing woman – a woman for all ages. You love her, and I love her, but not with the lust of my more youthful days. I find that kind of love in younger women, and I do not mean to be cruel, but my body does not yearn for Magda any longer, even though my soul will never stop wanting her brilliant, creative inspiration and her wisdom. You are an integral part of Magda's genius, Emil. I never was. I was always an acolyte to her.

I must tell you about another woman I met before I met Magda. She had a delicate waif-like beauty, wide lavender colored eyes, soft mid-brown hair. We were not romantically involved. She and her parents got caught up in the peaceful protest march in Moscow, December of 1905. They were badly beaten by the Tsarist secret police force, the Okhrana. The girl was raped while in prison. I happened to be in Russia at the time. Lenin suspected that the Okhrana had something to do with organizing the protest, in order to ferret out Bolsheviks and kill them, even if that meant killing innocent people, who were just marching for food and work, as were this particular girl and her parents. Lev Tashvin and I, and an American journalist, managed to break into the prison with the aid of inside help, and we rescued the family and took them to Paris, where they lived with the journalist. He taught them English, so that he could bring them to the States with him when he returned. He had fallen in love with the girl. After the cruelty she had suffered, it took time for him to heal the fear she felt for men, but she eventually came to love him."

"Do you perchance speak of Carson Shaw?"

The man, tall, strong physique, long grey hair tied at the nape of his neck by black string; face, a white mask, the skin tightened over the charred cheek bones, the nose truncated, the mouth pulled down at the corners, nodded.

"The very same."

"The son is his?"

"Yes. He wasn't born until 1915, some time after they'd settled in Boston."

"Did this young woman also love you? You cut a dashing figure before your disfigurement in the last war."

"I was an arrogant young man of eighteen. This gentle girl was not my type at all, but she and Magda are the two most impressive women I have had the good fortune to know and have love me, but they also knew how foolish that was. Magda didn't return to you and Miriam through any notions of duty or guilt, Emil. She eventually realized, or maybe always knew, that you were the deepest love of her life – her real hero - the man she could respect and love to the end of time. She must have told you this, Emil. I know that you must have tried to convince her to find fulfillment with me, especially when Magda was pregnant with my son, but she knew I was not cut out for fatherhood. You raised the boy as your own, and he is fortunate to have you for a father. You showed him love and support. You accepted him as your own, and believe me, I am so very grateful that you did. Magda loves you, Emil. Sex is not love. I know of your injury in the last war, and that you cannot give

Magda satisfaction that way, but she outgrew that need, and long ago realized what real love and fulfillment is in this life, and these she has found with you. She loves you deeply Emil. You are life and love to Magda."

"I do know this."

"Emil, it is imperative that you trust me in this. We have important work to do. I have told you of the Red Dragon society for which I work, keeping an eye on this cabal of evil, powerful men, who engineer war continually, generation after generation. You would make a perfect Red Dragon, but you work within the halls of power, aiding powerful men, and as such, you cannot be part of what we do. We must have no access to power, and can only work through brave people who can spill the beans on corrupt leaders and governments – what you'd call whistle-blowers. Can you work with us? Can you trust me?"

"Your people do good work for no personal gain. I admire that. I know Myrddyn, my dear friend, a brilliant man, back in Hamburg, belongs to your society. Hilda, his wife, I should imagine works for you as well, and does Cat too?"

"Not yet."

"I do trust you, Rudy. I need to work with you. We need such as you Red Dragons to watch our backs."

The men shook hands. Emil awkwardly embraced Rudy, who with more natural affection hugged him back.

"I must go. You know how to contact us?"

Emil nodded.

"At least have cocktails, some cheese and crackers with us."

"No, thank you. I think it is better if Magda never knows that I come here to meet with you."

"Ah, Rudy! She knows. Every creative fiber of her being knows when you are near."

Hollywood: 1940-1941:

Nessa had made great strides in her writing career since she had bamboozled Buckley Brentwood into hiring her. She had toed the line, and had carried out their directions to the letter. She had not added any of her ideas to their scripts, but, of course, she had given her opinion on how to better elucidate a point, add a touch of levity to better appeal, make the whole subject a little lighter and less ponderous. Her input added a fresh perspective, as their ideas, which once had been new and progressive, since had become somewhat repetitious and stale. Directors and producers noticed the change, and liked it. Harry and Pete were generous enough to acknowledge Nessa as the source of their inspiration, and before long Nessa was working on her own scripts from her stories, and being allowed to assist in directing.

Cukor had seen her in the cafeteria over the months since she'd been hired by "the boys". He'd taken part in lunch time gossip and cocktail hour conversations, speculating with Capra, Ford, Huston and Louis B. himself, as to why such an incredible beauty should turn down, so consistently, enticements to have a screen test for some role or other, when they knew she'd ace it. She was bound and determined to be, first a screenwriter, and then a director. They had let her stick around their sets, watching their techniques, absorbing the intricacies of lighting and sound effects. She'd been allowed to watch the editing process, to learn camera angles. They had been so helpful and generous just to have her around. She was lovely and witty, a fast learner, and she even had useful insights, much resented by most of the less talented stars.

Pete and Harry had been invited to Nessa's parents' place for Saturday night potluck dinners. They had described to Frank Capra and George Cukor, how inspiring it had been to listen to Jeb and his co-workers, and before long they came on occasion too, and their families. Buckley Brentwood and Duff invited themselves along out of curiosity, and Buckley made the startling discovery that these ordinary workingmen and women did not need rich people to think for them. They were perfectly capable of thinking for themselves, and were remarkably well informed, and not at all easily won over by political ideologies and fanaticism, but were practical, driven by common sense and a social conscience.

In March,1940, Nessa and Loretta returned from their sad trip to Wales to take Agnes's ashes home, a trip that had not been without its dangers, as Britain was at war with Germany, and U-Boats threatened the Atlantic sea lanes.

After her return from Wales, Nessa was approached by Cukor and Stan Moysee, a successful Hollywood producer, to write her own script from her stories, and to help direct the movie. Nessa knew the actress she wanted to cast in the leading role, and Cukor was in complete agreement.

Fiona Kyrke was a true professional, a writer's and a director's dream of the perfect actress – a working, thinking actress. She had played the glamour roles, the femme fatale, the seductress with a hint of menace, but she was also the girl next door, bubbly, vivacious, but always smart, not just in her high fashion clothes and hair-dos, but a girl with smarts upstairs, brains, clever, twisting the men around her little finger, and when they turned, she'd reveal vulnerability, not in wide-eyed overacting, tearing of the hair, sobbing, but by ever so subtle expressions in her small blue-grey eyes.

Fiona wasn't an obvious beauty. Her lively Irish Pennsylvanian wit, ever observant, constantly thinking, assessing, evident in the eyes, were what made her attractive. She had a slender figure and good legs. Clothes hung on her to the manor born, and even off screen, she was never scruffy, never caught by the press and camera without complete make-up or a strand of hair out of place.

She had been an orphan of the mean streets of Philadelphia, seeking a refuge in vaudeville as a dancer. She had been abused and used by the meanest sorts of men and women. She'd been feisty though, and even more importantly, she'd had incredible acting talent that came from her sad and cruel past. She never overacted. She achieved an authenticity with her eyes alone, and they, in their subtle way, spoke volumes.

Fiona and Lorna Trevelayan were of that late 1920's stable of MGM thoroughbreds. Hollywood had a bad reputation, fostered by scandals of wild parties, sexual shenanigans, murder, drugs, alcohol abuse and licentious living. Louis B. Mayer wanted to make the film industry socially acceptable. His stable of stars had to follow a strict moral code for public consumption, had to be perfectly attired with perfect manners, in other words, they were to become America's royalty. Fiona and Lorna, like so many other young girls of the 1920's, who had had hard lives, gave themselves over to Mayer's grooming, Mayer's strict code (at least in public, but behind closed doors was another matter), and Mayer's politics. They were Republican down the line; had to be.

Lorna had gone to New York to dance, and had been discovered in the chorus line. She'd hailed from Arizona in the desert southwest. The loving father she'd adored had up and left, and her mother had gone off with another man, leaving Lorna to fend for herself. Lorna had looks. She was blonde, with big blue eyes, tall, with the best legs in the business. Like Fiona, she'd had minimal schooling, but they were intelligent. They'd had to survive with street smarts and, an almost innate ability to learn what worked and what didn't.

Once they had become famous, they'd still conformed to outward elegance and moral rectitude, but privately they'd had their kicks, especially with the younger actors looking for someone with influence, who could bolster their careers. They'd had affairs with the older stars of their day too. Lorna had fared better in this than Fiona, and had a few famous ex-husbands, but now she focused mainly on wealthy older businessmen. Fiona had loved a famous handsome actor, and had lost him to up and coming beauties like Alisyn Kendale and Mandy Travis. She had not been glamorous enough to hold onto an actor. Old rich men didn't appeal to her like they did to Lorna. She'd played that role in her earlier days, and didn't like the control. She was free to be her own woman now. She'd have liked a companion of like age to enjoy the freedom with, a handsome son-of-a-gun, to show she could win one just like the beauties, but with her intelligence and her incredible acting ability, she'd have overshadowed him. Her looks could not feed the vain egos of young wannabe actors, who didn't value brains in women, but by then, she had ego enough herself, and it came from her abilities, not her looks.

Nessa had a plan of action for getting Fiona to accept the role. She knew that she was an untried writer. That she would be assisting in directing the movie would sound as if she were just another wannabe given favors for her looks. Fiona never would agree to being told how to act, if she thought Nessa had gained this kudos that way, so she'd waited until the day she was lucky enough to catch Fiona Kyrke sitting alone in the cafeteria.

Fiona liked to have time alone with the script to better get into character, and to figure out how to enhance the role. Everyone knew to keep his or her distance at such a time. Fiona wasn't given to shrieking displays or hysterical outbursts, or anything overt like that. She'd just turn to ice on one, and that would be that – completely axed.

She sat there that day in mid-brown velvet splendor. Edith Head had done her proud. She wore a brown velvet turban hat with a diamond clasp on her short lightly curled fair hair – fair, not blonde. Fiona liked her hair and make-up on the natural side. This enhanced her delicate small features and pale coloring better than vivid make-up, but her talons were blood red.

Nessa took a seat at a table in the far corner by a potted palm tree. She opened her brief case, and perused a script she had prepared, and she waited, not even glancing at the star, although she had chosen a table Fiona faced, so that, if she looked up, she'd see Nessa – couldn't fail to.

Fiona had registered Nessa's presence the minute she'd entered, and had been annoyed by it. She knew who Nessa was, a glorified script girl with ambitions any man who looked at her wanted to help her fulfill. Fiona had glanced up at her a few times, taking inventory each time: incredible looks, more naturally classy than Lorna; too tall for the actors then in vogue; too intelligent-looking for most men to hold any hopes; the usual slick sexy patter would die a terrible death; too self contained – didn't need anyone, as evidenced by rejections made to people who could have furthered her career, and too – well – goddamn annoying, sitting there, totally absorbed in her work, while putting her off hers. She wore casual clothes, yellow linen suit, jacket with upper and lower pockets, like a safari jacket, and a tie belt, A-line skirt and flat-heeled yellow open-toed sandals, and she looked like a front-page model for a high-class fashion magazine. She was totally infuriating! Little did Fiona know that Nessa's stylish wardrobe had been made for her by Loretta and Esperanza, Loretta's long-time close friend, and wife of Pedro, one of Jeb's co-workers.

Nessa looked up and met Fiona's critical appraisal of her. This is it, Nessa thought – axed.

"Miss Kyrke, please excuse my presence. I do have a script I want you to read. I wrote it. The part of Alyce I wrote with you in mind. I have discussed the project with Mr. Cukor, and he is willing to direct, only if you will take on this role. I know I have cornered you here, and I know how many other commitments you have, and I apologize profusely, and hope and pray that you will agree to read the script at least."

There was a long, overlong, period of silence, when Fiona fixed Nessa with her small blue-grey eyes that gave evidence, not in any particular movement or look, that her mind was working a mile a minute.

Fiona stood up and gathered her papers together. She walked towards Nessa without looking at her, and made as if to pass her by. She did, but she walked back and held out her elegantly gloved hand, again without looking at Nessa, or saying a word. Nessa placed the script in her hand, and Fiona walked away, head held high. Nessa smiled. Had she been able to see Fiona's face, there was a slight smile there too. Nessa's story was made into a movie that summer of 1940.

Mandy Travis was a blonde, blue-eyed American beauty, a sex-symbol, but Nessa made her develop acting skills as well as her physical assets. There was no depth to Mandy, what you saw was what she had to offer. She was sensual and seductive, sure of her ability to snare any man from boy to geriatric, but anything after sex, or other than sex, was not her forte, and her relations had no staying power. She was made for rapid high-school type flings, adolescent musical chairs, moving from one conquest quickly to another. She was an icon, nothing else, but Nessa made her question why she was like she was. Why did she rely so much on her looks and sexual allure? She discovered a Mandy who was kind, but who loved the freedom her looks gave her to bed any man she came across, take any man from any woman, and, when she failed in this, she didn't let it bother her. Her philosophy of life was that she'd be old soon enough, but for the time being she couldn't fail to turn heads when she entered a room, and men who rejected her were obviously aware that they could not hold onto her forever. She loved it when she drove them to distraction.

"There is only sex, honey," she purred.

"Why?"

"Well gosh darn it, everything else takes too much effort. My brain doesn't like to think, like yours does, Ness."

"Why?"

Mandy sighed, eyes wide with exasperation.

"Well I've never had to use my brain." She laughed. "Why the hell should I? Everything I want, I get without thinking."

Nessa got in-depth performances out of her nevertheless, by persisting and insisting, which frustrated Mandy and made her mad, then sad, and there it was – the performance of a lifetime!

The scene over, she'd cry and look at Nessa, who smiled with pride, and they'd laugh through their tears.

"Goddamn it, I hate you, Nessa Eiles!"

"I know. I know, but you were amazing. See what you can do, and you let it happen. I had nothing to do with what you showed back there. You were not just a sexy star, you were a goddamn fine actress!"

Mandy sobbed, and Nessa held her until Mandy pulled away and slapped her arm.

"Oh for goodness sakes, we look like a pair of lesbians! Let's go get a drink, a strong one, several strong ones. I need a man right now."

Alisyn Kendale had depth, inscrutable depth she took great pains to hide. She could have had rich men at her beck and call, but she chose to battle it out with fellows, who, like her, had come from humble beginnings, but aimed for the moon. She was a great actress. Her unusual beauty often hid this fact. She was from the South. Her family had been hard working and close. She had loved her parents, who had worked themselves to death for their kids. What pain she felt, she hid with drinking, partying, having casual sex just for the heck of it. The tender kitten had grown into the full-blown she-cat, with high cheekbones, black hair and up turned, narrow green eyes. She could drink and drink and still stay slender. She moved with the grace of a cat. She and Mandy became good friends. They shared stories of their sexual adventures, often having been with the same guys, but not at the same time. Mandy might have gone for it, but Alisyn was more traditional in that respect. It was a game for Mandy, an extension of adolescence, but Alisyn was more circumspect, more caring and sincere. They were rough diamonds with kind hearts.

Alisyn read to improve her mind, and she already had a pithy wisdom. She could assess a role and a situation better than anyone, including Fiona. Fiona would look for the angle that could be exploited, while Alisyn would look for the reason why, the excuse, the need to understand.

Lorna just wanted to succeed on her own terms, and have the resources to be independent herself and help others she cared for – in fact, to be the mother her mother hadn't been. She was sometimes ruthlessly exploited, but she was learning to grow a hard shell, as Fiona had done. It didn't stop her from wanting to be needed, and wanting to help, but as her own mother was callously selfish, so could Lorna be, as well as cruel, when thwarted.

Nessa worked as an assistant writer and director with these four actresses, and they marveled at Nessa's insight into their characters. She seemed to know them, even before they had shared their life stories with her as friends. Nessa's own stories had taken their fancy, and with the support of these actresses, who were box-office gold, and other talented women writers, Nessa managed to get producers interested in making films based on her writings, and in letting her direct them. She had managed to make that first film with Fiona Kyrke come in under budget, and it had gained an Oscar win for Fiona.

Sigi Andrus had arrived in Hollywood in early 1941. She was a Jewish refugee from Romania. Her parents were scientists. They had worked in the field of quantum mechanics. The whole family had been helped by British Intelligence operatives to escape to England before war had broken out in 1939. Sigi was a rare cultured beauty. She was well read, and had received an excellent education. She found Hollywood frivolous. She was bored sick by the party scene, and spent her free time with European exiles of a more serious mindset. She drove her directors to distraction with her somewhat arrogant approach to acting, but she responded to Nessa's direction, as Nessa only put her in parts that captured her air of mystery and her intellectual aloofness.

---

Fiona Kyrke's house in the Hollywood Hills: Late Summer, 1941:
"This is the life, Fiona honey!" sighed Alisyn sinking back into the soft creamy leather of the couch, her bare feet curled up beneath her, a glass of red wine in her hand.

Fiona, dressed to the nines in black sheath with diamonds, stretched back from pouring a glass of wine for Sigi in the glistening stainless steel kitchen, to glance at Alisyn on the couch in the all white lounge.

"Glad it meets with your approval."

"Sure does," muttered Alisyn to herself. Mandy, dressed in a vibrant peacock blue satin gown, came in from the kitchen, where the others were gathered, to join Alisyn on the couch, bringing a full opened bottle of wine with her.

"Here, move over will ya? So, what shall we drink to, or should I say which son-of-a-bitch are we toasting, I mean roasting tonight?"

Alisyn laughed her rich, throaty, naughty laugh.

"Lordy! Lordy! Now let me see, there are so many. You and I have racked up so many losers. Are you wanting one we've shared, or are you asking me about fresh game of my very little 'ol own?"

"Your own sweetie," said Lorna, elegant in short amber sheath that showed off her amazing legs. "Quite frankly, I am tired of you two dissecting some poor ham you've chewed up and spit out like lionesses on fresh kill." Lorna settled herself graciously in a wide armchair, also of creamy leather.

"Absolutely, Lorna," Fiona came sweeping into the room with Nessa and Sigi behind her. "I lost interest after you two dissected my ex last time you were here. It would have been in very bad taste, if I hadn't asked you to do it, and enjoyed every minute."

Alisyn became serious.

"If I hadn't been swacked at the time, I wouldn't have done it."

"Oh come on," laughed Mandy. "It was good to clear the air for all concerned. You were more hurt than you let on Fiona, but surely Alisyn and I both having him must have shown you what a loser he was. He was nothing to write home about, except maybe for you, and believe me darling, he'd have gone on having every little star-struck wannabe who batted her baby blues at him, and that would have been insulting for an actress of your caliber. We took him down for you before you had to go through that."

Fiona teared up some, and they all looked down at their drinks, except Mandy, who looked at Fiona straight on.

"Oh fuck it, you're right, but he was soooo pretty!" Fiona laughed and wiped her eyes with a handkerchief held out for her by Sigi.

"Hey, wait a minute," said Alisyn. "Nessa, come on fess up. How was your date with Mr.Oh-so-serious-politico man the other night?"

Nessa took a deep breath, and let it out slowly, thoughtfully:

"Well… and then again, well…."

"That bad eh?" Alisyn sat back and sipped her drink. "Honest to God, Nessa, why go for these mindy types, all talk? Why not have some fun with the mental low balls, but…." They all waited to see how she'd balance that sentence… "physically well endowed?" Alisyn finished primly. They all laughed.

"That's put me in the mood for something a little more exciting than wine," said Mandy, getting up. "Anyone else fancy a high ball?" They booed her, but laughed.

"Before we get really smacked," said Nessa (she, like Alisyn, was casually dressed in baggy silk top and capris: silver top in Alisyn's case, gold, in Nessa's), "I want to discuss my next script." They all groaned.

"Nessa, go find a man!" Mandy shouted back from the bar. Nessa gave a wry grin.

"Come on, Ness, relax tonight. You've got Oscar nominations for us all. We're grateful, but tonight we want a girls' night of letting our hair down, and our brows too. I don't think I have the energy to raise a brow to the height of your's and Sigi's tonight." Alisyn tried to raise her finely etched brows, making the others laugh. She flopped back and made serious love to her drink.

Nessa sighed:

"Alright, but I hope you can free up other commitments for April, next year, as I have plans for all of you."

"The plans of yours that I look forward to are going to your father's farm, and having your wonderful mother make us that great country dinner, and then having those gorgeous farmhands come over to play their guitars. I could gaze into their liquid brown eyes for an eternity." Alisyn stretched out sensually like a contented cat.

"Yeah, they are something," purred Mandy.

"No, no. I have known those lads since they were babes in arms, and I know how thrilled they are to come over with their parents, my family's friends, to ogle you girls, and ... no, absolutely not. They are too sweet, too vulnerable."

"I could do sweet and vulnerable, couldn't you, Ali? I was once after all. It'll come back to me."

"Honey, you were never that vulnerable," Fiona growled into her drink. Mandy gave her a pointed look by way of response. "Never," Fiona downed her drink.

They had gossiped and argued and cried and laughed until they were well into their cups. Sigi leaned out of the kitchen, and beckoned for Nessa to join her.

"Nessie, I want to invite you to a party at the home of a lovely German couple, Jewish like me, and refugees from their homeland. They came here in the early 1930's, just after Hitler came to power. Emil is a wonderful man, and well regarded by Roosevelt. He is a medical doctor, and he helps other refugees who come here seeking asylum. He is quite important. His wife, Magda, is a very talented artist and concert pianist. She is still an arresting beauty with a fascinating mind. They are so brilliant and creative, you would love them, and they would love your writings. They are very wealthy philanthropists, but they are not at all arrogant or snobbish. They are lovely, interesting people I thought you would like to meet. Emil is well up on quantum physics. My parents will be there too, so you can wallow in science and math to your heart's content. Please come. I think you will find it most enlightening."

"I'd love to Sigi. I always enjoy talking with your friends. I learn so much from them. They are all fascinating people, and I desperately need to touch base with my scientific side again. I miss it so much."

"Good. The party is here." Sigi gave Nessa a slip of paper with a Santa Barbara address on it. "It is next Saturday evening at seven o'clock. There will be a buffet and drinks, so no need to eat before you come. Emil and Magda always put on an amazing spread. There will be quite a few there, but the house lends itself to corners for interesting chats, and Magda will play the piano. It will be pretty intellectual, but fun too. I know you will appreciate it."

"Am I going alone? We are not going to go together?"

"I hope you don't mind, but I am taking my parents and two of their old friends. My car will be full."

Nessa sighed.

"No, Nessa don't despair! I thought of you. You see I am thoughtful, not entirely selfish."

Nessa laughed.

"Someone is going to pick you up at your apartment. He will also have a young Canadian couple with him. You will like them."

"I don't know Sigi. I don't know them, and I don't want to impose myself on strangers."

"You know the driver well, but I am not going to tell you who he is. I want it to be a surprise."

"Sigi this better not be one of your crazy set-ups. The last one; that way out musician who talked to the stars all evening…"

Sigi laughed.

"No. He is someone you like very much, an old friend. As for Ansel, he is a very creative person. He hears music in mundane everyday things. He hears music from the cosmos."

Nessa shrugged:

"I bet he does."

Sigi gave her a look of tried patience.

"Oh really, Miss Nessa? You don't find inspiration alone with your stars? What you hear in words, Ansel hears in rhythms, waves of different vibrations coming from out there beyond us, and from within us, and from the lives and things around us."

"I agree with him there. My Welsh grandmother taught Bobby and me that there is a cosmic din around us. She said that we are mostly a space filled with waves that translate into a reality we compose out of our four dimensional senses – those of which we are consciously aware, and those of extra dimensions of which we are not so aware."

"Was your grandmother a physicist?"

"No, Welsh."

"Oh you are going to enjoy your evening next Saturday," Sigi smiled, hugging herself with anticipation and smugness. "There is someone special who will be there for me too." Nessa was going to ask who, but…

"Can't you two come down to earth every once in a while?" They looked over at Alisyn leaning against the doorjamb, martini in hand.

"Oh yeah, and what is this then?" Nessa tapped Alisyn's glass, her eyebrows raised and a smile on her lips.

Alisyn coughed, shrugged and slouched into the kitchen, looking for more ice cubes. She opened the freezer, and peered back at them over the top of the door.

"Alright ladies, I am in search of more fuel to take my trip to the stars tonight. I guess this party next Saturday is for highbrows only?" she said, closing the fridge door and plopping cubes into her drink. Sigi and Nessa exchanged a quick look. Alisyn would get drunk and silly. She'd flirt. She couldn't help it. Oh she'd talk sensibly for an hour or so, even be clever and a quick study, but then the drink would kick in and she'd go over the top.

"Aw shucks, don't worry your little 'ol selves. I don't want to rain on your parade. I'll keep company with other little 'ol tipplers like the lot in there." She stretched out her arm, from which dangled solid gold bracelets, and pointed with a long red-nailed finger in the direction of the living room, where Mandy, of all people, was arguing with Fiona and Lorna about being Republicans. They hadn't named names, when Martin Dies had started an inquisition against possible Lefties in 1940, and they often played roles that supported the rights of the little guy, so Mandy accused them of being closet-liberals.

"You are only Reps because old L.B. said you have to be. That was in the twenties for God's sake!"

"Old L.B. was scared stiff then," said Fiona. "You maybe didn't realize how anti-Semitic America was in the 1920's, especially Los Angeles. L.B. didn't want to rock the boat. Jews were associated with communism. L.B. wanted no leftist stain anywhere near him. He insisted we all vote Republican, and it kinda stuck. Lorna and I did well by it. We had gone through hell getting to these dizzy heights, and, by damn, no one helped us on the way, but our talents, shall I say! I, for one, will be damned if I am going to share my hard-earned blood, sweat and tears – and then some – wealth with any of the shiftless masses. Let 'em get their own. As for political parties, I don't mind which really. Didn't Mark Twain say something about liking differences of opinion, cos 'they made for horse racing', or something like that?" They all laughed.

"To Mark Twain," Alisyn raised her glass. They all did.

"Well of course, Alisyn and I are too young to remember the twenties and thirties," purred Mandy slyly. Alisyn laughed, and the others threw cushions at them. "Okay, serious now – let's each say who is her favorite leading man, and how he is in the sack." They all groaned.

Party at the Franz house: Late summer, 1941:
Saturday night, Nessa waited in the foyer of her apartment building. She gave a brief laugh of recognition when an old Packard pulled up at the curb. Yes she knew the car and the driver well.

"Well, hello there, Steven, long time, no see."

"Surprise, surprise," he smiled. "Long time since last Saturday night's dinner at your folks'. Get in. Here are two delightful people I should like you to meet." Nessa sat in the front with Steven, and turned around to greet the two strangers sitting in the back.

"Nessa, meet Laura and Greg Macklin from the land of our dear and trusted neighbor - Canada." Nessa leaned over and shook their hands.

"Nessa Eiles," she said, smiling warmly. "Pleased to make your acquaintance." They smiled back readily. They were a couple of young fresh-faced kids, must be of her age, early twenties or thereabouts. "What are you doing here in Los Angeles? Are you on vacation during your leave from the Royal Canadian Air Force?" Nessa showed she recognized the uniform and insignia Greg wore. They laughed.

"You've got it," he said, smiling. He had a friendly grin, mop of light fair hair, boyish face, twinkling blue-grey eyes – handsome lad. Laura was smiling shyly.

"You in the services too?" Nessa asked her. The young woman, a brunette with upturned nose and brown eyes, lovely complexion, shook her head.

"No. I am a music teacher in Montreal, but I have been in the Yukon with Greg. I have been learning first aid, and rudimentary nursing to be of help where needed."

"Wow, cold! Bet you're glad to be in Southern California?"

Laura smiled and nodded. Greg replied,

"Yes we are. I have been stationed in the Aleutians, but I was summoned down here by my government to meet the host of our party tonight, and he told the authorities that I could bring my girl – sorry," he looked apologetically at Laura, who was laughing, eyes raised in amused amazement that he could forget the second he met a glamorous blonde. "My wife," he added, giving Laura a shy smile that asked for her forgiveness.

"You two are too cute for words," Nessa said, hoping that she didn't sound patronizing. A conspiratorial wink, and cuddling down in her seat, a dreamy expression on her face, showed she was teasing, plus, "I am so jealous," said with warmth and sincerity. "How long have you been married?"

"Two months."

"Oh well, of course. Congratulations."

Laura picked up the courage to ask Nessa about her film work, and then, where her real interest lay, about the leading ladies in her films. That took up all the drive time to the Franz house up in the hills on the coast just above Santa Barbara. By the time they got out of the ancient Packard, they were laughing like old friends. Nessa had been open, and as enthusiastic in answering as Laura had been in asking, an effective way to ease tension and forge trust and mutual attraction. They walked along the flagstone path to the big oak door, shoulders touching, heads together in animated gossip, while Steven and Greg followed on behind, and shared a smile of amusement at women's less complicated ways of getting on at first meeting, which somehow eased the way for them too.

They were greeted at the door by a middle-aged Mexican lady, whom Steven embraced and called Marisol. She took their coats, and led them into the crowded, yet warm, welcoming room beyond. There were people in ordinary day clothes, people in elegant evening attire, and men and women in military uniform. Steven was in his usual baggy, somewhat worn, academic attire: grey slacks, tweed jacket, rumpled shirt with frayed collar, scuffed Oxfords. Laura looked pretty and sweet in a short floral print summer frock. Nessa was elegant in flared black silk trousers and rainbow-hued sparkling sequined bolero jacket. She wore black satin pumps, so as not to tower over people.

A tall elderly gentleman with crinkly white hair and kind blue eyes approached them, beaming, with hands outstretched to embrace Steven, who beamed shyly back. They embraced.

"Now, Steven, introduce me to your young friends."

Steven introduced Laura and Greg, and then introduced Nessa. Emil appraised Nessa for a few seconds.

"Miss Eiles, I have seen you before, at your high school graduation back in 1935. I was very much impressed by your valedictorian address. I have wanted to meet you ever since, but we both have had busy agendas. My wife and I have followed your career in the movies. We have been deeply touched by your stories, and by your articles, which we also follow in the Atlantic Monthly. I had thought that your life would take a political turn, but you have taken a rather neat turn into analyzing life, and how people, mainly women, live life with no particular political notions, but try to lead good lives, helping others, trying to understand new notions. It gave my wife and me hope for the future – a new future with new, yes maybe, women's ways of doing things."

Nessa thanked him, but her eyes conveyed the futility of such hopes, at least in the foreseeable future.

"Yes, I understand, Miss Eiles. To attain Utopia, we first have to battle so many demons, that we dare not hope for too much. Let me introduce you to my wife." He beckoned to a beautiful older woman, tall like Nessa, with dark, almost black eyes, long swan-like neck. She wore a diamond studded black evening gown fitted to her long, graceful form. Her silver hair was swept back off her incredible face in a short pageboy style. She apologized to those to whom she had been speaking, and came over to join them. She extended her gloved hand to Nessa.

"Miss Eiles. I am delighted to meet you. I know of your work, naturally, and am very impressed." She then greeted Laura and Greg just as graciously. Steven, she was less formal with, and embraced him warmly, as befitted their long acquaintance. Nessa couldn't take her eyes off her. Magda Franz was a living work of art…intriguing, enigmatic.

Emil and Steven withdrew to talk. Greg and Laura were hailed by a young man in British Royal Navy uniform and his companion, a very attractive, tall, thin girl, who looked bored, until she smiled, and then she looked lovely, peaches and cream complexion, mid-brown hair, large, hooded blue eyes, upper class English accent.

"Miss Eiles…"

"Please, Nessa."

Magda paused and smiled. "Nessa. I am an old Yenta, but my musical soul detects vibrations emanating from certain people, and there is a young man here tonight, who I think may interest you. You both seem to occupy a rather rarefied zone of existence –extremely clever and talented, but sensual too. He has many talents. He is an extremely accomplished musician, a composer of innovative, magical nocturnes. He is also an adventurer engineer, and a pilot in the army air force. Will you let me introduce you to him? Will you indulge me in my imaginings, and let me see if I have read the music of the cosmos correctly?" She laughed. Nessa smiled, but inwardly, she sighed. These highbrow men, Sigi, and now this strange lady, Magda, wanted to throw at her, were always a letdown. Scott Freeman was the only clever scientific man she had been drawn to, and even he hadn't moved her beyond fondness.

As she followed Magda through the groups of people engaged in animated conversations, she noticed a man standing alone in a corner. He seemed lost in his own thoughts. He was tall, broad shoulders, well-built, could be the physical sporty type, not your ordinary working man type. He wore his evening tux with too much natural ease, so not averse to high society, cultural pursuits. He could be a business type, but could be a rugged outdoor type too. His face was interesting, sort of long oval, clean-shaven, eyes intense in an authoritatively aware sort of way, hair mid-brown, cut close to his perfectly rounded oval head. He may have kept it short to hide the curls that hinted at being apparent if his hair were any longer. He was very attractive, manly, no hint of affectation, no hint of being ill at ease. He'd come out of his reveries, and was looking around him, definitely interested in people there, but not ready to take part yet. His quiet natural self-assurance was very attractive. Nessa had never felt so intensely attracted at first sight to someone before. Magda turned to smile at her, a knowing sort of smile. Nessa wondered if Magda had detected her feelings, but for the man standing in the corner, not for whomever Magda was leading her towards. A woman stopped Magda to ask her something. Nessa took the opportunity to look at him again, and her eyes met his. A thousand volts of electricity seemed to pass through her. He looked guarded, curious, and she felt embarrassed, another first for her. Her face was on fire. She quickly looked away. His eyes were green, not friendly, more reserved, as if he were wondering why this stupid red-faced lanky blonde was looking at him in such girlish adolescent confusion. Never had she lost her cool composure before. Where was that ice princess she so relied on? He looked like the type who was attracted to cool, intelligent women, certainly sophisticated women, who were above all that uncouth blushing and giddiness. She tried to pay attention to the conversation in which Magda was engaged. She smiled with what she hoped was intelligent interest. She forced a look of charming reserve into her eyes. Yes, she could be that sophisticate to whom he most probably was drawn. She raised her head to look around casually, definitely not in his direction.

"Magda, may I interrupt? I haven't had the chance to thank you for your kind invitation to this party of yours tonight." Nessa turned, and there he was, in front of her. His voice had English inflections, such as Boston Brahmins cultivate, definitely American, but well-educated, most probably in England or Europe somewhere, in those fancy public schools, as they called the schools attended by the rich and well-connected over there. Well, Nessa spoke well. She and her parents may have used relaxed 'Ma and Pa' isms at home, but they used more sophisticated language when the occasion demanded it.

In fact, Nessa had acquired a more cultured accent doing theater in university. His voice made her melt, however. He had a friendly smile, but still a little on the reserved side.

Magda gave him a light kiss on the cheek. Nessa felt envious that Magda could be so relaxed and intimate with him.

"Drax, my dear, Phyllis you know, and may I introduce you to Miss Eiles." They were looking at her, smiles on their faces: Magda's sly, and his – sort of politely attentive. Nessa smiled and reached out her hand.

"My name is Nessa. I am sorry. Did Magda say your name was Drax?"

"I do apologize. I am so dizzy tonight, I didn't complete the introduction: Nessa, this handsome devil is Drax Shaw from Boston." Surprise! Surprise! She felt calmer now, more her old in-control self.

"Miss Eiles, I am pleased to meet you. I have read your articles in the Atlantic Monthly. They are very intuitive and enlightening."

"Nessa writes for movies too," Magda added.

"Your own stories or adaptations of other writers' works?"

"Both. I have been very lucky to have been given the chance to write scripts based on my work." He seemed to be considering the reason for that. She was still rather young to be so fortunate.

"I hope you will excuse me if I point out that you have achieved much in what must be a short time. When did you start writing for Hollywood?"

"I turned up there nearly two years ago, just after graduating, in response to an invitation from Harry Henderson, who had read one of my Atlantic articles. He thought I might be appropriate for the position of assistant screenwriter. They were working on a film related to what I had written about. Later, I had the audacity to show my own script to Fiona Kyrke and George Cukor, and they wanted to do the movie. Everything took off for me at that point, and I haven't looked back."

"Thank goodness you came across George. He knows true talent when he sees it, and he doesn't feel threatened by promoting clever women." Magda turned to Drax for confirmation. He seemed unconvinced.

"When he reads it, I think you mean Magda – true talent when he reads it in Miss Eiles' case." He glanced at Nessa. "And not, as is also appropriate as regards Miss Eiles, just sees it." Magda looked confused.

"I think Mr. Shaw has doubts about my writing talent having earned me my promotions. Am I correct, Mr. Shaw?"

"No. I know George, he is an old friend of my father's. Fiona Kyrke must have sensed a challenge in her character to accept it too. She is one of the more serious and competent actresses, one not given to frivolous roles."

"Drax, you are not implying that Nessa has gained her success through her stunning looks are you? If you are, I am angry at such chauvinism. We women have to fight so hard to be accepted for our intelligence, our minds, and men are always looking for easy explanations as to why we succeed, 'Oh well it was her looks,' or 'well, she had to seduce a man to get where she is.' I never would have thought you'd resort to such thinking. You have a brilliant mother, a gentle soul, totally involved in her art. Would you put her success down to her looks or feminine wiles? She is so ethereally feminine and beautiful, but she has been judged brilliant before people have seen her. You said Nessa's articles were brilliant. You thought that before you met her."

"I must apologize Miss Eiles. I found your articles brilliant, as Magda says. I guess you did take me by surprise. I was expecting a more academic, political sort of woman." Magda raised her hands in appeal to a higher judge. "Yes well, Magda is quite right to lose all patience with me. I guess I have put both feet in my mouth. I was so impressed by your work, that I was annoyed that maybe Hollywood had promoted you because of your looks. It wouldn't have been fair to you. That is what I meant, not that I thought your ideas were so banal that it had to have been your looks that brought you such success. I wanted your intellect to get sole credit, which it so rightly deserves."

"Oh, now Drax, that is much better. I apologize for misunderstanding you. I shall go and leave you two to get better acquainted." Magda clutched Drax's arm and hissed, "Now behave yourself, and be nice." She drifted off towards an elderly couple who were trying to get her attention, a charming smile on her incredible face.

"That's alright, you don't have to stay. I am not upset by any means."

"I'd like to chat to you some more, if you don't mind. Our eyes met before I joined you and Magda, and you looked a little confused, as if you'd met me before. The reason I ask, is that I feel as if I have seen you somewhere too. Have we met?"

Nessa was relieved that he had thought she'd merely recognized him from some previous encounter, and that he'd not thought she'd been so attracted to him, that she couldn't conceal the fact, but was as infatuated as a schoolgirl.

"I thought that you looked familiar, but I can't place where and when I might have met you, or whom I may have met that you resemble."

"Likewise." He scrutinized her so intently, eyes narrowed. She smiled, but she found this so amusing, that she felt like laughing. She felt bubbly. He noticed her amused embarrassment, and became embarrassed himself.

"I do apologize. I forget the social niceties when I'm trying to figure out things like where I must have seen you. I have never met anyone like you, so you do not resemble anyone I previously may have met. I can't let it go until the solution comes to me."

"We have not met before. I am sure I would have remembered you." Nessa gave a forced smile for emphasis. He laughed.

"That strange eh?"

Nessa nodded.

"Ah well, I should go and try to find some friends, who should be here by now," He looked around the room. "Goodbye, it is good to put a face to those clever articles of yours." He looked at her for a brief moment, shook his head, smiled, and raised a hand in farewell. He didn't get far. Laura and Greg grabbed him from behind, and Laura kissed his cheek. Nessa sighed again at how lovely it would be to be so familiar with him.

"Nessa, have you met Drax? He is our very dear friend. He and Greg learned how to fly together."

"Yes, we hatched out of the same nest," Greg smirked. Laura hit his arm, but laughed. Even Drax managed an amused smile, as he looked fondly at Laura. "Don't I wish," added Greg. "No, my nest was not so well off as Drax's."

"Look you Canadian love-birds, I am afraid that I have both insulted and bored Miss Eiles, and she must have been relieved that I was about to go off to find you two, so let's give her a chance to meet more exciting people. Goodnight again, Miss Eiles." Laura and Greg exchanged grimaces.

"What did this idiot do to offend you? I assure you he's harmless, well sort of, I think."

Nessa laughed, but couldn't think of what to say.

"Oh come on, let's all get a drink, and find somewhere to sit and chat. My shoes are killing me." Laura led them off to an unoccupied cozy corner, just as Sigi had said there would be. Where was Sigi in any case? Nessa glanced around. No Sigi in sight.

They got comfy, drinks in hand, and Nessa thanked her lucky stars Laura had saved the situation, so that here she was sitting hip to hip with him, just when it seemed she'd never have the chance to talk to him again. Their cozy contact was brief. Another couple bore down on them, and Drax was in the embrace of that beautiful English girl, who was with the handsome guy in Royal Navy uniform.

"Hi, I am Rory Ellis-Rhys, and this woman draped across my dear friend is actually my wife, Syb; emphasis being on my."

Nessa smiled wholeheartedly at him, and then at Sybil, who still had her arms around Drax's neck. She did free one arm to offer Nessa her hand.

"How wonderful! With a name like that, you must be Welsh." They looked pleasantly surprised.

"He is Welsh. I am sane." They all laughed.

"Don't mind her - Saesneg, you know. We have to make allowances, poor thing."

Nessa laughed.

"He means I am English," Syb explained.

"Yes, I know. I speak Welsh. My mother is Welsh."

"There now; I knew you had class." Rory looked pointedly at Syb, who sneered back.

"There must be some Viking in you. You don't look typically Welsh. They are all short and dark like this Taffy here." Sybil reached over to tousle Rory's silky black hair that had a slight attractive curl to it.

"I am not short. I am as tall as Drax."

"Yeah, yeah, and taller than I am," sighed Greg.

"And I love every inch," Laura threw her arms around her smiling husband, and was awarded with a brief kiss. They all sighed. Laura and Greg shouted, "Shut up!" in unison. People turned to look at them.

"Stop it. We are getting rowdy. How much have we had to drink?" Syb peered into her empty glass.

"Not enough." Drax took Syb's glass. "Here, I'll fill that for you. Anyone else thirsty?" They all handed him empty glasses.

"I'll come and help you," laughed Rory, taking two of the glasses.

"And you, Miss Eiles, what are you drinking?"

"White wine, please, and do call me Nessa."

He didn't look at her, and moved off through the crowd with Rory. Obviously he wasn't attracted to her. Was he the man Magda had wanted her to meet?

Sybil sat in Drax's spot next to her. She could still feel the warmth from his thigh as it had touched her's. Darn! He'd sit somewhere else when he returned. Sybil said that Laura had filled her in on all the movie news, and she was so very thrilled to meet her.

"I am only a writer, a minor one at that. They use my stories when they are hard up for anything better. I usually am just what I was hired to be – an assistant to the important screenwriters." The girls groaned.

"Please Nessa, we have read your articles, and we are fans of yours. We share your social concerns," Sybil touched her arm to show how sincere she was. Laura nodded, and gave a friendly grin. They were a fun pair.

"Nessa, there you are. I have been looking everywhere for you," and Sigi materialized out the cigarette smoke haze, a vision in a knee-length white silk cocktail dress, V-neck, short sleeves that just covered the tops of her arms, diamond brooch under the bust line, from which soft wide pleats fell to the hemline. Laura gasped and could barely contain her excitement. Here before her was the beautiful, mysterious Sigi Andrus. Nessa smiled and made the introductions. Sigi was relaxed and at ease with them at once. She graciously accepted their compliments, and answered their questions, enjoying the gossip as much as they did. Nessa suddenly remembered Sigi saying that there was going to be a man at the party, in whom she was very interested. It would not surprise her in the least if that man turned out to be Drax Shaw. He was Sigi's type. She and Sigi were usually attracted to the same types of men – and here he came, negotiating the crowds, glasses held high, three of them, and he hadn't spilt a drop. Rory followed, equally dexterous with his three glasses.

"Sigi, we saw you join the girls, so I brought you a drink too – your favorite, I think."

"Oh Drax, you are a marvel. Yes that is right, as usual. Well done! You are a dear." He bent down for her to kiss his cheek, which she did enthusiastically, letting the contact linger, and then they shared a smile that hinted at intimacy. Sigi's green eyes sparkled. He straightened, and continued whatever it was he and Rory had been chatting about on their way over. Sigi had that pampered cat look, a sly smile hovering as she sipped her drink. Nessa had her first experience of jealousy, and her first failure to get her man. This was sad. She liked Sigi very much, and admired her beauty and her intellect. Why oh why did Sigi have to set her cap at him? Oh this was torture! Was there any way she could leave? Would Steven give her a ride home? She looked for him across the heads of the other guests, and couldn't see him anywhere.

"Lovely house isn't it?"

Nessa jumped.

"Oh I am sorry. I startled you out of your reverie. You don't look too happy. Worrying thoughts?"

It was Sybil. She had that bored look again, but a knowing smirk on her lips. Nessa smiled. She liked this girl. She was so amusingly droll, and she and the winsome Laura seemed good friends. There was something about them that made Nessa feel as if she'd known them all her life.

"Do you perchance like our Drax? He is a fine figure of a man isn't he? He is a super fellow too, very easy to like, if you know what I mean." Syb moved her eyebrows up and down suggestively. "Not my type of course, I like them Welsh and other worldly."

"Rory is very good looking and fun."

"Clever too. You Welsh and your love of words! He didn't mention that he also writes. He writes novels and poems, oodles of words, and ones he makes up by bringing words together to make new words that capture a mood or moment so well. Greg does that too. They have lots of fun making up these words together. He seduces me with words, but he definitely backs them up with actions," Sybil rolled her eyes a la Groucho Marx and gave a throaty laugh.

Sybil was a little outrageous, like Alisyn, same languid air too, with a hint of devil-may-care about them. Sigi had stood to drink with the men. Greg had joined them. She was the center of their attention. Laura moved to sit with the girls. Sybil put her arm around her shoulders.

"Here is love's young dream. How goes it my Canadienne? Fella abandoned you at the first sight of a femme fatale? Join the gang." Syb raised her glass and drained it.

"Oh Lordy, there's Greg's Uncle Harold! Greg is going to introduce me to him tonight. I am terrified! He's with British Intelligence."

"Cheer up, kiddo. There is Kerr. He is so adorable. He's with the formidable uncle, who doesn't look too scary to me. He's kinda cuddly looking. Don't worry, Laura, Kerr helps ease every awkward situation." Nessa and Sybil exchanged smiles. "Kerr is super. He is one of our gang too."

"Are you all spies?"

"Look around you dear: Jewish exiles, exiles from all the occupied countries of Europe and the Far East, officers from foreign secret services, as well as American intelligence services."

"And Canadian," Laura added proudly.

"German anti-Nazis and Russians too – at least one or two from all kinds of subversive liberal backgrounds, so who are you really, Nessa Eiles?"

"Sigi Andrus invited me here tonight, said I might enjoy a more highbrow crowd for a change. My old high school professor disappeared into that study with Dr. Franz ages ago. I always knew there was more to Steven Etchberry than met the eye." Nessa trailed off as Sigi leaned over to tap her shoulder.

"How are you enjoying yourself?" she asked.

"Having a great time, as you promised."

"Is Drax an old flame of yours?" Sybil interjected, cheekily. She was like Alisyn.

"Oh I wish, but no, although I keep hoping. Drax and I have known each other for years. He and his parents visited us in our chalet in the mountains of Romania many times, when Drax and I were children. We really are good friends, and that's not just a coy, for-the-press, comment."

"But you fancy him?" Nessa asked.

"He isn't the one I was telling you about," whispered Sigi. "Although I wouldn't mind. I always have been attracted to Drax, but the attraction isn't mutual."

Laura gasped,

"You're kidding right? He must be attracted to you, and he is just playing it cool to challenge you, make you intrigued by his lack of interest. That always works."

Sigi laughed,

"Not in this case I am afraid. He's had too many chances, and he knows I'm a push over as far as he is concerned. No. Poor me has to look elsewhere."

"Yeah, poor you," Sybil sighed.

They all laughed. Syb smiled slyly at Nessa. She was incorrigible!

"So who is the lucky fellow you hoped to get together with tonight?" Nessa asked, her nerves as taut as finely drawn violin strings. Sigi decided to tease, and she put on a secretive smile.

"I think that Dr. Franz is signaling for you to join them," Sybil nodded in the direction of Dr. Franz's study.

Sigi turned to check.

"Oh yes, this is it, Ness. We'd better go in."

"Me? Why me? It is you they most probably want."

"No, Nessa, it is you they want to talk to. I was asked to bring you here tonight."

Nessa looked at the other two, and they merely shrugged.

As Sigi and Nessa crossed the room, Nessa felt curious eyes upon them. She had been bombarded by too many firsts that evening already. What lay in store behind that study door? Steven would be there, which was reassuring, although this wasn't the Steven she was used to. Sigi's presence was too whimsical and mysterious to be relied upon. Drax, Rory and Greg were following in their wake. She didn't want to have to respond to something complicated that would require careful assessment, in front of Drax. She had hoped that the evening still held the possibility of something a bit more romantic with regard to him. Too late, there they all were behind closed doors, looking at her: Greg, Rory, the fellow called Kerr and Sigi were smiling expectantly; Greg's uncle's hand was held out in friendly greeting; Steven had a somewhat anxious look on his face, and Drax looked full of doubt and reluctance? Why?

Steven introduced Nessa to Kerr Toddy and Colonel Harold Macklin, Greg's uncle. He then explained how they could use her intellectual talents as a go between for a very secret place in England and Emil's group here in California. They would by-pass intelligence services in Washington D.C. and the military, as they were not sure how reliable they were, and make sure that only FDR and Churchill received this extremely important top secret information.

"We have found that this war is not going to be won by the military or the politicians. It is going to be won by advanced knowledge of the enemies' intentions. This will give our leaders and our fighting men the advantage they will need to fight effectively. We cannot afford to have the hit or miss strategies and ineffective leadership that created all the carnage and wasted effort in the last war. Different branches of the military and different political interests in Congress and Parliament vie with one another. They are too competitive to be totally effective," said Uncle Harold.

"But isn't that democracy in action?"

"One would think so, yes, but actually it is not so. It is not freedom of thought in these cases, but more an expression of competing ambitions. Nessa, to win this war, we need to compartmentalize information, and keep certain crucial facts for those who need to know, and who can act without delay and debate. The British have brought together many clever and trustworthy people to work on breaking enemy codes. I cannot tell you how they are planning to do this until you agree to work with us. The extremely top secret work done by these people goes to FDR and Churchill only, no one else. FDR and Churchill have their detractors, who would love to see them fail. That is why they need a source of reliable information from people they can trust."

"And that would be you people here tonight?"

They nodded. She looked around her. Her eyes met Steven's, and they looked at each other for a long few seconds. She could sense his concern, but she knew then, that if he trusted them, she could too.

"Nessa, your mathematical expertise, as well as your analytical mind, make you a great asset as a go-between. Steven Etchberry has vouched for your character and your love for, and loyalty to, America, and through your Welsh connections, your loyalty to Britain."

"I also come from German stock, but I detest the Nazis with every fiber of my being," Nessa replied. "I would like to help free Germans of this foul Third Reich. I have wanted to do my bit for the war effort for some time now. Trying to raise money, clothing and food to send to Britain and Occupied Europe is helpful, but I have wanted to be more involved, more effective."

"It is possible that we may ask you to risk your life to get information from mathematicians behind enemy lines. Should you be of use behind enemy lines, it will have to be before you do your hush-hush work. We do not send our 'secrets people' into the fray in case they get caught and tortured. We cannot risk the Germans getting even a hint of what we do."

"I understand now why you kept sending me those magazines on mathematical codes and puzzles, Steven." Steven nodded, an apologetic grimace on his face.

"I do not want to put you at risk, Nessa. I could not live with myself if anything should happen to you, and I could never face your parents again."

"I do not want to be given safe assignments if I can be more useful elsewhere, even if that involves danger. My parents have family in Wales and Norway, and I think some in Germany. My father and Sam Pritchard went to fight in the last war before America was officially involved. I would be following in their footsteps, and proud to do so."

Emil smiled. Steven put his head in his hands.

"Now this next topic has nothing to do with the work you would be doing, Miss Eiles, but involves these young men here tonight. The Japanese have called up their forces. There has been a marked increase in Japanese radio traffic recently, and we fear the worst. Kerr and Drax, you have been involved in engineering projects in Indochina and the Philippines, building roads and bridges, not just as innocent helping hands, but to help build up their defenses, and to reconnoiter the regions for suitable bays and harbors, mountain strongholds, access routes through the jungle, points where we can join up with British and French colonial forces should war with Japan come to pass. You also were able to assess local attitudes to the Allies and the Japanese. Some nationalist factions in India and China and all former European colonies see the Japanese as freeing them from European colonial control. Communists function throughout Indochina. Russia may have great influence there, and Russia has no love for Japan. Thank God the Soviets are on our side now, although their neutrality pact with Japan is tiresome. Still Stalin needs to focus all his efforts on the Germans. He can't take on the Japanese as well. They are formidable, and have beaten Russia before, quite soundly.

For the last year or so, we have been preparing our vulnerable and, as yet relatively neglected, incredibly long and exposed coast of Alaska. The Canadians are building up defenses on their west coast. Alaska is nearer to Russian Siberia and Tokyo than it is to points in the contiguous United States. The Bering Sea separates Alaska by a scant fifty-seven miles of ocean from Siberia, which is another reason why we do not want to give the Japanese the excuse to attack the Russians. The Japanese navy has been unbeaten in battle for about a hundred years or so. If they take Alaska, they can bomb all our western cities, and armaments factories. We have no airfields, runways or adequate road or rail transports in Alaska, no adequate electrical power or communication systems, no military quarters or defenses, and no sufficient food sources to support vast numbers of troops and their attendant construction crews, services and so on. In fact, Alaska is wide open to invasion. It is a colossally difficult terrain, not to mention the complications posed by the weather and stormy frigid seas. We are trying the best we can to remedy the situation and attend to all these points of weakness. In the fall of last year, we sent construction crews to Alaska by sea. We are building Elmendorf Air Base in Anchorage, Fort Richardson for army headquarters, Ladd Field at Fairbanks. We have to lay runways that stay flat and smooth at temperatures well below zero. Everything has to come by sea through the Inland Passage, which is often foggy and stormy, and difficult to say the least. In the milder weather, the men are attacked by mosquitoes, but still they slave away to build up our defenses. The men have work, but what work! The conditions are primitive, harsh and dangerous, but it must be done. There have been sightings of Japanese submarines exploring our western coastlines since 1939. Needless to say, this does not look at all good for us.

Alaska is suddenly the focus of attention as a potential way to get Lend Lease weapons and supplies to the Soviets, who are badly in need of our help in that regard. It is not an easy route, but the shortest onto Russian territory. If Japan invades American soil through the Aleutians, they can attack supply routes into Siberia by sea and by air. All forces will have to contend with those god-awful storms they have up there. What are they called?"

"Williwaws", said Drax, Greg and Kerr in unison.

Nessa was shaken to her very core to think that America's western shores could be so vulnerable. Suddenly this whole evening's charade was deadly serious.

"Drax and Greg will be part of the eleventh army air force up there."

"Yeah, a regular winter resort –brrr," said Greg, and Drax gave a rueful laugh.

Emil took Nessa's hands in his.

"Nessa, you see how tenuous our situation is if Japan attacks us. We need you in England, doing this terribly important work that will relate to the war in Europe, and possibly in Asia. We shall need you in place by the end of the year, after Christmas, unless the worst comes to the worst, and we are at war with Japan before then. Naturally, America would enter the war ongoing in Europe at the same time that war is declared on Japan, and Britain will help us in the Pacific. Britain has extensive colonial presence in countries that will be threatened by the Japanese: Burma, Thailand, not to mention, the golden crown of empire – India, and Australia too, maybe even New Zealand, all dear to the British heart and pocket book," Emil smiled at Harold. Harold shrugged with his mouth turned down, and huffed. Emil continued; "I firmly believe that this war will not be won by politicians and the military. Oh they'll do the back-breaking, dangerous work, but they will win because of the work you and the others will be doing. They will know ahead of time where the enemy will be, and what he intends. What you will be taking part in may save countless lives, not just of troops, but civilians in harm's way too. We can use the military and wild counterespionage escapades by outfits such as Donovan's to make the enemy think we get our information to foil their plans from spies and commandoes, but we actually receive only a small part of our information on what the Germans and Japanese are planning from these sources. What we hope you become a part of, and Professor Etchberry has long been a part of, is our best-kept secret and our best hope. There is a Washington equivalent in the making, and their people will be trained in England. Drax, Kerr and Greg and Rory, as well as Sybil and Laura, have been trained there already. Are you going to join us?"

"I wouldn't miss it for the world. I won't let my peers fight my battles for me."

"Ah, I know another young woman of about your age, who is part of the anti-Nazi underground in Hamburg, who said those same words. You are both incredible young women, as are dear Sigi here, and Sybil and Laura. Strangely enough the young woman in Hamburg is also half Welsh," Emil shook his head at the happy coincidence.

"You are not just another Jewish refugee from Hitler's Reich, are you, Dr. Franz?"

They all looked at Emil, smiles on their faces.

"No, Miss Eiles, I am not."

He thanked them all for coming, and for listening to him and Harold go on and on, instead of enjoying themselves at the party.

"Go now, have fun, enjoy your time together, and pray the Japanese won't go to war. Yamamoto doesn't want to take us on, and he may prevail, but I doubt it. Rory, a word if I may? It won't take long, my dear boy."

"Now are you glad you came?" whispered Sigi.

"Overwhelmed, worried, yet glad of the chance to be useful."

Steven tapped her shoulder.

"We need to talk to your parents. Will you be there Wednesday as usual for dinner? They know what went on tonight, but they need to have their say."

"I bet my mother is dead against it."

Steven smiled.

"You may be surprised. She is Welsh after all."

"Oh you'll love England," Syb laughed, when they rejoined her and Laura. "Those huts are so cold in Winter and get smoked out, and so stiflingly hot in summer. I know that's hard to believe, but we do get some hot, muggy days in summer. It doesn't rain all the time, but summer rains make it hot and humid, and we don't have ice cold drinks. Our beers and sodas, called pops, are drunk warm. Oh it's just heavenly! There's always good old fish and chips to fall back on, served in newspaper with lots of salt and vinegar."

Nessa laughed.

"Sounds wonderful! I can work off all the fat I'll put on through water retention by walking or cycling everywhere. I always have wanted to see the lovely countryside, so green and lush."

"Oh you'll see loads of that and up close. Petrol, or gas, as you Yanks call it, is heavily rationed. You'll have to walk or cycle. If you go farther a field, you take the local buses, and to go into London, you'll be packed into railway carriages with civilians, the entire army, navy and air force lads on leave and randy as hell, all packed in together, smelly armpit to smelly armpit, like tinned sardines. Oh yes, sardines on toast, big treat over there!"

"Sounds lovely," Nessa sighed and grimaced.

"And did I mention the black-out and nightly bombing raids and sleeping in air raid shelters with some dirty old man's head in your lap, the smell of sweat filling your nostrils? I take eau de cologne down with me, and bathe in it. A handkerchief soaked in the stuff and held under the nose all night helps."

"Okay. I get the drift. I'll take several bottles over with me."

"Syb filling you in on the joys of life in dear old Blighty?" Rory laughed. He hugged Syb to him. "She's a regular tour guide and excellent promoter for our lovely historical isles, is our Syb. Aren't you sweetheart?" They all laughed. Syb gave Rory a forced cheesy smile. He kissed her on her nose, and arms wrapped around each other, they went off to dance. It was a slow number, and soon they were lost to all around them, with eyes only for each other. Greg pulled Laura to her feet and led her off to a dark corner to dance and smooch. Sigi, Nessa, Drax and Kerr stood there rather self-consciously. Drax looked at Sigi and held out his hand. She smiled and took his hand, and soon they were dancing. He held her close, but they didn't embrace. Sigi was whispering in his ear. Kerr smiled tentatively by way of invitation to join them, and Nessa accepted.

"You are going to be doing very important work you know."

"So I gather you'll be one of the pilots going to the Aleutians?"

"No. I shall be in Indochina setting up resistance groups should the Japs invade. I also am going to try and liaise with communist guerrilas in the mountains of China. They hate the Japs with a vengeance, so could form effective fighting and sabotage units. I shall most probably be there for the duration of the war, whether the US gets involved or not."

"You and Drax have traveled a great deal with your work. It must be exciting."

"It is. I love tackling difficult projects: controlling flood waters, building bridges across narrow gorges, with fast flowing rapids hundreds of feet below, digging ditches to irrigate fields for agricultural development, and so enable the people to grow their own food and lead better lives. Drax is a great guy, so clever. He can look at an impossible situation and see how it can be made to work. He's a wonderful composer too. He'd sit out on some precipice all night long, gazing at the stars, seeing how the terrain looked under the light of the moon, and the next morning he'd show us where to start work, and he'd have composed a beautiful piece of music that captured the beauty of the wretched place, a beauty we'd failed to notice before."

Nessa glanced over at Drax. Sigi was still whispering away, and he seemed to be thinking it over. The music stopped, and Drax and Sigi returned. The others drifted out into the garden to find even shadier spots. They replenished their drinks, and talked about what made up American music. Raw jazz and the blues were essential backgrounds for cinema noir. Nocturnes belonged to the romantic dramas of the thirties, but Nessa loved them. They created such an otherworldly ambiance. The band started up again, another slow dance for the older folks present.

"Oh for some swing," sighed Sigi. They laughed. "I can see some of these elegant elderly couples kicking up their legs to 'In the Mood', can't you Drax?"

"I like the slow ones. Nessa would you like to dance?" She thought he'd never ask. Sigi readily embraced Kerr, and he returned the favor.

"Wow, he didn't dance with me like that,"

"Does that upset you?"

"No. They make an attractive pair. Oh I am sorry. Do you and Sigi have something romantic going?" He laughed and pulled her into a close embrace, his cheek touching hers. Nessa could hardly breathe. She had longed for this all night, and here at last, she was in his arms, and he held her so firmly, so possessively, as if he'd never let her go, and she didn't want ever to leave his embrace. She rested her head on his strong shoulder. He radiated a sense of being in control, all protecting, decisive, capable, and yet he had a sensitive side, as evidenced by what Kerr had said about his music capturing the beauty of a situation. He rested his head on hers.

"Why Miss Eiles you are quite soft and cuddly for a warrior maiden!" She raised her head to look at him. He was smiling kindly, and she knew she had a dreamy expression that gave all away, but she didn't care. He seemed quite quietly amused at first, but the longer they looked at each other, the more intense his emotions seemed. He stopped smiling, and he lightly kissed her on her lips. He pulled back to look into her eyes again, with a more serious expression and then he kissed her once more with feeling. She readily reciprocated.

"Penny for your thoughts," Drax whispered in her ear, sending sensual shivers up and down her spine.

"I don't have thoughts for once. I have incredible sensations, feelings. I am bereft of words. Do you think it is the wine, or the ambiance, or both?" she murmured sleepily, her head once again on his shoulder.

"Well it could be, but I was hoping it was my humble self who created those sensations, and by the way, you're also pretty adept at creating incredible sensations yourself."

Nessa felt such joy! Her whole being had never felt so alive and sensual. She raised her head and he kissed her. They had somehow managed to find a dark corner in which to dance. He stopped moving, and they just stood there and kissed. Her hands stroked the back of his neck. He pulled her even closer. He finally broke away, and touched his lips. She looked inquiringly at him, a little confused, as if the light had been turned on and had disturbed her from a deep sleep full of wonderful dreams. He also looked somewhat confused. Nessa was too afraid to ask what was wrong.

"Forgive me, Nessa. I don't want to take advantage of you if you are not altogether yourself and under the influence of too much wine."

She laughed. "Nope, I am very well aware of how I feel. I am quite sober, and not under the influence of the wine, but I am intoxicated in a rather lovely way." He looked at her without smiling for a few seconds. She became serious too. "I am sorry. That must have sounded very silly…" He swiftly caught her up in his embrace and kissed her passionately. He kissed her neck, and between kisses, he confessed to being over the moon, and that he had never felt this way before, and wasn't sure how to proceed, but he hoped against hope that she felt the same way. She assured him, breathlessly, that she did, and that this was new for her too. They finally pulled apart, and with arms around each other, he led her out into the starry night and up the hill towards Magda's art studio. They stood on the crest and looked out over the sea, peaceful under the stars and moonlight.

"I'd like to know all about you Miss Nessa Eiles."

"Kerr said that you discovered beauty in the most unlikely places, beauty, that before, had not been apparent, and you turned it into something magical through your music."

Drax turned her to face him, and held her by her shoulders.

"You are beautiful, Nessa. The most beautiful woman I have ever seen. There is more to you than the beauty apparent in your appearance. You are of this earthly existence, and yet… I don't know. You have an ineffable quality. You are a dealer in words, ideas, and yet they don't capture you, and I don't think that even Greg could capture that special something in his art either, and he is so very good at doing that, portraying an essence beyond that he sees in front of him. What's the matter? You suddenly look sad."

"I have spent my childhood, all the nights of my life, gazing at those stars. Sometimes they console me, inspire me, and other times they make me feel so alone. I am on a new plane of existence tonight. I feel excited, as if I am setting out on an adventure, and yet I can't take flight. This too solid earth has netted us, you, me, all of us, in bonds of all too human making."

"Nessa, we have been given a rare gift tonight. Let us make full use of it, see where it takes us. If we only know this magic for a brief interlude amidst all the horror we have to face, then let it be so, and who knows, knowing now that we exist for each other, that we have something possibly wonderful, may well bring us through all this madness. Write a happy ending, where we meet up again, and go through the rest of our lives together. As for my composition for you, of you, I have that taking shape in my head already, and it is magical."

They embraced gently and kissed, silhouetted against a backdrop of shimmering moonlit ocean and misty starlight.

A lone figure moved away from the glass front of her studio, where she had been watching the lovers, and retreated into the shadows, her long, elegant fingers pressed against her smiling lips, and tears cascading down her beautiful face. She had translated the rhythms correctly.

They had almost three months to be in love, to enjoy their youth, to indulge in hopeful fantasies for the future, as around them, the darkness gathered ominously.

<hr />

La Jolla, San Diego: September, 1941:
They chased one another through the waves, playing like porpoises, with carefree abandon. Each of the couples indulged in intimate wrestling, squealing and salty embraces. They dried off by playing football with a large orange and pink beach ball: boys versus girls. The girls won by default, insisting that the boys hadn't played fairly, groping, holding, tussling and, well, just blocking and distracting in other ways.

"If that's how you guys play football with the other lads, I will have to rethink your sexual preferences," Syb struggled to readjust her halter top. The fellas laughed and rolled around together, getting all sandy, while the girls watched, hands on hips, lips pursed in slight smiles of amused vindication and eyebrows raised in question.

"Drax shook the sand out of his hair.

"God, I'm hungry! They all paused, looking from one to the other; then they made a mad dash for the picnic hamper. Drax won, but they all piled in after him, pulling out chicken legs, sandwiches, oranges and apples, chips and sodas.

Replete, they lay out on their towels on the warm sand.

"I love the sun-baked, salty tang on my skin," sighed Nessa. They all murmured drowsily in agreement.

"Oh, this is the life! I can't believe how lucky we have been to be able to stay here the month. It is beautiful in the Canadian Rockies now, but the evenings will be beginning to get chilly," sighed Laura.

"The colors are amazing," replied Greg dreamily. "I love all this sunshine and warmth, but I do not want to miss the autumn colors back home." A thoughtful silence ensued. The news was getting worse every day. They didn't want to miss anything that was special to them, especially sports and other activities, which, with their whole and healthy bodies, they had taken for granted before. They felt fortunate to have agile, creative minds, and couldn't face the possible loss of these abilities as a result of injury in war, or of the horrors they might see, or the crippling guilt of their having to kill innocent people, even children. Years of health, creativity and accomplishment should have been their lot, but these now hung in the balance.

"This is an amazing interlude in what has been Hell." Rory sat up, looking seaward, "But the horrible thing about being at war, is that you can't give of yourself fully to freedom again, even though each moment is precious, and you want it to last, to be reality, but you know you have to wake up and return to the bloody fray. Other young people, other innocent, ordinary people, have lost their lives or their loved ones today, while Syb, Laura, Greg and I have had this brief reprieve. I am almost impatient to return, so that I can get it all over and done with faster. I never could stand anything hanging over my head."

They all sat up, the carefree mood had passed.

"I am sorry all of you, I am so sorry."

Drax put his hand on Rory's back. "Don't let it bother you, Rory. I am sure that the war hasn't been out of any of our minds." They all sadly agreed.

"All this time, we have been preparing for it. That we have been free as birds has been just an illusion," sighed Syb. "You have been honing your fighting prowess, learning new techniques, how to fly new planes, perform new air battle tricks, and you are off to Alaska next week to learn how to fly under those impossible weather and terrain conditions. Laura has been learning how to treat wounds, burns and amputations under battle conditions, but her other talents are going to be used instead. Nessa and I have been sharpening our wits for the same purpose. No, I'd say we have not been free of the war."

"You have been at war for two years. I have been merely poised on the brink. My brother, Bobby, is now a fully-fledged pilot, and on the aircraft carrier Hornet in the Pacific, on alert, but not at battle stations yet. Drax and Greg, you have flown bombing missions: Drax as an observer, you as a fighter pilot with the Royal Canadian Air Force, Greg. I am being trained in armed combat, in case I may have to go behind enemy lines, but it doesn't seem real to me yet."

"Let's have another swim," said Rory, getting up, and pulling a reluctant Syb to her feet. They all ran to the ocean, which was a deep blue-green with hints of purple, and let the tumbling waves wash over them – no fooling around now, but rather a time for quiet reflections, as they watched the sun begin its descent into the west. They stood together arms linked.

"Do you think there are German and Japanese couples standing, like us, arms linked, hoping beyond hope that they get to live their lives, love and reach a healthy old age after a peaceful and richly creative life?"

"I hope so Syb."

"Then why the bloody hell do we let them do this to us generation after generation?

Fairbanks, Alaska: September, 1941:
The three men, kitted out in leather flight jackets, lined with thick white wool, big loose flight boots, into which their trousers were tucked, stood at the dock, where tons of construction equipment were piled up, waiting transport on tractor sleds to the building sites. Large tracts of open land near the town were churned up, teeming with workers and troops constructing airfields and runways, roads and rail tracks, and the necessary infrastructure to support army, navy and air force personnel. The sky was heavy and low, making the whole scene a study in grey, black and dismal. The black sea churned behind them, chilling them to the bone. The Inland Passage had been rough: roaring winds, stinging rain and fog as thick and unrelenting as a shroud.

"All this heavy equipment has to come by sea?" Drax muttered, looking around, an expression of quiet despair on his face. "How are we going to get heavy bombers and transport planes up here in large numbers? If we use this route for Lend Lease to Russia, we'll need to do it by air and road."

"Over the Canadian Rockies, through that permafrost-muskeg wilderness?" gasped Rory. "It would take years to complete!"

"Not necessarily. Kerr and I have built roads and bridges through dense jungle, over high mountain gorges, rapids and roaring cataracts in next to no time. With hundreds of workers, American and Canadian, going at it during the milder season, if such a thing exists up here, it could be done in reasonable time."

"Then there are the mosquitoes," sighed Greg. "They are the worst; swarms of them."

"Ah, we had those in the jungles too. They are horrible, but they can become just an extra irritation to which you get accustomed. No, it will be the intense cold, the storms, the ice and gales, the heavy snowfalls and white-outs and frost bite that present the challenge."

"FDR has had his Civilian Conservation Corps up here since 1933 doing great work under horrendous conditions. Man, those guys can work!" Greg narrowed his blue-grey eyes against an icy blast. "And this, guys, is a fairly good day for up here."

"Look at those guys, all colors, all ages, all sizes, all doing horrendous work with a laugh and a joke. God, they are bloody marvels!"

"Alright, to the point, gentlemen please. Greg, you've flown up here, what does it entail? What are the risks?" Drax grimaced as another blast of icy, stinging rain blew in his face. "The weather being an obvious one and the lack of suitable air fields, at least at present."

"Our Royal Canadian Fighter Squadrons protect the coast." As if on cue, a P-40 Warhawk roared overhead. "There, you see," Greg grinned at them "The 8th Bomber Recon. Squadron is here too. They all fly in here from the Yukon, usually to Elmendorf Field. They make it out to Dutch Harbor, but landing is hairy!"

"Our Eleventh Air Force will be out in the Aleutian Chain. I gather conditions are grim and basic."

"That's being optimistic, Drax. The heavy wet air blocks the carburetors. The planes get iced up. Visibility is in feet, sometimes inches. You will be flying in almost constant fog. Most planes don't have radar. You have to learn to start your plane in temps of fifty below, and keep the oil from turning to jelly before you get it in the engine. You can lose fingers to frostbite working the fuel lines. Rubber becomes brittle and breaks. Those perforated, flexible steel mats they put down over the spongy muskeg are like trampolines when you land on them. You bounce, and sometimes flip over. Heavy bombers ripple up the mats in waves in front of them. Living conditions are primitive. You'll need gas masks to deal with the fumes from the stove and the men." They laughed. "You'll be freezing cold all the time."

"I've heard of Williwaws. Strong winds right?"

"Oh, Drax, my naïve lad, you have no idea!"

"Worse thing there is, so I've heard," interjected Rory.

"The Williwaw is the main attraction of the Aleutians. The weather is nearly always stormy. The air is turbulent. The seas are black and rough, with waves towering to fifty, sixty feet or more. Another feature that fires up a Williwaw is that there are high volcanoes on most of the islands, which are a threat in and of themselves. The Williwaws come howling like demented banshees out of the narrow canyons among the jagged volcanic peaks. You can tell it's the Williwaw, because the fog is black and the icy rain is blowing sideways and upside down! Williwaws flip planes, ships and tankers like toys. They suck planes out of their revetments and blow them away. I can see in your eyes, Drax, that you think that Williwaws are bad, but rare right? Hell no, they are almost a constant danger, and they can dump several feet of snow in a second."

"I have always wondered why America and Canada never have been invaded through here. It is their closest point to Asia, and reachable from Europe."

"It is a strategic point. Japan can invade America from here quite easily, and maintain supplies through the Kurile Islands. Paramushiro is their heavily defended base at the extreme end of the Kuriles. They can get back and forth to Attu, the nearest point to Paramushiro at the end of the Aleutian Chain, in a day. Mind you, that goes for our planes too. We can easily reach Paramushiro from Attu and get back, no trouble at all."

Drax rubbed his chin in thought.

"We have no choice but to fight from here, if we go to war with Japan. It is our closest point from which to bomb mainland Japan, and to invade. The Japanese know this. That is why they made us sign that treaty, not to fortify the Aleutians. They said that would constitute an act of war, so they know we have neglected the godforsaken place." There was another icy blast of sleet and snow.

"Drax, that treaty was the only thing preventing the Americans from building up their defenses in the Aleutians?" Greg asked.

"That and Congress. FDR did want to start building up here when Japan started spreading out, but Congress vetoed it. They didn't want to provoke the Japs. FDR did manage to get his Civilian Conservation Corps started up here, emphasis on civilian, so he could claim it didn't violate the treaty."

"Clever old fox!"

"Ah, if only I wasn't sworn to secrecy!" Rory gave a tantalizingly knowing grin.

"Don't pay any attention to him, Drax. The Welsh always claim to have secret knowledge about everything. Why even God let them in on the secret of why we are existing at all, didn't he, Rory?" Greg laughed.

"Of course, me old canny Scot, but by-the-by, he happens to be a she."

Drax mumbled that he didn't doubt that for a second.

---

California: September, 1941:
Nessa, Syb and Laura nursed their drinks, lost in thought, while the band played soft jazz.

"Listen, music makes statements, sentences too, like language. The sections vary in length. Some sentences will be more important. They won't necessarily be repeated, but you can look for patterns that lead up to, or put emphasis on, a section of letters or notes. These patterns exist in messages, and can be used to crack codes."

"Have you heard any of Drax's compositions?"

"He played me a piece he'd composed based on Rory's short story, "Hiraeth". It is so moving. It captures the Welsh love for homeland, the frustration of being 'significantly insignificant' as Rory calls it, that results in 'bragsolation' – the consolation of bragging – about the Welsh 'mythability' or 'intangibence,' which I guess is an intangible essence. Drax captures it all."

"Blast him! He'd better let us hear it when he gets back."

"I have heard some of his compositions based on Greg's paintings of the Canadian Rockies, and the way he illustrates the close tie between an animal and its natural surroundings, showing how they fit like a lock and key. Drax captures that idea so well that you feel it. You feel the rhythms of the habitat mixing and swirling with the genetic rhythms of the animal to make a new, coordinated entity."

Laura sighed. "He captured the intangibence of Greg in that piece too."

Syb leaned in a tad closer, her gossip face on.

"Sigi and Kerr didn't last long did they?"

"The timing wasn't right. Kerr had to go overseas on a tour of unknown duration. Sigi was signed up to do two movies, one after the other. Sigi was inconsolable when Kerr left. She cried for days, well two days." The others laughed. "She met an Irish actor, very handsome, upper class guy, and what do you think? It is hush-hush, but they went to Mexico last weekend and were married. There'll be a press meeting and photo blitz set for tomorrow, when they return."

The girls were astounded:

"But Kerr is a wonderful fellow, isn't he, Syb?"

"I've always thought so, and they looked pretty smitten with each other. Was it all an act on Sigi's part?"

"No, I don't think so. She is a strange mixture of being intensely practical and very clever, outgoing, and then suddenly insecure, grabbing at reassurances, building ramparts, closing herself in."

"Let's see, Kerr has been gone for all of two weeks, and broken-hearted Sigi is now Mrs Irish Actor? That's quick on any scale of adjustment!"

Nessa agreed, but she was too fond of Sigi to judge her actions harshly.

"Sigi is transplanted in a new world. She doesn't think in the long term. The Nazis took that away from all the exiles. She told me that she loves Kerr dearly. She can see he is a wonderful man, the best, but he told her that he has important work to do to help get ready for war with Japan. She acknowledges the sacrifice, and is willing to put their love on hold, but she has an intense urge to hurry up on life. She wants to be married. She wants children. She told me quite frankly that, when Kerr returns, she'll dump this guy and marry Kerr. She said that Kerr would make a wonderful father, whether the children were his or not, and she is sure that, when he returns, they'll be together no matter what."

"Wow! How calculating can one get?"

"Laura, it's an innovative way of thinking," said Syb, trying not to laugh.

"Could you do that?" Nessa and Syb shook their heads. No, it was not their style. "Quite right," Laura nodded her head in agreement.

"How did you and Greg meet? High school wasn't it?"

"Not really. I was in the Montreal Conservatory of Music, and working part-time at the Canadian Pacific Shipping Office. Coming from a French-Canadian family of twelve children, I was number seven, I couldn't afford to travel, but that put me as close as I could get, booking all those exotic trips for others. I love those posters of our magnificent ocean liners, and I am so proud of them. Our Empress and Duchess lines show our national pride and strength." Laura teared up some. "In any case, in he walked, with his folder under his arm, a hopeful, cocky optimism on his face. He was only just out of art school. Mr Robertson, the assistant director of the poster department, looked his drawings over in silence, while Greg looked at him, with such an eager expression on his wonderful face, that I desperately wanted him to succeed.

I had seen artists, older than he, with more experience, turned away every week. I could see Greg's hopes fade, as the heavy silence went on. He looked up and saw me watching, an anxious look on my face. He smiled tentatively. At last, Mr Robertson closed the folder. He looked at Greg for several seconds with a grim expression on his face. Greg raised his eyebrows and gave him a weak grin. I held my breath. I thought my heart would break. Then… the man rubbed his chin thoughtfully and said that Greg had captured something. He liked the way he portrayed movement. 'Lithe strength', he called it. Greg's paintings of skiers almost made him feel as if he were shooting down those runs, the crisp air on his snow-tanned face, the sense of plowing effortlessly through all that inviting white snow under blue skies. We waited. Greg had sensed my nervousness, and glanced over at me a few times. I couldn't hide my tears. Mr Robertson smiled at last. 'I like 'em. How old are you, son? Twenty, eh! That's young, but you got what we're looking for. You're hired.' I just squealed with relief, and clapped my hands, tears cascading down my cheeks. They looked at me in surprise. Greg smiled at the man in joyful embarrassment, and thanked him profusely. 'Your girl?' Mr Robertson asked. 'She is now, if she wants to be!' Did I ever. We never looked back, as they say."

"That was beautiful!" Nessa and Syb hugged. Laura laughed.

"Oh, I forgot, and it was a bitterly cold, snowy day, and he met me after work. It was dark, and a blizzard was blowing, and we went to a small Mom and Pop Italian restaurant, more a café really, and he insisted on treating me to a spaghetti dinner, complete with a glass each of cheap red wine. We felt so grown-up."

"Now how did you and Rory meet, Syb? You both know how Drax and I met. You were there."

"I'd like all the details though. Drax is fun, but he's not a ladies' man. He is so reserved, and speaks his mind, that most girls find him hard to take. They find him devastatingly attractive, but not a push-over."

"You're right, Syb. He dispensed with the usual chat-up. In fact, he was very outspoken about my looks being responsible for my success, not a winning line with me."

"That sounds like Drax's usual charming approach. Rory and I met at Cambridge. I was doing something useful like math, and typically, he was doing something esoteric. He was studying languages, Hindi, Farsi, Arabic, even Mandarin Chinese, Russian and Japanese, trying to find common roots, where different languages had branched off, even pictorial, symbolic ones. He was especially interested in Indo-European influences in Brythonic Celt, which the Welsh, Bretons and Cornish people speak. The Irish and Scots speak Gaelic Celt.

Some boring date had taken me to a rugby match." Nessa and Laura laughed at the droll way Syb rolled her eyes in exasperation. "It was freezing cold, and we stood on the frozen grass, a brisk March wind blowing across the field. I had my big woolen hat pulled down over my more than bored face, and my arms wrapped tightly around me. My date was a cumbersome rugby fan, and he was jumping up and down with glee, yelling support. As far as I could see, it was an excuse for men to wrestle and stick their heads up backsides, big, heaving backsides. Most of the players had no front teeth, some had cauliflower ears and broken noses – Oh they were a comely bunch, but good-natured. I was standing there, looking positively angry and glum, when suddenly the mob approached at speed. I moved back in alarm. The whistle was blown, literally when they were just a nose tip away, and off they all sauntered, arms around one another, to the club house, but one remained standing in front of me, smiling. He had all his teeth, and they were white and well formed. His ears were normal too, and his very fine nose. His silky black hair hung over his mud-streaked face, in which, were the most fascinating bright blue eyes. I felt a sensual tug at the old heart strings, and in the pit of my stomach." Syb gave a seductive smile. 'Hello there,' he said. 'I've been watching you, and your enthusiasm is overwhelming!' I gave him a pointed glare. 'You with Brad Ross?' I told him that I wasn't any longer. He laughed 'Poor man! May I take you out for dinner tonight? I know your dorm. I'll wait at the lodge, say around seven?' I was rather taken aback, after all Brad was somewhere around, not quite cold yet, speaking metaphorically, but dead in the water nevertheless. It didn't seem right, but it took all of two seconds for me to decide it would be perfectly fine. He smiled that roguish smile, and ran off to the clubhouse. He even turned and waved before going in. Brad rushed over, 'I say, Syb, do you mind awfully if I join the lads for a pint and talk rugby?' I glowered at him, and told him to get lost. I was going back to the dorm to get hot tea and crumpets, and he could drink with the lads until the crack of doom. We were over. 'If that's how you feel, Syb. Cheerio then, see you around' Romantic devil! I never could stand English men. Their idea of romance is to be chums, not in the fair sense, you understand, but in that the old girl will do what he wants to do, stoically, faithfully, like-his-dog." Nessa and Laura shared a knowing smile.

"Rory was waiting for me that evening as I crossed the quad dressed in the height of fashion, just to emphasize from the outset that I was not the sporty type, though I think he'd got an inkling of that in the afternoon, when he saw me looking miserable, and dressed from head to foot in wool and boots. I had put on the glam, so he wouldn't think I was a bespectacled bookworm either.

I liked the look of stunned appreciation on his face as I approached. He held my hand, opened the door to his little sports car, and tucked me in. 'You have long legs,' he said, 'I hope you don't feel cramped or crumpled.' It was cold, and I was relieved that he had the top up and windows closed. He looked a little wind-blown. His beautiful silky black hair was mussed up, his cheeks red, and his hands had been cold to the touch, as if he'd driven to get me with the top down. I asked him if he had, and hadn't he been freezing. 'This is great weather to the Welsh. We love a brisk gale; a little rain now would have been even better.' I sighed, and thought I'd been fooled by his poetic looks and audacity. He really was like the other idiots. He smiled, noticing my sullen expression. 'Cheer up. We're not going to the fish and chippy, and then the pub, where I would have loved to show you off to the lads, but I have something else planned that I think will be more in your style.'

We drove way out into the countryside, to an old manor house. He parked the car, and a valet came out with an umbrella to help me through the drizzle that had started. I cast a baleful glance at Rory, and said he must now be thrilled to bits to have rain too. He smiled, and also exchanged a quick smile with the valet.

The man took our coats when we entered, and led us through a wood-paneled hall into a beautiful room, also wood-paneled, deep chintz armchairs and long couch in front of a huge fireplace, where a roaring log fire burned away. It was elegant and cozy. I noticed there was only one table, and it was set for dinner, superb china, gold plated cutlery and a bowl of Waterford crystal containing deep red roses; the whole shebang! We had to take a step up to the dining table, which was in front of a large latticed window; you know a cathedral window sort of thing. All the windows were latticed and charming. Rory told me that the house had been converted from an old abbey house. 'The gardens are exquisite. I shall bring you here in the daytime, so that you can appreciate them. It's too dark and misty tonight.' I was dumbfounded, and relieved that I had dressed for such a special occasion. I asked him if he lived there. I meant it facetiously. The valet hid a smile. I got the message, and Rory laughed at the look of stricken surprise on my face. His father was a bishop, and his mother was a sculptress. I had heard of her, Olwyn Price Ellis. She exhibited under her single name. I told him that I was rather disappointed. I had hoped that he'd been born and raised in the mining valleys, and that he'd pulled himself up by his bootstraps, and had gained a place at Cambridge on his own intellectual merits. He said that he was only a generation removed from the coal pits. His parents had come from the narrow, dark valleys of South Wales, from the heart of industrial Britain. In the previous century, Merthyr Tydfil, from whence his parents had hailed, had been the coal, iron and steel capital of the world. I was impressed.

I asked him how he had felt about Churchill's attack on the striking miners in the twenties. Churchill, then Home Secretary, had sent the constabulary into the miners' homes to beat them up in front of their families. He took several seconds to reply. His grandfather had been involved in that peaceful protest. The miners' families had been starving. The big iron and steel masters and the mine owners lived in luxury and wealth, while their workers lost their lives and their health to get that coal for them. His uncle had fallen into a smelting furnace, and had been burned alive. 'The working conditions were dangerous,' he continued, 'the hours long and the pay, a mere pittance, no pun intended.' He gave a bitter laugh. 'But a strange word, suited to the situation.' He took a long draw on his cigarette, and narrowed those blue eyes in the curling blue smoke. 'Ramsey MacDonald was right to rebuke Churchill. He should trust in the people, not bully them. Germany, France and Russia had their bloody revolutions, because their leaders did not listen to the people's grievances and attacked them. Churchill, as Home Secretary, was abusing that trust by attacking the miners, just as the Tsarist soldiers had fired upon those poor people marching peacefully for their rights in December, 1905, and just as the Republican government had the military fire on those poor protesters, who marched on DC in 1932, and the police in Chicago attacked peaceful protesters in 1937. The powers-that-be have begun the violence almost every time. Churchill admires force, a strong hand to control the masses and make them toe the line – a born-to-rule thing. That is a major fault among the rich ruling classes, along with their below-the-belt play. The Tories most probably contrived that Zinoviev Letter that hinted at Ramsey Macdonald's labor government's involvement with the Soviets. In any case, it brought down our first labor government. I hope and pray those days are on their way out. How about you, Sybil Brindley-Black, daughter of Lord Brindley-Black, Tory M.P? Where do your allegiances lie? I have heard intriguing gossip that you are a rebel, an advocate of women's rights and a socialist.' I asked if that was why he'd asked me to dinner. He smiled, and answered that it had been my long, wonderful legs that had attracted him to me, and my feisty attitude. He liked the fact that I didn't shrink from telling anyone and everyone what I thought. 'I am just plain old attracted to you Sybil Brindley-Black. I have watched you stride along King's Parade, books in arms, deep in thought, totally unaware of the men collapsing with desire in your wake. I have seen you put down sons of earls, and it is with trepidation that I offer my humble self, well not humble exactly, I think highly of my abilities.' I asked him if he were a socialist like his father, who, even though he was a bishop in the Anglican Church, was an active socialist. He was silent for several moments, and then he conceded that, if he weren't so apolitical, he'd be a socialist. I asked him if he would ask me over for dinner again. He laughed. 'How about every evening for the rest of our lives, Syb?' I said yes, without any further thought or hesitation. I had not liked my name being abbreviated to Syb, but with his soft Welsh-English accent, it sounded beautiful, and Syb I have been ever since. We were married during the summer of the following year, 1939, just before the resumption of hostilities that had been put off for twenty-one years. Perfect bloody timing, wouldn't you say?"

They sat in silence for a moment, peering into their glasses. Laura rubbed a finger along the rim of hers, making it hum.

"Greg and I met that December of 1937, and we married this last July, when Greg got leave to report here."

Nessa loved Drax with all her heart, but they had other important demands on them. Rory and Syb, Greg and Laura had made the commitment of marriage. It was only early days with Drax, three weeks since they had met. If he proved to be as sure about his love for her, as Greg and Rory had been for their girls, and if he did propose before going off to war, then she'd accept with no reservations whatsoever.

---

Fairbanks, Alaska, September, 1941:
"You think they'll fly planes up here from the lower forty eight by the inland route, over the Rockies? Man that will be some hair-raising flying!"

"Any route has enormous problems in this terrain: high mountain peaks, inhospitable weather, no adequate landing sites if you get into trouble, acres of unexplored wilderness to get lost in, if you survive a crash and are not seriously incapacitated."

"I thought you painted posters to sell this Yukon wilderness," laughed Rory. "God, Greg, I hope your paintings are more encouraging than your descriptions. What do you paint – travail posters?"

Drax chuckled. Greg gave Rory a cheesed smile.

"That's not all about this winter wonderland. Now if they do go ahead and build a highway from Edmonton to Fairbanks, a joint US/Canadian effort, then the pilots will feel a lot safer. They can follow the highway, and land on it if they get into trouble. They can be rescued more easily as well."

"It would make all the difference. They have to do it, no matter the cost. Saving the lives of those pilots would make it worthwhile."

"Come on lads, I'll treat you to a beer."

"Treating us eh? That must be his Canadian side talking, not his Scottish side, for our Greg here is a true Canascot."

"Right, Taffy, you can buy your own." Laughing, they all trudged through the mud to the local smoky hangout.

# MUSIC

Southern California: October, 1941:

H e looked at her, a mischievous twinkle in his eye. He grinned, raising a questioning eyebrow. She grinned back, invitingly. He looked at the ocean once more, a grimace of hesitation on his face that made her think he didn't want to return to bed, but really did want to go for a midnight swim, but then he turned and looked at her. Her confusion was evident in her eyes. He leaned over her, looking questioningly at her, and then he kissed her tenderly, until they melted into one another. It was the most gloriously sensual surrender of her body that Nessa had ever experienced, and Drax had abandoned any kind of control. Nessa was all there was.

Drax watched as Nessa ran through scrub bushes, leapt over streams and other hurdles, dropped in the long grass and shot repeated bull's-eyes on several moving target boards. She was lithe and focused and deadly. She'd need to be. She still moved with feminine grace, made fun of what was asked of her, still looked at him with warm, sparkling, sensual eyes, right after she'd just potted several rounds into "an enemy" target.

"I hope that I won't ever have to do this for real," she shouted over to him, as she approached in her baggy khaki trousers that concealed her long, perfectly formed, slender, tanned legs. Her long-sleeved, high-necked shirt was firmly tucked into her waistband, and her trouser cuffs firmly tucked into the tops of her big boots and socks, to protect her from ticks. She pushed her tousled short blonde hair back from those incredible cheekbones, tanned face, cheeks hint of pink that matched the color of her smiling lips.

She stood in front of him, smiling seductively. From Nessa's viewpoint he looked absolutely desirable in his army green T-shirt and baggy army pants, also stuck into big socks and boots. He was cool, not an ounce of sweat anywhere, but then he'd shouted instructions to her, she'd been the one on the run, diving in undergrowth, hoping no rattlers were around, spluttering through dirt, panting up scrub covered slopes. He appraised her calmly, then reached out to remove a strand of golden hair from her eyes.

"Not bad. You did quite well."

She glared at him, her mouth firm and pursed.

"I have grown up in the desert scrubland. I have hiked up these rolling hills in temps of 110 degrees with my father. I know these rocks, these formations, like the back of my hand."

"Okay, so we've established you are no Hollywood princess."

They stared at each other – her eyes as cool as ice. He raised a questioning eyebrow, a smirk breaking out on his lips. She grabbed him by the neck, pulled him towards her and then kissed him, ending by biting his lower lip. She turned and strode away towards the jeep.

He stood there a moment, licking his lip, and smiling in admiration, as he watched her stride over the rough ground as if she were on a red carpet. She got into the driver's seat. A sense of foreboding made him start to run. She ground the jeep into gear and, swirling to create clouds of loose earth that engulfed him as he drew near, she sped off, leaving him standing there, clutching his clipboard, his face red. He was sweating now. It was horribly hot under the unrelenting noonday sun.

He walked the seven miles back to the outskirts of the city. Luckily he'd had a flask of water in his backpack. As he came over the last hill, he saw her, sitting in the jeep, writing one of her scripts, the brilliant sun was beginning its mid-afternoon descent over the ocean in the distance. She raised her sunglasses:

"What kept you?" She held out an iced soda and a bag containing a sandwich. He was not amused, at least he didn't look amused, but he was.

"Nothing I haven't done before – many times." He said the last phrase, his face coming within an inch of hers. He kissed the tip of her nose.

"Me too. It's fun isn't it?"

"Not as much fun as this." He lifted her out of the jeep and pressed her against it as they kissed hungrily. He broke off and made a dash for the driver's seat, but she was too quick for him, and they struggled. She won.

"Come on, let's go for a swim."

He jumped into the passenger side, and off they sped into the setting sun.

They swam, her long slender form keeping pace with his strong, powerful body, as they cut through the surf. He took her in his arms, and they kissed, their cool bodies touching, seawater dripping from their hair onto their lips. They moved apart, keeping eye contact, each knowing this was something incredible, a feeling neither had experienced before with other lovers. The sun set on the emerald green line 'twixt sea and sky, and the warm golden glow left their bodies, plunging them into the deep indigo of night.

Drax got out of the bed, leaving Nessa stretched out on her flat stomach, her long legs draped over the sheets. He watched her for a few moments as he tried to capture the theme running through his mind: not words, but notes, cadences, that encompassed the feelings that had surged through him that day – feelings that he never had experienced before, and all tied up with the heat, the harsh chipped rock and shale of the desert, giving way to rolling yellow hills that, in turn, had given way to refreshing ocean and the shades of twilight. They'd embraced, Nessa's body promising the intimate sensuality of darkness, and through all these sensations, the ever-changing composition that was Nessa and her Southern Californian habitat; like lock and key.

After he had written down the music, he looked up, and Nessa was watching him, her turquoise eyes soft, yet thinking, always thinking. A gentle breeze stirred the drapes, and heralded in the dawn, rose and peach through gossamer grey, the gentle susurration of life stirring on the street, in the trees, along with the ever-present background rhythm of the sea.

He got up from the desk and moved to the bed. She looked up at him, his shadow shading her from the new day.

"I am not completely out of the music yet," he whispered.

She reached up to stroke his hair.

"I don't want you to be." Her voice was somewhat throaty from their lovemaking. "I have been watching you, but composing in my way..."

"With words?"

She nodded, smiling.

He got into bed, not losing eye contact. Her eyes flickered in a bliss she couldn't hide, even had she wanted to.

"Have you reached the end of the music?"

"Did you finish your composition?"

"Absolutely not, come here."

The remaining weeks of neutrality for Americans were running out; the respite offered Rory, Syb, Laura and Greg rapidly heading into memory. They spent cozy evenings out at Nessa's parents' new ranch house in the Sierra Madres. The air there was cool in the evenings. They sat out on the porch in the shade of a newly planted apple tree. The red and purple bougainvillea were covering the porch already. Loretta had transported her hive, done not without some stings and difficult moments, but the bees and humans had adjusted. She had her vegetable gardens and chickens. Randy and Riley had settled in well. Jeb's friends, his partners, had built in the canyons around them, and the men had cleared the scrub land and planted avocadoes, olive trees and some hardy lemon trees. They grew tomatoes, onions and lettuce, and joined the fruit and vegetable growers' cooperative that assured their produce would be bought, if they maintained certain quotas. Their produce was of excellent quality, and they were more or less their own bosses. They'd formed their own company: a multi-ethnic one.

Loretta, Jeb, Nessa and Bobby had been sad to see their little white shack pulled down. Jeb and Loretta had started their married life together there, and it was where Bobby and Nessa had been raised. It had been snug. They recalled fondly when they'd finally had a generator and electricity, when Jeb had built a small extension that had replaced the outdoor long-drop privy with a modern toilet, and a bath with hot and cold water and shower had replaced the tin tub in front of the pot belly stove on Saturday bath nights. The kitchen had been part of a small sitting room. A short hall had separated Jeb and Loretta's bedroom from Bobby's bedroom, which had been the size of a closet. Nessa's was next to the kitchen, and it had been from that window that she had climbed out onto the porch every morning. They had acquired a radio and a wall phone, and thought their life was blessed, their comfort complete. There had been many tears when O'Ruark had decided to turn the land into real estate. Modern, large ranch houses had taken over, with lush gardens, white picket fences. It cost an arm and leg to live on those acres now. The old farmhands had gone, to be replaced by wealthy business moguls and their families, who had made their fortunes in Los Angeles' current boom, soon to be increased a thousand fold by the industries of war. The whole economy was booming. The old Hollywood studio heads of MGM, Warner Brothers, Columbia and RKO were losing their power to the banks, corporations and ad agencies.

Jeb could offer consolation for the loss of their beloved cabin only by trying to salvage and replant what he could. They eventually were caught up in the enthusiasm of designing their own home, making it bigger, with all modern conveniences. Loretta liked it light and airy, easy to clean, with a big kitchen, complete with all available appliances. There were long wide windows all around the house, with beautiful views of the mountains. The porch had been extended into a wrap around verandah, with plenty of room for tables and wicker chairs to sit all their Saturday night guests. There was even room for a swing seat for two. The chickens had a bigger yard, with stronger protection. They'd need it. There were bobcat, cougars and coyotes in those hills, as well as rattlers. Jeb tried to make the house and garden safe from dangerous critters. Randy and Riley were kept close. They were older now, and never had been ones to wander off in any case. They enjoyed the warmth of the sun on the nice wide verandah during the day, and the warmth of the cozy new fireplace indoors at night. It was a vast improvement for them all, but they still had their moments of longing for the intimacy of the old house. Nessa had precious memories of studying at the small kitchen table, while Jeb read Sam's periodical and Loretta darned socks, and they had listened to the Lux Radio Theater on Monday nights, The Burns and Allen Show on Tuesday nights, and Edgar Bergen and Charlie McCarthy Show on Sundays, and the Big Band broadcasts and concerts. Bobby had built model planes on the rug in front of the potbelly stove, Randy snoring beside him. Riley had chased Loretta's ball of wool, until he'd give up, and settle on Jeb's lap. Those times had been precious, and the memory of them would see her, and hopefully Bobby, through whatever life had planned for them down the road.

Alisyn. Mandy, Fiona, Lorna and Sigi loved to join the gang at their Saturday night potlucks, and they now came up to the new house. Everyone seemed to enjoy these 'family' get-togethers of a Saturday night, when schedules permitted.

Nessa and Bobby had kept Wednesday evenings for dinner alone with Ma and Pa, and they usually slept over. Rory, Syb, Laura, Greg and Drax came for several Saturday night dinners with everyone present. Guitars were played, songs sung, views discussed. Nessa made what Greg called, 'Memages' that she would have with her always of these special moments of them all together, all her loved ones.

Greg, Laura, Rory, Drax and Nessa sang together around an old piano in their local Honky Tonk. They had good voices: Nessa's alto, Rory's and Greg's tenor, Drax's baritone and Laura's soprano. They had to persuade Syb to join in. Her voice, while untrained and weak, was sweet, but nowhere near as professional in quality as the others'. She eventually gained enough confidence not to care, and joined them enthusiastically when they burst into song at the drop of a hat.

Jeb and Loretta were introduced to Drax first on a Wednesday night, when it was just the four of them. Bobby had left on naval maneuvers with the fleet in the Pacific. Nessa had not brought a man home before, well not since Scott Freeman in their high school days. Loretta and Jeb were in a quandary as to whether they should wear their best bib and tucker, or just be plain and simple in their everyday clothes. They decided on the latter. Everyone would be more relaxed. Nessa told Drax to dress casually, and not stand on ceremony. The reason she took him to meet Jeb and Loretta was that he had asked to meet them. This had surprised her. He had not asked her about her family before, and she had not asked about his. He hadn't mentioned them, so she hadn't asked.

Before asking to meet her parents, Drax took her for a drive up the coast to a little mission restaurant in Santa Barbara. The Mexican food was outstanding, and instead of the usual Mariachis, there was one old man, who played a beautifully designed guitar. His fingers made that guitar express feelings such as Nessa had not heard before.

"I wanted you to hear him," Drax explained. "Doesn't he capture all the beauty of old Mexico, all the hardship and pathos too, as well as the depths of passionate love and longing?"

"There is also the hint of old California in the music. The sense of something foreign being imposed on the land, like a man forcing himself and his ways on a beautiful woman, so that she loses her sense of self, and becomes other than the free, creative spirit she once had been. Her natural vitality is quenched, and she has to conform to what he deems proper in a woman. She becomes a possession. She plays a role scripted by him for the rest of her life, but wait – an ominous tone creeps into the music, like the first tremors of an earthquake that will shake the tamed land and restore its untamed spirit, and the woman rebels, lets down her hair, and let's her wild creative soul soar." Nessa's narrative followed the music perfectly, or was the old man listening and following her words, and then again, maybe it was the guitar that was telling the story?

"Nessa, is that what you think I will make you do, lose your freedom and creativity, make you follow me around, conform to a behavior and lifestyle I want you to adopt?" Nessa was surprised. She hadn't thought that he would see her story that way, and told him so.

"I am not that devious," she laughed. "I saw the story as the guitarist played that beautiful piece of music. The music created the story in my head. Laura was talking the other day about how speech structure, sentences, paragraphs, their sounds are like chords and cadences in music. Colors come into it too. We see colors when we hear some tunes and melodies, and we use words and tunes to describe how colors affect us. I could just stare and stare at colors when I was a child. They had personalities, sounds, and so did numbers and everyday things around me."

Drax laughed.

"My mother is like that. Have I told you about my mother? I think it was Magda, who mentioned her, when she introduced us, and gave me the rollicking I deserved for what she saw as my chauvinism."

Nessa nodded, smiling.

"Magda said that she was a brilliant artist, who was very beautiful, but her talent had been acknowledged before people had realized how beautiful she was."

Drax held his wine glass in both hands, and kept his eyes on the glass, deep in thought, as he gently swirled the bright red liquid. Nessa waited. She could tell that he was hesitant. Was he concerned about how much to confide in her, or just trying to get it together? He was a careful speaker, his tone and words measured as to their consequences. It made her feel insecure. It emphasized that she was still a relative stranger, not in the physical sense, but still very much so in ways that really mattered; his thoughts, confidences, trust, his life. He looked up at her.

"I should love to hear about your family and your childhood back east, but only if you want me to know you that well. Are you afraid that I will turn it into a script, and that I'll flash your dearest memories and loved ones all over the big screen for public consumption? Relax, I am off to England soon. I have given in my notice already. As a cover for what I am really going to be doing, I told them I wanted to do something more useful for the war effort in Europe, and I was joining the Red Cross."

Drax shook his head and sighed.

"You have dinner every Wednesday at your parents' house. I know you keep that time for just the four of you. I have been harboring the hope that you would ask me to join you. It would be a chance for me to meet your parents and Bobby, without anyone else around." He looked awfully embarrassed. "I don't know, Ness, I guess I was hoping that I was that special to you. There I've said it. I want to be special in your life. I can't bear the thought of just being any old lover of yours." Nessa reached over to grasp his hands.

"Oh Drax, you know you are not any old lover. You know I love you deeply. You know you are very special. I just didn't want to push it, and introducing you to my parents may well have scared you off. You seem so reserved, as if you are holding back something of yourself, and so I wasn't sure that you thought of us in a more long-term way. I have told my parents how I feel about you. They know that we are in a delicate stage as far as our relationship is concerned. It's still new, and a long separation, maybe of years, is looming on the horizon for us. They know that I have strong feelings for you, and they worry that, as this is my first experience with love, I may have to suffer heartbreak at some point."

"Ness, the only time I would cause you heartache is if I could not return to you. I don't want to tempt fate by saying it…"

"Then don't," Nessa quickly put her long fingers over his mouth. He grabbed her hand and kissed it. His eyes closed, as he struggled with his feelings.

"Let's go," she said. "Let's walk by the sea, and hold each other so tight that nothing can ever part us."

Drax paid the bill, while Nessa glanced over at the old guitarist and blew him a kiss. He had watched them with wise old eyes all evening. He had played with all his soul for them. He bowed his head in response to the kiss, and smiled. Drax was about to put his wallet in his back pocket, then he remembered, and went over to the man to give him a sizeable tip. The old man shook his head, and held up his hand. Drax hesitated, then returned the note to his wallet, and smiled at him. The old man held up his fingers in blessing:

"Vaya con Dios, mi amigo, y muchas gracias."

"We should thank you for such a romantic and magical evening, Senor. Vaya con Dios, mi amigo."

The ocean lived up to its name that evening, and was as still as a millpond. The sky was a deep navy blue. Stars twinkled, and the half-moon hid seductively behind a thin gossamer thread of cloud. The sand was cool between their toes. The moonbeams played in Nessa's hair and eyes, as they sauntered along at the edge of the flat, caressing waves. The only sound was a mere murmur of moving water at their feet.

"I wish I had time to take you to the Cape to meet my parents, but I don't. They won't give me leave at this juncture. I still have a lot to learn about flying in snow, fog and gales, and landing on makeshift runways. It isn't that much different from taking off and landing on aircraft carriers, and I can do that. God, I hope this all comes to naught, and we don't go to war."

"I suppose I won't be going to England, if we don't go to war. I wonder if I'll get my job back with the 'boys'. I hope and pray we stay out of it. Poor Laura and Greg, Rory and Syb are still involved. I hope and pray they win, and stay safe and unharmed and alive. They have become very dear."

"I may just go to fight with them." Nessa looked up at him in alarm. "They are my dearest friends, Ness. I want to fight alongside them. They are fighting a vicious, evil foe. I don't think we Americans should stand by and let them fight alone. They may well be fighting a battle for us that we'll have to face at some point."

"If you go, then I will go, and work in the Red Cross, or help in those ways we can't discuss. The Nazis can't win against the six of us." They smiled at the thought of the six of them, arms linked, marching off to take on the foe.

They sauntered on a little farther.

"Ness, you'll love my mother. She is so, I don't know, ethereal I guess, magical for sure. My Russian grandparents are also very special. The three of them marched in that fateful protest in 1905, and were attacked by the Tsar's soldiers and the Okhrana, who had set up the protesters' march and the consequent attack upon them. They were imprisoned, and my gentle sweet mother was raped." Nessa gasped in horror. Drax had angry tears in his eyes. "Some of the Bolsheviks, who had marched that day with the people, managed to get into the prison in disguise, and they rescued several people. My grandparents and mother were fortunate enough to get out with them.

My father was a journalist from Boston, covering events in Russia in the early 1900s. He was somewhat of a lefty himself, definitely liberal in his outlook. He had helped the Bolsheviks with the rescue. There were two great fellows, one a big kind Cossack named Tashvin, and the other a young, handsome, dashing fellow named Rudy, who was half German and half Russian. He had a wild creative spirit. My father had met them in Paris, where Rudy was a revolutionary in many ways. He was an artist, friendly with all those avant-garde fellows, such as Braque and Picasso, and he was a close associate of Lenin's. My father went with them to Russia. After the rescue, he managed to get my mother and her parents to Paris. He taught them English, so that they could come on to the States with him. They already spoke French and German. My grandfather had taught languages in a little school in a village out on the Steppes. My grandmother had taught music. My mother recalls fondly the little shack in which they had lived. It had a big stove, those curvy, prettily decorated ones they have in Russia, and a big samovar that was always on the boil to make tea around the clock. The snow would be piled as high as the roof in the winter, but they were snug and warm. 'We had tea, books, music, our sewing, my paints and art pad, Annushka and Katrinka,' my mother said. 'What more could we want?' Now Annushka and Katrinka were their cats, big furry ones, one tortoiseshell, the other marmalade.

My grandfather gained a teaching position in the University in Moscow, and they moved to a tiny apartment in a loft of a big house in the city. They sided with the poor workers and destitute families, and so they took part in that march in 1905. When my mother and her parents were rescued by Tashvin, Rudy and my father, they insisted on going back to their small loft for the cats. Rudy had refused point blank to get the cats, but Tashvin won him over, and back for the cats they went. My grandfather had made small wicker baskets for the cats to bring them to Moscow. My grandmother had lined them with quilt, and they popped the cats in those, and off they went into the snowy night." Nessa sighed with relief. "I knew you'd like that part about the cats," Drax kissed her lovingly, and then continued: "Well, after many close-calls, and dreadful weather conditions, they all made it to Paris safely, cats and all. Don't worry, Ness, the cats came to Boston and lived to a ripe old age before they moved on, as cats do, to another cosmic adventure. My Russian family are rather fey, not entirely of this world, I assure you."

"When were you born?"

"I am getting to that, if you'll bear with me. My father was hopelessly in love with my mother. She was, and still is, petite, slender, with light brown hair and huge lavender blue eyes. My father and grandparents helped her through all the nightmares she suffered over the years. My parents finally married in 1911, after settling on the Cape. My father always has been very gentle with her, as if she were made of the finest Dresden china, but she has a strong will, and, as she claims, made herself heal. It worked, for they finally consummated their marriage, and I was born in 1915, April 13th."

"So you are two years older than I am?"

"Like you, I had a magical childhood. My father's family, snobs of snob hill, Boston Brahmins, I guess they are called, did not welcome these Russian waifs to the family tree and fortunes. My father was furious, and never had anything to do with his parents again. He bought a little grey house out on Cape Cod. It was situated in a little wood behind sand dunes and sheltered from the storms, hurricanes and sea surges. My mother and grandparents loved it. It reminded them of their little home in the village on the Steppes, surrounded by a sea of waving grasses.

The Cape house was cozy in winter; beautiful in fall and spring, with all the trees around, and in the summer, my grandparents would sit in the garden, the kitchen door open, and enjoy the balmy sea breezes. My grandfather found work in a small bookshop in the town, and my grandmother taught piano, and my mother worked in a small seaside art gallery. At home, they made things. My grandfather liked working in wood and wicker, and my grandmother sewed beautiful quilts, and embroidered on these quilts, figures from my mother's drawings and paintings. My mother painted Russian peasant figures from her childhood. I guess you'd say they were a bit too patterned, but they were quite light and easy on the eye. They were symbolic of Russian village life in a magical, otherworldly way. I loved them, and my grandmother's quilts wrapped me in their magic through the nights of my childhood."

"Where did the music come in?"

"They were all musical. My grandfather played the violin, my grandmother, the piano and balalaika, as did my mother, as well as the harp. My father was pretty good on the cello. I grew up knowing how to play notes and chords before I could speak. I loved it. The sound of my grandfather's violin was a part of the sea and sky, the dunes and the woods. I smell the sea breezes, the rain and sun, the apples in our orchard, the wicker and wood when I hear a violin. I smell tea and custard cakes, the burning log fire and fruitcake, when I play the piano. I smell my mother's paints, the musty smell of old books, and the onset of snow when I hear the balalaika. I see colors too. The balalaika is all shades of blue; the piano antique brown-gold; the violin, all colors in rapid succession like lightening; the harp, silver, like water, and the cello, heavy."

Nessa laughed.

"That's not a color, but a sensation."

"The cello is bloody heavy. My father, although a tall, thin man, is rather heavy too. He is a writer and a journalist, published many times, an authority in some areas, but he is not light of heart as my mother and her parents are. He has curly white hair now. He was blond once. His eyes are green, like mine. In fact I am like him, only broader in the shoulders, and I have a more oval face, like my mother.

Your story tonight sort of captured their relationship, and that was why I was so upset. My father thinks for my mother. She is often reprimanded if she goes off on a fey tangent when he has his serious, intellectual friends to dinner. He loves her. She is the free spirit he can't be. His friends, those serious intellectuals, love her. They always want her to join in their conversations. She has lots of literary and artist friends of her own, like the Edward Hoppers, the Dos Passos'. My father joins them, talks for a while, and then escapes to his study. He does that when I bring my jazz and swing friends home too. I have great difficulty finding a common ground with my father. I resent his patronizing ways with my mother and grandparents, though they don't seem to mind. They have fun, and work around him somehow. I love them dearly, and I feel sorry for him. They know how to enjoy life and enhance its diversity with their creativity. They don't give money or prestige a second thought, and, although they like to share their ideas, they don't care how they are received. My father, on the other hand, is preoccupied with money and prestige; how his writings are judged by the academic community, and he doesn't need to be. He is very highly thought of, and he has oodles of the green stuff. He is a very clever businessman, although that's not something of which he is proud. He likes to think he is above that sort of thing, but he has made some very good investments, and he enjoys it, but won't admit to it. He inherited his father's investment and banking business, even though they were estranged up to his father's death. I never knew my Boston grandparents. There isn't a day that goes by that my father doesn't moan and groan about what an imposition the business is, and yet he works away at it, and can't bring himself to sell out. I am not at all interested in business and banking. I love engineering, making bridges and roads, and seeing music and art rendered in steel, wood and concrete. I design my own works, so you could say I am an architect/ artist/engineer/musician. I told my father to say that when friends ask him what I do for a living, and he flipped. It sounded like a 'jack-of-all-trades and master of none' to him. It was beneath his dignity. It wasn't academic or intellectual enough for him. It was too practical, too physical, and also too out-there." Drax hung his head, and self-consciously studied his shoes. "That's my family life to date, Ness."

Nessa held his face in her hands and kissed him. They were lost in their intimate embrace, as dawn peeped over the mountain rim in a misty haze, and its silver light spread across the water in ripples, the black stillness retreating before it.

Next Wednesday, Nessa took Drax to dinner at her parents' home. There were just the four of them, and Randy and Riley. They got on well. Nessa and her mother watched Jeb and Drax, as they stood talking in the orchard, the November moon rising over the Sierra Madres behind them. Drax bent to scratch Randy's head, while Riley wound himself around Jeb's leg. The men were illuminated by the light of the lamp on the table on the verandah, while Nessa and Loretta swung gently on the swing seat in the shade of the bougainvillea.

"They are of similar build and height, broad shoulders, narrow hips, strong legs." Loretta and Nessa shared a look, and laughed quietly.

"Honestly, Ma, I don't know about you!" Loretta blushed, and they laughed some more.

"You love this man, I know, and I can see why. He is in every way a capable man, and he seems very considerate of your views, and he certainly knows your work, your writings, and seems to hold them in high regard. He is sensitive to a woman's point of view. He asked me what I thought about things, and seemed to be as sincerely interested as your father, Sam and Steven are. I can't stand men who condescend to women."

"He doesn't do that. He was quite challenging when I met him, and I have seen him withdraw within himself when women put themselves down, or their men do it for them. He detests that."

"I like him, Ness. He is easy company, and I can tell your father feels at ease with him as well."

Nessa watched the two men, the dark of night behind them. God, she hoped this would last! Was it all too good to be true?

December 8, 1941:
Six people sat on the wind swept beach. They sat in silence, looking out over the grey-green rolling waves. A fleet of white clouds tinged with grey, raced across the sky. The three men and three women huddled together to keep warm. They wore slacks and big sweaters. Syb had pulled the wide collar of her sweater up over her lower face, so that only her eyes showed, and they had a bleak expression that matched those of the others'.

They had been as startled as everyone else, and as outraged. The Japanese had attacked Pearl Harbor the day before, sinking most of the fleet, destroying planes on the ground. Many of Drax's fellow pilots were dead, or badly wounded. Rory said that he'd called Emil Franz, and Emil had told him that there had been a delay in the Japanese Ambassador getting through to the State Department with the declaration of war, because it had been Sunday, so the attack had come without war being officially declared: "A day that will live in infamy," as the President had said.

The forces had been called to arms. This was their last day together. That night Drax was bugging out to Seattle. Rory was off to Washington in the wee small hours, to liaise with the allied naval intelligence services. Syb was going back to England on the Queen Elizabeth out of New York. The luxury liner had been converted into a troop carrier. The journey was not without its risks. German U-Boats patrolled the Atlantic in packs, and they'd had huge successes in attacking convoys taking much needed supplies to the beleaguered British. Rory had expressed his concern, but Syb, on the point of tears, showed a nonchalance she couldn't possibly have felt, and said that the Queen could easily outrun U-Boats, which was true, but not if they got a sighting on her unawares, and fired their torpedoes to intercept her amidships.

"That's why the big old girl makes a zigzag course across the Atlantic." What Syb didn't tell them, was that the British had been well aware of where the U-Boat packs were operating. They had captured a U-Boat, and obtained the codebooks and 'officer only' signals, and so had been able to read German naval messages by June, 1941. They had to guard this secret advantage. The messages only went to those at the top, and were classified as ULTRA secret. It had taken a great deal of effort to crack the German Naval Enigma codes. The advantage they had gained by tremendous luck, hung by a thread, for any hint that their naval codes had been broken would make the Germans change their Enigma enciphering rotors. Then, horror of horrors, the Germans went and changed them anyway, in November. It had thrown the cryptanalysts at Bletchley Park into near panic, until a German U-Boat cipher operator blundered, and from the mistake, the Bletchley crew were managing to re-break the U-Boat code, but it was taking time, time when shipping in the North Atlantic was once more vulnerable, and Syb knew it. The Germans had increased their U-Boat fleet ten fold as well, which increased the danger. Syb hoped and prayed her fellow cryptanalysts at Bletchley would figure it all out by the time she had to set sail. U-Boats had been skulking just outside American coastal waters already. Rory did not want her to make the trip, but she was due back with all the information she had gathered from scientists and mathematicians at Caltech and Princeton.

Greg was leaving to join his 115th squadron in British Columbia that night, and Laura was leaving with him, but she'd fly on from Vancouver to Ottawa, and then to New York, to liaise with William Stephenson, head of Canadian Intelligence. He connected the British Secret Service with the FBI, and ultimately Washington. They were all taking up their posts ready for the battle ahead. Their romantic interlude was over.

"I can't stand this silence," said Greg. "We are lost in our gloomy thoughts. Come on, let's sing." They groaned; singing was the last thing they felt like doing. Greg stood up, swallowed a few times to control the emotions he felt, and sang the haunting Skye Boat song to the sea. He choked as his emotions got the better of him. Drax and Rory stood up and joined in. Greg shrugged off his tears, and they all sang out bravely together. Nessa joined in, and finally, Laura. Syb stood up to sing too, but she couldn't carry the tune, and they laughed.

"Oh shut up, the lot of you! You are all so bloody great at everything. I have no talents. I am useless at everything."

"You are not, Syb. You have a wonderful talent," Rory winked at her suggestively. Syb lashed out at him.

"Oh great! Sybil Brindley-Black is a terrific fuck!" and she ran off down the beach. They all just stood there, mouths open.

"God, we love you, Syb," Greg said softly. They all smiled.

"I am a thoughtless fool," said Rory. "Look at her sitting there on that rock, her sweater over her head."

"Go to her, Rory," Laura pushed him on his way. They watched Rory kneel at Syb's side and take her in his arms. After several minutes, when the rest of them had sat there, gazing out to sea;

Laura in Greg's arms, Nessa in Drax's, Rory and Syb returned. She apologized. They all hugged.

"Let's go eat and have a pint," Greg said, and off they trooped through the sand. Rory was reading a note Syb had put in his pocket. She had written it while under her sweater. Rory stopped, and burst out laughing. Syb turned and smiled.

"What's up?" Drax asked.

"Listen to this incredible composition from our incredibly talented Syb here: 'Poor Sybil Brindley Black/ for talents, she did lack/ she died all alone/ and they put on her stone/ at least she was good in the sack.'" They hugged Syb, and laughing and arguing they trudged off to the bar. That night, Syb's limerick in mind, that made them smile softly at the fond memories of their time together, they went off to war.

# EMOTIONS

The Franz House, Santa Barbara: December 9th, 1941:

Rory had arrived at the house while it was still dark, having left Syb sleeping in their hotel room. Marisol had served their breakfast of coffee, juice, eggs and toast on trays set on the coffee table in front of a roaring log fire. Emil was dressed in a big old sweater over his pajamas, and he sat huddled in the deep cushions of the couch. Rory was in uniform, and sat on the ledge near the fire.

"What happens now?"

"For you, nothing changes."

"I want to return to active duty. I have been here six months"

"Time to let you heal. You had some close shaves."

"I lost dear friends on the Hood when she was sunk by the Bismarck. Bletchley proved its worth back in May, when the code breakers discovered that the Bismarck was coming into Brest." Rory gave a bitter laugh. "We got the planes up, and arranged a reconnaissance flight over the old girl; three in fact, so that the Germans wouldn't think we had cracked their naval codes, but discovered her by chance. I took a hit, and was rescued by the Dorsetshire, and so was in on the kill. As dangerous as the Bismarck had been, a magnificent creature sank into her final berth beneath the sea, and we saluted her. I saluted her flat on my back of course. It is always very moving to see ships go down. We watched in silence, even though we had cheered wildly when the last hit put pay to her."

"You were involved in the stand-off with the Graf Spee outside Montevideo, and saw her destroyed in 1940."

"That was sad too, though she'd given us a lot of grief as well. I guess I just love ships and airplanes. They extend our experiences here on earth up into the skies, and across massive oceans, where we could not go safely otherwise."

"Yet many ancient peoples did brave the oceans in lesser crafts. Your people's ancestors and mine for instance, way before recorded times." Emil nursed his coffee cup and gazed into the dancing flames. "I can understand that you want to return to the fight with your mates, but you may be more useful to us by returning to your surveillance of those in DC, whose sympathies and business interests side with the Germans. Emil sensed Rory's anger. He glanced over and saw the defiance in those blue eyes, the hard lines of his mouth, the tense posture. He looked back into the flames. They began to talk at the same time. Emil acquiesced, letting Rory have his say.

"Syb is returning to the war zone in London, Nessa too, maybe. Greg and Drax are actually fighting, giving their all, and you want me to sit at a desk in Washington, feeding filtered information to the Russians, so that they know where and when the next German offensive will be. They are our allies, who are locked in a deadly battle with the Germans. They are dying in ghastly numbers to help us. We should not need to justify our helping the Soviets to bloody paranoid capitalists safe in their mansions here and at home. I am trotted out to cocktail parties – the gallant war hero – to chat up bloody useless, in my opinion, super rich socialites, who didn't want America to go to war, unless it was to fight Russians, and who think that we Brits kept information from them about the Japanese attack. I detest them, Emil. Let them keep their goddamn money for all I care. I don't care what they think. I have no respect for them. I do not see the communists as such a threat in the future. I think I shall fear the extreme Right here even more.

I must fight, Emil. I must rejoin my squadron on Ark Royal. I detest the Fascists. I deplore our class system, though I would retain our constitutional monarchy for the sake of continuity and tradition. I prefer a traditional figurehead, who stands for the people, to a political or religious one, who stands for some goddamn ideology, gang and myth. I detest rampant capitalism, the worship of the god almighty buck."

"Rory, Stalin must believe his British spies are getting this information for him. He must not know about the work done at Bletchley. The more effective the Russian forces fighting in the field are, the closer we are to defeating this evil fascism."

"Philby caught on. He was astounded to learn we knew of the German battle plans against the Soviets. He put two and two together. He knows what spies we have behind enemy lines, and all our covert operations, and he knows the information hasn't come from those sources. He guessed that we have broken the German codes."

"Yes. Well done, Rory. You see how important it is that he could tell you he'd guessed that, that he thinks you are one of them."

"But you know what information they are giving the Soviets. Harold has known what they are up to since their Cambridge days. Stalin checks their information, and Harold makes sure it is authentic and verified by other Soviet sources of intelligence, but Stalin still doubts us, and is reluctant to act on our information."

"Stalin's generals made him see sense, thank God, otherwise the Germans would now be standing in Moscow, victorious, and we'd be in a devil of a pickle!"

"I have problems there too, Emil. I think these goddamn spies are just young Englishmen who are hurting, not helping, socialist goals. If these spies are uncovered, they won't have won points for communism. They will serve only to frighten the masses back into feudalism, and they'll put pay to all the hard work genuine socialists have done in trying to support the workers and have a fairer, more balanced, progressive society. Our socialists will be tarred and feathered along with the communists, as will all liberals who stand up for peoples' rights. The spies are only serving the capitalists they seek to oust, and serving them bloody effectively at that." Rory sighed and hung his head.

"You were severely injured in the air attack on the Bismarck. You have an excuse for the desk job in DC…"

"No, Emil! I am fit for air combat. Please let me go. I feel unclean spying on these Cambridge friends. I sympathize with them in wanting justice for the working classes, but that won't come from Russia. I detest the oppression and paranoia of Stalin's Russia, and I feel bloody sorry for American workers too, the poor deluded bastards!"

"We need to know what these spies know, other than the stuff Harold feeds them on purpose, unbeknownst to them of course, so that we can warn British and OSS agents to get out when their covers and operations are blown. You are the only one who can do this. They trust you. You are one of them. It has taken years for you to perfect this cover, and you have been of immeasurable help. It is only a matter of time before these fellows are uncovered. British Intelligence lets the communist spies at Bletchley get certain tapes. They are deliberately left in their way, so to speak, and they get them out of Bletchley, and hand them over to their Soviet controllers. Believe me, if that were information we did not want the Russians to have, they would not get it, and those spies would be caught and incarcerated, but it suits British Intelligence to just watch them, and keep them operating, to see whom they contact, who their controllers are, know what the Soviets are learning. Anything they miss, you catch. You are a very important asset."

"I know. I just want to take a more active part in defeating the Nazis. I feel the Soviets are our allies now, and they are putting their lives on the line for us."

"Rory, what you do, the information you get, only goes to me and Harold. We try to help FDR in a way that won't get him into trouble. Fascism, the evil of the Nazis, the suffering of my people, the hegemony of the Japanese in the Pacific, may well be strengthened, and our enemies may prevail, if we leave things up to the influence of certain rich, powerful people in our governments. The freedom of the World, the balance of power, depends on these men of honorable and fair intentions, like FDR, and although Churchill has a weakness for strong dictatorial leaders and a return to the days of Empire, he realizes that Britain has to change with the times. The British people and their loyal Commonwealth allies have held out so bravely, fought so magnificently for the mother country, they have earned their just rewards. Their sacrifice was not acknowledged sufficiently with any meaningful social change after the last horrible carnage. This time the people have the example of the social change effected in Russia on behalf of the working classes, and they will demand more of the same after this war. They will not tolerate a feudal class system. They will demand their rights and justifiably so. This terrifies the rich capitalists, but if they are wise, they will give in a little, throw the people some harmless bones to pacify them. The people can be trusted if treated fairly. They do not want any further upheavals in their hard lives. They've gone through a colossal depression and drought, two terrible wars. Oh God, they have been marvelous! They deserve some socialist programs to help them out. They have earned them, and then some.

You may, even more importantly, as far as we are concerned, inadvertently hear something about who is arming the communists in Russia and China, and elsewhere, to provoke new wars after this one. We cannot let military intelligence, and the sted FBI, OSS and even MI5 and the rest of MI6 in on what we do. It is such a delicate situation. We can't let politicians and these other intelligence services destroy this network of ours with grandstanding political zeal and misplaced, self-serving patriotism. I can pretty much guarantee that those who keep blowing the trumpets of war are in the pockets of these evil and corrupt war mongers and armaments dealers. Now, more than ever, we need to keep up our secret surveillance of those who are the real power in controlling world events. It is a constant struggle to keep everything in balance by some sort of sleight of hand that never can be acknowledged."

Rory raised his head, a very thoughtful expression on his face. He seemed as if he were drawing away, but then...

"Oh damn you, Emil. Alright, I'll return to DC, but know that I want to fight Fascists. I want to destroy their evil. I want to be able to look Drax and Greg and my navy chums in the face again. Emil, if I thought that all this is just to be used as some sort of sick devious way to make rampant capitalism look good, and to frighten the people with the idea that there are commie spies everywhere, who are operating beyond our control, I'll expose those rich profiteering bastards, who get rich off perpetual war. I swear I will. I don't want to be part of giving them the right to eliminate our civil rights, and hone in on our personal lives. I swear Emil, I will fight it with every breath I take, but then," Rory gave an almost hysterical laugh, "I will have been discredited as a commie spy too, won't I, and rendered bloody useless. The people don't stand a chance do they?"

Emil's conscience plagued him yet again. He was out of his depth, and not sure what was right anymore. He'd have to rely on Rudy's Dragons, that they would save Rory and Syb from such a fate. Rory's battle for fair play in this world would be going on long after this war was over, and he and Syb would be making incredible personal sacrifices to play their roles effectively.

Rory calmed himself, although he was unsettled by the new look of doubt on Emil's face.

"Is there any way that Syb can be released from her duties to join me?"

Emil eased himself out of the depths of the couch, smiling.

"American cipher encryption and decryption services need help from Bletchley. I think it may be possible to send Syb to DC. Nessa will go to Bletchley to learn their techniques, and Syb will come here to help the Americans to get up and running. Nessa will return too, after she does her stint at Bletchley. Laura is in New York with Stephenson, so not so far away either."

Rory smiled.

"Thank God for that. The girls will be together at some point at least. I had harbored the hope that I might be able to join Drax and Greg up in the Aleutians, but I know that is unlikely."

Emil laid a hand on Rory's shoulder as they headed for the door.

"In war, you never know. The unlikely is not impossible. God speed my boy. I have a very deep regard for you, Rory. Keep safe and alert. You'll need your more than capable wits about you." The two men embraced. Then Rory left. Emil watched the car until it had disappeared around the Monkey Puzzle tree island on its way back to the road. He came back into the house and closed the door.

"Does he have to be sacrificed if those spies are uncovered?"

Emil looked up at his wife standing there in her emerald silk dressing gown.

"He'll have to be, if we want the Soviets to believe that all the information fed to them by these Cambridge men and Rory is authentic, but I don't think that will happen, unless the Americans become paranoid about communism after the war, and institute a witch-hunt. Then they may be uncovered, and, unfortunately, Rory with them."

"They will be taken in by Russia?"

"I think so. Russia owes them, and can't afford to have them turned or questioned. They also can't afford the negative impression it would give to their other sympathizers worldwide, if they refuse to help out those spies who risk all for them."

"I can't believe that America and Britain would want to advertise the fact that they have had traitors working undetected in their halls of power."

Emil laughed, more of a sneer really.

"But that is exactly what they want to shout from the rooftops. They want to show how devious and underhanded communists are. They want to frighten the people, as Rory said, so that they can control them and take away their hard-earned liberties. That is exactly what the extreme Right here wants, Magda. These spies are just what they want to expose, to put down socialism and leftist liberal policies. They want to frighten the people away from ever going that route. These spies, not Rory of course, may well cost us in the West our freedoms."

"Rory and Syb have to end their days in Moscow to achieve such an insidiously awful outcome?"

"What is more, Rory has tumbled to it. He knows he has been used, and coming from the Welsh mining valleys, where genuine socialism flourishes, and which he supports with all his being as the true way, he is devastated. Oh God, Magda, I didn't see the big picture at all. Your hero, who thinks of everything, didn't foresee this horrible trap." Emil gritted his teeth, tears of anger and frustration ran down his cheeks. "But I swear by all that is holy, that if these spies are uncovered, I will do my utmost to ensure that Rory and Syb are not used to serve these evil ends of the war mongers. I swear I will fight this with all the powers I possess."

Magda took him by the hand and led him to the couch by the fire. She put her arm around Emil's heaving shoulders, and they sat staring into the flames.

"These young people, Emil, they are like strains of music crying out for hope, for peace, love and freedom in the horrid symphony of death and corruption that is war. They should not be so expendable. Their rhythms are healing ones of life, unlike those of the evil ones, who profit from suffering and destruction."

Emil did not respond, but joined her in gazing anxiously into the fire's dancing flames.

North Atlantic, January, 1942:
Syb stood at the rail of the big Queen as she plowed through the turbulent icy waters and thick fog. She huddled in her navy duffle coat, pulling the sides of the hood around her face to protect it from the stinging sleet and salty winds. The bars of the rail were caked in congealing ice, and the deck underfoot was slippery. They had said goodbye to their destroyer escort just outside the three-mile limit off the New York coast. Syb knew that U-Boat packs would be waiting, not to mention the odd iceberg or two.

The elegant ocean liner, now a transport ship, still offered comfortable quarters and good food. Syb smirked to herself. Yeah, she was traveling first class! They maintained radio silence, and the sailors were on constant watch. There would be no air cover way out in the Atlantic, and under these weather conditions. Syb hoped and prayed Bletchley was deciphering those new German U-Boat codes.

The evenings were spent playing cards with the 'boys'. They were a jolly bunch, although they all shared her anxieties. Open ocean was U-Boat hunting ground, and their numbers had increased markedly, as had their successes since changing their codes.

"Ah the Queen is a big strong ship, ain't she lads? She can outrun any old Kraut sub." They all laughed and nodded their heads enthusiastically, or rather desperately, in need of the reassurance.

Syb lay awake at night in her bunk. She thought of Rory in Washington. He had been so depressed about not being able to join in the fight. Spying was a soul-destroying game, as was his task of trying to convince isolationist Americans that giving the Soviets important information to help them beat the Germans was the fair thing to do. She reflected on the possibility that they might have to end their days living in Russia. The privations didn't worry her, but they would be in the Bear's cave so to speak, and if Rory's cover was blown…well she didn't want to think of that.

She thought of the times with Laura, Nessa, Drax and Greg, and her heart ached. She would miss them dreadfully, if she and Rory were tarred and feathered as communist spies, and had to go to Russia. They'd miss their family, well his family, and the good, loyal servants who had raised her. They would be shocked to learn Rory was a communist spy. They would hate them, despise them, and it would be all a dreadful deception. She rebelled at the thought of the incredible sacrifice they were making. Could they be exonerated? Could these loved ones ever know what they were doing really, how brave they were? Oh God, she thought, is the image tarring and feathering worth it? Is spying on the Soviets worth it? There was a gentle knock on her cabin door. She sat up and tentatively asked who was there.

"Sorry to disturb you, Miss, but do you have your life jacket on? Please put it on if you haven't. Our lookouts have sighted suspicious activity. We are putting on speed, so should be okay. If you are alarmed, we are putting the boys in the main ballroom, and you can join them, if you'd feel better in company."

"Thank you. Yes, I think I will." Syb got her things together, and put her passport, house key and money in the waterproof pocket of her coat. She had secret documents from American scientists to British scientists fitted into the waterproof lining of her coat. She slipped on her lifejacket.

The men were sitting on the floor of the big ballroom. She sat down with them. Windows and portholes were closed. Lights were extinguished, except for two hurricane lamps on the floor. They maintained silence. All you could hear were the ship's passage through the water, a creaking, whooshing, sometimes a metallic ping, the rustle of men changing positions, cards dealt by a ring of fellows in the light of the lamps, a cough or two, a sneeze, quickly, self-consciously, stifled. You could feel the zig-zag course followed by the ship. The stately lady was zig-zagging for all she was worth.

Syb leant back against a side couch, closed her eyes and prayed to Fate to be kind.

Day broke, and they were making some speed, still zig-zagging, but not so fiercely. They could chatter now, quietly, and the staff brought them cereal, porridge of course, and boiled eggs and toast and tea and coffee. The shutters were opened, and Syb could see sailors with binoculars lining all sides of the deck. They were armed with automatic rifles too. The troops in the ballroom also were armed. Syb had her own gun tucked in the waistband of her slacks. She would use it on the enemy, should they be boarded, but, more importantly, she would have to use it on herself. She could not be taken alive, knowing what she did about the work done at Bletchley, and before taking her life, she would have to find a surreptitious way of destroying the papers in her coat.

The day wore on. Syb had gone on deck to get some fresh air. The big white clouds were racing across the sky, and the green-grey sea was somewhat turbulent. The big liner cut through the waves like a sharp knife through butter, creating a huge foamy wake. Gulls screeched overhead. That was a good sign, wasn't it, that they were nearing land? Syb peered ahead, but saw only ocean. Then the warning siren went off to take cover. Syb fled back into the ballroom. Men were rushing to the windows and gazing out, trying to see what danger was out there.

"I don see nuffin'" said one lad, craning his neck to look up at the sky.

"Maybe them U-Boats are under us, you twit. You can't see 'em."

They all braced themselves for a sudden hit.

"It's a plane! I can see planes," yelled the same lad. "See, I warn't wrong to look up."

They all peered up at the sky, leaning over one another to do so.

"Whose goddamn planes are they?"

"Can't tell yet." In any case, thought Syb we must be nearer land.

The anti-aircraft batteries opened up.

"Theirs." They all sank to the carpeted floor, expecting the worse, but the planes were outgunned and they left.

"Just reconnaissance, I bet." They all nodded in agreement and relief, well until the planes passed on their coordinates to the U-Boats.

They spent many sleepless nights crammed in the ballroom. The ship zig-zagged at speed on occasion, and then nobody played cards. They all just sat and listened to every sound.

In the cold light of dawn, Syb and the others went out on deck. It was hard to see anything. The sky and sea were shrouded in a grey mist. They had slowed, and seemed to be barely moving, as the fog and mist covered them like a shroud. It was eerie. They asked the ship's officers if they were going so slowly because the enemy was around.

"Doesn't hurt," was the only cryptic reply they got, and the day, and then the night, wore on. Some managed to sleep, but not Syb. She felt the stealthy motion in her bones: the softened noise of the engines, the eerie whoosh against the ship's hull, the sudden clanking of metal parts – then a full stop. Lights had been off for several nights, but the darkness always felt ominous. The lads sat upright, listening, straining to hear what could be out there. Syb's mouth was dry. No one spoke. After an hour or so, the big ship started up her engines and moved at a slow pace again. Syb would have loved to be on deck, just to breathe, but they were kept in the ballroom, portholes shuttered. Suddenly the alarms sounded shrill and urgent. They all nearly jumped out of their skins. Oh my God! Oh my God! Boys fell to their knees and prayed. An officer carrying a rifle came in to give them the news. The ship was moving at speed, and zig-zagging for all she was worth.

"It's okay lads. Just had to sneak around a bit. The fog was so thick, didn't want to hit an iceberg."

"Then what the bleeding hell was that alarm about, fair stopped the old ticker it did?"

"The fog cleared, and the old girl is running to save her virtue. Look-out spotted U-Boats off the port bow."

They could feel the engines straining, and the mighty mass of the ship plowing through the waves. This went on through the night, and much of the next day. The tension was awful. Syb's bones hurt. She finally fell asleep, and awoke to gentle motion. She roused herself, and seeing the shutters open, and the men standing on deck, she joined them.

It was foggy again and cold. She wondered where they could be. She couldn't see a thing. Then:

"Oh my! Oh look there!" a young lad shouted. "Oh my God, Oh Sweet Jesus, just look!"

Syb peered through the mist, and it began to clear a little. And then she saw what the lad had seen. There, approaching rapidly through the grey waters, were destroyers. The clouds closed in again.

"Did ya see whose they were?" a soldier asked the lad.

"Na, didn't see 'em long enough to identify 'em."

"Wait for it, my lad, we are going to be in a sea battle sure enough."

"No," shouted Syb, almost hysterical with joy. "I see them. They are ours. Oh God, what a beautiful sight!"

They were in home waters. The destroyers had come out to escort them home. They cheered and waved, and the destroyers gave quick whoops of greeting. The beautiful stately Queen replied. Everyone was cheering, hugging. Syb hugged the others, and let herself be kissed on the cheek. She stood at the rail, and tears cascaded down her smiling face. What a beautiful sight! God, she loved her country! She loved her brave, wonderful little island home. Her heart lurched momentarily at the thought that she might have to leave it forever, should their cover be blown. She would be considered a traitor, and yet she and Rory loved their country and her dear brave people so very much.

The Queen stood regally at her mooring in Liverpool. Syb, her bags around her, looked up at the brave lady, and blew her a kiss of thanks; then she headed to the train station and home with a thankful heart.

Santa Barbara, January, 1942:
Emil and Magda asked Nessa to dine with them. Steven and Harold also would be there. Emil had returned from a secret meeting with the President. Nessa had been waiting to go to England, but she had received no news of a departure date, and was working as a liaison between Naval Intelligence headquarters in San Francisco and the University of California at Berkeley.

Something was in the air. Physicists at Berkeley had been fired up by a visit from British physicists back in August, who had written a report that detailed their suspicions that Germany was developing an atomic bomb. Washington had been slow to act on this, so the Brits had come to Berkeley to urge the physicists themselves to act.

They had got in touch with scientific advisors to the President, and they sent scientists to England to assess the situation, and the validity of this report. They had confirmed the fears of the British, and since then FDR and Churchill had developed an Anglo-American partnership in making and producing an atomic bomb to counter that of the Germans. Since Pearl Harbor, which put the Americans in the war officially, these efforts had increased dramatically, and scientists and the army were collaborating in secret to get this project going as quickly as possible. FDR kept Congress on a need to know basis; the fewer who knew what they were doing, the better, and again there was no time for debate and delay. The Nazis didn't need to get even a hint that the Allies hadn't been developing such an awesome weapon until now. No one knew how far along they were in the process. They might be ready to launch an attack, and after the preemptive strike, with no warning from Japan, the Allies could no longer rely on their enemies following the proper conduct of war.

Nessa had been involved only in a minor way, just passing information back and forth. She didn't know about the possibility that Germany had developed an atomic bomb. Emil, Steven and Harold discussed their concerns over dinner that January night.

"I have some disturbing information to relate to you, information that can go no further than those of us here tonight. Nessa, have you kept up with papers on atomic research? I gather you have a close friend at the California Institute of Technology, who is working in the area of quantum mechanics, and is using his expertise for Naval Intelligence."

"Scott Freeman. He is in the navy, as is his wife. She is also a scientist."

Emil nodded:

"Yes they are a very clever young couple. Have you kept up with such work?"

"I enjoy trying to keep up with that work, but I am an amateur I am afraid."

Steven gave a chuckle, but kept his eyes down, a wide smile on his face. Nessa and Emil looked at him and then at each other and smiled.

"Steven does not believe that is so."

"He maybe has a higher opinion of my knowledge in that field than is merited."

"What do you know of nuclear fission?"

"I guess that you are talking about dividing a nucleus, releasing formidable amounts of radioactive energy? The atom has been split. The nucleus can be, but to form a workable amount of energy, you'd need a sort of chain reaction. An element with a large atomic weight, that breaks down easily, giving off radioactivity, such as uranium, would be ideal."

"Yes, producing barium for example? Word has reached us that Otto Hahn has produced barium by neutron bombardment of uranium. Lise Meitner worked with him at the Kaiser Wilhelm Institute in Berlin before Hitler came to power. She is Jewish, and Dutch colleagues helped get her to Sweden. She informed her nephew, Otto Frisch, who works in Copenhagen with Niels Bohr. Niels Bohr and Rudolf Peierls have had success in separating isotopes of uranium, Uranium-235 and Uranium-238, by thermal diffusion. They reckon that they can separate enough U-235 to make a bomb. Two Hungarian physicists, Leo Szilard and Eugene Wigner, feel absolutely certain that Hahn's work, and that of other quantum physicists in Germany, like Heisenberg, could well produce a nuclear chain reaction."

"Germany has access to large uranium deposits in Czechoslovakia, and if the Germans are developing it, and the fact that they have stopped all exports of uranium from Czechoslovakia after their take-over gives some proof of this, then we must pursue developing such a weapon ourselves to counter the Nazi threat. The effects of such a weapon would be so catastrophic that, if the Germans knew we had the same capability, they would think twice about using it."

"Szilard and Wigner took their fears to Einstein in August, 1939. They were not sure how best to act. They decided to write to Alex Tanner, an advisor to the President and to me. We advised them to go directly to FDR.

In October, this last year, FDR authorized the Manhattan Project, made up of scientists and military personnel, to construct an atom bomb in the New Mexico desert, with subsidiary work underway at Berkeley, the University of Chicago, Caltech and MIT. The headquarters to coordinate efforts and funding are in Manhattan, hence the name of the project, which is also a diversionary tactic, to turn attention away from the actual building sites. Washington D.C. is of course involved, and extra building and research sites will be constructed in Tennessee and Washington State. The construction required will be enormous."

"Have they produced a nuclear chain reaction yet?"

"Not yet, but the scientists at the University of Chicago are making some headway."

Emil could tell that Nessa was knowledgeable enough to know what such a weapon could do. She had paled visibly when he had mentioned a nuclear bomb. She was deep in thought, and it took several long seconds for her to get her thoughts together. Steven and Emil exchanged worried glances.

"This is an apocalyptic moment in our history, in the history of life on this planet, to be able to produce and harness the power of the forces that made this universe. It scares me to the very roots of my being. Trying to get my mind around what it entails is overwhelming enough, but what really scares me is who is to be in control of such power. Obviously, we cannot let the Nazis get their hands on this awesome power over life on Earth, but from my experience with certain of our powerful and wealthy profiteers, I would not want them to have such control either. They have been horribly ruthless with human lives to gain their wealth. If such knowledge and capability become general knowledge, then we would live in fear for the rest of our lives, and so will generations after ours, for every nation, every crazy megalomaniac, every psychotic leader, every rabid profiteer and gangster could blow us all to kingdom come."

"The enormous amounts of energy, if carefully harnessed, could provide all people with food, clean water, possibly medical treatments, for such power can also heal as well as kill. It could replace oil, coal and other toxic fuels. It is, if precautions are observed, a very clean energy source," Emil pointed out, though his optimistic words could not conceal his worried tone.

"Ah, Emil, you forget the human factor. We can take all the precautions required, but you and I know that the room for human error and carelessness is vast. One slip, and it would produce terrible damage, poison all life, and make total desolation of this beautiful earth of ours."

"It may make people think twice before going to war, if all nations possessed such a weapon. One nation could destroy its enemies, but there would be retaliation from some quarter, and the initial aggressor also would be destroyed."

"Then no one nation can have such a weapon. We all must have it."

"These are certainly important moral and political questions. Unfortunately, if this knowledge is not used now by us, or by the Germans, it is still knowledge that is a hair's breadth away from becoming available, from becoming generally known and developed."

Nessa slumped down in her chair, and held her head in her hands.

"I guess this had to come eventually, but why now, before we have means of controlling the knowledge. We need to ensure it will never be developed as a weapon, and can only be developed by people and nations and concerns who are responsible, who are caring, not greedy, ruthless and fanatical about their beliefs and ideologies, with psychotic delusions of being master races with God given rights to have the power over life and death."

"You have sobered us Nessa, but if Germany has developed such a weapon, then the situation is urgent. No time must be lost in checking them with the threat of instant retaliation."

Nessa did not raise her head, but with a voice utterly devoid of hope and full of helpless resignation, she asked what they wanted her to do.

"We need to know how far the Germans have gone in developing this bomb. We are almost certain that they would use a secret plant to work on it. We need to see where their top physicists are, and if they are being gathered in a certain place, as we are doing with ours now. We need to see if Heisenberg and Hahn have disappeared from their usual laboratory positions. Durner is a mystery, but important. We think he may be involved in work on neutron production using beryllium and polonium, and in making pure polonium chloride."

"The OSS and SOE have people on the ground trying to find out where a possible plant could be, where resources are being diverted. You speak fluent and idiomatic German, with Swabian inflections. Durner comes from that region of Germany, and he works in a chemistry laboratory near Ulm. It is a hard place to find, and is sort of hush-hush with the locals. Our agents had difficulty finding it, let alone finding any information on it, and who works there. This makes it a most suspect place in our book, and almost fits the bill for this type of research. We want you to track down Durner, and find out what he is doing. Our other agents do not have your understanding of nuclear physics. It is dangerous, but of immense importance. You will have help. We have a man undercover in the SS. He will meet you and tell you what to do."

Nessa's blood ran cold. Harold and Emil made it sound so easy. Oh it was very exciting. Any movie star would kill for such a role, but this was real life, and she would be going behind enemy lines.

"Nessa? Will you do it? It is of the utmost importance I assure you. Steven did not want us to ask this of you, but he realizes that you are the perfect choice."

"I cannot bring myself to tell your parents, Ness," Steven choked on his emotions.

Nessa looked up at Harold.

"I want to do this. It is what you have trained me to do."

They took their leave of Emil and Magda, and Emil closed the heavy oak door and laid his head on it and sighed.

"I take it Simon will be the SS contact?"

"Yes, Rudy and Lev will be there as back-up too."

"Good." Magda took Emil's arm and gave it a loving squeeze. "And you arranged it all, so every step is thoroughly worked out. No one thinks of every detail as you do, my love."

Emil grimaced at her trust in him, but gave her the reassurance that, of course he had thought of every last thing, but nevertheless he was anxious. The Nazis were slippery and clever in their cruelty, and just as thorough in the details. He hoped and prayed that Simon and his group of communist lads ensconced in the SS had not been discovered. They were such brave lads, and Nessa was such a fine and wonderful person. Good had to win out here, not just for these incredible young people, but for the whole of humanity. He patted Magda's hand.

"I am so very relieved that Rudy and Lev will be there." He watched her reaction, as she knew he would. She smiled a teasing, chiding sort of smile.

"Rudy has such a flair for intrigue and defying danger. He won't let himself lose to the Nazis. He took on Stalin in Moscow and in Spain, but he is not my hero, Emil. You are my hero. You take on Hitler with every breath you take, with every thought that occupies that clever, and often devious, mind of yours."

"Ah yes, quite the intrepid, dashing hero, inspired by my lady fair in all I do." Arms around each other, they retired to their bedroom.

Santa Barbara Coast, February 23, 1942:
In the days, weeks and months after Pearl Harbor had been attacked, Japan's victories were overwhelming, as country after country fell to their control. The Americans kept their fleet at sea, and maintained radio silence. It was imperative that the Japanese could not track them.

Emil descended the wooden steps from Magda's studio back to the house, balancing the tray of empty plates and glasses, the remnants of their supper, and trying to hold the flashlight steady. The air was cold, and the hillside studio, the house and trees were shrouded in heavy sea mist. Emil stopped and peered out through the overhanging branches of the evergreens to the grey ocean beyond, obscured in the swirling grey air. Good cover he thought for enemy submarines to penetrate the coast's defenses. He could hear foghorns way in the distance. Our ships were out there. Then suddenly there was a series of sharp explosions, and great balls of orange flame along with heavy black clouds rose into the February sky. Good God! They were under attack! Emil put the tray down on a rock and ran back up the steps to get Magda, but she was already hurrying down to join him, Mindy, her dachshund in her arms."

"Oh my God, Emil! What is it? What is happening?"
"Come, come, Magda. We must take shelter."
"Where, dear God, where?"
"The stone basement. Come on."
"Where is Frou-Frou?"
"Asleep by the fire. I'll get her."
"She'll be terrified."

"No she can't hear so well. Ah, here she is. Good girl. Come to Papa, Frou!"

Emil opened the closet door in the kitchen, and they climbed down the stone steps into the cellar. Emil held Magda's arm until they were safely on the ground. He put on the storm lamp and turned off the flashlight.

"Do you think the Japanese will hand us over to the Nazis?"

"Oh no. Come on Magda. There is no way the Japanese can take over America." Emil was worried though. He didn't want to alarm Magda, but it was possible that this attack, obviously on the refineries on the Santa Barbara coast, could be a feint, and a raiding party could well have been sent to kidnap him. The Japanese and the Germans would like to get hold of Emil Franz. No! Impossible! There is no way the Red Dragons and Rudy would let that happen. They must know of this raid. They must be protecting the house. Rudy was in Hamburg with the anti-Nazi underground, but other Red Dragons would be out there.

"Oh Emil, do you think they have come for us?"

Emil hugged her close and shook his head,

"Ach no! What we do here is in no way common knowledge. How would the Japanese know of us?"

Suddenly they heard footsteps tramping overhead. Mindy barked. Magda tried to soothe the dog. The door to the cellar burst open, and booted feet clambered down the steps. Soldiers, American soldiers, four of them, armed with rifles, came into view.

"You alright, Dr. Franz, Mrs Franz?"

"Oh are we glad to see you! Mindy calm down."

The men led them back up to the kitchen, while Magda laughed, and told them about her fears that the Japanese had invaded. The men laughed, and reassured her that it had been a bombing raid on the refineries only. Not that that wasn't bad enough.

"Jap I-class sub offshore. Some of them carry three folding wing seaplane bombers. They bug our coastlines from the Aleutians to San Diego, but do little damage"

"They torpedoed the freighter Absaroka outside LA harbor back in December, didn't they?"

"Sure did."

The men had reassured Magda, but they secretly indicated to Emil that they had a more serious message to impart. They got Magda settled in bed with a cup of hot chocolate. Mindy and Frou-Frou, her beautiful Persian cat, huddled with her.

Emil offered them coffee, but the men declined. He took them to the front door, and once outside with them, they hurriedly told him that they had intercepted a raiding party of four men, Germans, who were on their way up through the trees to the house. The Japanese sub had dropped them off.

"So the hit on the refinery was timed to distract us from a kidnapping attempt?"

"'Fraid so, Dr. Franz. Don't worry, we had you well protected."

"Thank God for that. Thank you too. No-one was hurt I hope?"

"Not any of us, but I am afraid the Germans didn't fare too well. They are not dead. We need to question them, but they are not friendlies."

"Do we need to move?"

"We'll let you sort that out with your powerful friends."

"You are American soldiers?"

The man smiled,

"American soldiers, yes." He gave Emil a wink and a salute. Ah Red Dragons then, Emil thought to himself, and smiled and shook their hands.

The next day, FDR sent soldiers to take Emil, Magda and their animals and cherished possessions to a secure location near DC. Marisol and her family would protect the house until they could return safely. Unbeknownst to the Franzs, they were Red Dragons too, and well trained.

# ACTIONS

Germany, late spring, 1942:

Nessa alighted from the steaming behemoth that still panted and belched as it released its passengers. There were mothers and small children, soldiers on leave, waving to frantically ecstatic wives or girlfriends who waited at the barrier. There were businessmen, elderly couples, women alone, workers... and spies, thought Nessa. She was not at all cavalier about this. She was as scared as hell. They lined up for identity card and travel pass inspection at the gate. She played with her travel pass, but realized that made her look nervous, so she changed the motion to a more flippant, impatient tapping. She tried to look arrogant, as if this were beneath her. Harold had told her not to lick her lips incessantly, no matter how dry her mouth was, and it was. She felt her lips sticking to her upper teeth. She was sure that, if she had to speak, her voice would crack and her nervousness would be obvious. Her name was Carla Berg. She was a widow. Her husband, Heinrich Berg, had been killed in a car accident while they were traveling in Italy before the war. Should they check her story, their identities had been forged, and were in the appropriate files in Italy and Ulm.

Finally, it was her turn, and she'd find out just how valid her papers were.... one second, two, three.... and...she handed over her travel pass and papers. Her hand didn't shake, but his did when he looked at her, and he dropped a sheet. He bent down to pick it up, embarrassed, red-faced. He scanned the pages and pass thoroughly, however, just to keep her there, make her look at him, with those magnificent blue-green eyes. They had been cunning enough to keep her in snow-bound New York until her California tan had paled, even so....

"Have you been skiing, Frau Berg?" She gave him a questioning look, and with an arrogant nod indicated her travel pass. He looked at it again, a bit flustered. "No. I can see that you haven't. You have a slight tan. I do not think our weather has been sunny or warm enough yet to produce a tan."

"I am an avid gardener. I work hard at my allotment. We need fresh vegetables. Now the soil is a little softer, I can dig and plant. Every little bit helps, isn't that so?"

"Highly commendable... and you are here for what purpose?"

"I am delivering books on gardening to my friend who lives here." One could tell that he wanted to ask if the friend were male or female. "Frau Grinker and I were in school together. We both love gardening." He looked as if he were struggling to come up with something to keep her there. This persistent attention could mean he was suspicious. She held out her hand for her papers. People were beginning to grumble at the hold up. He let her go reluctantly.

"Please give my regards to Frau Grinker."

She walked off with a determined and confident stride. No smiles. No thank you. No interest. God, did he know Frau Grinker?! She wouldn't have known Nessa, but they had hoped she wouldn't have been needed to corroborate Nessa's story. It was the weak spot in the plan. They had to use the name of someone who really lived there, in case the guards knew the names of all the people in so small a village.

Risky, but she was through the initial hurdle, and now she hoped to make a hasty departure before he got off duty, and had the notion to find her again at Frau Grinker's. She hadn't liked the look of him. He had dead eyes, hooded, cold, predatory eyes, and a long face with a long nose. He had made her skin crawl just to be in his company. The marked visceral response she had to him was a warning. She'd have to be careful, and hopefully not encounter him again.

She walked down the narrow twisting streets, lined by high roofed houses with dark wooden beams set in the outer walls, as in houses of Tudor design. It was a warm day. The sun's rays reflected up from the clean sidewalks. The shadows between buildings were sharp. She felt as if she were in an Escher print, and thought how Hitch would love those black lines on the sunny pavement – the quiet, peaceful, seemingly innocent village, making the effect even more ominous. Well I am living a Hitchcock movie, she thought, and she desperately wanted it to be over.

Nessa approached the village center with its stone fountain. The bus out to the next village left from there. She watched as a large black Daimler, flying tiny side flags with the SS insignia on them, pulled into the square. It came to a stop in front of her. The few people around looked on in fear. What had she done? What danger had she brought to their quiet, loyal little village?

A very handsome high ranking SS officer got out of the back of the car, and laughing happily, embraced her. She could feel people relaxing, but they were still curious and almost servile, now that she had acquired some admiration, trust and respect from the SS. They should have felt revulsion for her. How awful to see this servility to thugs, but then again she also had seen this back home.

"Darling! I am so sorry to have kept you waiting." He was a tall, elegant sort of fellow, with blond hair, kind blue eyes, fine features, charming in a relaxed friendly way. "How wonderful to be with you again!" They embraced briefly. To the casual observer, they made a handsome couple, positively stunning Aryans – tall, slender, elegant, blond and blue-eyed.

Once they were seated in the car, Simon introduced himself.

"Miss Eiles, I am very pleased to make your acquaintance, but our time together must be brief. The officer who examined your pass may well decide to visit Frau Grinker when he gets off duty. Oh yes we had a man standing behind you in the queue. The officer gets off duty at five o'clock. We must be done with our task and out of here by then. An airplane will be waiting for you at a secret field not far from here. The plane has German markings, so you should be safe. The pilot has submitted all the necessary flight plans, reason for trip etc., and should get clear passage. You will land near a German base in France, and from there the Resistance will row you out to a waiting British sub, and off you'll go to dear Old Blighty, and then home on a bone-shudderingly cold transport plane, and hopefully you will have with you the information you were supposed to obtain."

"You make it sound so easy."

"It can be, but the Nazis can ruin even the best laid plans, and we have a few complications already with which to deal. First, the security around this lab is formidable, even I, as an SS officer, cannot gain access without written permission from someone high up, and not even our contacts in the high command and German Intelligence know who this high-ranking person is. Any interest in the lab is suspect, and uninvited guests are arrested and questioned.

We have been following one of the scientists who works there on his days off, which are few and far between. He and his wife live in a rather isolated cottage, way outside the village, and they keep very much to themselves. The reason he can leave the facility at all, is due to the fact that he is only a menial scientific worker. He is not directly involved in Durner's work. We wondered why he led such a reclusive existence. Sometimes their nearest neighbor, who lives about half a mile away from them, gives him a ride to work in his car. They do not visit each other beyond that brief connection. The wife shops in the village once a week. She cycles in and back. She does not draw official attention by growing vegetables, which of course have to meet certain quotas, and cannot be hoarded, so people watch for things like that. They do not keep animals for the same reason. We left a person to watch them for several weeks, and we had one lucky break. The wife brought out her aging and infirm mother to enjoy the spring sunshine last week, and there behind her was a child, a deformed child. They are obviously hiding the child, for, as you know, the Nazis euthanize children who have physical or mental handicaps."

Nessa felt sick to her stomach.

"I had not heard that. God, these Nazis are vile. It must be terrible for you to see what they do and have to ignore it."

"We try to rescue the ones we can. Everyday we persist in our work, seeing it as one less day, one less victim. Some of our men, who are not part of our group within the SS, frightened these poor people two nights ago when they broke into the cottage and told them they could be rescued if the man did something for us. We felt awful for doing this to him, for it involves no end of risk. It was a risk he was more than willing to take to get his family out of Germany.

We watched as he went to work today, and he looked awful, but then he is usually a nervous sort, so nothing out of the ordinary there to attract attention. He got a ride to work with his neighbor, and he had his bicycle tied onto the back of the car. This is not an unusual occurrence either. This neighbor often gives him a ride to work, and our scientist cycles home.

The lab is expanding, and a field is being cleared behind the main buildings. This was a lucky break, as we have managed to get a man into the work detail. The security is less stringent, as they don't enter the facility at all, and there are guards who make sure they don't. Our scientist has to take the brave step of finding a way into Durner's lab to appropriate the necessary documents, and then get them out to our man in the work detail." Nessa looked at him in horror. "I know – a formidable task, with very little likelihood of success, but human lives are at stake, so we have to try to do this."

"What do we do, just wait?"

"'Fraid so."

"This man better get the highest medal for bravery there is."

"Oh Miss Eiles, there are so many who deserve such recognition. We come across poor desperate people everyday who take on the system, armed only with their sense of morality and common decency towards their fellow man spurring them on, making them overcome their intense fear. What did FDR say about only having to fear fear itself? Well these Nazi thugs are pretty scary, and use diabolical means to control the people. Even if one did do a brave act of defiance, their loved ones, people not even involved, may have to pay the price, such is Nazi retribution on people who defy them, but we must persist in trying to defeat them."

"How will we know if it has worked?"

"When we see the workers go home at four. Our man in the work detail will be wearing a green kerchief, indicating that he has the papers, and if he hasn't a green kerchief on, then we know it didn't work. We'll just have to hope that our little scientist is still undiscovered. He and his family will go out with you, when you leave, whether he succeeded or not."

Nessa gave him a huge smile and heartfelt sigh.

"I am so relieved to hear you say that."

Four o'clock, and the workers left the field in the early gloom. Clouds had come up, and rain was beginning to fall. They sat in the car, hidden in the deep woods across from the lab, but they could see the gates quite clearly. They had come in along a rutted track, by-passing the road that ran in front of the facility, and so their approach had not been observed. The rain pounded on the car roof, exacerbating the tension they felt.

"There he is," Simon and the driver, Klaus, said simultaneously. "No kerchief." They slumped back in their seats.

"What now?"

"Wait, there is our scientist. He is leaving for the day. I am glad he is alright, whether he tried to get those papers or not."

"Why isn't he getting on his bike, Sir? It looks like he may have a flat tire."

Simon and Nessa sat up and watched him struggle with his bike.

"Our worker is going over to help him. They are laughing, and he is carrying his bicycle for him. Can we follow them?" Their driver quietly reversed out of the wood, back onto the rutted track, and drove as quickly as he could to join the main road. They were in time to see the pair struggling to get the bicycle on a bus. The rain was coming down in earnest now. The conductor would not let them on. The bus drove off.

"Pick them up, Klaus. No, wait. Let that SS staff car go by first. Right, go now."

They slipped out of the side road, and drew up in front of the two men, who, by this time were soaking wet. Simon rolled down the window.

"Can we be of help?"

The worker gave Simon the finger, but laughed as he did so.

"Thanks, Lev, I needed that. What the hell is going on?"

"Get that anxious look off your face. Our brave man here has the papers hidden in his flat tire." They gasped with disbelief and relief at the same time.

"My God, how?"

The little scientist was trembling with terror on seeing the SS car, and Simon and Klaus in SS uniform. He thought the SS had set up the plan to trap him. The worker reassured him it was alright. He had stripped off the tire, and he handed the papers wrapped in waterproof covering to Simon. There were quite a lot of them bundled in there, and yet he had done it very cleverly. Simon had the door open to conceal their actions from passing drivers. The worker got in the front with Klaus, and the scientist squeezed in the back with Nessa and Simon. He was very wet. The bicycle was tied on the back of the staff car. They drove off at speed. SS staff cars traveling at speed with civilians inside was not such an unusual sight. Nessa wondered if the people they passed would offer up a silent plea for them.

The scientist told them how he had gone to Durner's lab at mid-day, when the scientists usually had their lunch. He had not been allowed in, but he told the guard that he only wanted to give Professor Durner a note from Professor Schleidt in the next building. Schleidt's work was top secret too, but the two professors often conferred throughout the day. Schleidt was still busy, and had not yet gone to lunch. He was told by the guard that Durner was at lunch already, and to give the note to him in the canteen. He went around the corner and peeked back, and as he had hoped, the guard had sneaked off for a smoke, not far, but far enough so that he could slip in through a side door. The lab had windows that opened onto the corridor, so he'd had to crawl on the floor, just raising his head to grab papers lying on the work benches. He left through the same door and got away. He went to the toilet and wrapped the papers in waterproof coverings around his body, but there was no way he could get out to the field unseen.

At four o'clock he left with the others, and went to the bicycle rank right in front of the security guards. He fiddled with his bicycle lock. It had gone dark, and rain was beginning to fall. The guards were not watching him, but were signing out scientists leaving in cars and on bicycles, the weather making them hurry, and so they were not as observant as usual. He kept fiddling with his bicycle, but in reality he was fitting the papers in the flat tire. Some had glanced his way and given a sympathetic shrug, thinking he was trying to fix the flat. He was of no consequence in any case, and had no access to the important work labs, so why worry about what he was doing?

Nessa could have hugged him. He was barely five feet tall. He had big sad blue eyes, frizzy brown hair and a gentle voice and smile.

Suddenly he screamed out:

"Wait, where are you going? We are heading out of the village on the wrong road. My house is on the other road."

Simon reassured him that they had removed his family already.

The man broke down in tears. Nessa put an arm around his heaving shoulders, and struggled to control her own tears. Klaus, Lev and Simon kept quiet, but Lev reached for his handkerchief and blew his nose.

"There is still quite a way to go until we will be safe, but hold good thoughts."

"Where are they now?"

Simon glanced at his watch;

"We are not far off. Klaus, here is the track." Klaus swung the car off onto another muddy track through a wood. A man stepped out of the trees. He was tall, broad shoulders, dressed like a workman. He had long grey hair tied back at the nape of his neck. His face was something else – it was pinkish white, scarred, his nose truncated, his mouth had no lips, and was pulled into a sneer. His black eyes and his fine physique somehow dominated the horrendous damage to his face, so that he still had a certain mysterious attraction.

Simon and Lev jumped out of the car:

"We have a problem," the scarred man said, "But I'll get to that. Did you get the papers?" They nodded, but were impatient to find out what had gone wrong. "I collected the family just before you left work at four," Rudy replied, looking at the scientist. "I have them with me now." He opened the doors to a baker's van hidden in the trees. The little man squealed with delight, and ran to his wife, and they embraced, tears pouring down their cheeks. They jabbered away, in what Nessa realized was Polish, and they touched each other's faces lovingly. While the family greeted one another, Simon asked Rudy what had happened.

"The infatuated officer at the train station got off duty early, four o'clock. He ran to Frau Grinker's and, of course, found out that she didn't know a Frau Berg, and was not expecting a visitor from Ulm. Your beauty, Miss Eiles, is a liability. He was desperate to see you again, but when he found out he had been duped, that infatuation quickly turned to anger and resentment. He is, unfortunately, the sort of man who likes to beat the women who attract him, beat them into submission, take out his sick revenge on them, whether they elude him and snub him as you have done, or if they succumb to his attentions. In any case, he tore off to his superiors, fired them up, and right now they are most probably searching for you high and low, and have guessed that, if you are here under false pretenses, then it is the lab in which you are interested. They have established roadblocks on every road out of here. There you have it."

"Damn and blast!" exclaimed Simon.

"Anything you can do without getting into trouble?" Lev asked Simon. Simon and Klaus exchanged looks of concern.

"I am not supposed to be here. I have no official reason to be here, and with the lab so close, it would make Himmler suspicious. He is keeping an eye on me as it is."

"I have been thinking this over," said Rudy. "Weren't you and Klaus in Ulm several weeks ago, some SS liaison thing? Well, how about you becoming infatuated with the beautiful Frau Berg too? You have a bit of spare time now, and so have come to renew her acquaintance. It would be perfectly understandable."

"But the missing research documents from the lab, it is too much of a coincidence."

Nessa went over to join the scientist. She didn't give her name, but the little man was thrilled to introduce his family:

"This is my darling wife, Trundl, and my lovely daughter, Alvissa, and my mother-in-law, Agata." The wife shook her hand, and thanked her profusely. Nessa smiled. The little girl was sweet. The old lady was in her own world, but seemed happy there. Nessa bent to kiss the child's cheek, and kissed her teddy bear too.

Looking at Simon, Nessa asked if she could see the papers the man had taken. The smiles vanished, and the man and wife looked terrified. Nessa had guessed correctly. Simon handed them to her. She tore off the wrappings and perused them. She could tell at a glance that they were just lists of lab rules and regulations, with his research notes in for good measure. She could tell also that, while there were hints of isotope separation experiments, they had achieved nothing. She had guessed as much just by looking at the place. No atomic bomb could be made there. They were not set up for any kind of chain reaction. She looked at them, and the man and woman hung their heads in shame.

"What is it?"

She handed Simon the papers. He scanned them and sighed. He looked at the couple, waiting for an explanation. It came thick and fast. He had been too scared to try to get into Durner's lab. It was impossible, but he desperately wanted to get his family out of Germany. He was a good scientist. He knew all about chain reactions, about isotope separation, nuclear fission, he had worked with Otto Hahn in Berlin. He was Polish, and so of no consequence to the Nazis. They were delighted to stick him out here, and give him menial tasks to do. He hadn't wanted to tell them what he knew and was capable of doing. He was a very good atomic scientist. Hahn had thought highly of his expertise, but thank goodness he hadn't told the Nazis. They sent him to work with Durner. He knew all Durner knew, and Schleidt too, and it was nothing. Nessa questioned him about the polonium, and he said they hadn't got any.

Uranium yes, but not polonium. He quickly realized why she was interested in polonium, and was intrigued at the thought of such a route to a bomb. He knew his stuff alright, and assured them that the Germans were only into experiments with heavy water. They knew what was needed, but hadn't fully developed the capability yet. He assured them that they had made a better catch having him, rather than Durner's research notes.

Simon led Rudy and Nessa off a ways:

"What do you think? Is he telling the truth, or making himself out to be more than he is, just because he was too scared to get the real thing? He could have grasped bits and pieces, so that he sounds as if he knows what he is talking about, but maybe he is nowhere near understanding the processes involved, and we could trust him, and think the Germans are nowhere on developing a bomb, and they could well be. There are still others, Heisenberg and Hahn, who are the really big shots, and they would know how to develop an atomic bomb."

"Well this is, or is not, a bust, and we shall most probably carry on in any case, just to be sure. We can still rescue them can't we?'

"If we can rescue ourselves at this point."

"What is his name?"

"Andrei Bronstein."

Nessa laughed,

"My God! I have read his papers. He is a goldmine." She ran over to them, and hugged Andrei and his wife.

"You are Andrei Bronstein. I have read your papers. They are brilliant, but you do biological research on the structure of the spindle in cell division. How could you have helped the Germans in any way related to nuclear fission?"

"Well, I understand the physics, even if I am only a cell biologist, but Hahn knew of neutron bombardment of the atomic nucleus. He was experimenting with beryllium and polonium. They produce neutrons. He hadn't got a chain reaction going. I don't know why the German scientists are so slow, maybe they don't want the Nazis to get the bomb. They were okay sorts, but I tell you now, the Russians are not so slow. Do you remember an article in the journal Physical Review, dated 1940, but I forget the volume number? There was a letter to the editor, in which neutron bombardment and isotope separation were mentioned." Nessa nodded. "Well since 1940, publications on American and British atomic research have ceased quite abruptly. "I don't know why the Germans didn't catch on." Andrei continued, but we Poles and the Russians did. The Russian scientists studied your pre-war papers, and with the sudden cessation in publication in these matters, they put two and two together, and figured you were doing secret research on nuclear fission. They are already into isotope separation by gaseous diffusion."

"How do you know this?"

"We Poles keep abreast of what Germans and Russians do, but in this case, Trundl's sister is married to a Russian physicist who works at the Leningrad Institute for Physics. She got the information through to us by the Polish underground. Believe me, there are connections, and there are connections, like a rabbit warren. We Poles and Czechs, we are not totally down and out." They all laughed with relief, and expressed their respect for these brave, clever people.

Simon became serious.

"Now how to get out of here?"

"There will be nothing amiss at the lab to arouse their suspicions, until you don't return to work tomorrow?' Rudy said.

Andrei nodded.

"Those were my harmless jottings and musings, and I had put them in my bicycle wheels last night, that is why they fit so well. I could never have fitted them in like that in front of lab security, even with the distraction of rain. I got a lift to the lab this morning with our neighbor, and he tied my bicycle on the back of his car. I didn't have to ride it."

"Good. Well then, all of you back in the van, except you Nessa. You go with Simon and Klaus. Lev and I will drive the bread van. I suggest that when you reach a road block, you two look cozy and romantic in the back seat."

"Ah the things I have to do in this line of work!" Simon sighed, a huge smile on his face. They all laughed.

"Come on Miss Eiles, for God and Country."

"We will follow right behind. You'll be our cover."

"You do have bread in there I suppose?'

"All neatly lined in stacks, and flour made from turnips. The 'flour' sacks, stacked on the floor, will cover Andrei and his family. Andrei, for reasons I am sure you understand, we will have to sedate your mother-in-law and daughter."

"I will do it. I am a biologist with medical expertise."

"Okay then, let's go."

They drove out of the trees and back onto the road, after ascertaining all was clear. They approached the roadblock out of town, and were waved down to a stop. Simon held Nessa's hand, and they snuggled shoulder to shoulder, smiling at each other. Klaus handed the guards their papers. The soldier looked confused. Simon's eyes suddenly became cold, his voice arrogant and harsh; it was a complete metamorphosis into the real thing.

"Is anything wrong," he snapped.

"No, Sir, but we have been instructed to look out for the lady." The soldier related their suspicions. Simon and Nessa burst out laughing.

"She was meeting me, you idiots! Frau Berg is indeed a brilliant gardener, and knows of, but doesn't actually know, Frau Grinker. She used her as an excuse, instead of saying she was meeting me. She didn't know just how secret our assignation was meant to be. Honestly, that officer is an arse! Tell him he is being sent to the Russian front forth with, and to keep his lust to himself in the future. How dare he assume such a beautiful lady would be interested in him."

The man was loyal:

"He was just doing his work, Sir. He was suspicious when the lady's story was found to be a lie."

"Russian Front," Simon snarled as he rolled up the window. The soldiers let them through.

"Are you sending him to the Russian Front?" Nessa asked casually. She hadn't liked the man, or what she had heard about his treatment of women.

"Absolutely, and I hope the Russian women teach him some manners. I shall send a note ahead to some people I know over there." Nessa laughed. He was so droll, and so out of place and time. He should be sipping gin cocktails at some country estate in England.

The bread van got through easily, now that Nessa had been discovered. Rudy was waved on through. They reached the hidden field, and the plane with German insignia on the wings was waiting. Nessa took her leave of Simon and Klaus, and thanked them profusely. They thanked her for her bravery in coming. Rudy and Lev flew with them to France. Their pilot radioed in to the German air base that they needed to land in a field. They had engine trouble and would radio back when safely on the ground. On landing, Rudy and Lev quickly handed them over to the French Resistance men, who were waiting for them. There was no time for goodbyes. The rest of the trip, while still a little unnerving, went without a hitch. They had been terrified, rowing out in the complete darkness of a rainy night to the British sub, waiting off the Coast of Brittany. The sea was rough, and there were huge gun emplacements all along the cliffs, but fortunately, they passed undetected. The flight back to the US was uncomfortable and cold, and they got fired at by a German destroyer as they flew overhead, but they landed safely at last in New York. Then they took the train down to DC.

Emil had arranged for the family to be set up in comfortable hotel rooms, and their needs were rapidly addressed.

"What will happen to them now?" Nessa asked, as they watched the family, still crying tears of gratitude, leave Emil's house in an army staff car. They had hugged and kissed everyone, and were so relieved to be in America.

"They will go to New Mexico, where he will be part of the Manhattan Project. They will have help from social workers in caring for the old lady and the child. I do hope you don't mind, but no respite I am afraid. You are overdue for your training in England."

"I have just returned from there."

"I know, but first you will need to liaise with intelligence here, Naval Intelligence, before going to England. Great strides have been made, but our intelligence guys still feel as if the British could share more, and the Brits resent our access to industry and resources that enable us to develop their ideas ahead of them, but bit by bit, it is working. Too many are involved over here for the British to feel comfortable, and rightly so. They like dealing only with Churchill and FDR on an absolutely need-to-know basis."

"How will they feel about me?"

"You're okay. You fly in under the wire so to speak, working for me, and I am in that group of absolutely need-to-know. You need to come up to speed with our recent developments in code cracking before you go there. Your involvement in this work means that there will be no more forays into enemy territory. You'd be much too valuable for the Nazi torturers to get their grubby, meaty, blood-soaked hands on you."

"Don't sugar-coat it Emil. I heard enough when I was there to give me nightmares forever more. I can understand so much better why we need this bomb."

"And now you will learn another, more civilized way, of defeating them."

Nessa was about to take her leave. She stood at the open door, but closed it again.

"Emil, those men were so brave, especially those undercover in the SS. I take it Simon wasn't his real name?"

Emil just smiled and patted her shoulder as he re-opened the door. She stood for a moment, debating whether to pursue the matter, but she thought better of it, and took her leave. Ask no questions, give no answers, she thought. She would have to follow that creed to the letter where she was going.

There were several letters from Drax awaiting her when she reached her apartment. There was a postcard from Alisyn down in Mexico, and she was in love with a bullfighter. There was a long letter from Sigi. She had divorced her Irish husband, and she bemoaned the fact that he hadn't even made her pregnant. She resented Emil for not telling her what Nessa was up to in DC, and decided she might visit her in the summer, when she was in DC on a war bond rally with Mandy and Fiona. They were busy entertaining the troops at the USO in Hollywood. They danced all night, and their feet ached, but the fighting boys deserved all the fun and attention. They were all nice lads. Lorna was the partner of choice. She could cut a rug, and the guys appreciated her gorgeous gams. Sigi wrote:

"They took a vote one night, and the boys decided that Lorna's gams were better than Betty Grable's. Mandy and Alisyn are the pin-ups of course. There isn't a locker room, barracks, ship or plane that doesn't have photos of them all over the place. I am open-minded, and like arousing men as much as the next woman, but those two revel in it."

Nessa smiled to herself, but she shuddered. That experience with the German officer at the railway station had made her feel dirtied in some way. She never had given her looks a second thought, and had felt in control of how men responded to her. She knew that Fiona, Sigi, Lorna, Mandy and Alisyn had had trouble with the wrong sort of men, who threatened them, even hit them and abused them, but she'd had some sort of protective intuition, and had avoided those men. She was tall and athletic, and they most probably thought she could do them serious harm, for in no way did she appear weak and helpless, or not in total control. She thought she had appeared that way to that German too, but men were at war, and this seemed to mean that the low life scum, the angry and vengeful men, whose insecurities and weird tastes tended to put off most women, didn't seem to have to observe the niceties. They went for what they wanted, beating women into compliance. She wondered if the uniform had that effect on them, gave them extra power to inflict themselves on women, who normally would have given them a wide berth. Nessa shuddered again. She had not felt fear of this kind before, but there had been something about that man, that she felt unclean just thinking of him, and decided to take a long hot bath. Come on, she told herself, you could beat him to a pulp if you had to. Did she want to be a pin-up? Hell, no! Right now, she wanted to be covered from head to foot like a nun.

She went to bed to read Drax's letters. They were so reassuring. He loved her. He had dreams of her appearing like a snow princess out of the violent (censored), but she guessed Williwaws. He wrote that the guys had thought him nuts the next day, when he'd stood there, arms outstretched, letting the blizzard buffet him about.

"I imagined it was you in all that snow and ice, and somehow I don't mind those stinging blizzards anymore, because you are my winter princess, and you are in them. You asked, in your last letter, if I am composing music. Yes I am. Greg is painting, sketching too. He sends his love, and please give mine to Laura. Give hugs to Syb and Rory, if you run across them." The rest was of a more personal intimate nature that made her feel delicious to the tips of her toes. The sentiments were explicit, but tender and beautiful. She could almost hear his music in them. She cuddled down in the soft bed, and let these thoughts take her into sleep.

Nessa met Syb, Laura and Rory for cocktails the next evening. As Emil had promised, Syb had been seconded from that secret place in England to Naval Intelligence in DC, to help train personnel involved in enciphering and deciphering enemy codes. Laura had come down from New York to bring papers to Hoover at the FBI. Naturally, they did not discuss their work.

"This is amazing that we are together. I think Emil is a magician to get us all seconded to DC." Syb cast a quick glance at Rory. "Although I know that Rory would rather be on active duty."

Rory was not the warm, friendly guy he had been in California. He was moodier, and resented having to do the social rounds required of British Embassy military personnel in DC.

"I swear, if I have to wine and dine one more arrogant bejeweled hag with uppity notions of how very lucky we are to have FDR on our side; for if it had been left up to her and her friends, they would not have gone to war to save us, I will not answer for my actions."

"You know that most of us don't feel that way, Rory. All the young men I grew up with are fighting on your side. My father and Sam went to war before America joined in in the last war. I think we have ample proof of how abominable the Nazis are, just ask the refugees to these shores we see everyday, ask Sigi. Mind you, there are certain elements here of a Nazi frame of mind. I saw the swastika-bedecked rallies in Los Angeles not so long ago."

"In England too," added Syb. "Certain of our aristocratic set favor the Nazis, even our former king, apparently. Thank God he abdicated! His brother is a much better man for the job."

"There is the chance that I may get to see some action soon. The Soviets are in town, first time Soviet diplomats have been to DC on an official visit, hopefully putting the last details into the Lend-Lease route through Alaska and Siberia. They have put up so much flak about it all. They are afraid that the route is too close to Japan, and they don't want to violate their neutrality with Japan. The Russian pilots are to take over in Fairbanks and Nome, and fly across to Siberia, also over dangerous terrain and under difficult flying conditions. They don't trust us flying over their air space, and yet we will have a whole load of them over here in Alaska for training on the planes and other vehicles we send them."

"Will you be flying up there then? You three boys together again would be great."

"I may, Ness, if Emil can swing it."

"Greg is doing some 'real' painting; capturing the beauty of the wilderness scenery, so his letters are happy, well the parts that aren't censored." Laura giggled, "And then again there are parts that should be censored." They all smiled.

"Here I am with three gorgeous ladies, and I am wasting my time being miserable. Come on, let's go to a jazz joint and drown our sorrows."

They left the bar and went to a basement club where great jazz was played every night. Rory began to brighten up, and lost himself in the rhythms. They could relax and let their hair down. The company beat, hands down, that of the high society cocktail set, with their inane and acerbic gossip.

---

Pacific Theater of War, June, 1942:
May 15, an American Navy cryptanalyst in Honolulu made a stunning breakthrough and broke the Japanese naval code. The Japanese fleet planned to attack Midway and the Aleutians. The Americans were hopelessly outnumbered, and Alaska was in no way prepared for an invasion force. The decision was made to send only a small force to defend Alaska, and concentrate all efforts on Midway.

The army and navy argued how best to go about the defense of Alaska's vast coastline, with its many inlets and bays. The fog and many rainstorms easily could conceal an enemy invasion force.

The Royal Canadian Air Force flew in to reinforce the American forces on the Aleutians, so at least Greg and Drax would be facing the invading forces together.

※

Washington DC, June, 1942:
Nessa had followed the news from Midway from her post at Naval Intelligence in DC. She begged them to let her stay until it was over. The situation had been so one-sided. She waited eagerly for each report, and as the battle had worn on over June the third and fourth, it was becoming apparent that a miracle had happened, and the vast Japanese armada of destroyers and planes was being given the beating it so deserved. The aircraft carriers had taken hits, and the relentless determination of the brave dive-bomber pilots off those carriers had carried the day, but not without heavy losses. The Japanese had withdrawn in disgrace. Their Banzai suicide pilots had wrought terrible damage on the Americans, but the sacrifice those young pilots had made for their Emperor had been in vain.

A few days later, Nessa sat at her desk too afraid to think. The words of let him be alive, let him be alive kept running through her mind, even when she was making conversation and discussing work. Let him be alive, please, let him be alive. There was a gentle knock on her door. She got up to open it, knowing it would be about Bobby. She was surprised to see Scott Freeman standing there, and then she knew for certain that Bobby was dead.

Scott took her in his arms and led her to her seat.

"I thought it would be better coming from me."

He waited as Nessa hung her head, and the sobs came thick and fast. He put his hand on her shoulder and waited it out. Nessa thought of her parents, and the pain twisted her heart again, and she couldn't breathe. Scott knelt and held her shoulders firmly as she gasped for air through her sobs.

"Ness, please breathe. Do you need a doctor?" She shook her head, and forced the panic of losing Bobby to subside. Gaining more control, she stood up and wiped her eyes, nose and mouth.

"I am sorry, Scott, but the tension has been so horrible the last few days. I knew he was in the thick of it. As the number of pilots being killed rose, I just knew, he wouldn't make it. He was so gung ho. He'd have flown right into all that flak to get a hit."

"He was brave, Ness. He flew repeated sorties. All the pilots did. Only one survived on the Hornet. Only a few made it on the other carriers."

"He died in battle?"

Scott nodded:

"Unfortunately, his plane took a direct hit. It blew up into pieces, and so…"

"No body to recover?"

Scott looked down at his shoes, anywhere, but at Nessa's grief-ravaged face.

"I have to go home to be with my parents. Do they know yet?"

"Oh no, Ness. You have access to privileged information. They won't know for a while."

"Then I must go home to tell them."

Nessa was given compassionate leave for two days, and she was flown home in a navy transport plane. It had broken her heart to make that drive up into the hills. Friends greeted her from the surrounding orchards. They were so happy to see her home.

"Your mother and father will be so happy to see you," Abe shouted. She just smiled a sad smile and waved back. The waves and shouted greetings faded away. The men stood among the fruit trees and looked at one another.

"It is bad news I think," Juan said. "Let us get our wives. I think Jeb and Loretta will have need of us in a little while."

Jeb had been coming down from the water pump when he saw Nessa pull up. She was in naval uniform. He hadn't seen her in uniform before. She looked so smart, and he felt such pride in them both, Ness and Bobby. His heart beat with joy to see her. Oh dear God, how he had missed her and worried about her, and here she was. He broke into a run, waving his hat. Loretta came out on the porch, and squealed with delight,

"Oh my darling girl." She pulled off her apron and ran down the steps to throw her arms around Nessa. Jeb came puffing up behind, and noticed Loretta's look of alarm, and then he saw Nessa's face too, and he slowed to a walk. They stood before her, anxious looks on their faces.

"Ness honey, what is it?"

She couldn't hold back the tears. They were choking her. For a moment she couldn't find her voice. Then out it came, that god awful devastating news, and she saw her parents' hopes and dreams collapse before her eyes, and they seemed suddenly smaller, shrunken into themselves, suddenly old, as if life had been drained out of them in an instant. Loretta fell to her knees and started keening. Jeb knelt down and held her, the tears streaming down his weathered cheeks. Nessa knelt with them and embraced them, sobbing herself. Jeb raised his head, and saw their dear friends standing at the gate, hats in hands, tears coursing down their faces. The women sobbed, and the husbands held them close. Jim and Suki Chang had lost their son a month ago in the battles in Italy. Tom and Vede Yellowhorse had lost their son and nephew in the fighting in the Philippines. Loretta couldn't see anything. She was lost in a whirlwind of denial, of begging that it wasn't so. She screamed out his name over and over again. Steven drove up and gently made his way through the group at the gate. Jeb got to his feet and they hugged. Sam came up the lane as fast as his lungs would let him. He broke down when Jeb told him the news. He couldn't breath. Steven had to take him to the hospital in his car. Jeb stood there watching the car drive off in a whirl of dust, and he clamped his hand over his mouth to stop himself from screaming. Oh God, were they going to lose Sam too? He shook his head violently as if trying to deny what had happened.

Suddenly, Loretta stopped keening. She sat in the dust, still, not focusing on anyone, just staring into the void that once had been taken up with daily thoughts of her boy coming home, needing dinner, trying to ride his bicycle when he was a child, chattering on about planes all his short life, tumbling with Randy in the dirt, his freckled face wreathed in smiles, his wonderful laughter, teasing her, and how they enjoyed a good run around, chasing him with her broom, and when he stood there in his uniform, looking so proud, his red hair catching the sun:

"I am a man now, Ma. I must do what men do when their countries and families are threatened. I'm doing what I know best. I'm a good flyer Ma. No one knows planes and loves them as much as I do."

Nessa and Jeb and the others watched in amazement, as Loretta took a deep breath, and suddenly stood, and calmly walked into the house. Loretta closed the door to all the sunshine outside, and stood in the darkened room. She wouldn't hear Bobby's shout of greeting as he came through the gate anymore. She looked at the door, almost begging fate to let him open it, and stand there, tall and handsome, smiling warmly at her.

"I've seen some right pretty girls, Ma, but none as pretty as you."

Oh to hold him in her arms again! Loretta hung her head in pain, her heart feeling as if it would burst. She raised her eyes to Heaven and screamed. She should have been with her boy. She should have been holding his freckled hand, as she had done when he'd been very young. Her hands stretched out almost reflexively to take hold of his.

"Oh my boy, my boy!"

That evening, Nessa and Jeb sat on the porch with Randy and Riley. Randy hung his head, and looked at them with mournful eyes. Riley too rubbed his head gently against their hands.

"Your mother never ceases to amaze me. I know it's going to be hard on her, on us, and you Ness, but she's found some strength from somewhere. She always does."

"Love, Pops. Ma gets her strength from her love for us."

"Well I sure love her and you and…" Jeb choked. Nessa held his gnarled old hands.

"We all loved him so much, Pa, so very much."

Jeb wiped his eyes with his handkerchief.

"When do you have to go back to DC?"

"Day after tomorrow, but I'll see if they'll extend my leave."

"No, Ness. You have put yourself in harm's way to help end this monstrosity called war. We know you are safe in DC now. Steven has told us a bit about what you have had to do, and we are so proud. Go do it, and end this insanity once and for all by using that fine brain of yours. Bobby tried his best, and it is what Bobby would want you to do too. Only please keep safe and well." He broke down and hugged her to him. Loretta stood behind them, and she moved in and joined the embrace.

"You are my world," Nessa cried. "You gave Bobby and me a wonderful life and wonderful memories. Just know you are in my heart always, as you were in Bobby's."

"I just wish I could have been with him, holding his hand," Loretta said.

"I bet you were, Ma, and Pa too, right there with him every minute as you are with me."

"Are we, Honey? Oh God, I hope that we are. We are, you know, every living second."

"What about Madge Cooper? We need to tell her. She was Bobby's best girl as I recall."

Jeb nodded towards the gate. Nessa turned, and saw Madge standing there, a tiny figure, lost and forlorn, her chestnut brown hair blowing across her face in the evening breeze. Loretta walked down to her, and the two embraced.

"She's a real fine girl," Jeb said, standing. Nessa stood up too, and watched the two women walk back up the drive. Madge's blue eyes were red and swollen from crying.

"I have loved Bobby ever since we were in kindergarten," she said. "This may not sound too proper, but I wish with all my heart that I was carrying his child, just some part of Bobby that would be with me always."

Nessa's heart lurched, and she thought of Drax, and how she would feel the same way, but not wanting to tempt fate, she quickly brushed the thought away.

They talked and reminisced well into the night. Steven returned at about midnight to tell them Sam had died. They had been almost resigned to it, but their hearts broke yet again. He had been such an inspirational and loving presence in their lives.

"Sam went to keep Bobby company," Loretta said. They nodded their heads in agreement, but the harshness of loss irredeemable, could not hide itself yet in such comforting fancies.

"Did he ask for me?" Jeb asked gruffly.

Steven shook his head.

"He was gone before we got to the hospital. His will couldn't help his lungs this time. He didn't have the breath to say a word."

"Just as well," growled Jeb. He got up and, as he strode off to his orchard, he said through his tears, "He talked too much in any case."

Madge looked confused. Loretta kept her eyes on her husband's back as he disappeared into the gloom of the trees.

"Jeb has lost his boy and his closest friend today. He and Sam were like brothers, always."

Riley stood up, shook himself, and looked up at the sky. Randy stirred and stood up. A whirl of dust blew up around them, and Randy barked.

"And Bobby is with us," Loretta said, smiling. "I had a short nap in there, and begged I would wake up, and this wouldn't be real, but I had a dream. I was collecting honey, and the gate swung behind me, and I turned, and there was Bobby smiling away. I woke up with the shock of the relief and joy I felt to see him happy and alive, and when I realized it was only a dream, I felt strange, not drained of life as I had felt. Something remained with me. I felt such consoling warmth and loving reassurance. I don't know. I can't explain it, but I know Bobby is okay. Sam too. Sam needed the release. He's suffered too much for far too long."

Steven drove Madge home. They went inside, but Ness looked back, and Riley was watching the dust disappear into the deeper blue of evening in his all-knowing, inscrutable feline way. Bobby is on his way to the next big adventure, she thought, just as Iorwerth and Agnes had believed. They had believed in a continuity of being, something persisting where nothing should, at least according to our limited senses and perceptions. Nessa winked at the evening star, and it winked back, bringing a smile to her face. She stood and saluted her brother, and blew him a kiss.

The Aleutian Islands, June, 1942:
Out on the storm tossed seas, hidden by heavy sea fog, the Japanese invasion fleet bided its time. At 0545 hours on the morning of June 3rd, 1942, fifteen Japanese planes broke through the heavy cloud cover and attacked Dutch Harbor. The Alaskan defenses had some warning from the deciphered Japanese naval codes that an attack was imminent. They just were not sure where. Dutch Harbor was a diversionary attack. The main force landed at Kiska and Attu islands and dug in. The US navy had taken precautions and evacuated the Aleuts off the Pribilof and Atka islands, but the inhabitants of Attu were captured by the Japanese and sent to Japan for the duration of the war.

June 11th, the weather cleared, and Colonel Eareckson ordered his untried pilots into action. The first run was a bust. Heavy bombers at high altitude were too slow and easy targets. Eareckson ordered in B-17s, and so Drax arrived on Umnak Island, along with Greg, who flew in with the Canadian 111 Squadron in P- 40 Warhawks.

Eareckson decided the best way to avoid anti-aircraft batteries dug into the revetments would be to come in low through the narrow mountain passes, and bomb individually rather than in formation. They came in low, about 1200 feet, through the mountains, and took the Japanese by surprise. The enemy was dumbfounded. Our pilots hit their targets. They arrived back on Umnak in jubilation.

"God what a thrill! I don't know how we did it. You were right, Drax. Eareckson is something else. He's a great flyer!"

"We're not so bad either, Greg. Take a look at your windshield. That's mud on it. We came in that low."

Drax sauntered off to the makeshift mess hut, leaving Greg standing there, goggles in hand, mouth open in disbelief."

Midway had been a disaster for the Japanese, despite their huge superiority in aircraft carriers, destroyers and planes. The attack on the Aleutians was a huge success. They had invaded America.

The 11th Air Force kept up an almost constant bombardment of Kiska and Attu. If they couldn't see their targets, they just dropped their bombs through the fog. This kept the Japanese on constant alert. They even flew in under the fog at 700 feet. Japanese transports and cargo ships were damaged, and several Zeros shot down. Downed US crews were rescued by an accompanying Navy PBY. No one lasted too long in those turbulent frigid seas. Take-offs in thick fog were achieved by the pilot in front radioing back to the next in line once he'd cleared the runway.

At the end of August, Drax requested that he go in with the landing forces on Adak Island, which was much nearer Kiska than

Umnak. The engineers were going in to lay a runway, and Drax wanted to help out.

Landing was no picnic. Adak had steep cliffs, and they landed in strong storm winds. Antiaircraft batteries had to be set up, and heavy construction machinery had to be landed and hauled by manpower over muskeg and basalt, the consistency of quicksand. Nevertheless the engineers got a lagoon drained, and had a runway up and operational by early September, and Eareckson was the first to land on it. Eleventh Air Force arrived in strength. They were 400 miles nearer to their targets, and Eareckson led them in bombing attacks at deck level, which were very effective. He had developed delay-fuse bombs that came to be used throughout all the theaters of the war. They could bomb at deck level and veer off again before the bombs exploded.

Drax had been involved in many difficult construction projects throughout Asia and Latin America, but the Williwaws were something else. They blew down buildings repeatedly, and construction crews had to tie themselves on buildings to prevent being blown off. That is how Greg found him, when he flew into Adak with the Canadian 111th. Drax was roped onto a roof hammering in planks that the winds were raising up and loosening behind him. Greg jumped up to help him and got blown off immediately. He landed in a puddle of mud, much to everyone's amusement. Drax grinned down at him, as Greg managed to slither to his booted feet after slip sliding all over the place.

"God, you look a mess!"

"And no hot water showers right?"

Drax nodded.

"No hot food either. The mess was blown over ten minutes ago. The guys are busy fixing it again as we speak. Should be up in twenty minutes or so."

That night, as the williwaws raged outside, the men huddled inside around the foul smelling heaters.

"I have never seen anything like this before," Drax said. "Horizontal rain - it is an amazing sight!"

"I hear Eareckson has you boys flying in at zero altitude."

"Yep, and you fighter boys have three minutes to knock out their guns before we come roaring in behind you."

"Three minutes – that long eh? I could grow a beard in that time," Greg said nonchalantly, but his gut felt otherwise. They laughed, as Drax threw a sack cushion at him.

Greg punched his sleeping bag into some semblance of comfort, and thought God, three minutes! That's no time at all. He lay down and pulled out Laura's photo from his wallet. She was sitting on a ledge up in the Rockies, her black hair blown around her lovely face, her eyes and lips smiling at him. He sighed, propped the photo up on his pillow, and then checked that his will was in a waterproof envelope. He'd hand it in to the HQ hut tomorrow before taking off. He looked over at Drax, who was already fast asleep, Nessa's photo held against his chest. Greg closed his eyes before the tears took hold.

Greg and Drax had the utmost trust and respect, even love, for Colonel Eareckson. He took great risks, but he never let his pilots do any maneuver he hadn't tried out repeatedly first to perfect it.

The Williwaw raged for several days, dumping a ton of snow on them, and then it blew itself out to just a brisk gale. They dug out. They refueled, risking frostbite as they tussled with hard frozen gas nozzles. Their planes were freezing cold. Drax got settled in and cleared his windscreen to check on Greg, who was just about ready. He glanced up and peered over at Drax through his frosted windscreen. He smiled and gave a thumbs-up, and started off down the bumpy runway, praying he'd get through this and Drax too. His airplane wobbled in the gusts, but it responded to his touch, and up they rose into the turbulent grey sky, and were immediately encircled by thick fog.

Drax had watched him take off, his heart in his mouth. He smiled, and felt tears of relief start behind his eyes:

"Good old Canascot – you certainly know how to fly. God Speed."

Greg tried to peer through the fog. His pilots were in formation behind him. He gave them coordinates. God only knew how they'd spot enemy destroyers below. They'd have to fire blind going into Attu.

"Try and get a direction on the tracers when they fire on us. It might help the boys coming behind." Greg thought of Drax coming in low through this muck. Drax was an expert flyer, like Eareckson, brave and daring, with absolute trust in his plane. "Okay lads, here we go, ratta, tatta, good luck!" They descended to 700 feet and roared in, guns blazing. The Japanese anti-aircraft batteries hidden in the hills and on the harbor opened up. Red tracers soared by them.

Greg saw that Cal was hit, and heading for the high seas. He saw Cal bale out, and hoped and prayed the old PBYs would be there to rescue him before he froze to death in those waters.

The ships were out there, but it would most probably be some brave PBY guy who would pick up the downed pilots and crew, and he'd have to do it in minutes, while under attack from enemy zeros and ships. No one survived for long in those frigid, tossing black waters with forty-foot waves. Greg turned, his squadron followed, and they headed out just as the B-17s came roaring in at deck level, Eareckson in the lead, Drax behind as wing man. Greg wiggled his wings in salute.

"Well done, Canucks. Go home to tea.

"Boys down in the drink."

"We know. PBY at site. They've been picked up, and all ok, over and out."

Greg breathed a sigh of heartfelt relief.

"Too cold for a swim, so cut and run for home after party."

Drax laughed,

"Will do, keep home fires burning."

Drax followed Eareckson out and away. Japanese destroyers lay smoking in the bay.

"I think we got a few," he ventured.

"We'll verify with photo boys when back at base." Eareckson radioed back, "But I think you're right."

Suddenly there was an ear-splitting explosion, and Drax was surrounded by flames. He called back to the bomb crew. No response. He used his extinguisher to dowse the flames in the cockpit. He adjusted the controls, and pulled himself free. He peered into the back of the plane. His men were lying in a pool of blood, but they were alive and groaning. Good sign. Drax decided not to down the old crate, but try to make it back to Adak.

The fog got thicker, the wind wilder. He couldn't get much altitude out of the old bird. He flew just above the foaming crests of the tossing waves. His windscreen was covered in sea spray that was freezing up. He couldn't see a thing. He radioed into base. He gave his coordinates.

"Drax what the hell are you doing? Are you going for a swim?"

"No, sir. Conditions too inclement, and boys not in swimming shape. They are hurting, burns and concussion from strike. Will need ambulances at air strip, over."

Eareckson radioed back:

"Will do. Can you make it? Nix that. See you soon."

"God willing, yes Sir!"

There was only the god-awful cold, the ubiquitous fog and sounds of howling wind and sea. Drax was determined this wasn't going to be it for him or his men. He had to get back to Nessa and his mother and grandparents too, even the old man, as rocky as their relationship was. He trusted in this old bird. It would get them back safely.

Sea level was a dangerous approach into Adak, but he may be lucky and come in under the thick fog. He'd get wind-tossed, but he may make it in one piece, hopefully just shaken about a bit. He heard a voice behind him;

"Going in for a landing at base, Cap?"

"Yep, hold onto your innards. You guys ok?"

"Hick has a head wound and is groggy. Rest of us beat up, but not serious. Need help?"

"No, fine. Just prepare for usual rocky landing, bumpty-bump time."

"Sounds like fun, right? Just no flips, Cap"

"Try not to. Good luck. Here we go, hold tight."

Greg stood with Eareckson and the others watching the stormy black sea. They were buffeted by strong gale-force crosswinds carrying snow and icy sleet.

Nobody said a word. Greg guessed that, like him, they were all praying to whatever force that cared. Drax, come on, old chap, let Nessa guide you in on a wing and prayer. Then they saw him – at wave level for chrissake! Lord above! Greg and the men watching were too scared to think, to speak. The old bomber tossed about. Drax must be breaking his bones to keep her steady. He needed to pull up to land safely. He'd hit the strip coming in so low.

Drax was busy praying himself to the old bomber. Come on old girl, my lovely old battleship, come on. You can get up, yes you can. Come up for Papa.

He pulled on the stick, and after a pause that seemed like an age, the old crate lifted her nose, and brought her tail end up with her, up, bit by bit, up, up. Drax yelled, "I love you, I love you." The plane rose above the waves into the swirling air.

"God, he did it! He got her up! Oh Lord!"

Eareckson looked over at Greg, and smiled, but they knew Drax still had a hell of a fight to land her in these conditions. They couldn't see him now. They couldn't even hear the plane's engine. Fire crew and the ambulances waited at the strip. Everyone peered up at the sky. Several anxious minutes passed. They were too afraid to say anything.

"Here he comes," Eareckson bellowed. "Get ready!"

Drax had turned and was descending. His landing gear was down, but the plane was wobbling about, buffeted by the crosswinds. Lower and lower, touchdown, but too fast. Drax brought her up again, and turned for another try. He circled for several more minutes.

"That's my boy! Slower, come on, come on. You're the best goddamn pilot I've ever seen, you can do it. Next to me of course," Eareckson smiled, and Greg concurred. "You're not too bad either, Canuck."

"That's a great compliment, Sir."

Drax came in again, but he encountered a strong crosswind. He turned into the wind. He managed to break free and circled again. This time he came slower, lower and landed, but bounced about a bit, up-down-up-down, and then a skidding stop, the plane being blown right around to face the direction they had come in, but she juddered to a stop and defiantly challenged the wind face-on. Everyone cheered, tears in their eyes, even Eareckson! They all ran to the plane. The ambulance was there, also being buffeted some, but they got the guys out, and before they headed off to the hospital tent, Drax checked with each one, and they were ok. They chided him a bit on his flying, but their faces beamed with gratitude and relief.

"Remind me to fly another airline next time," Hick shouted to those waiting. They all smiled and chuckled. Drax shook their hands and patted them on their shoulders as they lay on their stretchers, the sleet and snow falling relentlessly on them. They all held on to his hand a little longer by way of deep, soul deep, thanks.

"Man alive, Drax, that was some flying!" Greg grasped him in a bear hug, closely followed by Eareckson. Everyone slapped him on the back.

"Beer all around," yelled Eareckson. They cheered, and made their way back to the mess hut.

"You, okay?" Eareckson asked, his hand on Drax's shoulder. He could feel Drax shaking through the flight jacket, and he could tell that Drax had his teeth firmly clenched to avoid the chattering, not just from cold. He slapped him on the back, and walked off, letting Greg and Drax walk back through the wind and snow together.

"Amazing bit of flying, Drax"

"My arms and hands felt strained to their limits. My neck and shoulders ache like I've pulled a massive rock behind me. That old girl is a corker! Hey, look after my girl well. Spoil her a bit," Drax shouted back to the ground crew.

"Sure will, Sir. She'll get super-star treatment. She deserves it."

"She sure does."

"Come on, you're due for some super-star treatment too – a few beers, a hot tub and a rub down and massage by Miss Fifi, aka, the rough and callused hands of our old Doc Krinsky, so sought after by the rich and famous." They laughed.

"I swear he hauled coal in med. school with the hands he's got," Drax added with a wry grin of anguish.

July, 1942, England:
The train pulled away, and as the steam settled, Nessa found herself on a deserted platform in the semi-dark of a British summer night, not a light visible anywhere, and she felt that, black-out not with-standing, she was in the middle of nowhere. Bletchley was about fifty miles north of London, an important rail junction town, with lines to London, Oxford and Cambridge, the main wellsprings from which Britain obtained her brightest and keenest minds. There were iron steps that led up to an iron bridge. She crossed the bridge, struggling with her bags and brief case. There was a large chain link fence with rolls of barbed wire on the top,

and beside this ran a footpath that led up through the grass to the top of a slope. A voice muttered out of the surrounding gloom, making Nessa jump with a start:

"Miss Eiles, is that you?"

She replied in the affirmative, giving also the code she had been given before setting out from London. The man responded with the correct answering code. He took her bag, and they walked in silence along a country path, beside which was a wooden fence.

"Ah, here we are now Miss."

Dawn was beginning to break, and Nessa could see a concrete sentry box and gates, from which the lane wended up through the trees. The sentry asked for her code, and signed her in. She continued on up the drive by herself, until, through the wide spreading branches, she spied a huge house. It was an amazing sight. The design was Victorian, with all the fancy gables and turrets, some turrets like those in fairy-tale castles, some domed, wide glass conservatories, with roofs fringed in castle-like crenellations, loads of chimneys, some short, some tall, the whole house seemed to ramble on for ever. There was a big lake and lovely gardens in full bloom, paths that wended through fields, and paths that meandered through woods. There was the ubiquitous croquet lawn that Nessa discovered was an essential addition to most of these English country houses. She smiled when she remembered Steven saying that the English gentry got their exercise in the fresh air by playing croquet. He had added, "But they think out a lot of strategies and puzzles playing croquet, so be warned, and they play it quite ruthlessly, I assure you."

"Not so fair and gentlemanly then?" She had asked.

"Absolutely not, and remember 'fair and gentlemanly' did not gain an empire that spread over two-thirds of the globe."

Her papers were examined again at the entrance to the huge house. She had noticed that much of the grounds outside had been taken over by huts and a red brick building. Paths ran from hut to hut like paths through a maze. Inside the big house there was a large staircase that seemed to go up and up to different landings, and, what had been a family home of some warmth, despite its size, was now whitewashed offices. Despite the early hour, people of all sorts, some in uniform, navy, army and air force, and some in civilian attire, some in swimming trunks, and others in white tennis gear, were milling about, running up and down stairs, disappearing into offices, or tearing back out to the huts. This is extremely hush-hush? It was not what she had expected. There are almost as many personnel here as there are at Naval Intelligence HQ in DC, only more civilians, and more casually dressed, as if guests at the country estate, yet she was aware that they were working flat out at a frenetic pace to keep up with the huge amounts of German and Japanese codes coming in at a horrifying rate. It was an all out national effort to win this war, and encouraging to see. Nessa hoped she'd become a useful cog in the process. Remember, she told herself, no questions, and no discussing work with others, unless permitted to do so.

A woman in Royal Navy uniform, a WRN, 'Wren', took her papers, and smiling, told her she'd be taken to another manor house close by, where she would live for the duration of her stay at Bletchley.

"Do you cycle? We have a bicycle here for you." She took Nessa out, and leaning against the wall of the house was the oldest, most decrepit bicycle Nessa had ever seen, but it had a new basket attached to the handlebars and a working bell. The woman smiled apologetically.

"It's fine," Nessa said.

The next day it poured with rain, and Nessa's trip through the beautiful countryside was a less than pleasant experience. She was soaked. She did not wear US naval uniform, but was dressed in civilian clothes, a light summer skirt and blouse and raincoat, with a scarf for her hair – no protection from the intense British summer downpour, but the old bike took it in its stride, bouncing over ruts, and sloshing through puddles as large as small ponds. They had sent a private bus for her, but she had missed it. Two Wrens took her to a local hotel, so that she could have a warm bath, and one of them brought her a change of clothes and a cup of hot tea, reinforced with a tot of whiskey.

"Just the ticket to guard against those nasty summer colds. They can be even worse than the winter ones."

Nessa had been surprised to find out that there was quite a sizeable town outside the train station. There was a huge brick factory that accounted for the smell of burning clay and grit in the air. At night, the town had been cloaked in semi-darkness, not a light anywhere, as were most towns and villages throughout the British Isles. The night was short in the summer. Secret arrivals and departures from Bletchley had been timed for those brief hours of darkness.

London, of course, had a vibrant nightlife. People stumbled from theaters, cinemas, restaurants and nightclubs, mostly in the dark, even the taxis and double-decker buses kept their lights off or covered. It was a strange world with a plucky atmosphere of making the best of what was available, and having fun where it could be found.

Nessa found that Syb had in no way exaggerated the discomforts of sleeping in underground stations while bombs dropped fast and furious above, but usually someone started a song and they'd all join in, children ran around playing tag, old women and men gossiped, mothers read bedtime stories, some darned socks, some did each other's hair and make-up, lovers cuddled – in short, life went on underground, and only when the blast shook parts of the roof down on them and the ground shuddered, did they fall silent. Some closed their eyes in silent, fervent prayer. Children whimpered, infants cried, but within seconds it was back to normal, and then relative silence as most of them, one by one, fell asleep.

Nessa found that when she attended dances or parties, the partygoers only made slight concessions to the air raid going on, and kept dancing while all fell around them. The Brits treated the raids much as they would pesky wasps at a picnic, running for shelter only as a last resort.

Nessa loved the diversity: every night in the pub there were academics, military men and women, army, navy and air force from all the British Commonwealth countries and other allies, all colors and creeds. The conversations ranged from the banal and idiotic to the extremely high-brow and deeply philosophical in a matter of seconds. Never had her brain had to work so fast just to keep up. It was like a cerebral switchback, plunging from heights to shallows at high speed. Her fellow workers at Bletchley were an amazing bunch. They were winning the war with their advanced knowledge of enemy movements, gleaned from cracking enemy codes. Their Bombe machines were derived from the original deciphering of German rotor codes achieved by brilliant Polish mathematicians, who had, in turn, gained the information from a French intelligence officer, who had a spy in the German code service. The British designed the Bombes, and these huge ticking machines, hence their name, analyzed tons of enemy coded messages every second of every day. The young women of the Royal Navy, who tended these data, and diligently examined them for clues, personified devotion to duty and country. It was demanding, stressful work. Win by outsmarting the enemy, outthinking them. That was the way to make war obsolete. It made Nessa feel optimistic about the future. There would be no point in going to war, when all plans could be uncovered ahead of time.

One beautiful summer's evening, Nessa was walking home across the meadow, when she caught sight of Alan Turing, dressed in shorts and sports vest, running towards her. Her curiosity had been peaked about him by friends at Caltech and Princeton. He worked in Hut 8, and was quite brilliant. She did not know what they did exactly, as was the rule, but she knew that he had designed the "Bombe" machines that deciphered the German codes. She knew he was somewhat eccentric, and kept to himself, or to the company of people who worked closely with him in Hut 8, but he had been quite sociable when he'd been sent as a scientific liaison between Bletchley and the Americans. It crossed her mind for a brief second that he might very well like to chat about inconsequential things, science not associated with their work, but as he drew nearer, she dismissed the idea. It came as quite a surprise, therefore, when he raised an arm in greeting as he approached, and he stopped, hands on his knees, head down to catch his breath.

"Hello there. I have been meaning to welcome you to Bletchley." He extended his hand, and not wishing to embarrass him by pointing out that she had been there several weeks now, she smiled and shook his hand.

"Nessa Eiles," she said. "You are Dr. Alan Turing. I have been looking forward to meeting you. Several colleagues back in the States wanted me to extend their kind regards to you."

"Yes, I should imagine the same fellows who recommended that I have a chat with you."

They sauntered on together. He dispensed with small talk, and launched straight way into his dreams of creating a thinking machine that could replicate the processes that went on in the human mind. How did thought and imagination arise from the normal functioning of cells? Were just nerve cells and the great coordinating brain involved, or were all the cells in the body necessary contributors? Nessa raised a point that had fascinated her. Were humans the greatest thinkers in the animal and plant kingdom, or did we require more hardware and software to achieve what other life forms managed to achieve with more compact, efficient means? Were human systems of analyzing data and responding too cluttered? Had our big brains unraveled, and did we have to reacquire abilities to which other organisms had ready and immediate access?

Turing was interested in machines that could do huge mathematical equations with rapid ease; that could correct for moods and errors. He asked her if she knew of the mathematician philosopher, Ludwig Wittgenstein. She did. Turing went on:

"I attended his course at Cambridge. We did not see eye to eye on my ideas. He claims that all the experiences, the learning, the emotional input, the social networks that make up a human brain cannot be replicated by a machine.

One human being cannot know for sure how or what another human is thinking or feeling. We have to rely on cues of information. We can communicate, but even then, we are not fully aware of all that is involved in what we decide to say or take notice of, so how can a human and a machine be of like mind and understanding, when they do not even share the same way those ideas and feelings and experiences came to be? They do not share the same basic experience, social or intellectual."

"He has a point."

"Like your unraveled human brain, he has clutter. A machine may be able to simplify all that, and reach the same end result."

"Have you heard of a psychologist who works in the field of animal behavior at the University of Hamburg, Von Uexkull? He, like you, feels that animal sensory systems have to be designed to sort through clutter in their environments, so that they can focus on sensory information that is of the utmost importance to survival: cues of food, danger, mates etc."

"I have heard of him. That is the kind of thing I believe we can achieve with machines. Machines can select out of an array of information, patterns and facts of importance to the problem in question."

"Generally though, you want to develop machines that will compute, solve long difficult equations for us by following mathematical rules?"

"Yes. Down the road that may well be feasible. Well, not so far down the road, Nessa, at least I hope not."

That night, Nessa thought over the notion of calculating machines. Would it be possible for machines to write stories? Could they select a topic, select characters with certain characteristics, put them in situations, and then through logical deductions come up with a story of how these characters would react to the situations in which they found themselves? When she wrote a story, she selected along similar lines, didn't she? Fiction, painting, compositions in music are decided. They are on track to a logical end, but reality, while predictable to a certain degree, is not totally so. The more complicated the parameters, the more chaos will out, but at the heart of chaos is an ultimate organization. She was involved in searching for patterns in speech relating to military actions everyday. Finding these patterns helped break the codes. It was essentially what Laura had been discussing that day in the bar on the beach.

That night, alone in her room at the manor house, Nessa was so caught up in Turing's idea that she couldn't still her imagination enough to sleep. Will we some day be able to predict world events and avoid drastic ones?

Nessa got up and jotted down some ideas. There was a story in all this. She just needed to think it out some more. Drax could do the music, and Greg, the visual backdrop. Rory could create new words for new notions.

Nessa felt her time at Bletchley, as well as the time she'd spent at Berkeley, Princeton, Bell laboratories in New Jersey and MIT in Boston, gave her insight into a brave new world, with a lot of potential for peace through better communication systems world wide. Better understanding might hopefully eliminate war and violent confrontations that, by right, should belong to a bygone age. She smiled fondly, remembering Scott's valedictorian speech at their graduation. She had met some exciting, brilliant people, some of whom were somewhat eccentric. Many of the brilliant men she had met at Bletchley had gone to Cambridge University like Syb and Rory. Some were homosexuals, and most of them had been of a more left, socialist frame of mind, usually as a result of the horrors of the last war.

Her mind strayed back to the brilliant homosexuals. Life did not conform to human limitations of what was 'natural'. Life thrived on diversity. Genius, as she had found in her work at Bletchley, and in her escapade behind enemy lines, lay in thinking off the grid sometimes. The Nazi idea of a master race, their programs to sterilize the mentally challenged, the physically handicapped, those they considered degenerate, had followed similar procedures practiced in America. These foul actions claimed to ape (what a pun, Ness laughed to herself) Natural Selection by Survival of the Fittest, but what humans forgot, was that Nature was a much wiser selector of what constituted 'fitness' than humans, with their narrow, self-centered perspective on life.

Drax had written. Her personal mail had to go through a PO Box number in London. They had learned by now how to write to each other without resorting to information that had to be crossed out. They kept it intimate, the language of lovers. Like most Americans in the lower forty, she was not aware of the Japanese invasion of American soil in the Aleutians, nor of Drax's and Greg's daring feats to loosen the hold the enemy had on Kiska and Attu. They, in turn, did not know of her adventures in trying to outwit the Germans and the Japanese, and in planning for a new way of doing things after this war was over. There is always a downside to every hope for something better. This new, exciting and innovative existence would be developing under the shadow of the most catastrophic weapon yet devised by man. This worried Ness, but there might well be more hope-inspiring contingencies, if the weapon terrified people too much to make war.

The Aleutians, Spring, 1943:
The Alcan Highway was completed in November, 1942, and the ALSIB, Alaska-Siberian, Lend Lease route became functional. That winter of 1942 was one of the worst on record. The winds were unrelenting, and blew in tons of snow in a continual whiteout. The pilots and crews played endless games of cards. Greg was given the job of recording, in sketches, the lives they led on those islands. He also drew portraits for the men to keep or send home. This became a very popular pursuit with everyone. He did a portrait of Eareckson with his husky dog, one of Drax waving out of the cockpit, men smiling through icy blasts, struggling up basalt ridges from narrow bays pounded by storm tossed seas with waves as high as mountains.

"There you go my lad – a genuine Macklin. It may be worth something one day. You hold on to it." They would scoff at that, but they had to admit that he had a great talent. He captured some warm pre-war essence of their personalities that was not immediately apparent under all that fur, wool, hair, dirt, frostbite, fear and desperate longing for home, loved ones and the sanity of peace.

In the winter they bombed at night by the light of incendiary bombs dropped usually by Greg, whose plane went out alone about a minute ahead of the main flight. By January, the navy moved in in force, and prevented supplies getting through to the Japanese on Kiska and Attu.

On February 13, the B-17s flew their final mission. The Staff officers went to San Diego to plan the invasion of Kiska. Before he left, Eareckson went down to the landing site to watch Drax land after a hair-raising bombing run on Attu. He had done an incredible number of missions. He had risked life and limb coming in at wave level to bomb Japanese cruisers. On more than one occasion, he'd got salt water in his engine and had crashed into the black, tossing sea. Luckily he'd been noticed, and his coordinates sent to the PBY that miraculously rescued him within minutes. The men loved those old PBYs. The Russians admired them too, and asked for them to be included in their aircraft quota under Lend-lease.

Drax climbed out of the cockpit, and was surprised to see Eareckson standing there, waving a chit of paper.

"Got you a break at the 'country club' in Ladd. You are overdue for some R&R, you lucky son-of-a-gun. Get your gear. Your flight awaits. Two days, that's your lot. Make the most of it."

"You're kidding right?" Eareckson shook his head. "Greg too?"

"Nope. He's got leave from his Canucks to go to Annette for two days. Hard to break up you lovebirds, but them's the shakes. Take it or leave it. Actually young Macklin has bugged out already."

"He has, has he? What a selfish bugger!"

Drax grabbed the chit, and ran for the plane waiting to take him out of there. He shouted his thanks back to Eareckson, who yelled for him to take a good hot bath when he got to Ladd and tidy himself up." Drax just laughed.

"Who the hell for?"

Eareckson smiled to himself as he watched the plane take off.

⇌╬⇋

Ladd Field, Fairbanks, 1943:
Drax was shown his room – a real bed, with soft clean sheets, blankets and quilt. He had his very own sparkling clean bathroom, with hot water! He indulged in a luxurious bath, and while he dozed in the steamy air, he thought over all the horrors he had experienced. They came on thick and fast. He just lay there, the water up to his nose. He had relived all the close calls at night in his nightmares, and he couldn't quite shake them when awake. He let out the water and just sat there. There was a soft tap at the door. He got up quickly, and wrapping a big white fluffy towel around him, he stepped out of the bath, but a shape already had materialized in the doorway to the bathroom. When the steam cleared a

bit, the shadow took form, and what a form! He couldn't believe his eyes. There she stood, looking wonderful. He felt the emotion bubble up inside. He collapsed on the floor and sobbed, and she knelt beside him and held him, tears cascading down her face, her warm, incredible face.

They spent the two days in bed. Food was sent up to them. They made love and talked quietly, their bodies entwined, while snow fell, and the winds howled and buffeted against the windowpanes.

They had been through a lot, and they opened their hearts to each other. She held him tightly as he recounted the dangers of flying in the Aleutians, and how brave the men were, and how brilliant Eareckson was, and Greg too, and then he comforted her, when she told him that Bobby had been killed at the Battle of Midway. Nessa finally allowed herself to give vent to her sorrow and anguish; then Drax asked how her parents had taken the loss:

"Mom was amazing. She'd had a dream of Bobby, in which he'd told her that he was okay. I think that a healthy mind, threatened by something so devastating, comes up with its own defenses through dreams. We can't just accept our imaginations when awake. They are too contrived, but in our subconscious dreams, we can accept a soothing sort of reality. It worked for her in any case. Dad and I found relief through work, not that work made us feel the loss any less. Memories are alright, but we keep him in the present for now. We have sensed him near us, all three of us. I expect such sensations will soon pass, and he'll be consigned to memory. The thought of that makes me sad."

She couldn't tell him about what she was doing, or where she was exactly, or that she had been behind enemy lines, and neither could he tell her everything he had done.

"I don't suppose I will ever know what you are doing." They looked at each other, and she smiled apologetically. "It's okay. You are doing a great job, Ness, if our recent intelligence is anything to go by. Whatever you have been through, I am grateful that you are here now, safely in my arms."

After the lovemaking, Drax's face assumed a look of deep concern.

"You know, Ness, we fighting men are fed the honor/glory schtick, and we do not believe it. Most of us know we are fighting guys who are as deluded as we are supposed to be, and maybe they are having doubts too. We know they have to save face, and fight to the death for their Emperor. This is thumped into our heads, that we are fighting fanatics, who are determined to kill us. It makes us fight fang and claw too. How much of that is mind games – on both sides? The music in my head has such sinister undertones to the notes of triumph and patriotism. Good and evil themes intertwine, and notions of today's heroes being tomorrow's villains – what goes around comes around – echo through my mind, and the music."

Nessa raised herself on her elbow, and ran her bare foot up his leg.

"Have you composed any music?"

"Hmm." She was so sensual, so warm and close. "Not necessarily harmonious. There are too many jarring moments: camaraderie and fun one moment, then discord, anger, suffering, that reinforce the loneliness, the sense of menace. Feelings that unite: caring for one another, having your back covered, covering another's back – all in this together. Then feelings that divide: mistrust, injustice, cruelty, the feeling others aren't pulling their weight, or are putting you at risk; feelings of jealousy that others are being praised and you are being overlooked. Then feelings of joy at another's good fortune, of being generous and putting others before yourself. The music in my head reflects these contradictions. I have had feelings of intense love for my fellow man, seeing the sacrifice, the good-natured giving of self, of life, without doubt or question. I have seen the anguish of young men dying, or horribly mutilated, not really knowing why. Their perfect young bodies and minds are now damaged goods, heavy, ungainly, ugly. There is nothing more tragic than good young people killing good young people, because others threaten them with dishonor, treason and cowardice if they don't. I composed a piece called 'White Feathers". It is full of overpowering notes with insidiously evil rhythms. These depict the self-righteous people, safe at home, who hand out white feathers. Then the quivering rhythms, with tones of quiet, yet conspicuous harmonies, are for those with independent, from the crowd that is, reasoning abilities, who know intuitively that all this is wrong. These gain in strength, until they overpower all other strains.

Greg, quite independently of my music, has done some wonderful sketches of the men and the hostile wilderness and the isolation. They capture what I am trying to achieve with my music."

"I must hear these pieces sometime. Is there a piano around somewhere?"

"There is one in the restaurant, but I don't want to leave this room, this bed. I want to be with you for as long as possible, just the two of us."

They made love for the rest of the night, not just the physical act of love, but the silent moments in each other's arms, lost in their feelings for each other – the wonder that they had found each other in such times, and after such horrendous experiences.

Nessa flew back to DC the next morning, and Drax returned to Adak, where preparations were underway to invade Attu and Kiska, and drive the Japanese off American soil.

---

Washington, DC, 1943:
Nessa stared out of the window of Emil's sitting room at the rain pouring down outside. Emil put down the phone.

"The scientists are moving in at Los Alamos. There are communist sympathizers among them, but loyal Americans I am sure. There may come a time, when we will have to question our consciences about developing such a weapon. You are getting to me, Nessa. If we get our bomb up and going, do you think we can trust those more rabid capitalist profiteers with their rampant paranoia about communism? Do you think they will want to hit Stalin first? You know, hit the Soviets before they hit us with no warning like the Japanese did. The only way to forestall such a catastrophe would be to balance the power by letting the Soviets in on the secret."

"Then we could all get annihilated? Stalin is no saint. He is just as paranoid."

"Well the thought of that outcome should act as a deterrent. Let the communists and capitalists face off on a more equal footing."

Nessa sighed and smiled sadly.

"We go in for defending dichotomies. We fight tooth and claw to defend one view or the other, failing to see that behavior and beliefs are most probably a compromise of many determining factors. Behavior is like music, you need an instrument and a player to produce it. In the case of behavior, you need genes and learning. America and Russia take opposite poles, and wars result. Peace may come out of the middle way, the compromise. I see this taking shape in Britain after the war, a nascent socio-capitalism, and in the rest of Europe. Do you think these Dragons, you have told me about tonight, can maintain an even course of compromise?"

"Using brave whistle-blowers? Those guys better have the courage of their convictions, for they'll be putting their lives, and those of their loved ones, on the line, and may well be considered traitors, albeit for the general good. Unfortunately, all good guys usually have to pay the ultimate price for advocating fair play and a social conscience, don't they? Look at Jesus and all the advocates for peace and love down through the ages. They never advocated greed, avarice and selfishness. They were quickly dispatched to the useless levels of gods and martyrs, and their ideas for social reform just as quickly institutionalized by those in power, so that they could maintain their control over the people. Once this was achieved, the original teachings died an awful death, along with those who had preached them."

Nessa looked out at the rain. God, I hope these Dragons are effective, she thought to herself, quietly, peacefully effective. She now saw their reason for working behind the scenes. They neatly avoided deification and martyrdom that way, and so could remain an effective force with which to be reckoned.

---

The Aleutians: May, 1943:
"This insanity has gone on long enough," Greg said, when Drax met him off the plane on the runway back on Adak.

"My sentiments exactly."

"What horror ride have they got lined up for us now?"

"We are invading Attu."

"How did Nessa react when you told her that you had sprained your shoulders, arms and hands, so that they are not so finely coordinated to play the piano with your usual sensitive touch?"

"Oh she said that all that will return once I stop putting continual strain on them." Drax strode off, whistling. Greg stayed put, a frown of doubt on his face. Drax turned back. "Come on, then. What's the matter now?"

"You didn't tell her, did you?"

"As I said, why bother? The ability to play will return. The doc said so, once I get some proper treatment, and stop flying missions."

The landing forces ploughed through snow, fog and below freezing temperatures, gale force winds and rough seas to secure beach heads. No shots were fired. Planes dropped food supplies, but the wind blew them into deep crevasses. The Japanese were hidden on the high ridges, and finally opened fire on the troops as they struggled up the slippery slopes from their beachheads. The fog was so bad that planes crashed into the high mountains.

On the 23rd, there was a big air battle. Drax and Greg were in the thick of it. They weaved and dodged, downing many Japanese Zeros. Finally the Japanese pilots conceded defeat, and flew back to the Kuriles. They would not be coming back. Desperate hand-to-hand combat went on for several days. In the end, Japanese officers committed suicide, using grenades. Survivors were taken prisoner. Attu had been liberated.

Now the Eleventh Air Force and their Canadian allies turned their attention to Kiska, and bombed it day and night. The weather was deadly. June to August, williwaws reeked havoc.

July 26th the naval cordon around Kiska broke up to chase some blips that appeared on their radar. A Japanese evacuation force had arrived under heavy fog while the American ships were off chasing blips. All of the Japanese forces on Kiska were quietly and efficiently loaded onto the ships, and they slipped away. The Japanese got back to Paramushiro without any loss of life, or a shot being fired. Luck and the weather had been with them.

Kiska was covered in fog, and the Americans kept bombing it long after the Japanese had gone. They landed on August 15th 1943, to find dogs waiting to greet them. It was a great embarrassment for the generals, but the men were relieved. Drax and Greg had very close calls, but they had prevailed under conditions that no aircraft and pilot should have been able to survive. They knew their planes well, and put great faith in them. They flew with skill and daring, and never would have attributed their survival to sheer guts, but, in reality, that was what it had taken most of the time, and great planes and ground crew.

The generals and admirals in Washington decided that the war in the Aleutians was too embarrassing for the close scrutiny of the press, so our heroes went unheralded. Many Americans never knew that American soil had been invaded, and held by the Japanese. Many never knew the west coast had been bombed by the enemy. Such news would not be good for morale, especially the news that the US fleet had been hunting all over for blips on a screen, and let an entire Japanese force escape without a shot being fired, and they never knew that many of the American and Canadian fatalities on Kiska had been the result of friendly fire under conditions of zero visibility. Nevertheless, the men fighting in the Aleutians had gained a victory, and a significant one, heralded or not, for now they were poised to strike against Japan itself.

Fairbanks, Alaska, Lend-Lease Route, 1943:
By early, 1943, the ALCAN, ALSIB routes were working well, right through from Great Falls to Ladd Field, Fairbanks, where the Soviet pilots took over and flew everything onto Russian soil. The terrain and the weather conditions were hazardous, but after a lot of initial hiccups, and loss of planes and other supplies, it all went relatively smoothly. American supplies of airplanes arrived at the Eastern Front in time for the defense of Stalingrad. Bletchley code-breakers had given Churchill information about where and when the Soviets could expect a German assault, and Churchill, with due care to conceal his source, passed on the information to Stalin. Stalin, true to form, did not believe any of it, but luckily for the Soviets, he was persuaded to act, and the Germans were defeated. Advanced information from Bletchley, and airplanes and other military equipment from America via Lend-Lease, had given the Soviets a decided advantage, and time to build their own weapons factories.

FDR's hopes of buying Soviet trust and friendship in the post-war period were not looking too promising. The Soviets appeared to be guarded, and not at all overly grateful for the thousands of planes, equipment and food supplies that passed along the ALSIB route, but then again, the US was doing very well out of it. There was an enormous increase in industrial and agricultural production, and they were being paid well by Britain and Russia for these desperately needed resources. The Russians were aware also of how some powerful figures in America were gearing up to take on their preferred enemy, namely them, and from a position that held all the advantages of wealth, resources, armaments and effective, relentless anti-Soviet propaganda to frighten Americans into another war. America was giving shelter to Russians who had fled the revolution, aristocrats born to rule and finagle, as if American profiteers and racketeers needed any help in that regard.

One dark late afternoon, in a howling gale and blizzard, a radio operator named Ned, noticed a British Naval officer hand over papers stamped 'Top Secret: The Manhattan Project', to a Soviet dispatch flyer.

"What in Hell is going on?"

"Oh, let it go, Ned! It seems we're making a bundle out of it, so why worry?"

"The ungrateful bastards could help us fight the Japs, instead of staying neutral. What's that all about then?"

"Ned, perhaps it has escaped your notice that thousands of them Ruskies died fighting at Stalingrad, and them other battles on that so-called Eastern Front. They have their hands full with the Krauts. The Japs whipped their ass not so long ago, and took Manchuria and other chunks of territory. Even with us supplying 'em, they can't fight all our battles for us. Stalin wanted us to form a second front to help him out against them Germans, but we didn't, so it is only fair that the Ruskies can't risk helping us out with the Japs, and fight on two fronts for us."

"You a Commie lover, Chuck?"

"Ah go soak your head."

"Some fancy name that British guy had."

"You caught it?" Chuck asked in surprise.
"Yeah, I listened good. Here I wrote it down."
Chuck looked at Ned's hasty scrawl: Arliss-Reese.

Shemya Air Base, November, 1944:
Drax drained his cup of bitter coffee, grabbed his flight gear and left the warmth of the operations room to brave the stinging sleet and dense fog to run to his B-25 craft sitting out on the runway. A welcoming light indicated that his crew was aboard already, checking the radio and other equipment, medical supplies and survival chest. Some guys had been shot down over the Kamchatka Peninsula, and had needed to survive under harsh conditions, until they could be rescued, either by our flyboys, or by the Soviets – always a dodgy prospect, as the Soviets had a neutrality pact with Japan. They had to intern Americans forced down in Soviet territory according to the rules of international law that pertained to neutrality under the Geneva Convention.

His co-pilot, Art, a tow-haired college professor from Kansas, watched as Drax settled into the pilot's seat, and handed the flight plan to his navigator, Jeff.

"Okay, jazz-hot off, ready to go," Drax looked over at his radio man.

"Jazz off, Cap, Sir. All systems go."

"Good man. Your girl sweet?"

"My Gibson Girl is sweet, Cap. Sure hope we won't need her to sing out."

"She better sing out loud and strong, if we need her to, Ned."

"Roger that, Sir."

"Karabuzaki bound?" Art asked.

"Yep, and Suribachi." These were Japanese air bases at the southern tip of Paramushiro, in the Japanese Kurile Islands – their Pearl, and main jumping off point for attacks on the

Aleutians and U.S. Pacific Fleet. Paramushiro lay eight hundred miles away from Shemya, an easy 'there-back home' distance for the B-25. They flew in a squadron of six planes, keeping contact in the dense fog by radar. The radar reassured them that they were not all alone in that surreal world. There was life beyond all that swirling grey.

The sky cleared the farther south they traveled, until at last, they had some blue sky and blue ocean beneath them.

"My God!" Art exclaimed. "What is that bright shining golden orb in the sky?" They all smiled to themselves.

"That would be the sun, Art. Remember the sun?"

"Wait, a distant memory is beginning to form in my frozen mind. The sun – yes, I remember. It was warm, even hot at times, and I think I was stupid enough to take it for granted, and my farming folks prayed for rain. Can you imagine that? They wanted the gall-darn stuff!"

"Farmers need the rain as well as the sun, Cap."

"Yes, thank you, Ned," Art made a grimace at Drax. "Just getting a little melodramatic there, Ned, putting on a little theatrics to stimulate the old brain. Ever tried that, Ned?"

"No need to find brain fodder in lies, Sir, straight old truth as I see it, is fine by me."

"Good lad," Art shouted back, emphatically, but he gave Drax a pointed stare. Drax laughed.

"Good old boys keeping you academics with your fancy notions honest, Art?"

"Yeah, democracy in action." They laughed.

They made landfall over Kamchatka, and headed south to the eastern shore of Paramushiro. South of Karabuzaki, they turned north for their bomb-run. Japanese Zeros appeared out of the sun, guns blazing. Drax made a mad dash for cloud cover, and they found themselves in a blizzard in no time.

"Wowee! What luck! How do you feel about the snow and fog now, Art?"

"I love them. Oh God, how I love them!"

The winter storm had come in fast, and it had chased off the Zeros, but they had been hit.

"What's the damage?" Drax yelled back.

"Not good, Cap. Radar is out, and we've an engine out."

"That is only too apparent, I'm afraid. Hell, now the second engine is acting up!"

"Roger that, Sir."

"Keep your eyes peeled for a hole in all this cover, Art. We're going to need to land, but need to unload these bombs first."

Art groaned,

"Make damn sure that we don't unload over Russian territory, Jeff. It looks like we are going to have to rely on the hospitality of our so-called allies, and dropping a bomb load on them will not have good repercussions in that regard."

"Jeff, where the hell are we as regards landfall? I can't see a damn thing through this white-out."

"According to my reckoning, we are still over ocean, Cap."

"Ken, let 'em loose."

"Sure thing, Cap, but will have to open bomb bay manually, doors jammed."

"Go help him, Ned and you, Jeff." Art went along too for good measure. The plane made its' usual shudder, telling Drax that the bombs had gone. He prayed that they were still over open-ocean.

Art slipped back into his seat, Jeff and Ned into theirs.

"Bombs away!" Art sang out.

"All of them?" Drax asked this just for his own peace of mind. It had become a ritual sort of thing. Art nodded.

"Jeff, where are we?"

"We were over open-ocean, Cap. Unloaded just north of the northern Kuriles, and way south of Kamchatka, so clear of Soviet territory."

Drax breathed a sigh of relief, but shared a worried glance with Art.

They almost glided over the southern tip of the Kamchatka Peninsula. Drax found an isolated stretch of beach, and brought her down in a beautiful, classic, soft bellyflop. They cheered with relief, but then they looked around, and the situation was bleak – very bleak. Highly flammable fumes were rapidly filling the cabin and flight deck, so they scrambled out, as fast as they were able, into the driving blizzard.

"We might as well find some spot to shelter through the night, and see if it is safe to use the radio tomorrow. Our guys will come looking for us, when the weather clears some."

"Hope they beat the Ivans to it," sighed Jeff. "How about our Gibson?"

"I have it," Ned shouted. Jeff had the flight maps and papers, and Art had the medical chest. Drax and Ken had hauled out the survival chest, which contained blankets and dried foods and tools, and some water, and a dinghy. They set up a rough shelter over the whitened, dried out skeleton of a tree using tarp and rope, and they settled into the rubber dinghy, all five of them, and pulled a canvas sheet over them. Ken, the bombardier, had a deep cut on his hand, made when he had tried to open the bomb doors. Art cleaned the wound, and dressed it with bandages and meds from the medical kit, and suggested Ken keep his big gloves on.

"You don't want to get frostbite in that wound. In fact, we should all cover up every exposed part." The rest of the survival chest was in there with them too, and they had dried food to nibble on and clean water. "Keep the food locked up," Art added. "There are tigers and bears in these forests."

"Oh My!" they all shouted and laughed,

The wind howled and tore at the tarp all night long, and they could feel huge mounds of snow building up around them. They could have found a more sheltered spot in the forest behind them, but Drax didn't want to get too far from the plane, well far enough to be safe if she blew, which was unlikely now the fumes had cleared and it was freezing cold, and he also wanted to stay on the beach, where they could easily be found, should someone come looking, again very unlikely.

The next morning, they dug out of the snow, and looked around them. The sky was black. The sea was black. It was a black and white world, but they were used to that, having been out on the Aleutians for more than two years. Ned cranked up the emergency transmitter, the bright yellow Gibson Girl, with yellow box kite attached to its antenna, and it began sending out SOS signals at a regular frequency. A patch of blue sky appeared over the ocean, and it began to spread out, which was a hopeful sign. Ned managed to get the radio working. By the early evening, they had got through to the base on Shemya. In the meantime, Art and Drax had gone off with hatchets to cut some wood, and they returned to say there was a fresh water stream nearby.

They got a good size fire going, and they sat around the blazing embers, hands clasped around tin mugs, sipping coffee, relishing the taste and smell. The Gibson Girl was still sending out signals.

"At least they know we are alive and well," said Ken. They all nodded.

"But they can't pick us up. They can tell the Russians where we are, and they will come for us."

"And then?" They all lapsed into worrying speculations of their own. Ken watched as Art re-dressed his hand. "How is it looking, Art?"

"You'll live. You must rest it for a few days more, but the cut is healing nicely."

While they huddled in their 'tent' that night, Drax suggested that they blow up the plane. Ned, Ken and Jeff protested:

"Oh gees, why, Cap? The Ruskies know all about our B-25's, so why destroy her?"

"I hate to do it too, Ned, but I feel it is our duty to do it. If the Japs know we've landed on neutral soil, they may demand the plane from the Soviets as a gesture of good faith, and proof of their neutrality. The Russians have to intern us, of course, but I am not that sure that our plane would be. I don't want to risk it. We are duty bound to prevent our air planes from falling into enemy hands."

"Well the blaze should bring the Ivans in no time," Art gave a droll chuckle. They all smiled, except Ned.

"I am not looking forward to being rescued by the Ivans." Drax leaned over and patted his shoulder.

"They are okay, Ned. My mother and grandparents are Russian. They weren't Bolsheviks, but they supported the workers, the Russian people. They've had a hard life, not knowing whom to trust, but when they warm up to one, they are great folks."

"At least you speaka da lingo, Drax," Art said. "That reassures me a lot."

"Yes I do, so no worries right?"

The next day, they blew the plane by setting a fire within it, so the remaining gasoline would catch. They'd had to run for it, way down the beach and into the undergrowth of the forest. It seemed to take ages, but the fire spread in the cockpit and through the fuselage, and then…Wham! When the smoke had cleared, hours later, they gazed at the blackened skeleton of the B-25, and Art said a prayer.

"She was a good old bird." They nodded in agreement.

"And a piece of home in this godforsaken place," added Ned, sadly.

"Nothing inhabits this godforsaken place but us." Art stood hands on hips, and gazed up and then down the coast. "You know this place has a multitude of volcanoes, but then so do the Aleutians."

The black smoke was still curling into the white sky for the next four days.

They went through another week of living rough. They didn't fare too badly. They had fresh water from the stream, and wood all around. Their supplies were running low, and they were on the point of going out to reconnoiter the forest for food, when a Russian plane flew over and dropped tins of food. There was a note attached, which notified them that they needed to send up a flare. This they did.

It wasn't until nightfall that seven Russian soldiers arrived in a patrol boat. Drax told them how they got there, and that the plane had blown up spontaneously, and fortunately, they had all been quite a ways off when it had. The Russians examined the charred remains. The inside had been totally gutted. They seemed to have their doubts as to Drax's veracity. They demanded a detailed account of how long the men had been there before the plane had blown. Drax had to be careful, as the Russians most probably knew exactly when they had been forced to land after the air battle, and when they had started transmitting distress signals the next day. He told them that there had been fumes, but they had dissipated. He said that snow had got under the plane and had built up around it, and maybe, as they hadn't exactly witnessed the event, the plane had suddenly toppled and that may have set off the fire. The Russian officer smirked and shook his head.

"Good job you all stayed well away from it," he said at last, and turning he grimaced and did a little shuffle for his comrades, and they all laughed.

Drax and his crew packed up their supplies and dinghy, and put them on the boat, which then took them through rough seas to a military post. They were drenched and sore. If they had been expecting better food, they were sadly mistaken. They got stew, and then the interrogations began. The boys would only give their names, ranks and serial numbers. The Russians wanted to know the whole set-up at Shemya, the bombing schedules and targets, but they got nothing. They pointed out that they were allies, but Drax pointed out that in the Pacific Theater of the war, they were neutral, so not allies. They had fired on American planes flying over Kamchatka, and had downed a B-25, killing all the crew. They interned other American crews shot down over Russian territory, and while this was in accordance with their neutral position, interrogating American servicemen on matters that might aid the Japanese, was not.

"You are flying into our airspace with bombs and radios. You could be spying on us. We have every right to ascertain your true objectives. You would do the same to us, if we flew planes loaded with bombs and radios into your airspace. These actions are not part of the Lend-Lease deal. You are not part of Lend-Lease. You are, as you cowboys and Indians say, part of a war party." He laughed, and so did the other Russians standing around, armed with machine guns.

"It is interesting how many of you fly boys shot down here speak Russian. Are you working for your intelligence services? Are you selected by them to be part of aircrews flying over Russian territory, so that you can understand what we say among ourselves? You destroyed your plane and its bomb load. Why? Did you have special features on that plane for carrying out spy work?"

"Drax Shaw, Captain, U.S. Army Air force, serial number...."

They spent the next month in some holding station, where the conditions were primitive. The new year of 1945 wore on. They just hoped and prayed everyone back home knew they were alive. Eventually, they boarded a Trans-Siberian train and headed off across the vast distances of Mother Russia. They slept on wooden bunks in carriages that rattled and rolled along. They saw many Russian towns and villages. The people seemed desperately poor, even in areas where Russian industrial complexes stretched for miles, and transport trains taking wagon after wagon of tanks, trucks, guns and planes to the pacific coast were in great abundance.

"They seem to be gearing up for war against Japan, one hopes," said Art, after they had been held up for two days as armament transport trains rumbled by.

"They have benefited from Lend-Lease. Now they can make their own planes and tanks and ships, taking the opportunity to improve on our designs, or at least copy them. Do we have any secret weapons left?" Jeff asked.

"I don't think so," said Ned. "I saw top secret papers from some Manhattan Project changing hands between us and the Ivans at Ladd."

"Well then, we don't have any secrets they don't know," Art pointed out.

"The guy I saw handing over top secret Manhattan Project papers, whatever that is, was a Brit, a Royal Navy officer."

"Well FDR and Churchill share everything. I am sure that this Manhattan Project is a joint allied effort."

"I ain't so sure, Cap, I saw…"

Ned's speculations were cut off by a loud roar of steam and clanking, as their train started up again, and Russian soldiers hastened them back to their bunks.

Their final destination was a U.S. base near Teheran. Art was optimistic:

"They couldn't chance the Japs seeing them return us Statesside on the Pacific coast. The Japs have spies everywhere, and so do the Germans. We are here, I bet, because an exchange can be made more surreptitiously."

It was not until the end of May, after peace had been declared in Europe, that they finally were flown home.

When they landed at Andrews Air Force base, they were loaded on buses to take them to flights that would take all of them to their homes and families.

Drax had waved them off. He had seen her, waiting there behind the wire-link fence, smiling through her tears. God she looked good, and she wasn't in uniform, thank God! Nessa had been taken aback at how much thinner he was, but he hadn't lost that confident air, or his good looks, on the contrary, he looked wonderful, tall, tanned, strong, the same casual elegance and sensual smile. His eyes were full of love, and that was all she needed to see until he could hold her in his strong embrace again, and they could kiss longingly and lustily, and melt into each other.

※

Emil Franz House, DC, early June, 1945:
"You look quite well, considering your experiences. You are thinner, but your medical file claims no physical or psychological traumas." Emil looked up at Drax over the rim of his spectacles.

"Kerr, Biff, Ben and I have survived worse conditions and treatments. Am I allowed to ask how they are?"

"All three of them are in China. Biff is married, and has an infant son. His wife is in our organization. She is of French and Vietnamese heritage, and before China, she and Biff were with the Maquis in the South of France. She is an extremely competent asset, quite deadly too."

"Is she there to help regain France's colonial possessions after the war?"

"Absolutely not."

Drax raised his eyebrows: "More of an affiliation with her Vietnamese side then, but working for us?"

"It depends on what you mean by 'us'."

Drax raised a questioning eyebrow. Emil didn't bother to elucidate further. Drax thought for a moment, actually debating with himself over whether to mention it or not. He decided to go ahead.

"I know this is most probably just gossip from the lads working that ALSIB route, but my radio man claimed he saw some weird goings on up there at Ladd: gold bullion coming in, papers going out. He even saw a British naval officer handing over top secret documents." Drax watched Emil's response to these disclosures. Emil seemed passively interested, even a little dismissive.

"The Soviets are paying us back big time, and with gold and cash."

"The top secret papers? My guy saw papers about some project called the Manhattan Project. That ring a bell?"

Emil shook his head.

"It sounds familiar, but it is out of my sphere of operation. It might be a military op."

"I know that FDR and my father treasure hopes that, after all this generosity, the Soviets will be our friends after the war. What do you think? I'll tell you now that I do not have such an optimistic outlook for our future relationship with the Soviets."

"I miss FDR terribly, for after this war, those who detested his New Deal projects that helped the ordinary people, will hold power. Truman, and any president who follows, will not be able to bring these conservative capitalists to heel. Rampant capitalism, with no checks or regulations, will hold sway. The rest of the world is going to be pulled apart by these opponents, and it will ruin the chances newly independent colonial countries have for establishing any kind of democratic solutions. They will have to pay court to one or other of these stiff-necked giants. I do not think that America and Russia will let them choose their own way. Their freedom will be just an illusion.

Americans put misplaced trust in the wealthy, and are hypnotized by the snake-oil salesmen, yet balk at trusting those of their number who need a little help. Look how quickly they have come to despising FDR's projects, projects that saved them when they were in dire straits, but the minute they are back on their feet, they scorn them, and return to an almost feudal state of trust in wealth."

"Emil, the Soviets have a huge military capability. The Japs are going to be made aware of Soviet revenge soon enough, I should imagine, and then we'll have the Soviets knocking at our door through the Kuriles. They questioned us relentlessly about our attack plans on the Japanese bases and industries in the Kuriles, about our flight plans and bombing runs planned to go over Russian territory, Kamchatka. We didn't give them anything but name, rank and serial number, but those are the routes they'll use to attack us, once they take their lands back from Japan. They have learned a great deal about our defenses in Alaska from the ALSIB route."

"The Japanese still have a very powerful fighting capability. Stalin would be mad to take them on. We bomb Japanese cities relentlessly. We have retaken many islands occupied by them. We will win in the end, and Stalin realizes the immense industrial power that is America. He knows he is in no position to take that on. We most probably will shore up our northern frontiers. If they plan to attack us from the Kuriles, and they do not have sovereignty over those yet, and may never have it, then so can we attack them from the Aleutians, and possibly the Kuriles, if we control Japan. No, I do not see us going to war with the Soviets, not an outright 'us and them' war, but small territorial and political wars of influence and support only, avoiding actually fighting each other. Russia and America will gain at the expense of these poor newly freed countries. I pity them, I really do. They will have so much suffering ahead of them when this war is over, and all just to satisfy the egos of the paranoid Soviets and our profiteering, self-serving, self-righteous, patriotic zealots, who give the Russians every excuse for being paranoid."

"Then it is same old bloody same-old. We will have more wars, just not on each other's home turf, but in someone else's back yard. Sounds rotten! Emil, I have had too much experience of Japanese and Russian tactics to ever trust them. Japan has set a precedent of attacking before declaring war. Others will follow suit. I don't blame us for feeling paranoid."

"Working relationships cannot be fostered under such mistrust and fear."

"They haven't been established through aid and trust either, Emil. The Soviets do not, and never will, trust us, FDR's generosity notwithstanding."

"I am putting my faith in the plans for a new United Nations to replace the old League of Nations, but it will only work if all nations, no matter how small or poor, have equal say. It must not be dictated to by the powerful nations, or Russia and America will hold sway, and render the whole global effort null and void."

"God, Emil, look how useless the League of Nations was. This new one will be just as ineffective in keeping world peace."

They sat in silence for a while. Emil concerned with Drax's outlook and mood, and Drax wanting to leave, but somehow or other being incapable of doing so on such a pessimistic note. He needed to believe in a better world, and to him, Emil was the man to inspire the hope that this could happen. Emil spoke at last, changing the subject:

"Greg and Rory were involved in the fighting to end the war in Europe. They were part of the D-Day landing forces. Rory was involved in work for British Naval Intelligence in DC up until the end of 1942. He was much relieved to be able to fight the actual foe again. Laura, Sybil and Nessa have been involved in hush-hush work States-side."

"They have nothing to do with this Manhattan Project?"

"I don't know. They work closely with the military intelligence services and the OSS. Laura is go-between with the FBI. The war is not over for any of us yet. I gather that, by special dispensation, you are joining Kerr in the northern provinces of Viet Nam and China?"

"There are flyers to rescue from behind enemy lines in Indochina."

"Yes, and a potential battlefield to reconnoiter and study. I hope that you will be keenly observant of who is funding these elements and arming them." The two men exchanged looks that implied questions they dare not raise. "Truman is having a time of it trying to control all these factions giving him advice and orders, and threatening him too. We are arming Chiang Kai-shek, but one of the Chinese warlords working supposedly for him, is giving the weapons to the communist groups in Yunnan and Tonkin Provinces, so here we are arming both sides of a battle yet again."

"I leave for China the day after tomorrow."

"Nessa was a pale shadow of her former self while you were in Russia. Fortunately, we knew you were alive and well. Your parents asked me if I could put them in touch with Nessa, which I did. They got together whenever Nessa's schedule allowed. They like her very much. Magda and I joined them when we could. Drax, I hope you will excuse me if I ask, but do you still feel the same way about Nessa? Please forgive me for asking, but I sense a change in you, Drax, and I am not sure in what way."

"Neither am I, Emil. There isn't another woman. I love Nessa, to the exclusion of all other women. I admire what you and my father are trying to do, which is keep America honest, but we are facing ruthless adversaries down the road. I'd always thought the Russians were brave to change the system in favor of the people, but they didn't, did they? With all our talk of liberty and individualism, we don't really care. We're a sink or swim lot. People who succeed rarely turn around and help others to make it, unless they get a tax break by so doing, but at least we don't hide that fact. We broadcast it loud and clear, so people are stupid if they think America has a social conscience. Russians say they do, but the powers-that-be there do not. They are out for themselves too, so they are hypocrites. I am leaning more to our way. At least it is more open. Nessa and I have discussed these things, and she disagrees with me, of course. Nessa won't accept rampant capitalism or communism. She still hopes we'll develop a fairer society based on that socio-capitalism of hers."

"Maybe you are right, Drax. Maybe Nessa, with her socio-capitalism, and I, with a more global outlook along similar lines, are being idealists. We want a world with a social conscience, not a national one, not a religious one, not a political one, but a fair system, with no hidden self-serving agendas."

"I think that is pie-in-the-sky thinking, Emil, and when I tell Nessa this, I see a light go out in her eyes, and she looks at me, as if I am suddenly alien in some way. The horrible thing is, that I keep wanting to provoke her, not come around to her way of thinking. I feel that way with my father too. This is an awful turn of events. I love the woman desperately. I hope and pray this is just a reaction to being exposed to the horrors of the Soviet system for too long, for I also now doubt what FDR was up to. I am thinking like these right-wing extremists here, and fear, the fear instilled in me in Russia, has brought this about. I cannot shake it off." Drax put his head in his hands. Emil got up and put a hand on his shoulder.

"People who go through similar experiences to yours in Russia either come away loving and idolizing their captors, or detesting them. Were you horribly afraid?"

"No, that's the thing, I wasn't; not any of us were. They were suspicious and didn't trust us, that was for sure. They were not friendly, but I suspect they'd have been in trouble if they had befriended us, and I came to see their ingratitude for all we'd given them in that light too. The poor buggers would be punished for showing any interest or friendship towards non-communists, especially capitalists. We could tell them how good we had it, and as such, I came to see that we did have it good compared with them. I guess we were used to things being great under FDR, well better, at least. I guess we'd forgotten the horrors under the Drought, Dust Bowl and Depression and the bad old days of the chiselers and racketeers, and folks living in make-shift tents in Central Park, and the god awful fundamentalism and feudalism of our extreme right, not to mention the evils of racism. Our Negroes fought bravely for America, and I dread to think how they'll be rewarded when they get back home, especially those who live in the South. I watched those Blacks work on the ALCAN Highway under horrendous conditions, along with other poor working class stiffs, and believe me, they were amazing. They were cheerful, while sleeping in freezing cold tents and huts, inadequately heated by foul-smelling stoves. To my mind, the government could never have paid them enough, yet they were glad to have jobs and any kind of payment. I suppose you are right, Emil. Our workers don't exactly live the dream either. They are exploited as much as the poor Russians."

"I think you sound quite balanced, Drax, so why should Nessa doubt you?"

"I am not so fairly balanced with her, Emil. I want her to know the fear of communism as well as she knows how to fear ruthless capitalist exploiters and fascists, and I am sure she does already… Oh, I don't know what I am about really. War breeds mistrust, fear and so many contradictory notions that may well sow the seeds for future wars, and evil men cash in on this."

"I am afraid that you are like many young people returning from the horrors of war. Your lives have been on the line too many times. That must shake your sense of security. You have learned to be both resourceful and, at times, completely helpless. That plays with the brain in most profound ways. I am so full of anguish that all this isn't over yet for you, Kerr, Nessa, and others still involved in the fighting in the Pacific theater of war. I hope, most desperately, that you will all survive, and that, as young survivors, you will not tolerate any of the selfish, exploitative ways of thinking that went before, but that you will be more innovative, liberal, global, less self-involved."

Drax's eyes held an expression Emil found hard to describe. He saw Drax to the door. Drax was about to leave, when he stopped, and looking, not at Emil, but out into the night, he said that his man had heard the name of the British naval officer, who had handed over top secret papers to the Russians at Ladd Field.

"Arliss Reese, does that sound familiar to you, Emil?"

Emil's heart missed a beat, but he shook his head and smiled. He watched Drax walk through the dusk of a summer's evening to the waiting car. There was the scent of newly cut grass on the air, and a hint of honeysuckle. In his heart, Emil wished the young man good luck in China, and hoped that he would find some sort of peace within himself, and come to trust again that Nessa would not let anything, especially different political views, stop her from loving him to the depths of her being. It would help that he would be with Kerr again. Kerr was a good, sound influence. He also prayed for Rory and Syb. The situation was coming to a head more quickly than they previously had thought.

⇌

Washington, DC, June, 1945:
"So here we gals sit again, without our men, just as women have done down through the ages."

"Women have done a great deal on the home front, and at the front lines, to win this war."

"And women doing men's jobs will have to give them back when the guys get home for good…not fair!"

"You wrote a film script on this, didn't you, Ness?"

"Yep, from the last war, and I tried to see both points of view: the women resenting their loss of independent income, and yet trying to see to their poor ravaged men too, and men trying to adjust to new values on the home front, while resenting having given their all for no apparent purpose, except change for the better, that didn't necessarily include them at first. It starred Fiona, Sigi and Lorna."

"So, Ness, off to the mysterious Orient to join Drax?"

"Guess so. I am excited about going, even if it involves the same old tedious data collection and analyses for me, while Drax will be out exploring the high mountains and jungles for hidden prisoner-of-war camps."

"I am being dispatched to the jungles of Ceylon," sighed Syb. "Also doing same old, same-old."

"I think that you are both lucky. I am stuck in New York with Canadian Intelligence."

"New York, Oh poor you!"

"Shut up, Syb! I like change and adventure as much as the next girl."

"I'll feel sorry for you while I am sweating in jungle temps and humidity; when my hair drips sweat into my reddened eyes, and mosquitoes attack my peaches and cream skin in droves, and the nights I lie awake cooking in my own juices, while poisonous snakes slither around me, and nasty things swim through my blood stream. I'll think, poor old Laura having to walk through snow and ice to some fancy nightclub and restaurant."

"I hope you'll think of me freezing to death waiting for my crowded street car, of me eating my meager supper all alone, while my husband and dearest friends battle the foe in some exotic locale, near some tropical beach. I hear what the gals and guys who return from Ceylon say, and it isn't all hardship. They have fresh fruit on tap, laundry done for them, gin slings at sundown, no black out, parties at charming tea planters' luxurious houses, with servants to wait on them hand and foot. Yeah, it is some miserable posting alright!"

"Stop it, you two. We are just war-weary. I am sick of it. We are almost twenty-nine years old. We were twenty-two when this started. Six bloody stupid years have gone by, years in which great evil has been perpetrated against innocent people, while others rake in the cash." Nessa broke down into tears. Syb and Laura exchanged worried glances. Ness was a brick, a tower of strength – what had happened?

"Ness, dear, is everything alright? Are you and Drax okay?"

Nessa shook her head, and taking out her handkerchief, blew her nose.

"No, Syb. We are not alright. Drax was frustrated by having to sit out the end of the war in Europe, when we were all pitching in to win. Rory and Greg were flying missions. We were doing intelligence work, and he was cooling his heels in the Russian camps. He understandably detests communists. Our fighting forces have to believe they have been fighting for a system, our system, and they have killed innocents for it, so it must be the best there is. When our far Right screams of the communist threat, they must have grounds for so doing… no wait" Nessa held up her hand to stop Syb, who was in the act of protesting. "I know, Syb, the rich are playing the old fear factor again to control us, and keep us, well let's face it, well-kept slaves, but Drax is shaping up to take the far Right view that communists should be rooted out and sent packing. I argued that this is not the democratic way. Trust the people. They can absorb lots of different views. 'Oh yeah,' he said. 'Even racism, fascism, bigotry? The people have liked those views too at one time or another. The wonderful people you trust in can go pure psycho like the Germans, the Japs, the southern racists. Maybe people need to riot, pillage, kill and rape, using a cause they think they can believe in as an excuse for the violence that lies simmering within. Look, Ness, all comers: Catholic Inquisition, Protestant comeback, French and Russian revolutions, the wealthy and powerful killing on a whim, the poor and middle classes terrorizing their own to get ahead. Look at the Mafia, formerly Robin Hoods, now murderous thugs. They all feed on the ordinary people. I tell you, Ness, we are sharks in a fighting frenzy – that is what all life is about.'"

The girls sat in stunned silence for a moment.

"Time we girls took over. Go get Drax sorted out," Laura laughed. Nessa smiled, but not with her eyes. She looked over at Syb. Syb also seemed lost in not too pleasant thoughts.

---

K'ung-ming, China, summer, 1945:
Nessa lived with a wealthy Chinese family in a beautiful pagoda style house up in the foothills that overlooked a picturesque lake to the north of the walled city. The foothills led up to high snow-capped mountains. She had her own set of rooms, and was attended by servants, who saw to her every need. This embarrassed her somewhat, but they didn't seem to mind. They chided her good-naturedly, when she tried to save them work by doing things herself. She told them that she came from a farming family, and had lived simply, with basic fare, but they laughingly dismissed that as of no consequence.

Nessa had buffed up her knowledge of Japanese and Chinese; some learned while growing up in California, and then more thoroughly acquired in crash courses held in DC for operatives going into the field. Her facility in picking up languages, thanks again to Agnes and Loretta, had helped tremendously.

The father of the family with whom she lived was a banker, and he had spent considerable time in San Francisco and New York. He had studied economics at Columbia, and his wife and two daughters and son had joined him there. Evenings were spent reminiscing over time spent in Manhattan, and how they loved New York, and missed their friends there, and the life they had led there. They were close friends of General Chiang Kai-Shek and his intelligence chief Kang Sheng, and traveled frequently to the Nationalist headquarters in Chungking. The names of the top American military commanders, as well as OSS representatives, slipped easily into their conversation as close associates. They were only too glad to show her their hospitality on behalf of all these important people they knew. They had tried by polite, yet devious, ways to ascertain why she had to live separately from the other ladies of the OSS, of which there were quite a few. She must be there on a very important assignment. Nessa slowly shook her head and smiled. She was just a nobody, who was charged with the most tiresome secretarial duties. She had arrived late, and they didn't have a spare billet for her. The housing officer had suggested she approach the family, as they were such good friends of important Americans, and ask if they could put her up until a billet became available. She feigned regret at having to impose on them, and begged to be allowed to be of help to them in some way. They politely shook their heads. She wasn't an imposition, and she brought them many American delicacies they could not get in K'ung-Ming and Chungking. They were grateful to her, and she should not feel that she was a burden. Yet, in many unspoken ways, they conveyed to her that her presence wasn't just an inconvenience, but that it also raised many doubts and suspicions in their minds about her actual agenda. Nessa smiled to herself.

The father was in the pay of the Japanese. He had hoped that, by his support of, and kindness and generosity to, Americans, he could gain enough of their trust that he'd learn, in passing so to speak, from careless chatter, the whereabouts of downed American crews, hidden by native peoples in the jungles of China and Japanese occupied Indochina and Burma. He had provided information about secret Japanese prisoner-of-war camps deep in the jungles to gain the trust of the Americans, but his information had become suspect. Missions sent to reconnoiter these areas had discovered Japanese forces hiding in the jungle all around, but no sign of any camp. They had managed to withdraw again without being detected. Nessa had been placed in his home to watch who came and went.

There were some factions, seeking to promote independence for their countries after the war, who saw the Japanese as liberators from colonial exploitation. They hoped for Asian hegemony in trade and business in the Pacific. China, India and the countries of Southeast Asia could form a trade alliance with a victorious Japan, and thus trade with Europe and America on a more equal footing, as their own independent nations, and not under the control of colonial powers. Nessa's host family belonged to this faction. Fortunately, most Chinese, Burmese, Indian and Indochinese peoples detested the Japanese. They all had suffered horribly under their occupation, but especially in the central provinces of Viet Nam, where thousands had starved to death in a holocaust on a par with the one that had taken place in Europe. The Japanese had taken their rice, and made them grow crops that furthered the war effort, providing oils and sacking, rather than food.

Local Burmese helped to locate hidden prisoner-of-war camps in their deep jungles. Other indigenous peoples helped in finding camps hidden on isolated offshore islands. Allied rescue forces would then attack these camps and rescue the poor men and women, who were usually in a terrible state of malnutrition, who had suffered torture, or had been made to do backbreaking work. Natives also provided information on hidden Japanese forces, and American and British bombers flew in to destroy them. Drax and Kerr were part of these search-and-destroy missions. After such sorties, they would return to Chungking, or K'ung Ming, for new instructions. This would provide Drax and Nessa with the chance to meet up.

The evening was magical. They sat on a blanket on the lakeshore. The moon's rippling reflection competed for attention with the lanterns set afloat on tiny platforms. Flowers, large lotus blossoms, blossoms off the trees around the shore, also dotted the tranquil waters. The snow-capped mountains formed a stunning backdrop.

"It would be hard to find a more exotically romantic setting anywhere," Nessa sighed, as she lay in Drax's arms, her head on his chest. He murmured by way of reply, his eyes closed. He and Kerr had looked exhausted when they had turned up after their last mission. They were haggard, and had deep dark patches under their red-veined eyes.

"The war certainly seems far away, another place, another time."

Nessa smiled. The lake was a twin of the dark star-lit sky above. She found that, despite their close embrace, she was having difficulty in finding what to say, and maybe this wasn't a moment for words. There had been too many of late. This was a moment for peace, and the contentment of being safe and together, but there was some irksome vibe that disturbed her equanimity and cast a troubling little shadow over the evening. It was like a small blemish, one couldn't quite hide. She was about to ask him if he still loved her, but he spoke first:

"What did you think of my parents? Was my father in any way difficult or distant?"

"No. They were very welcoming, all of them, your grandparents too."

"Did you go with Emil and Magda?"

"No. I went alone. Emil and Magda were there on only two occasions. We had a lovely time. The apple trees were in bloom, the sea was blue, with tumbling white frothy waves of early spring. Everyone was concerned about you, not quite understanding why the Russians had not released you. Your grandparents played some beautiful pieces of music, some of their compositions intermingled with variations of Debussy and Vivaldi. Your mother sketched the while, and then played the balalaika for us. She said that she hoped the music would travel to the Russian soul, and they'd release you."

Drax snorted:

"Not much chance of that. Russians' souls are trapped in the ice of dogmatic dialectic."

"You know, Drax, that being Russian, your mother and grandparents saw it more as if Mother Russia were keeping you safe in her arms until the war was over, even though they knew that you would detest that."

Drax removed his arms from around her, and struggled to sit up, making Nessa have to sit up. She leaned back against the cushions, but he remained sitting upright, his hands clasped before him on his knees. He hadn't quite shaken her off his chest, but Nessa had felt as if he might as well have done. It had been a distancing gesture.

"No politics, Drax, please."

Drax hung his head, and looked back at her, sitting there amongst the colorful cushions. He had a smile on his face.

"You are an incorrigible optimist, Ness."

"Do you still love me?"

"We have gone through so much in the last few years, life-changing experiences, the both of us. We haven't had much time to be just us. We've had to let in lots of other considerations and people."

"But has our love remained inviolate?"

"The 'we' we used to be – young lovers, idealistic, romantic, a source of magical inspiration for each other?"

Nessa nodded, a worried expression on her face.

"Am I, Ness, still your only love, the love of your life?"

"I am afraid so," she smiled sadly as a tease.

He made a feeble attempt at a laugh, raising his head to gaze up at the stars. He sighed.

"Look, Ness, I love you, but my mind is so confused. I know exactly where you stand on things. You haven't changed. You love being with people. You see something special in everyone you meet. You want to be involved in championing a just cause, but you see… I do not. When all this is over, and God willing, I am hale and hearty in all respects, I want to travel. I want new experiences. I guess having lived on the edge of survival, taking on nature in all her rages, and man at his absolute worst, I can't settle to pampering my fellow humans. I don't want anything to do with them, or their crazy notions. I want to be cleansed of them. I want to be alone with my music, without human interference."

He turned to look at her. Her face was obscured by darkness, the moon being eclipsed by a long line of cloud. Her voice came out of the shadows, lost and forlorn, but only momentarily, and then it had an edge, bordering on almost a cold, practical acceptance. He could not see if her face reflected the same acceptance. Was she sad, disgusted with his wimpy excuse, or relieved? His new lack of confidence had given rise to doubts. Hidden in her shadows, Nessa felt as if her heart had been torn into shreds, both from his cold words of alienation, and that look in his eyes that seemed questioning, challenging, doubting, assessing her love, testing her love. She had heard of this doubt from other girls, this paranoia in their men returning from battle. Love had carried them through the separation of war, only to find this cold reaction in the men they loved, the men with whom they had been longing to be reunited. She thought she and Drax would rise above all that. As she looked at him, she saw how foolish she had been; of course what Drax had been through would have affected him. He had seemed so self-reliant, so self-assured and confident, but there had been hints of something else – she just couldn't put her finger on it.

"Should I not have met your family, or not have met them until you could be there to make the introductions?"

"It would have been a very special moment for me; you and my mother meeting for the first time. I guess I do feel cheated out of that."

"Varvara instigated it, but I was happy and eager to oblige her."

"You didn't think I should be there?"

"Well, yes I did, but we were so worried about you, we wanted to get together to commiserate, to console each other, I guess. After all, we are the ones who love you the most."

"Ah." Drax resumed his study of his joined hands. Nessa felt the slow burn of anger rising within her. If he were playing with her deepest emotions, he could go to blazes, and she'd be well rid of him. This doubting, cynical man did not deserve her love, but this had been a momentary feeling. It subsided almost as soon as the notion had come to mind. She'd been prepared for physical deformities and disfigurements, burns, complete paralyses, even the inability to perform sex again. She had encountered all these in the men she had seen come back from war. She was prepared for shell-shock, terror, nightmares, irrational fears, all the scars of battle, but not this. It may well be the result of battle fatigue, helplessness and doubt that all prisoners had to face, a separation and alienation from all they'd known before. Her heart went out to him. Her love for him returned with the moonlight on her face. Drax could see her now, and he was startled by the look of deep love on her face. She was his rock, his safe haven, of that there was no doubt.

"I love you, Drax, always will. You do what you have to. You deserve your freedom after all these years of sacrifice for others. We all do. I'll be waiting for you, until you tell me to move on, that you have no need for my love, maybe that moment is now, and so be it. I'll have to live with it, but if you still have love for me, but need to resolve other emotions, I shall wait you out, and be there for you. We were rather carried away by it all, maybe we need a cooler, more cautious reflection now that the threat of war looming on the horizon has been realized and dealt with, or will be soon. Oh Drax, what a romantic evening, so magical, so beautiful …" Here Ness broke down, tears spilled over and ran down her cheeks. Drax just sat there, not looking at her.

They folded up the blanket and picked up the cushions and handed them to the servants who waited to take them. A cold wind had drifted down from the surrounding mountains. They stood facing each other, but he could not bring himself to look at her, until she, looking at him the while, touched his shoulder, then dropped her hand and turned away. He raised his eyes to watch her walk back through the trees, her back straight, her head held high. She strode along with her usual unhurried, elegant, confident stride.

Drax arrived back at his room to be greeted by Kerr, who was in a state of great agitation.

"Drax, where is Nessa?" Drax replied that she had gone back to her lodgings, and why all the concern? Kerr hurriedly told him that, as Nessa had told the family that she wouldn't be back that night, but staying in town, the banker, Mr. Ling, had arranged to meet with his Japanese friends. He had checked that Nessa's alibi, Drax, was actually in town, and they had watched, as he and Nessa had gone out to the lake. Taking this as a sign that no trap had been set, Mr.Ling had gone ahead with the secret and treacherous assignation at his house.

"How long ago did she leave you?" Drax had meandered around some, so checked his watch, and Nessa had left him twenty minutes ago.

"Blast," Kerr said. "We have only just learned of the meeting from one of the servants at the house. She could not get away until the Lings had dismissed the servants for the night. They had to prepare a meal for the visitors, but had not been allowed to see them. The girl took an incredible risk in spying through the screen at those gathered for dinner. She had to creep out of the house, and get down the mountain track without being detected by the Japanese soldiers on guard."

"The meeting may have ended before Nessa got back."

"The girl said it had taken her an hour, after setting out the dishes, before she could get away, and another forty minutes or so to reach us, which was just before you came along. I think the meal and discussion would take longer than that." Kerr wondered briefly why Nessa and Drax had not been together for the night, but whatever the reason, Nessa's safety was his main concern.

Nessa, by this time, was approaching the gates to the courtyard of the house. She had been arguing with herself, going over and over in her mind every minute detail of the evening. She could hardly wait to meet Drax, to see him standing there, so handsome in his officer's uniform, deep brown jacket, tan trousers. He wore his uniform well with his broad shouldered physique and strong legs. She could hardly wait to feel his arms around her, and then… a luke warm greeting. He was tired he said. He'd had another close call. Alright, that she could understand. She was a little preoccupied herself. The Lings had been suspicious of her night-out, checking repeatedly that she would not return. They did not want to lock the gates, and leave her out in the dark, they had offered by way of excuse. These were dangerous times. The thought had crossed her mind that this would be their opportunity to meet with a Japanese courier.

She was about to hurry on, when a long, thin, black cat stopped her in her tracks. He was friendly and rubbed against her legs. She bent down to stroke him. He purred and butted her hand with his small head. She was reminded of Riley and home. She was about to murmur this to the cat, when the cat tensed and looked ahead to the house. Nessa suddenly felt the darkness grow ominous and oppressive. She could sense danger all around. The cat looked back at her, and then at the gate. Nessa rose slowly. She then realized that she couldn't see the gate in the deep darkness. It was always well lit, and the courtyard beyond. Lanterns burned throughout the night. A cold shiver went through her, along with the brief thought that this horrible night might not yet have finished with her. She had her revolver in her handbag. She reached for it, holding it, still concealed, in her open bag, and cautiously approached the gate. As she drew near, she saw that the gate was slightly ajar. Should she withdraw? She looked behind her, and sensed she was being watched. The cat had disappeared among the rocks. Everything was too still, too quiet. The darkness was heavy with 'presence' of some sort. She could not go back along the track to town. If they ambushed her, they could make it look like she'd stumbled in the dark, and pitched headlong down the steep mountainside to her death. Forward was her only option. Should she slowly push the huge gate open enough to let her slip through? Should she wait just in case someone was on the other side? Should she push the gate wide open quickly, maybe hit or startle them? She could jump for cover at the same time. Lord, what to do? She raised her revolver clear of the bag. She pushed on the gate, but it didn't swing wide, it got caught on a heavy bundle of something just behind it. Oh for some light! She reached around with her foot, and poked the heap of what seemed like rags. No, it was a body. Her foot slipped in something slick. Then she realized she could smell blood. She crouched down and crept around the body. Suddenly a light appeared in the servants' quarters, a small hand-held lantern by the look of it, and a quiet voice called her name. Was this a trap?

"Miss Nessa?" a man's voice, that of Peng, the watchman. He had pushed up the bamboo shutter that covered the window just enough for the light to be seen. "Miss Nessa, please answer if it is you." She slowly stood up, hidden behind a cherry tree.

"Yes, Peng?"

Before she could say more, the shutter came down, and the light was extinguished. It was dark again. She listened for movement. Suddenly, out of the darkness, Peng was in front of her, grabbing her arm and pulling her onto the path. She resisted, raised her gun. Lights flashed on all over the place, and she was blinded. A group of people stood before her. One, a tall woman of middle age, but extremely beautiful. She seemed to be in charge.

"Ling and his family are in our custody," she said. "Their Japanese guests are dead. Their guards are dead." She pointed to the pile of rags at the gate. "The others you can now see lying around you in pools of blood."

"Who are you, Kuomingtan or communists?"

"Friends, Miss Eiles. I am sure that you can deal with this now. We have to leave. Don't worry, we have taken care of the servants with dubious loyalties. Peng here is reliable. Sui has gone to the city to warn your people."

"Who are you?"

The woman frowned in consternation, and snapped out orders. The others with her left as silently as they had come, disappearing into the night. The woman stood alone, except for the black cat at her feet. She had a rifle over her shoulder. She looked at Nessa for several seconds. Nessa was too dumbfounded to do or say anything.

"Viet Minh," she snapped, and then she too disappeared into the surrounding darkness, the cat followed. That made sense, Nessa realized. They hated the Japanese, maybe more than the Chinese did, and with cause. God, what a night!

Kerr, with soldiers in tow, but not Drax, appeared some minutes later. They had literally run all the way, and were breathless.

"Viet Minh! Wow! Great!" said Kerr. "They did a good job. They also delivered the Ling Family to our compound. The man and his wife are under arrest." Nessa just sat on a rock. Kerr knelt beside her.

"Are you okay, Ness?" She looked up at him, and her expression, or maybe lack of one, said it all.

"Drax came with us, but he saw that you were safe, and felt it might be easier on you, if you didn't have to see him again tonight. I have no business asking, but have you two split?"

Nessa nodded. Kerr patted her shoulder gently.

"I had hoped that you two would come through this bloody war with your love intact and strong; that your love would beat the odds. It may still, Ness. Drax has changed. I have noticed that. He wants out, wants to get back to his music. Cut him some slack, Ness. Love may yet win out, and you and Drax have something so very special. We all could sense it."

Nessa gave him a weak smile in response.

"Yes, Kerr, we did. We had something so very special."

Kerr put his arm around her, and they joined the others in making their way back down the mountain. As they stumbled along, Nessa had to ask who the woman was, who had been in charge of the Viet Minh band.

"I am not sure, but if they were Viet Minh, as you say, and if she is who I think she is, then she is very special, Ness, an incredible woman. Her name is Minh Li."

A month later, Hiroshima and Nagasaki were destroyed by the most terrifying weapon on earth. The war ended, but not because the Japanese were shocked into surrender by the bomb to end all bombs, or by the suffering of their people in these two cities, but by the declaration of war made on them by the Russians. Stalin joined in at the last second to reap the rewards. Japan had hoped that Russia's late entry meant that they would not have to make war reparations to the Soviets, but only to the Americans. Such was not the case. The lands Russia had lost in the earlier war with the Japanese were once again hers. Manchuria and the Kurile Islands became Soviet possessions, and the route that once had been a lifeline for them in desperate times was sealed and fortified against their former allies.

# THE PEACE?

Hamburg, Germany, 1946:

Emil stepped out of the British army staff car that had been sent to bring him to the headquarters of the British Occupation Forces, and raising a hand to hold his grey felt homburg on his head, he peered up through the summer sun's blinding rays to scan the old federal building, still being rebuilt, but showing evidence of its former Hanseatic splendor in a new way. He shook his head and smiled. He loved this old city. It had faced destruction by flood, fire and plagues throughout its history, and by many wars, and yet its citizens always got back to business, starting, as now, from the ground up – ever resourceful, ever resilient, ever practical, ever creative. He was glad to be home, and no fanatic Nazi was ever going to tell him he didn't belong here again. He had fought for Germany in the first awful war; he had cared for Hamburg's poor and sick to the best of his quite considerable ability, and while in enforced exile, he had fought to free Germans from the Nazis' horrifying excesses and insanities, and helped to relocate the terrified refugees who had sought sanctuary in America. He was a Jew, a German Jew, and proud of it.

Colonel Harold Macklin rose from behind a massive mahogany desk to greet Emil as he was ushered in by an officiously impatient young WAC, with admittedly, a mountain of paperwork on her desk in the outer office. Emil, ever the gentleman, smiled and bowed his head in sympathy - the while, stroking the brim of his homburg in his fine, age-spotted, hands. The young woman, somewhat mollified, could not resist a blush, and a smile of apology in response. Harold placed his hand on Emil's elbow, his raised eyebrows and knowing grin, an acknowledgement of the magic of Emil's charm on the fractious girl. Emil greeted him, and then, with a look of pleasant surprise, greeted the others seated around the desk. They were balancing cups of coffee in their hands, and Harold handed one to Emil, as he led him to a seat alongside his own, behind the desk.

"Ben, how wonderful to see you; Myrddyn and Johannes, you too, although we only parted earlier this morning, after one of Amalie's delicious breakfasts." The others sighed in agreement.

"I apologize, gentlemen, but all I can offer is a tin of assorted Peek Freans biscuits." They eagerly reached for one as Harold offered the tin around. Settled with coffee and cookie, they began their business.

"Ben," Harold began. "You are determined not to keep up with your work for the OSS?" Ben gave him a look that brooked no wavering on his decision. There was a brief reflective moment of silence. "You are right of course," Harold continued. "I regret the loss of your fine observational skills, wise judgment, courage of conviction and undoubted loyalty. We have need of you. Biff Chatsle, Nika, or, using her new name, Celeste Chatsle and Kerr Toddy of course, are still involved in important work. We were hoping against hope that you and Cat would change your minds and join us. Unfortunately, my nephew, Greg Macklin and his wife,

Laura, also are determined to return to a normal life. We have lost so many fine and brave souls. I am thinking of course of 'Simon', known to us fondly as Max von Alt, and his brave lads, Kurt, Addi, Danny...and the incredibly brave Fraulein Schrenck, dear Marthe. Addi, of course is alive and still working for us. I cannot say where. They… all of you young people… have been incredibly brave, sacrificing your youth and your well-being, not just physical well-being, but your peace of mind also, under horrendous conditions that would have driven most of us mad. We can never thank you enough, and because of the precarious position, yet again, of the peace, we cannot acknowledge that bravery publicly, with medals and such…"

"That's alright, Colonel Macklin. We don't set any store by such things in any case. To us, those medals are almost an insult. We do not need to be singled out from all the other brave people who fought for the general good. You and Emil gave us tasks to do, and we did them, at least as well as we were able under the diverse and difficult circumstances in which we had to operate. Cat and I, like Greg and Laura, want to return to normalcy, and work in ways we hope will improve conditions for all life on this planet. We hope to go to Africa; Cat to study animals, after she finishes her training in veterinary medicine, and I will continue to help those who have need of my medical expertise. We don't want to take, but to give back. I know that leaves poor Biff to try to infiltrate, and hopefully expose, those war mongers and profiteers within our governments and corporations, but he has Nika guarding his back. I worked with her in France, with the Maquis, and she was not only incredibly beautiful, she was deadly. I saw her in action. She strikes with the speed and accuracy of a cobra, and moves with the stealth and agility of a cat. I was relieved that she was on my side."

"Nika only just has been told of Biff's undercover work, and that she is not part of it, but is part of ferreting out bad guys within the American intelligence networks. She is one of the good guys in the OSS, but other OSS agents, newly recruited, have agendas that bear watching. Needless to say, she is not pleased. Biff's undercover work has trapped him in a difficult situation of a personal nature, and Nika is furious. It has created problems in their relationship. Biff's role, in which he has to acquiesce to the pressure brought on him, and Nika's impatience in swiftly and irrevocably removing all evil sources of irritation, are not at all compatible. She is impatient with all this pussyfooting around, but Biff has to help expose a vast network of evil. Nika would be removing only a chip off the tip of the iceberg."

"And I assume, Colonel Macklin, that governments of all political leanings are compromised and infected by the greed of this cabal of wealthy and powerful people, who gain more wealth and influence by perpetuating wars?"

Harold, Emil, Myrddyn and Johannes nodded in solemn agreement.

"Now that the war is over, Myrddyn and I have terminated all our armaments industries. We shall no longer build, or design, weapons of war. We are going to fund and promote research into new technologies that will promote better communications throughout the world, better standards of living, agriculture and medicine, and share the profits, as Gustafsen's always has done, with its workers. We will offer our services to this new United Nations, when it is up and running effectively. We will welcome your input, Ben."

"I think that is highly commendable, Johannes. I only wish more big corporations operated as you do; with such a social conscience as Gustafsen's always has had."

Johannes smiled at Myrddyn.

"Yes, well Myrddyn's Welsh grandmother was instrumental in giving Gustafsen's a social conscience."

"So Cat has told me, many times," Ben smiled, and the deep love he felt for Cat was reflected in his kind brown eyes.

"I have something more immediate, in which Cat may be of immeasurable help, but it will cause you great pain. It concerns a young woman, an American, you know her, Ben - Vanessa Eiles - that young woman whose valedictorian speech we listened to back in 1935."

"God, yes! What has happened to her? I saw her last in China, just after VE Day, and just before the atomic bombs were dropped that ended the war in Asia. She was working with Kerr Toddy, and she was Drax Shaw's girl, as I recall – beautiful girl, also very clever. She spent some time at Bletchley didn't she, Emil, while working for your organization and American Naval Intelligence? Then, like the rest of us, she was in the OSS in China after the war in Europe was over."

"She has had a rough time of it, Ben. Much to my and Magda's utmost surprise and deep chagrin, Drax ended their romance, somewhat abruptly, and apparently without any justifiable reason that we could ascertain. Kerr is his closest friend, and Drax didn't confide in him, and Kerr claimed that, as far as he knew, Drax was head-over-heels in love with Nessa. Drax was not the sort of fellow to take love lightly, and not the sort of fellow to do something as cold as ending the romance with no explanation at all. We were all mystified and stunned about it, Magda especially. Nessa also lost her brother during the war. He was a fighter pilot on the Hornet, and was killed at the Battle of Midway. This devastated Nessa and her parents.

Before returning to Hollywood to resume her writing and directing career, Nessa decided that she wanted to help repair lives destroyed by war, so she came over here to work in the displaced persons' camp just outside Hamburg. She helped in trying to reunite families separated by war, and helped to find homes for orphaned children. She worked mainly with children from the concentration camps, deeply traumatized children. I know Cat has been doing such work. Nessa, like Cat, has a rare gift in reaching these poor children. Evil, however, even infiltrates these camps, where we are trying to heal and restore relative normalcy to these devastated lives, for scattered among the genuinely tortured souls are extremely dangerous and virulent ex-SS, trying to hide from the authorities. They wear ragged clothes, and pretend to be inmates of the camps. They come and go as they please, helping to bring in supplies, and pretending to help agencies locate families who live within the city and surrounds. This, as you may guess, is a dangerous thing. They can give those names and addresses to SS hiding outside the camps, and in this way, their evil can be perpetuated. They will hang for war crimes if caught, so what do a few more murders and rapes matter to them? They will take out as many Jews and anti-Nazis as they can before they take their last sick breath.

Nessa did an undercover job for us in Germany during the war. She assisted in the rescue of a Polish scientist and his family. While so doing, she aroused the suspicions of a particularly nasty pervert, fairly typical of the type the SS attracted. With the help of Simon, Rudy and Lev, she managed to fulfill her task and escape, and Simon had this man sent to the eastern front. His experiences there served to further establish Nessa in his sick delusional fantasies as an object of both desire and revenge. Nessa had escaped being harmed by him in that brief encounter, but she had her first taste of being exposed to a man of unutterable perversion and evil, and he has haunted her nightmares ever since. I think that the brain registers both present and future danger with almost a prescient ability."

"I wish Cat had taken heed of such intuitions before she leapt from that plane to save her cats."

"Ah, Ben. Cat had to live with evil every day. If she had paid heed to warnings from her brain, she wouldn't have gone out. She'd have hidden herself away, but she didn't. She fought them with every breath she took, and when it came to saving herself or her cats, she chose them. She always had waded in fearlessly on behalf of those the Nazis victimized. Nessa's family also had suffered injustice and brutality at the hands of ruthless profiteers; her two grandfathers were killed while championing workers' rights. To continue with my present sad story, however: you can imagine how excited that SS psychopath was to see Nessa here in the camps – the subject of all his sadistic sexual longing. He got his gang together, and they followed Nessa's movements to and from the camp, with the intention of waylaying her, and exacting their dreadful revenge.

In the interim, a friend of Nessa's from California, Nessa's brother's former girlfriend, one Madge Cooper, had arrived to work with Nessa. On the evening set for the attack, Nessa and Madge were walking back to the hostel together. The men attacked. It must have been terrifying for Nessa to see the man who had haunted her nightmares there before her in the flesh. There were too many of them for the girls to fight off, though they bravely tried to do so. The girls were beaten, and Nessa was held by this maniac, and made to watch her friend being brutally raped by the other men. She was told her experience would be even worse. She would learn never to treat him with such scorn and arrogance again. By the time they would finish with her, she would grovel at his feet. Nessa fought, but to no avail. She inflicted some damage nevertheless. Madge had stopped struggling, and they had finished having their way with her. She lay in a pool of blood, her shredded clothes around her. They turned their attentions to Nessa. The man wanted her first. He wanted the others to hold her down, and then he intended that they could have her. He wanted to see them take her with the utmost cruelty and depravity."

Ben, Myrddyn and Johannes were overcome already, recalling what Cat must have gone through, with no help at hand, and how Myrddyn would have longed to have been there for his beloved daughter, to have had the chance to kill the monsters. Emil continued through his tears.

"Nessa had the slimmest of chances, but she managed to struggle free momentarily, and pull from her coat pocket a sharp metal nail file she kept there just in case she was attacked – a flimsy thing I know, but in desperate hands, a formidable weapon. She plunged it into the man's carotid artery with all her strength, and ground it in. They were covered in his blood. He was on top of her, his hands around her throat, but she would not give an inch. His body blocked the others from helping him. He was in his death throes, and Nessa kept on grinding in that file relentlessly in her anger and terror. They could not pull her away. She kicked, she bit, she clawed, and slowly she had him beat. The others were about to pounce, but some workers, on their way home, heard Nessa's screams and ran to her aid. The sight of poor Madge lying there drove them to a fury, and Hamburg workers have no love for the Nazis. They had taken their unions from them, and incarcerated their hero, Thaelmann, their communist leader, in a concentration camp. During Weimar, there had been bloody clashes between the workers and the Nazis, so the sight they saw before them, the barbarity those SS detritus had inflicted on Nessa and Madge that night, made them lose all control. Justice was quickly and finally served. Nessa had killed her monster with her own bare hands and…a humble nail file.

The workers helped Nessa to her feet. She broke free to run over to Madge, but Madge was dead. Nessa had strained her vocal cords, and had a dislocated jaw, a broken nose, broken ribs and ruptured spleen. She has required urgent surgery to repair the damage. It was fortunate that she avoided being raped. Her parents are on their way here with Steven Etchberry and a friend of Nessa's mother, one Esperanza Lopez. It is a tragic thing to happen to such a loving family. Their friends, the families who work their small holdings with Jeb and Loretta, all wanted to come to help, but they had to be realistic. They needed to keep the fruit orchards operating to keep up their quotas." Emil paused and, looking at Ben and Myrddyn in turn, his face etched with worry and doubt, he began tentatively, "I apologize wholeheartedly for putting you through this again. The wound in your hearts is still raw, and I wouldn't ask what I am about to ask, if Cat, herself, had not been so open and ready to help all others, women and children, raped and abused by the Nazis, as well as those raped by the liberators. I am afraid there are such horrid men on all sides in war. When they get here, her parents and friends will help Nessa heal, but I think that Cat may be able to reach her, and help a little, before her loved ones arrive."

Nessa awoke from her surgery, and tried to focus through her swollen eyelids on the flickering blurred image before her. The figure rose, and sat on the edge of her bed. Nessa tried to clear her vision. Gradually the blur took the form of a young woman, dark hair, not curly, but not straight either, kind, wide set dark eyes, but not brown, more like the colors of the forest. The woman smiled tentatively.

"Hello, Nessa. I am Cat Kieffer, a friend of Emil's, and wife of Ben Robie." Nessa was stunned, in that this woman spoke to her in Welsh. "I understand that you speak Welsh, but if you prefer, we can speak in English."

Nessa whispered that Welsh was fine, more than fine. It had been the language of her beloved grandparents, the language that had soothed her fears when she'd been hurt as a child. She felt the same healing effect now, deep within her. Cat noticed this effect in Nessa's eyes, and explained that the old language had helped heal her spirit too.

Cat told Nessa all about her experiences at the hands of the SS. She showed her the scars where she had been bound hand and foot with barbed wire. She told her also of the scars that were not visible. Cat and her family and close friends, along with her cats, had been escaping from the SS, when the cats had become separated from them as they'd run for the plane that had been sent to rescue them. The plane had to make a rapid take-off under fire, but Cat had flung herself out of the plane in an attempt to get to the cats. She hadn't realized that they had been rescued already by a friend who had been watching from the woods.

"You worked with him on your German mission," Cat said smiling. "He is Rudy von Silvren." Nessa, without thinking, shook her head in disbelief at such a coincidence, but the pain that wrought was unbearable. Cat got up, and made Nessa lie back against the pillows. She asked if Nessa needed any pain relief, but Nessa replied that the pain had dissipated as quickly as it had come. Cat could tell that, no matter how brief the pain had been, it had left Nessa exhausted. She could relate so well to this. Cat had not been able to run for it, as she had injured herself in the fall, and so she had been taken prisoner.

Nessa had listened. She had seen Madge's torn and bloody body before her as Cat had spoken. Madge, the quintessential Californian girl: bright blue eyes, shiny chestnut brown hair tied up in a ponytail, that had swung jauntily back and forth as she'd walked along, freckles over her pert nose, white-toothed, broad smile. She had radiated health, fitness and innocence. She'd been Bobby's girl. Bobby's American sweetheart, faithful and true to him and his memory. Nessa felt like screaming out in protest at the cruel injustice of such a fate. Madge deserved a much kinder end. She had come to help people, not her own, for God's sake! She had come willingly, eagerly, to help, to give hope to wretched, suffering people that there was still goodness and kindness in this world.

Nessa did not feel sorry for herself. She felt numb. How many had died, or suffered alone and exposed, with no help in sight, as Cat had done? Bobby had been one, though she knew in her heart that Bobby had plummeted to his death in the ocean, firing for all he was worth at an enemy who had dared to take him on. Hadn't she and Madge also fought with the same zeal to kill those who had dared to take them on, and who, in the end, had desecrated and killed Madge. Now this Cat had done the same, put her life on the line for her cats. Hadn't they all, all of those in these hellish things called wars done the same?" Had they done it for the 'greater good', as defined by their leaders? What a rotten deception and lie! Biff and Kerr were even now in the process of proving that it was for this cabal of war mongers' own good, not the greater good at all, that innocents suffered and died. There were no honorable wars, when children, old people, animals and innocents died, homes were destroyed and lives desecrated, torn apart. She saw the evidence of this everyday in these camps. How dare these warmongers go back to their mansions and neat, protected, privileged lives, while the mass of the people suffered like this? How goddamn dare they, and how goddamn useless were the folks who let them do this, generation after generation?!

Cat had stopped speaking. Nessa hadn't wanted that soft, lilting language to cease. Cat sat there, her head down, looking at her hands. Nessa sat up, wincing against the pain. Cat looked up, a look of concern on her face. Nessa shrugged it off and held out her hands. Cat took them, and then made Nessa lie back against her pillows, and gently put her arm around her shoulders. Nessa laid her head against Cat's arm.

Nessa asked her, in Welsh, if the abuse she had suffered had affected her in more personal, intimate ways, her response to Ben, for example. Cat thought on this for a while, and Nessa feared that she might have gone too far. They had only just met after all, but Cat quietly told her that her love for Ben was different, it healed, was gentle and reassuring, whereas the other had been an act of violence and intended desecration. She never at any time had been their victim. She had escaped in her imagination to her childhood, to memories and experiences she held dear. Her body was hers, and as such was beyond violation. Those men were the victims of evil, and they capitulated to it out of weakness, revealing their inferiority, their cowardice, in every way. She just wished that she could have killed them as Ness had done. She hoped that Ness did not feel guilty about that. Nessa could relate to this. At no time during the attack had she or Madge been victims, their bravery and moral courage had remained inviolate, and she did not for one second regret killing that monster. Cat hugged Ness to her, and Ness felt the blessed release of sleep. That is how Jeb, Loretta, Esperanza and Steven found them, when they arrived later that afternoon with Emil.

Madge's parents and sister arrived the next day. They were deeply traumatized on seeing Madge's body. Nessa and her parents wept with them. Nessa told them how brave Madge had been, and how wonderful she had been with the children in the camps. They were beyond consolation and angry. Cat took them to a camp for war orphans, some of whom had been raped and beaten. Faced with the sight of small children so abused, Madge's family realized why their daughter had tried to heal them, even at the cost of her own life. They returned with Madge's body to the States, but before leaving, they visited Nessa again, and told her that they would return to continue Madge's work. Nessa thanked them, and thought that would be a fitting tribute.

Nessa felt such horrible guilt that she had survived the attack. Jeb and Loretta couldn't help giving thanks in their hearts for their narrow escape from such horrendous sorrow, when they witnessed the Cooper family's grief. Cat told them that she too, would never get over her guilt, the guilt of surviving when so many innocent souls hadn't, and the guilt she felt as a German, and how she felt that she should have done so much more to get rid of the Nazis.

"Oh my goodness, Cat, you risked your life to fight the Nazis, and to rescue their victims, human and animal. What more could you have done?"

"So much more, Nessa, so much more; from the very start we should never have let the wealthy establishment, with their fear of the rising popularity of communism and socialism, put the Nazis into power to control the Left. The workers never fell for the inclusion of 'Socialist' in Hitler's all inclusive title for his party. It was an extreme Right wing party from the start, ultra-conservative, bigoted fascism. We stood by and watched all the wrongs done; maybe we acted as individuals, but as people, we did nothing. Oh there were moments of sanity, when it seemed we had come to our senses finally, but the fact that there were still many who adored Hitler, who screamed themselves hoarse with love and support for these fiends, somehow or other kept the rest of us uncertain and guarded in the face of such mindless frenzy.

"Oh Cat. Believe me, every nation has such crazy people, and the powers of evil feed their fear, their sick need to be superior in some way to those who are different. Leaders use these unthinking masses to control those of us capable of rational, independent thought. The extreme capitalist Right is doing that now in my country, whipping up fear in those who are always ready for a fight, who are susceptible to bigotry and mass hysteria of some sort. In the present case, their victims are those of all leftist, liberal persuasions."

"Churchill has turned back to his true colors. He has done a lot to fire up the Americans against the socialist left. He is back to his usual Tory shenanigans of keeping money and power in the hands of the conservative classes of privilege."

"Americans were amazed that he was voted out of power after the war. It seemed so ungrateful, but now we can see that he does not have the interests of the workers at heart. Europe, as a whole, sees the need for some sort of socialist backlash. These returning troops must be given more support than the troops who returned after the last horrible war, and they must not just be psyched up so that they can go out to fight again."

Nessa had healed quickly once her parents had arrived. Cat, Ben and Cat's parents often joined them as they sat taking tea on the hospital terrace in the warmth of summer afternoon sunshine.

Hilda and Myrddyn Kieffer were thrilled to learn that Loretta's parents had come from Penydarren, a suburb of Merthyr Tydfil. Myrddyn's grandmother, the redoubtable Blodwyn Kieffer, had come from there. Hilda came from the neighboring village of Pantyscallog. In some cases, they even knew the same families, and could share tales.

Nessa smiled, a broad smile:

"Cat, you are going back to Nature to learn from our biological roots. Well, I intend to continue writing fiction, as I think the arts, works of the imagination, pre-empt real changes in human societies."

Nessa felt a momentary flicker of sadness. How she would love to have worked with Drax. His mind had an almost intuitive sense of mathematical and verbal relationships and their concomitant musical rhythms, but it had been his love that had made everything so magically wonderful…no, she wouldn't go there; she couldn't go there. She'd get Laura and Greg to help her. Rory and Syb too, but here she had to pause. Emil had told her of his worries after his talk with Drax. She would have dismissed the idea that Drax could betray Rory; that he would put such nonsense above friendship, but Drax had changed, and she, like Emil, had a terrible foreboding of things to come.

Hollywood Hills, Autumn, 1950:
Nessa had returned to movies after an eight-year absence. She had continued working at the Displaced Persons' camps in Europe until the spring of 1949. Her work in helping families find loved ones who had been sent to the Nazi death camps had been heart-rending. The harrowing emotions seemed ever with her, despite the warm consoling feeling of being home with family and friends, safe and loved.

She curled up among the soft enveloping cushions of Fiona's deep creamy leather couch, nursing her martini in silence. Alisyn was holding forth on the current tension in Hollywood:

"This is fucking ridiculous! Those guys joined the communist party under the delusion that they stood for a fair deal for the common Joe. This country is going backwards not forwards. What the hell did we all fight for for the last eight years? Remind me now – didn't we fight the Nazis because they were racist bigots, psychos and anti-Semites? They were anti-Communists, anti-Socialists, anything that represented the freedoms of Weimar, such as homosexuals, Negroes and jazz, anything, anyone, who offered the chance for enlightenment. They burned books and incarcerated, or worse, liberal writers. They thought for their people. They told them what it was to be German. Anything anti-Nazi was UnGerman. Any of these things ring a bell, ladies – a goddamn clanking big ugly old bell? Certainly not a Liberty Bell – no - hell and gone from any kind of freedom." Alisyn burst into tears and buried her head in her arms in frustration.

"The Nazis hated Weimar, as much as our conservatives in the Democrat and Republican parties, hated FDR and his New Deal. I just don't understand these people. Is it so wrong, so frightening, to help everyone have a chance of getting ahead?"

"Oh you just said a mouthful, Sigi. Be careful now, Dalton Trumbo only wrote one line in a script that said, basically, we should all share, and look at the trouble he is in."

"You going to name names, Fiona?"

Fiona scowled at Mandy, who sat there with a challenging smirk on her vermilion lips, her blue eyes cold as ice.

"I should ask you to leave my house and never come back after that comment, but I'll put it down to drink, you miserable lush." They stared coldly at each other for a few seconds; then Mandy laughed and sipped her drink. Fiona kept looking at her, a look that could kill, until Sigi gently shook the diaphanous sleeve of her negligé to change her focus. "Careful, Sigi! This cost the earth."

"Nessa, you're pretty quiet. Let us in on your thoughts."

Nessa had been lost in re-living the horrible sight of Madge lying there, torn to shreds, her body desecrated. She had been worried by the thoughts that had crossed her mind at that moment. She and Bobby had shared their feelings growing up, and he said it had helped him better respect and understand women after talking things over with her. What had come to mind at that horrible moment of looking at the ravaged body of Madge, had been a talk she'd had with Bobby one evening after they had attended a rally for Mexican fruit pickers' rights. The beautiful, vibrant Valda Torres had spoken. She was a socialist activist, and her speech had been very moving. She made sound sense, but the owners would never accept this. They and their bully boys had stood around, their rifles cradled menacingly in their arms. They had called after Valda, whistling, chiding, taunting her with lewd and disgusting gestures. Bobby had been more angry than she had ever seen him. 'It isn't fair,' he'd shouted. 'Valda made sense. She was brilliant. I am scared for her, for all of you women who dare to speak out for justice and fair-play.' Nessa had replied that Valda was respected in her community, and those she had grown up with, like the two of them and all their friends, they would see that she would be protected. Then Bobby had confessed to being very attracted to Valda. She was sure of herself...she was... 'Sexy?' Nessa had suggested smiling speculatively at him. Bobby had frowned, then smiled softly. 'Yes. God, Ness, she sets me on fire. I feel like I could do anything, be something, with a woman like that, but then I think of Madge, and how she dotes on me, and I feel so guilty, no not guilty, trapped.' Nessa had pointed out that Valda was very deeply involved with her cause, and she was attached to Feliciano Guttierrez, one of the labor leaders. 'I know, Ness. She is way out of my league. I can't hope to compete with Feliciano. Oh well, it is just a rather lovely dream, even if it is so goddamn frustrating.' Nessa had put her arm around his shoulders, and pointed out that Madge was a beauty in her own right and had good grades in college. She was more traditional that was all. 'I admire her, Ness, I really do, and know that I am a lucky guy, as all the guys tell me, but … well…it's silly things, like we pet around, and she has to break it off to go freshen up! I ask you, it kinda puts a fella off. She is worried about freshness all the time. She sheds talcum powder all over the car. It makes me sneeze. Valda now, well she is lovely and smells of night-scented jasmine, and I love her shiny black hair that has a hint of midnight blue in it. I bet she doesn't obsess about her looks like Madge. You don't do you, Ness?' She had laughed kindly and shaken her head. Strange what stays in one's mind and pops out even at such horribly inappropriate moments. She wanted to smile at the memory, but wouldn't let herself. She had to remember how Madge had looked lying there in such a foul mess. Why? Oh, why?

"Oh, I'm just wool-gathering, Mandy, but you did raise a loaded gun with that naming names comment, you know."

"As Ali said, most of those guys joined the communist party when they thought communism was a good thing. They discovered that it was too controlling. Why it took over their lives, and told them what to think and write, so they left. They left when they saw it was just as controlling as fascism, so I don't know why we've got this witch-hunt going on. It's just like Germany, when the Nazis came to power. Now our courts are like the German courts, where any kind of refusal to name names of anti-Nazis was seen as contempt of court and Un-German, only here we have to name communists and lefties, or we're seen as being Un-American. Goddamn! We didn't beat those guys in Germany; we inhaled them and got infected."

"We are experiencing a backlash by the wealthy conservative establishment now that FDR has gone," Nessa said, sipping her drink. They are getting back in control by pushing those fear and panic buttons FDR so detested, and it seems like the people are responding. They have been so stoic, brave and self-sacrificing, and now they are looking for some kind of justification to be self-serving again. It also keeps up the excitement levels and prevents the inevitable let-down that follows the hectic pace of war."

Nessa, unlike the others, was aware that, after finding the Venona Papers on a battlefield in Finland, and, from these, cracking the Russian codes, they had uncovered people high up in the State Department, and in various international agencies, who had worked for the Soviets. She was aware of how many of her friends in the OSS, and even at Bletchley, if not communists themselves, had been of a leftist, liberal, even socialist bent. They had been appalled by the willingness of some of the extreme Right-wing to sell out the Soviets during the war. Many scientists working on the bomb at Los Alamos, also had been appalled to learn that they had created a weapon, not so much to defeat Nazism and the Japanese, but as a way of preparing to take on the communists. The most virulent conservatives were so afraid of the Left in any form, that they even considered using the doomsday bomb in a pre-emptive strike against those who dared to differ from the American way. If the Soviets had seemed ungrateful for American aid during the war, it was because they were well aware of how American and European conservative factions felt. They knew that many among the wealthy classes wanted to destroy them. America had got very rich off war, and American corporations were busy buying influence, resources and monopolizing future air routes all over the globe. Even Churchill had been alarmed at this. While other nations had fought for their lives and freedoms, Americans had quietly established control, and Stalin was out to beat them at their game. The warmongers watched with glee. They would own the next century.

"We all trust one another right?" Alisyn said, raising her tear-stained face. "Cos, you said what I think, Ness, but …"

"I am not, nor ever have been a communist," Nessa parodied the phrase doing the rounds in the current congressional purge. "Neither do I know any communists. I like some socialist programs, and I would like to see them instituted within a capitalist framework, a fair one, not a crooked one."

"Not any of us have joined the communist party either," said Lorna suggestively, examining her long red talons, and flexing them as she raised her eyes to look at Mandy.

"Artie is just a pseudo-intellectual. He joined the communist party to be just like those other intellectual writers and leftist liberals. It was all the rage under FDR, but he got out quick when he learned they wanted a sizeable share of his income, and wanted to tell him what to do."

"If he gets named, you may be subpoenaed to give names of friends he associated with, communist or not."

"Oh shut it, Lorna, I didn't go to those meetings with him. Our relationship is based on sex. We don't share anything else. I don't know who was there, or who, of his many friends, are commies."

"You better hope they believe you. A congressional witch-hunt does not follow the usual laws of a court of justice. With these guys, you are guilty until proven innocent, and you are guilty by association."

"Hollywood chased off those fascists in 1940, and I don't know why they don't do it again. People love going to the cinema. The big agencies can stop this persecution by threatening to stop making movies."

"You forget, Alisyn dear, that the people now have television. Movies may become a thing of the past."

"No way, Fiona! Teenagers can't cuddle and grope in front of the television, with all the family there, like they can in the dark back rows of the movies."

"Trust you to think of that," Fiona sneered. "You and Mandy are stuck at the adolescent stage of development. Grow up!"

"Ah, she's just jealous because she didn't have any young boyfriends to grope around with in her youth. Did you, Fiona? She was the plaything of dirty old men."

Everyone tensed. Fiona and Mandy stared at each other with such hatred, neither willing to look away first, and the others watched them nervously; each ashamed of Mandy for retaliating so unfairly. Nessa put down her glass, and changing the subject, she prattled on, hoping to diffuse the tension:

"It's different, Mandy. In 1940 we were not at war, and many people pulled back from communism when Stalin made a peace pact with Hitler. These leftist intellectuals were Americans, after all, and never wanted to be controlled by a foreign power. They wanted to start their own brand of socialism. A little bit of this, a little bit of that – a working compromise good for all. I don't know when, or why, compromise became a dirty word here. Those old profiteers and gangsters made it so, I guess. Now we are told that Americans don't compromise. They assert themselves, and after all, we carry a big stick. We can force other countries into our way of thinking. If we used cataclysmic power to get the Japanese to capitulate, then we can use it anytime, anywhere, against all who may like to reach a compromise between rampant capitalism and communism. We do not tolerate an 'on the fence' position. Now everyone has to take sides, like gang warfare, and we are forcing that view on the rest of the world. Here at home, people, like these congressional witch-hunters, employ the 'love us or leave us' tactic. It is not their America, least it wasn't last time I checked with the ordinary, sensible, not-easy-to-scare, folks."

"Damn right, it isn't their America alone. If anyone is being un-American, it is McCarthy and his lot."

"I don't know, Alisyn, we have been kind of fond of persecuting people who are different in some way. Look at the Salem witch-hunts, carried out by the Puritan establishment against women with their own free views; learned women and women of property, and anyone who defended them. Look at the lynch mobs in the South, and the horribly unfair, criminal treatment of Blacks there. Look at the way we have cheated Native Americans out of their lands and heritage, and now we are persecuting communists, and in the wake of these persecutions, there are those ever ready to jump on this bandwagon to make a rotten buck. McCarthy's hearings pick on communists past and present, and they do at least require two independent informers, but others in our industry make wild accusations with no proof, and then the so-called Hollywood watch dogs take a pay-off from those accused, often falsely, to clear their names. It's like those awful dispensations the Catholic Church handed out to pardon sins, and it has the same sanctimonious air of 'repent and ye shall be saved' about it too – all horrible and criminal infringements of human rights. Honestly, don't our politicians trust us? We'd never take to being controlled by a foreign power. In Europe now, they have socialist and communist parties. They have socialist health care programs and education programs. The people are willing to pay more in taxes for these programs. They help one another. Their leaders are wise enough to let the communists stay out in the open, where they can keep an eye on them. We are going to force our communists underground, where we can't see what they get up to. Honestly, all this is political grandstanding by the same old profiteers and gangsters, who want to control our government, and make a buck from all this fear-mongering, and make us too afraid to protest. We may need to take precautions against communism, but why not do it without going off half-cocked; screaming 'Red Menace', using lurid propaganda posters and campaigns. It makes us look like the bloody Nazis for goodness sake! It makes us look like scared wimps, compared to people of all the other nations. They trust themselves to be exposed to many different kinds of political thinking, and, hopefully, to come up with a good one that benefits all, and what is more, their governments trust them to be so exposed. Bottom line, our politicians don't trust us. It's not the Reds, Pinkos and Liberals that scare them, it is us: 'We, the People', who scare them. It is us they oppress and punish."

"Yeah, they do make us jump through hoops. I blame our bosses, who agreed to refuse to hire anyone who was, or is, a communist, and to fire those already working, who are, or were, communist. God! We have to write a letter to the American legion, asserting our innocence, groveling and repenting every step of the way for any liberal idea we may have had."

"It is criminal, Alisyn. It is against the law to refuse employment to anyone, no matter their political creed."

"Oh Sigi, these bullies are above the Constitution, the law. Why they imprisoned the lawyers who tried to defend those accused of being communists! The FBI is illegally involved with some attorneys to set up their clients. Take the Fifth, and accuse yourself, and then refuse to name names, and you are blacklisted: no chance of getting work or being reinstated. Take the First, and you go to jail for contempt of court."

"It is very frightening for us exiles from Nazi Germany. Jews are often associated with communism, socialism and liberal politics. We are leftist intellectuals. The Jewish Leagues are too scared to defend Jews accused of communism. They fear they will be tarred as communist associations. Defend communists, and you must be one."

"It is also more insidiously evil than that, Sigi. We are in a competitive industry. People can inform in secret, behind closed doors, and this way they can get the parts, or work, for which those they accuse were chosen."

"Oh, Ness, this is awful. This is how it was in Nazi controlled Europe. It was horrible how people rushed to inform with no proof."

"And they have done so here too, out of fear, out of greed, out of jealousy and revenge."

"Wait a minute, Ness. Some of those who informed are genuinely patriotic, and they do sense a terrible threat to our freedoms, our country, from the Soviets. They have the atom bomb now too, and China has just gone communist. Russia is over-running their neighbors brutally. We are already at war in Korea against the communist North. China is threatening Formosa's independence again, and other islands off their coast. That iron curtain Churchill talked about, warned us about, is becoming a reality."

They had to acknowledge the truth of what Lorna said.

"Let's take a look at these communist leaders; they are men from working class or middle class backgrounds, some are intellectuals. They are not used to power. They have reasons aplenty to mistrust the rich and powerful. Stalin and Mao have to contend with leaders from wealthy European and American families, who have been trained to rule. FDR made Churchill pander to Stalin. Stalin knew he was being set up. When FDR died, Stalin must have known that Churchill would return to his roots, the wealthy establishment, and their right to rule, and Churchill has, raising the fear factor. His people didn't fall for it. They voted him out, and social reform in, but Churchill will be back in control soon. Someone I know said that he'd heard that even Stalin does not think that communism will survive the propaganda, the spin the western media are so good at, and the incredible force the West will employ to destroy it. These men from the people do not know how to combat these men born to rule, born to cheat and corrupt through their governmental and banking institutions, even using their gangster element. They just try to copy them. What other example do they have? They know how ruthless the wealthy classes can be. They, like the French revolutionaries before them, know they have to be just as ruthless and oppressive. They have evidence that kinder leaders do not last long."

"I say give the United Nations teeth. Get rid of warmongers and their trade. Look at the way the Marshall Plan has won the people of Europe to our side. We provide food and clothing, while the Soviets threaten their freedoms by military take-over and isolation from other countries. I think the Marshall Plan is a good way for us to go. Give aid and trust, don't bully."

"Yeah, Ness, but old McCarthy thinks General Marshall, and even Truman, are suspect for trying to reach a compromise with communists, and dear old Eleanor is way out there on compromising and helping in their book. There's you're dirty word, compromise, again, Ness. McCarthy and all zealots like him are a flash in the pan; grandstanding to enhance their political careers, and the others see their chance at making a quick fortune out of others' fears and vulnerabilities. Thank God for Broadway, their theaters don't discriminate. They give jobs to actors and writers who are blacklisted or grey-listed. This rather sick moment in our history will pass, and hopefully we'll recover our good old American fair play and trust." Fiona seemed to have regained control. One had to admire her. She was sensible enough to realize that the past was just that, gone, and she used it only as a prop for her acting, and never as a crutch, or an excuse, or even as a wimpy way of manipulating a win in an argument.

"Oh shucks, let's get drunk. I don't want to think about all this anymore."

"Are you going to stay in an alcoholic hibernation until this all blows over, Alisyn?"

"Yep, and I am going to do it in Europe. I am going to live in Rome. I may never live in the States again. They can come and find me if they want me to act in their goddamn films. I've lost all respect for this industry."

"I am scared, but we exiles have nowhere else to go. I can never trust Europe again. I trust you all, all my friends here. We can ride out this insanity. Oh God! What am I saying? We said that in Bucharest, when the Nazis first appeared on the scene." Sigi got up to replenish her drink.

Nessa knew deep in her soul that this would all blow over at some point. The Republicans would get in, and there would be more laissez-faire economics, that would lead to another crash and depression, and then the Democrats would get in, and there'd be more programs to help the people build up their spending ability, and the economy would recover, and then the people, not wanting to pay taxes, or to share, would bring in the Republications again, and so on and so on.

The girls talked on, arguing pretty much along these lines. Nessa withdrew into her thoughts.

She had received a long letter from Emil, who was recuperating after a severe heart attack. In it, he had brought her up to date on what Drax and Kerr had been doing in China and in Indochina.

They had stayed, after the war was over, to locate more hidden prisoner-of-war camps. The local people had been most helpful. It now looked like America would be the force governing the future of the Pacific Rim countries, and those seeking freedom from the former colonial powers of Europe were eager to win Americans to their side.

Emil wrote:

"Many former OSS operatives and American military personnel, like Drax and Kerr, who fought side by side with these freedom fighters against the Japanese, sympathize with their cause. Some, formerly stationed in the Far East, are now serving in the State Department and Treasury back home. They urge President Truman to side with the nationalist forces in Indochina. The pro-European factor at State push the 'Red Menace' panic buttons, claiming these nationalist rebels are communist led, and so America must support France. Britain was in charge of Indochina immediately after the war was over. They were there as an independent body, to keep the peace, but when they left, they ensured that the French could take-over from a position of strength and advantage. This is so unfair."

Emil went on to say that his son, Marc, had been with Drax and Kerr in China. He had flown missions with them against the

Japanese. He had fallen in love with a Chinese doctor, married her, and now was working in aeronautical design at the Lockheed Plant near San Francisco.

"Marc has three daughters. Magda and I love them very much. We have been most fortunate, but as you may, or may not, know, we lost our daughter during the war. She was a beauty, like her mother, only she had deep rich red hair. It breaks my heart to write of her. She left her husband and three boys to go off with a Hollywood screenwriter. It didn't work out, but her family has moved on. Her husband re-married, and the boys love their new mother. Miriam was bereft, and took her own life. We see little of the boys, which is hard on us, for we love those boys very much. We write to them, but only Samuel writes back occasionally, and never mentions coming to see us. At least we now enjoy being close to Marc, his wife, Tsai, and their girls.

It is amazing how life works out. All these connections between different stages in one's life are so reassuring, at least I think so. Ben Robie, Kerr and Biff Chatsle were with me that day when you gave your graduation speech. You impressed us all. You see, it is a funny old world. Now you have caught up with Ben's life in Hamburg, and you have met Cat. Our story is so complicated, so many events that brought us all together.

Magda joins me in sending you our love and best wishes. We hope that you have come to terms with the news that Drax, after spending time in Indochina, has returned to the States to lose himself in the rhythms of the Bayou. Carson and Varvara are worried about him, but I think he will be fine, once he gets what he has to get out of his system. Magda said to tell you that her heart is with you."

Nessa thought how Emil never changed. He was so open, so all-embracing, but also enigmatic, with some little mystery that kept one out of the fold, so to speak: You are family. You are not family. She always felt these vibes when with him and Magda.

"Will you look at that, Nessa has fallen asleep while we've been yammering on. Look at that little furrow between her brows. Her dreams must be disturbing ones…" Alisyn realized too late, that, of course, after all Ness had been through, her dreams would be worrying, if not terrifying ones. The others, while aware of her gaff, didn't call her on it, but were lost in their own thoughts of what Ness must have endured; some of them having shared similar brutality, when they should have been too young to deal with it, but somehow they had.

"Let her sleep on, Alisyn. I'll throw a blanket over her before I go to bed."

They left, and Fiona made sure that Nessa was snug and warm under a soft knitted blanket. She turned off the lights, and went upstairs. Nessa rubbed the tears from her eyes, waited until she was sure Fiona was asleep, and then got up, folded the blanket and tip-toed out, resetting the alarm, and locking the door behind her.

A door opened upstairs, and Fiona stood there in her elegant white negligé, then returned to her room, closed the door, and addressed the darkness,

"Poor kid!"

As she walked to her car, the moonlit ocean, a whispering backdrop, the tall palms, black silhouettes against a navy blue sky, Nessa had decided what to do. Enough with this living in the past, she was thirty-three years old, and she was going to begin a brand new life. She had written to an old screenwriter friend in Paris, Pete Gardener, Rangy Pete. He had gone there to escape McCarthy's witch-hunt. She had asked if he could find her a job, and she'd had the reply that day, but had kept it to herself. The French film writers knew of her work. They had enjoyed her screenplays and her movies, and were over the moon in their eagerness to have her work with them. The salary was a pittance compared with the one she was getting in Hollywood, but she wanted out, and could make do. She just had to tell her parents, but she was determined to go, start a new life. Randy and Riley had passed, quite peacefully, on to their other lives. She'd been with them at the end. Now she was going to put the war years and the present insanity behind her, and enjoy the creative freedoms and free-for-all social and political tussles that was Paris.

Cape Cod, Autumn, 1950:
Carson Shaw noticed the dark green Morgan pull into the sandy drive way. Drax parked it under the golden leafed maples, and sat there. Carson hung his white-haired head with its thinning curls and sighed. This wasn't going to be easy. He made to get up, quickly scanning the papers on his desk to make sure he knew where he was in his work, and so easily could return to it when Drax was settled in his room, or with his mother and grandparents. He heard her cry out, and was relieved that Varvara had noticed Drax had arrived. That would take the edge off their meeting. He stood by the ivy covered door, and watched Petya and Lisabetta embrace Drax, tears running down their beaming, wrinkled, old faces. He had envied the ease with which they and Varvara could express their emotions, show their love. Why couldn't he run to embrace his son? Why couldn't he cry with heartfelt relief that he had come through the war apparently unscathed... or had he? They had great difficulty understanding Drax's rejection of Nessa Eiles. She was a stunningly lovely and clever girl, so kind and unaffected, a rare thing amongst the high-class beauties Drax had been used to. They had felt so at ease in her company, when she had visited them. He and Varvara had been so relieved that Drax had found such a love. He obviously had been unhappy and very critical of the girls he had been thrown together with before he'd met Nessa.

Finally they stood facing each other, father and son. Drax smiled and held out his hand. Varvara managed to stifle an outcry of protest at such a cold gesture. Carson smiled, and found that, as he did so, tears formed and ran down his cheeks. He pulled Drax to him, and burying his face in his neck, he shook with silent sobs. They looked on in surprise. Drax had tensed; Carson could feel it. He controlled himself sufficiently to stand back and place his hands on Drax's shoulders.

"I love you. I am so overwhelmed that you are here safe and sound."

Drax stood there, not angry, not resentful, but as if he was trying to find a way to respond to his father's outburst. The other three had silly smiles on their faces. Varvara's beautiful violet colored eyes were sparkling with love and…what - amazement or relief, that at last Carson had let himself go?

After a few moments hesitation, Drax hugged Carson, and arms around each other, with Varvara and Lizabetta hanging on their arms; Petya, his hand on Carson's back, obviously a sign that he understood and approved, they entered the house laughing and talking excitedly, expressing love, joy and wonder that he was there at last. He had come home to them, and 'for how long'…was pushed to the back of their minds.

They had dinner: roast chicken, roast potatoes, beans and carrots from the garden. Wild flowers lay in garlands around apple pies, made from the apples off the trees in the orchard that were sheltered from the strong sea breezes by the high grassy dunes. They sat out in the garden, under the huge sycamores, whose leaves had turned to gold, russet and brown. They wrapped Lizabetta's quilted throws around their legs, as they watched the sun set over the sea. The gentle susurration of waves on sand; a nudging breeze that loosened several big yellow leaves from their last tenuous link to the overhead branches, that creaked a sad farewell; the soft whisper of regret, as the leaves floated down on them, these were the opening notes of the composition forming in Drax's mind. His grandfather seemed to sense this, and picked up on the themes, almost telepathically, with his violin. Varvara and Lisabetta joined in with their balalaikas. Drax waited. He wondered if Carson would throw in the heavy notes of his cello. He had disappeared into the house, and sure enough, here he came, clutching his cello. Drax had resented that, but when Carson gently captured the subtle cadences and then enhanced them, Drax was astonished at how he had missed this before. It finally brought home to him how he had misinterpreted his father in all things, choosing a theme for him that had been totally wrong, that had jarred. Instead, he should have listened, not trammeled by resentment, while Carson tentatively had revealed his true nature; his anxiety over intruding on the harmony the other three had created for themselves, as they had created this small corner, this home, so in tune with its natural elements, as close as they could manage to the little loft apartment in Moscow and the little wooden shack out on the Steppes. Where, Drax thought, they had been cosy and warm: wrapped in their music, stories and crafts, while the blizzards had raged outside. Each season had brought with it inspiration, a sense of oneness with Nature. As Varvara had said, they had been minds exposed to the natural elements through a small window, a bubbling samovar and log fire, yet still a part, even as translators and observers, of this magical adventure called life. Not always as passive observers, Drax thought, they too had suffered and been uprooted by life's quixotic about-face. The evil human world had invaded that nest of theirs in a brutal way, and yet they'd survived, due in no small part to the gentle, compassionate intrusion of his father, who had let them weave a new nest in a new land. Why had he not seen this before?

They stopped playing, concerned, questioning looks on their faces.

"I can't join in. The fact that I survived to be here with you now, is due to some literally jarring flying on my part, so jarring that I strained my hands and neck muscles, and I have lost the delicate touch I once had. That I can no longer express with my fingers, the subtle shades of emotions, and the mysteries of nature in all her moods, prevents me from playing. I can't stand the coarseness of my touch. What really hurts is that I can feel and create in my mind, but can no longer express how deeply and how magically the subtle shades of Nessa's being affected me; shades which she translated so brilliantly in her singing, with that rich, moving alto voice of hers. My music seems fractured."

They sat there, stunned. Varvara began to weep.

"Will you recover, son?"

"The doctors think so, in time, but I know how naturally that touch came, and now I fear I will have to learn it, practice to achieve what came naturally, and I fear that I may lose something in the process."

"No, Drax. It will return. The instruments will help you. Your fingers and muscles will remember once they recover. I just know they will." They nodded in agreement with Varvara.

"And Nessa, will I regain her?"

Varvara closed her beautiful eyes as if in prayer.

"Time, Drax, time will tell."

The next morning, after breakfast, Drax and Carson walked along the seaweed-strewn beach. The breeze was colder and stronger, the waves tumbling, frothy white in a steel grey sea. Seagulls wheeled and dived, their harsh calls and chuckles filling the air. The two men pulled the collars of their heavy navy pea coats up around their red windblown cheeks. The wind, with its astringent salty tang, stirred up the sand and made their green eyes red-rimmed and watery. They were alike in stature, and in the impression they gave of a reserved interest, that could be translated by the more extroverted and garrulous, as cold and judgmental.

They talked about Drax's experiences in Russia, and how he felt the people were still suffering just as they had under the Tsar's rule. "They still live in fear. They still are told what to do, what to believe, what cannot be spoken." Carson smiled, and said that he felt that the Russians thrived on this. Physical and creative restraint, maybe challenge was more appropriate than restraint, only made them more daring and innovative. They thrived in adversity. Carson laughed, and said that, even as exiles living a fairly good life elsewhere, Russians were miserable. It had become their 'act', their public persona, what they thought made them fascinating and mysterious as a people.

"They test their freedom with provocative statements wrapped in old-world Slavic charm."

Drax was going to contend this, but he realized that there was a measure of truth in it.

"In any case, I hated the Bolsheviks. I hated their bleak, cold, grey-black world. There wasn't any color anywhere. I could only hear iron on iron, grinding through lives, squashing all life under, and shoveling the torn and bloody shreds into the massive maw of a ruthless, relentless industrial monster. There was no music."

Carson listened, with a look of concern on his face that seemed to be debating with the more optimistic notion that this would pass. It was a natural reaction to all Drax had gone through. He knew that a large part of Drax's frustration lay in the long enforced inactivity he'd had to undergo in Russia. He'd been an active part of the war. He had triumphed over death many times. He'd fought the enemy with cunning and skill. His time in Russia had rendered him ineffective, not in control, helpless to do anything. The war in Europe had ended in a victory that had been denied Drax – a victory in which he hadn't played an active part. After all that bravery and highly charged energy, his war had fizzled out on a whimper. Of course Drax hated Russia and communists, but surely he had resumed his fight against the Japanese? After all, Drax really had not fought in the European theater of war, except for a few months before America had gone to war. Drax's war had not ended on a whimper, unless he had resented the atomic bomb depriving him, yet again, of a hard fought victory. No, that was crazy! Drax would have been relieved to end the carnage that would have happened if the war had been allowed to go on.

Drax looked at him as if he read his thoughts.

"I know," he said, "I feel rotten about sitting out the last months of the war in Europe, while my friends fought on bravely, giving their all. It was why I resented them, wanted to avoid them..." He paused, as if struggling to come to terms with how he felt. "It was why I left Nessa so abruptly, so coldly, and she had been in danger... Oh God! I have been so stupid, stupidly absorbed in myself. I am glad that I could fight to free our POWs in secret Japanese camps, and help destroy the Japanese forces of occupation throughout China and Indochina. I know that before my time in China, I had felt as if my war had ended like a fart from a collapsing balloon. I don't feel that way now. I fought hard and long in China. It's something much more insidious than that." Drax paused. He obviously had something that lay heavily on his conscience.

"Drax, get it off your chest whatever it is. I want to help you."

"Dad, I need to talk. I feel as if I have done something terribly wrong, and I may have hurt a friend, all of them actually, irrevocably. On the other hand, I may well have done the right thing, and this friend may have deceived us all."

Now Carson was very concerned. He feared the worst, and hoped and prayed that Drax had not fallen into the web of deceits created by these evil times. He placed his hand on Drax's shoulder and suggested they go indoors and talk by the fire in the study.

Petya seemed intuitively to know that the men needed time together, and he kept Varvara and Lisabetta in the kitchen. Varvara longed to spend every second with Drax, but the fact that he had reached out to his father, changed that moment of resentment to an unexpectedly warm feeling that flooded her being - the realization at last of a longed-for understanding between father and son. Now they all could enjoy the time they had together in these ever-changing days of fall: warm to cold; rich colors to grey; apple scented days and evenings to smoky, salt-laden gales, harbingers of icy Winter.

Carson lit his pipe and sat in the high-backed, velvety deep armchair by the fire, the crowded book case an ever-present background to the man, or so it seemed to Drax. He could not imagine his father in any other setting: books, papers, pipe in his mouth, the glow of a log fire. Drax opted to sit on a low footstool and tend the fire with the dragon-headed poker, while he got his thoughts straight.

It had turned stormy outside, and wind driven rain spattered against the window.

"Something my radio man said, when we were traveling across the vast expanses of Russia, kind of stuck in my mind, and gnawed away at me. Finally, when we reached States-side, I collared him and asked him to tell me again about the British naval officer he had seen handing over top-secret papers about the Manhattan Project to the Ruskies in Alaska. Had he heard his name? I tried to be careful, but Ned was the kind of guy that picked up on something shady going on. He had a big long red honker that he forever was sticking into other folks' business." Carson had to smile at how Drax had picked up the vernacular of his comrades-in-arms, while still retaining his Boston Brahmin accent. "I said that it had struck me as strange, and I'd wondered if I had come across the guy in my liaison work with the British. Ned said he'd made a mental note of it, and he'd never forget it - Arliss Reese; tallish guy, had a big navy overcoat on, so Ned couldn't tell if he were well-built or slender; dark hair, well what he could see under his officer's cap, fine featured face, and when he'd turned to the light of the big old swinging light bulb over the door to the Ruskies' quarters, to better read some paper, and shield it from the raging blizzard, Ned had thought his eyes were blue, not dark in any case. I told Ned that was quite a feat of observation, considering the weather, and that it was in the fading light of an Alaskan afternoon. He agreed, but said he was so curious, that he tried to get closer to take in as much as he could, and that's when he heard the Ruskie call him Arliss Reese.

I tried it out on Emil, when I got back. All I got was that kind slow smile of his, his eyebrows raised in question. He didn't know this name. I thought of pointing out to him how close this was to Rory's name – Ellis-Rhys - but Emil just shook his head and pulled down the corners of his mouth in that dismissive way he has.

The six of us just had so much fun together, Dad. They were so bright and clever. We shared ideas. We sang. We swam and hiked, and oh, just shared so much fun. I was fond of them all. Nessa, of course, I loved, but let's not go there. I let her down badly, when she may very well have had dire need of me."

"We liked her very much when she came here. Your mother and Nessa took long walks along the beach together, no doubt talking about you. They'd return arm-in-arm, smiling and suntanned, their eyes bright. After dinner, we'd all sit in the orchard, and we'd play our instruments and Nessa sang. Your mother and grandparents were brought to tears, as Nessa sang those old Russian folk songs with deep rich emotion. She said it was how she sang in Welsh, and pointed out that the Welsh and Russians love those slow emotional songs, especially when they are sung by male voice choirs. Now what did she call it? Oh yes, Hiraeth, or something like that. It means love and longing for one's homeland. Of course your grandparents and mother responded wholeheartedly to that – tears and hugs and so forth. I sound detached, but actually I wasn't. I was quite moved." Carson was lost in his thoughts of those evenings for a moment, and Drax realized even more what he had lost. "She's a lovely girl, Drax. We all thought so."

"Her parents are exceptional people too. We spent evenings at their little farm up in the Sierra Madres. The discussions were lively and fun. Their friends would play their guitars. The Mexican food the women brought was out of this world. We sat in the warm scented air of night, under the soft glow of Chinese lanterns, Randy, their dog at our feet. Riley, the big ginger cat on the balustrade of the veranda among the purple and red bougainvillea... God, it was the perfect idyll, or exile, as Magda called it."

"I am glad that you had that enchanted place to fall in love, to be in love, before you had to go off to war."

Carson saw the spasm of regret pass through Drax.

"Goddamn war! Am I the only one who was weak? Laura and Greg survived it all. Rory and Syb are together. Why was I the one to drop the ball?"

"You were wrenched out of the war, Drax. You had to find your feet before being plunged back into it again, and you never really had the chance to do that. I gather from Emil and Magda that Nessa is giving you space and time to recover, to see if you can still love her?"

"Is she? I don't know how forgiving she can be, and she has a lot of forgiving to do. I never have stopped loving her."

"Did you find some solace in your music in New Orleans?"

"I've got some good ideas for compositions in my head, but I am having some difficulty in getting those subtle influences expressed when I play. I've lost the delicate touch and rapid finger movements. I do the exercises the physio docs tell me to do, but the flexibility still isn't there. This is another avenue closed off to me, whereby I might find some solace. I don't deserve it I guess."

Carson shook his head in denial.

"It is frustrating, Drax, and I feel for you. I know how music heals the soul. It did for me, and for your mother, especially for her. I was looking forward to hearing your compositions. I see very clearly, usually from modern pieces, the way jazz and the blues and spirituals translate into nocturnes, but how to retain that raw, intense expression of the soul in classical cadences?"

"What reaches your soul and makes tears of longing come to the eyes in the music of Fauré and Debussy, is also in blues, jazz and swing, just more exposed, raw, as you say."

"To think that Schoenberg and Stravinsky went atonal to be more realistic to life than those romantics with their ethereal airs, and here you are combining the two."

"I assemble influences, hopefully staying true to each."

"So, Drax, you are afraid that the British officer was Rory?"

"Do you know anything, anything at all, that Emil, or Greg's Uncle Harold, may have dreamed up that involves Rory in some way?"

Carson sat up and leaned forward, his elbows resting on his knees, his hands clasped together.

"Drax, I have something to tell you. As you know, I have been working with Emil and some important men, former advisors of FDR's, and Colonel Harold Macklin, who work in a very hush-hush offshoot of British Intelligence. Well let's just say that these fellows keep an eye on governments, and all the intelligence services, in an attempt to keep them honest." Carson sat up and gave a brief laugh. "Harold will say that the safety of the British people cannot be left entirely in the hands of the English Upper classes, or even the English. We Americans value the 'God Almighty Buck' so much that we hold the wealthy in high esteem. We cannot put all our eggs in this one basket of the rich and powerful. Besides, society needs a diverse pool from which to draw to realize all its potential. We have benefited from immigrants from all backgrounds and creeds. We should maintain this diversity of talent.

You asked me before the war started if I knew of any special work you could undertake. You knew Kerr was involved in some 'special' work, and you'd like to do the same. That was how you met Magda and Emil and all your friends. All of them were doing 'special' work for their governments as well as ours. Their work was mainly keeping an eye on things."

"And your involvement with Emil?"

"I have been keeping an eye on business people. After all, I am one of them, one of those city boys who deal in high finance. I had no intention of ever becoming a committed capitalist, but Emil and Harold and some of FDR's closest confidantes, knowing of my 'integrity', as they put it, asked me to come out of my academic cloisters and get involved with Wall Street investors, bankers and giants of industry to keep an eye on their connections with those in the Senate and Congress and the military and intelligence services, as well as the press, the propaganda boys, I guess you'd call them. This I have done, making friends with ruthless businessmen, bankers and industrial giants I never would have associated with if given the choice. I do not like what I have discovered. They have this country in their iron grasp, and they dictate who has power, and how it is to be wielded, and those ways serve only their coffers. The rest of us are slaves to their wishes, and they do not have our interests at heart at all, only their own."

Drax hung his head smiling.

"Nessa used to say we should get rid of money, and then these profiteers would have to fix their own cars, clean their own toilets and do their own laundry like the rest of us."

"Oh what a precious idea! Get rid of money? Well why not?"

"She wants to get rid of ologies and isms too."

"Why not? Our political and religious institutions are stale and increasingly self-serving. They serve only to fuel wars and fanaticism."

"She also thinks women are better suited to run democracies."

"She's right. They are better suited to run true democracies that is."

"So Rory is in the clear?"

"That I don't know. I am sorry. Every organization, even Emil's and Harold's, can be exploited by spies, not that I think Rory is one. What do you intend to do?"

There was a long silence as Drax stared into the fire's flames, shades of anger, doubt, helplessness reflected in his face. Carson watched him anxiously, wishing he could ease his torment.

"What have you done, dear boy?"

Drax looked up at him in anguish.

"I told my superiors about my suspicions as regards Rory. I was hoping that they'd keep it within the naval intelligence community, or even the State Department, with its ties to British intelligence, and they'd come up with some clandestine reason as to why Rory was in Alaska, giving top secret papers to the Russians. I hoped and prayed that there was some legitimate reason for what he did. Unfortunately, they have passed the information on to a senator on the House Committee on Un-American Activities. I have been subpoenaed to testify in a secret session, closed to the press and outsiders, next week."

Carson's blood froze in his veins.

# CHANGES

Santa Barbara, Autumn, 1951:

A black sedan emerged from the heavy mist and downpour, and wound its way up the driveway lined by the tall feathery evergreens, in which the mist hung like cobwebs. Emil had been watching for it. He moved to open the big oak door as a man in a trench coat and broad fedora pulled down over his head to shield him from the rain, emerged from the car and, clutching a big leather briefcase to his chest, ran up the path. In even that short distance, the man's raincoat and hat were soaked, and Emil took them, and handed them to Marisol to dry out.

"Dr. Tanner, thank you for coming. Come and get warm by the fire. Would you care for a coffee, or would you prefer wine, bourbon, a cocktail?"

"Coffee, please, Dr. Franz, with a scotch chaser if possible?"

"Absolutely, and Magda and I will join you. It is a cold, raw evening. Come sit near the fire."

"Are you glad to be back here, Dr. Franz? This is a lovely home, so secluded and charming." Alex looked around the room: the log fire was lit, big comfortable cushions on every chair and in every nook and cranny, the smell of freshly brewed coffee and apple pie on the air, and that gentle, caressingly soft glow from the lamps on the side tables.

"Very much so. Magda and I did not feel at home in Washington after FDR died, although President Truman couldn't have been kinder to us, and we feel so sorry for him, having to assume power in these dangerous and complex times. The intrigues got to us, even though, during the war, we were part of all that in a way. Now, of course, our role, or function, has been terminated. We no longer have refugees to rescue from the Nazis, and many former Nazis have been recruited into American and Soviet intelligence services. This absolutely stupefies me, but both sides are gearing up for another conflict, and who better to muddy the waters, fudge the truth and by-pass any and all ethical considerations, than the Nazis? I am heartily relieved not to be part of the rampant paranoia being instigated. I will reiterate that I feel sorry for President Truman, what with the Korean War, Stalin's land-grabbing in Eastern Europe, and China falling to the communists, not to mention that all now have the ability to develop nuclear weapons. Still America's lead in that regard would have been momentary in any case, even if spies at Los Alamos and elsewhere hadn't been involved. Oh they helped shorten the time gap, helped the communists develop the bomb earlier than they otherwise would have done, but given this horrendous backlash to FDR's New Deal here, maybe it was for the better. It gives all potential combatants pause for thought."

Emil handed Alex Tanner his scotch, as Marisol brought in the coffee, along with slices of her apple pie. Magda followed close behind, a vision in navy-blue silk. Alex rose to take her long, elegant hand bedecked in diamond and sapphire rings.

"Dr. Tanner, how are you?"

"Physically fine, Mrs. Franz, but spiritually… not so good."

Magda sighed and raised her hand in agreement. She sat in the deep leather armchair opposite his at the fireside, and Emil pulled up his old tapestry-backed rocking chair to sit between them.

"Well, Dr. Franz…"

"Emil, please."

"Okay, Emil, what are we to do? You'd think, wouldn't you that with wars lined up for most probably the rest of this century, the old warmongers would be happy? But, no, they have to keep their pots boiling."

"God, it's an awful world we live in! How did we let their evil ways control our lives?"

They lowered their eyes to gaze into their scotch and ice, as if it were only there, in those tempting amber depths, that they could find solace, escape. Alex looked as if he'd partaken of that consoling route a little bit too often of late. He looked tired, disillusioned.

"I miss the get up and go, the optimism FDR showed, even if he didn't always believe it; the reassurance he gave us that all would be well, that we could overcome everything thrown our way, even fear. Truman has his plain-speaking, dry, pithy wit, that brooks no martinets, but he faces the relentless tidal wave of paranoid crap bearing down on us. God, I detest these goddamn self-righteous, self-serving profiteers."

Emil and Magda shared a look of concern for Alex. After a few moments of reflective silence, Emil, looking into the flames, said,

"That's how Rory felt, poor boy! What are we going to do about him and Syb?"

"I thought that you and Harold had some plan or other," Alex said, looking up in alarm. Emil hung his head. Alex looked from one to the other of them, his anxiety mounting to near hysteria. They must have had a plan. Emil raised his eyes to look beseechingly at Alex. Alex felt an intense fear take hold.

"There was a meeting, Alex, in London, after Klaus Fuchs confessed to his espionage activities for the Soviets at Los Alamos and in England, espionage work he didn't agree to perform until the Soviets were our allies. The heads of our new CIA, the FBI and the Offices of Strategic Operations and Policy Coordination, OSO and OPC, were there. What an alphabet soup! The British intelligence services were there, MI5 and MI6. Stephenson was there for Canadian intelligence. The Canadians have their atomic spy problems too.

I was there, along with Harold Macklin, to explain our undercover work for FDR, which was to rescue innocents, keep an eye on infiltrations, especially at Bletchley, and our main research facilities here and in Canada, including the ones where research on atomic weapons was being conducted.

Harold's section had been following known spies for the Soviets for some time, especially the men from Cambridge University, and he had used these spies, unbeknownst to them of course, to our own advantage, by letting them feed useful information to help the Russians defeat the Nazis, and feed disinformation when necessary. Rory, as you know, was Harold's spy on the spies, if you will. A role that caused him much anguish, for he did not want to betray fellow Cambridge men, yet he disagreed with the route they had taken to oppose the system, namely spying. Such underhand work to serve a foreign power makes people feel insecure; the precursor to fear, and it thereby puts pay to their trust in socialism, or any other new progressive ideas, even homegrown ones.

FDR and Churchill used us, because they knew the OSS and military intelligence services, the State department and Treasury and other government departments, including the FBI, had been infiltrated, both by communist spies, and for some considerable time, probably from their inception, by those in the pay of the warmongers. How did FDR and Churchill know? That's where we were useful. We had help from another organization, who has deep sources within German, Japanese and Soviet services, as well as American and European governments. These people I cannot name. I don't have access to that information, and neither does Harold."

"By God, Emil, then who runs this network? Who are these people?"

Emil just shook his head by way of reply.

"Don't worry, Alex, they are extremely trustworthy. They are there to try to safeguard the people, all ordinary people the world over - a losing battle if ever there was one - but at least they try. I am not part of them, neither is Harold. They are not funded by any agency of government, religion, dogma or policy. I do not know how they are funded. I suspect that maybe they aren't."

Alex gasped.

"Is Rory one of them – these deep spies? Is Rory going to be sacrificed? Will he have to flee to Moscow like Burgess and Maclean? Drax has linked him to handing over top-secret Manhattan Project papers to the Soviets. How will you get Rory out of this?"

"Yes, Alex, I know. The Americans are very angry that the British have let Burgess and Maclean go, but, as we now know, they had served their purpose. They had been used to give the Soviets information that had helped them win the war for us. They also gave the Soviets information that resulted in the deaths and torture of our agents in the field. This is why the Americans cannot just let them go unpunished, and neither should the British, but they did, and I wonder why. I think the Russians also wonder why. These idealistic Cambridge spies have been rendered useless to both sides, haven't they? The Russians had to take them. It wouldn't look good if they didn't support their fellow communists who had worked for them, but they'd never trust them again. The Soviets have never trusted us. It must have seemed most fortuitous to them that, despite really shady affiliations with communist parties, these spies of theirs managed to get into high positions in the Foreign Office and the secret services. No, the Russians do not trust them and will not give them access to anything important now they are in the Soviet Union. I think that the British see this as punishment enough. These men are British, of the old school tie establishment. If they sought to change the old class-system, well then let them end their days in that classless society they so revered. It would be just desserts from the British Establishment point of view. Hauling them through the courts, as the Americans would wish, tarring and feathering them as traitors, may result in making them heroes or martyrs. These men are perfectly capable of justifying their stand for the working people, the ordinary people, and believe me, with all the pro-communist and socialist factions in Europe, who are very popular, I may add, this would be the last thing the ruling classes in England would want. American powers-that-be relish witch-hunts as they frighten the masses and let them be controlled, but beware, these are complicated times. No, the British conservative classes were wise to let them go to the loud accompaniment of social outrage and opprobrium heavily meted out by the press and other propaganda machines. This way, only the Establishment's point of view gets across, and having an opposite point of view is reviled so much, that the people get to doubt, which leads to confusion and resorting to their best bet, which is do nothing, wait and see, and…snap…the powerful and wealthy classes have them where they want them."

"Rory was your double agent."

"And he proved invaluable. He saved the lives of many of our operatives in the field, but there were so many secret organizations involved that Rory couldn't cover all of them. He didn't have the access to MI6 ops that Philby had. He didn't have access to all Foreign Office secrets that Maclean had. He had some lucky breaks, that's all. The Cambridge spies and Bletchley spies did not coordinate their efforts. They worked independently, so Rory had to too. We may have spoon-fed some information these men passed on, but certainly not all of it. Rory was the only one we could spoon-feed with information for the Soviets, as Rory was our man."

"Why not have let them go and kept it all under wraps?"

"Well, you see Alex, they were used for a far more important purpose. MI5 and MI6, as well as your intelligence services, could afford a little image tarnishing, in that they had been incapable of preventing huge Soviet spy networks from operating in their countries, and operating from important positions. Why, and for what possible purpose would our services want to look like such dupes? Well, I'll tell you, Alex, to frighten the people into believing that commies were all around. Strict measures now have to be taken to ferret them out. People will have to give up their civil liberties; the Constitution and the judicial system will have to be bent to accommodate the likes of McCarthy and his ilk.

The Russians had gained some sort of victory in having spies in high places in Europe, Britain and America. The Americans and British had egg on their faces at being duped, but they had achieved a much greater victory by having the means to terrify their people, and discredit any further socialist or communist influence in their governments, or in their societies. The Americans will be more successful in their anti-communist campaign of terror than the more adaptable, but nevertheless cunning, British, who will let their communists and socialists function where they can keep an eye on them, and so by, maintain the semblance of a democracy. America, of course, sacrificed her right to claims of being a democracy, by using massive propaganda to promulgate fear and threat of loss of livelihood for those who dare to hold different political beliefs from the wealthy establishment.

To sum up, the capitalists gained the most, but at a cost to their claims of being democratic. Their propaganda press, however, can spin any old lies for the less well-informed public, and if they keep pushing the life, liberty, pursuit of happiness slogan, and how Americans have it so good… and that all-blinding cry of "God Bless America" to end the possibility of anyone raising any doubts or complaints, well then, who will realize they have been bamboozled? This communist witch-hunt is a crime against the American people. It shows they are not trusted to think for themselves. It deprives them of their freedoms."

"But, I don't understand. What will happen to Rory?"

"We were aware that some in the CIA are operatives in the pay of this wealthy-military-press-intelligence cabal that controls DC, and that they were present at this meeting. Harold and I told them that Rory was our man, which, of course, he is. I told them, and Harold nervously complied, that Rory had been sent, stationed actually, in Alaska, as he'd requested, to keep an eye on diplomatic traffic going and coming through Ladd. I reminded them that their secret services were well aware of this coordinated effort with British intelligence. The secrets from Los Alamos left for Moscow from many places, usually as part of the Soviet clearing house for the Lend-Lease program, under the cover of an import-export agency. They had too many outlets for us to cover effectively, even using combined efforts.

The British and Americans have decoded Soviet messages through their lucky decryption of the Venona code book found in Finland. They have been reading Soviet mail and radio traffic between Moscow and the Soviet consulate in New York since 1944. We know their networks, and they know ours, but you'll find no record of steps that were taken as a result of our all knowing this.

We said Drax's source had seen Rory hand over information from Los Alamos. It was harmless stuff, but useful enough to allay suspicions that we'd tumbled to the spies the Soviets had in Los Alamos and elsewhere, with the help of a dear man, a scientist, we had rescued from Germany during the war – Dr. Andrei Bronstein. Thanks to Dr. Bronstein, we could 'doctor' some information passed by the Los Alamos spies. Rory passed on this doctored information in Alaska, through his role as a Soviet spy. We used other agents at other ports. The Russians had so many outlets that some very important information did elude us, but we caught some of it, thanks to dear Andrei. Rory was part of our network working the ALSIB route."

"What our guys are furious about, are all these other clandestine efforts on our turf. They know the British whisked off Maclean and Burgess to prevent them falling into CIA and FBI hands. They claimed the Brits stood by their own. It was the old school tie thing you know: 'They are spies, but they are Englishmen, by Jove!' What our intelligence guys can't take is that the British let them escape all the way to Moscow. Our guys were denied a witch-hunt, but they are making up for that now."

"In any case, Alex, Harold was raked over the coals for having a British spy operate on American soil, even if he had recovered and saved damaging information from reaching the Soviets, even if he had worked in cooperation with certain CIA efforts. They want Rory. He will be their catch. They want to know what Rory learned in his undercover role with those spies.

Harold and I told them that Rory must maintain his role as a Soviet spy. He must be allowed to escape to the Soviet Union, as the others had, otherwise the Russians would not believe anything he had given them, or was now feeding them. If Rory was questioned and pardoned, which he should be, of course, he is not a traitor; then he and Syb would have to go into hiding, as the Soviets would seek revenge. Rory and Syb can only live an open life, free from fear, if they carry on with this charade. If he is arrested and questioned, the Soviets will know, even if it is all done behind closed doors. We must forestall all attempts by McCarthy and his ilk to bring Drax's accusation into the public domain. Rory must be able to contact his Soviet controller to say that someone has damning evidence of him passing information to them at Ladd, and he is afraid, and wants to come in from the cold before the Americans can question him. The Russians will take him in. He knows too much of their set-up, but we must not be seen to have questioned him at all. We can put an obvious surveillance team on to him, and the Russians will be watching, and notice this, and they will rescue him before he gets arrested."

"Oh no, Emil! Please do not let them do this. They can never return to the States. They can never go home. Please Emil, make them see sense."

"This is the only solution, Alex. The only good outcome is that Rory's role will never be made public, so his family and Syb's won't be compromised in their supposed treachery. We'll tell their parents the truth, and swear them to secrecy, and I think that they will readily comply to avoid the onslaught of the press and public indignation. Rory and Syb are really heroes to do this, to make this sacrifice. We must not let the extreme Right in Britain and America use Rory to further their campaign of 'Red Terror'. Rory would never condone that. He is a socialist after all, as is Syb. He would never let himself be used by the Right to suppress socialist efforts to help the people. We must do this for him. He and Syb have earned it, and then some."

"Syb did top secret work at Bletchley, and she knows we have cracked the Russian codes, so surely, we can't let them interrogate her?"

"The Russians do not know Syb worked at Bletchley, or in Ceylon with our intelligence services. That has been the best-kept secret, and we have taken the utmost care in covering her movements. She has appeared to the Russians here and in England as a math teacher. The only time she didn't follow Rory around, was when she was in Ceylon. We had her return home to her family's country estate for the duration of her time in Ceylon. She disappeared into that mansion, and, on occasion, was seen walking in the grounds. That was a double, hard to detect from a distance, and wearing a scarf and dark glasses. Syb, of course, had left from her home under cover of darkness to go to Ceylon, and had left her double in her place. Her parents, though avid Tories, complied, as she was spying for us. They would want to avoid all connections with her if her defection to Moscow were made public, even if they know she is really our agent. They may well like to tar and feather all socialists and the Labor party with this spy propaganda, but not with it being so close to home."

Alex knocked back his scotch and re-filled his glass.

"My heart bleeds for them, going to that frozen place. Rory will not be able to write the kind of stuff he wants to write. Commies hate socialists as much as capitalists do. Socialists care for the people. Oh, Emil, we can't lose such fine kids as those two. We just can't."

"When we undertake such clandestine work, Alex, we never are aware of all the possible ramifications of our actions."

"I don't think the commie hunters will let Rory escape the attention of their propaganda press, and their toadies in Congress will howl for blood to get good press, to grand-stand."

"We have all agreed to keep Rory's defection under wraps. There are no records. What secret papers there are concerning Rory's work for us, are among other top-secret operations that cannot be made public as they protect American security. McCarthy and his ilk are bloody liabilities. They are jack-booting it over all our and the good CIA's covert espionage ops. Most of our and the Soviet espionage activities ensure the peace. The good guys on all sides are aware of this cabal that perpetuates war, and we sort of work together to thwart them at their evil game. Believe me, we good guys are walking on tightropes to keep this world safe and at peace. The good guys in the Soviet government will protect Syb and Rory from the bad element in the pay of the war profiteers' cabal.

In any case, Alex, we are discussing a fait accompli. Rory and Syb have flown the coop. They were smuggled out by Kerr Toddy and 'others'. They are in Leningrad. It helps to give them secret sanctuary from the Russian point of view, in that Rory's parents are active in Britain's socialist party, even though his father is a bishop in the Anglican Church. I see no conflict of interest there, as he is a man who follows Jesus' teachings, and is often a thorn in the flesh, a fitting pay back, don't you think, in the political body of the establishment's religious institutions? As of course was Jesus."

"Is Rory one of these secret guys you can't name, the independent ones? Is Kerr one of them too?"

Emil shook his head,

"I do not know, Alex. What can I say?"

"What about Drax?"

"Carson knows all this, but Drax can never know. He will not know, but he'll suspect that a deal was cut, and Rory got off, maybe that he was too important a leak to ever be acknowledged. He'll just have to deal with that, and hopefully feel justified in his betrayal. I wouldn't want to be him, if he finally decides that friendship with Rory and Syb was worth more, much more, than his betrayal of them, which served to promote political grandstanding of the extreme Right. He knows his parents and Rory and Syb, and especially Nessa, would never condone this. Drax's betrayal, in their eyes, would not only be of Rory and Syb, but also of the American people and their freedoms."

"But Drax thought he was doing the right thing."

"That is what is so horrible. These young people have been trapped in the web of evil being spun by the powers-that-be. They should be celebrating peace, the resumption of their creative, caring, talented lives - after all they have more than earned it. They have given so much to win the peace and defeat an incredible evil, and yet the battle goes on.

Sadly, Nessa knows all. Steven Etchberry told her. She, like you, hates the sacrifice Rory and Syb have to make, and she finds it hard to forgive Drax. In any case, she is getting on with her life, and that does not include Drax.

Harold let Greg and Laura in on it all. They sympathize with Drax, and with Rory and Syb. They dearly want to tell Drax all, but they can't. They are not sure of just how mired Drax is in this communist paranoia, but they remain his friends, and they keep up with Nessa too. They even want to write to Rory and Syb and visit them, but that would be impossible. The Russians would never allow it, and neither would we, as Laura was an integral part of our code breaking and intelligence work. We can't let her fall into the Russians' hands."

Alex left, a man bearing a heavy burden of guilt. The fact that they had put these youngsters' lives on the line to spy for them never had sat well with his conscience, but it had proved to be a very effective way of winning the war.

After they had seen him off, Emil and Magda exchanged a heartfelt sigh of relief. Magda kissed her husband, and claiming that she was exhausted, she went to bed. Emil cleared away cups and glasses. He sensed a presence. Rudy emerged out of the shadows. They faced each other in silence, and then Emil said,

"Thank you with all my heart, thank you. You will have your Dragons keep an eye on Rory and Syb? They are very dear, very brave."

"It is over for you, Emil. You and Magda have been working so hard for so long to help others. You can devote yourselves to your philanthropic endeavors."

"And you, Rudy?"

Rudy winked, and opening the back door, he disappeared into the deep darkness of a cold and cloudy moonless night.

# ENCOUNTERS

Washington, D.C.: Early spring, 1954:

It was such a memorable moment. Alisyn was amazing. Dressed in a bright red, beautifully tailored suit, she stood before the congressional committee, surrounded by their pack of photographers and press, and took the Fifth Amendment, refusing to name names. She had been brought before the committee for a speech she had given at a Hollywood function to raise money for orphans of war. She had talked about a more balanced society, where wealth and work had equal status and influence. Naturally, she was summoned before a congressional hearing chaired by McCarthy himself.

With her black hair, mid-length, shiny, slight bouncy curl, her perfect cheekbones, her flashing long green eyes and scarlet lips, she looked amazing as she told them about her America. She finally revealed that she was of mixed blood; her father was of Irish ancestry and her mother was a Mulatto from New Orleans. She proudly told the press present that they should spell her mother's heritage with a capital letter 'M'. She said that the witch-hunt against socialist

Americans was a travesty, as they were loyal Americans, who never would take to being told what to do by a foreign power. They just wanted to bring socialist programs, as most of Europe was doing now, to hard-done-by American people, those who could not afford health care and a fine standard of education, who could not, therefore, hope of giving their children a step up in life.

We needed people wealthy enough to create work, to support charities and the arts and education. We needed workers to do the work for these rich people. Both employer and employee were necessary to make America great, and both were American on an equal footing. Both wanted to follow the tenets of their wonderful Constitution. She was American, as her parents had been. They had died, giving their all; doing backbreaking work to build America, and no one was going to tell her that she was Un-American. She said how congress had taken Paul Robeson's passport away; the great singer had been blacklisted for refusing to name names. Robeson had replied that his family had slaved to build America, and it was as much his as anybody's. She felt the same way. She was not, nor ever had been, a communist. She knew people who had been communists, but had given it up, and people who were communists, and they were as American as apple-pie. She would not give their names.

McCarthy tried to drown her out with his bullying, inane questioning, but she stood there, head and shoulders above him in all ways. She conceded that such hearings were necessary to protect Americans from harmful and crooked influences. She tried to hide a smile when she said the word crooked, and she coughed slightly and looked pointedly at them. The spectators present laughed. When asked to explain that pointed remark, she related a history of how many, considered sterling Americans, had gained their wealth, and had badly treated their workers who had asked peacefully for a fairer deal. Why, in some cases, these wealthy employers had cheated Americans out of their rights and their livelihoods in the process of building up their wealth. Was this backlash against socialism a guilty reaction by the wealthy in America, afraid that the workers might be justified in looking for some way in which their wrongs could be redressed, their wages made more commensurate with the work they did? She was warned that she was getting dangerously close to contempt. She looked surprised and concerned, and asked in what way she could possibly have held the hearing in contempt? More laughter broke out.

She didn't mind wealth. She had money and lived in modest luxury. She had a much more comfortable life than either of her parents had had. People were not created with equal abilities, or equal starts in life, but those less well able to get by should not be cheated or treated shabbily so others could get ahead. People with different points of view should not be persecuted either. To her mind, this was Un-American. She had been treated badly as a youngster, because of her mother's heritage, and that was wrong too, and what she considered to be very Un-American.

Oh, Alisyn was blacklisted, but then that wasn't anything new for her. She had her platform and she used it. Many admired her stand. Greg did a painting that resembled in style, the painting done of the signing of the Declaration of Independence by the nation's forefathers, except that the central figure in his painting was a beautiful Mulatto woman, standing proud and tall in a flaming red suit.

Alisyn worked in plays performed on and off Broadway, and was a sensational hit. She finally showed her depth as an actress and as a person, an American. This is what Nessa said to her after the hearings, which Nessa, Jeb, Loretta, Steven, Esperanza, Laura and Greg had attended, offering her their support. Fiona, Lorna, Sigi and Mandy were told by Alisyn not to attend. It might compromise their careers in movies. The movie heads felt the same, so they dared not attend. Movie stars and their weavers of imaginary heroes were made of celluloid after all. Only some deserved the mantle of hero and heroine in real life, putting other considerations before their livelihoods and fame, like friendship, common sense, standing up for what they believed in, no matter what, and yes, their careers in movies paid the price.

⇌⇋

Paris: June, 1954:
The city lay under dark thunderclouds. An early gloom had descended, along with a deluge of rain. It matched the mood of the people running to catch buses and trains to get home, or to meet friends at cafes, as Nessa was on her way to do. The French forces that had been held under siege for several weeks at Dien Bien Phu, a last-ditch hold out, deep in the jungles on the border of Viet Nam and Laos, finally and bloodily, had been defeated. It had been France's last stand, and the bravery shown by both sides had been incredible. French honor had been restored in some way, even though they had lost, but that honor lay only in struggling to the end in what was a futile battle against inevitable change. Colonies were out. Independent new nations were in. The whole world had watched in horror and suspense as General Giap's forces had closed in for the kill. The French combatants had been composed of men and women of France and her remaining loyal colonial forces. These colonial forces included women who had followed their men of the Foreign Legion from North Africa to the steaming jungles of Indochina, and who had fought bravely with them. French doctors and nurses, helicopter pilots, some of whom were women – all had fought to the bitter and bloody end. The Vietnamese finally had won their freedom… from France, at least!

Nessa took off her beige colored raincoat, and pulled off the soaking wet brown and beige scarf from her sodden hair. She shook them gently, and handed them to the waiter, who waited with outstretched hand to take her wet things. He wore the usual white high-necked starched shirt, narrow black bow tie, black waistcoat and trousers and long white apron. After a brief exchange of views about the weather, he indicated a table, way in the back of the room, by the large side window, where her friends were sitting. She thanked him, and wended her way around the seated diners, apologizing if they had to pull in their chairs for her.

"Ness, at last! We were going to send out a search party." Helen Gardener greeted her, a wide grin on her face. Helen and Pete Gardener, along with their teenage son, Russ, had moved to Paris in the late forties. They hadn't liked the political atmosphere back home. Both were writers of a leftist, liberal persuasion. They were in their fifties and had Russ, their son, late in life. They had given Ness a home, until she'd found a lovely, but basic, loft apartment in a house in the Marais, within walking distance from their apartment.

Eight other friends, two couples, three men and one woman, all of them American journalists living in Paris, made up the rest of the gang, who met regularly to party, to discuss world events, and to reminisce generally about life back home. Nessa enjoyed their company. They were light-hearted, with stimulating opinions and ideas. The single woman, Harriet Bigelow, was a great friend, and she and Nessa met often to discuss their love life. Harriet lived with a French writer, who was not always faithful, but then neither was Harriet. Nessa had little patience with her, when Pierre flirted openly, and Harriet would rush around to Nessa's to weep on her shoulder and lambaste men generally.

In the last three years since she'd arrived in Paris, Nessa had concentrated on her writing. She had written the screenplay for a movie, articles for journals, and one of her stories had been turned into a script for a play then being performed in local theaters to full houses. She'd found time for two brief romances, in neither of them had she been in love, and so, when the men had become upset at this, she'd ended the relationships. Now she was thirty-seven years old, and felt that maybe that was it in the love department.

Nessa was caught totally by surprise, therefore, when, with the usual gang at the Café des Bons Mots that night, there was an extra man present. He had fine features, friendly grin that spread in wide furrows across his narrow face, definitely furrows, not dimples. His nose was fine, not too long, nor too short, his teeth were good, dark silky hair, with silver strands throughout, hair long, compared with current lengths for men, a length favored more by academics, just below the ears, and his absolutely best feature, out a list of good features, were his eyes, that were a clear and intelligent, but also friendly, sky blue. He stood to be introduced to her, and he was tall, although not much taller than she was, broadish shoulders, compact build, tanned face and neck, which made his eyes seem even more blue. Nessa felt a frisson of sexual attraction flow through her body. She hadn't felt this way since Drax. She couldn't take her eyes from his as they were introduced, and she didn't care. She was dazzled. She could feel her eyes shining, her mouth was moist, she felt just delicious through and through. He looked steadily at her too, with a broad smile of obvious appreciation, reflected also in his eyes. Helen's voice, making the introductions, seemed to fade away. Helen and the others also had picked up on the obvious attraction between the two of them. They quietly resumed their conversation, but they kept glancing up at the couple, who, without a doubt, would soon be romantically involved with each other. After exchanging names yet again, they noticed they were still standing, and sat down with only slight embarrassment. They couldn't have cared less what the others were thinking.

They had spoken mainly to each other after they had been introduced, swapping life stories, and even when talking to the others, their eyes had kept meeting, and it had been with great difficulty that they had looked away. Eventually, the others relented and said their farewells, leaving the two of them alone together.

Nessa and Raf walked along the banks of the Seine. The night was chilly and moisture-laden, the pavements sleek and shiny after the deluge. He had explained earlier that he had got his tan in Viet Nam, where he had joined the soldiers who were trying to get into Dien Bien Phu to help rescue the men and women fighting there. He was a free-lance journalist and ex-soldier. He had been part of De Gaulle's army-in-exile in England, and had returned to France to work with the Maquis, the brave resistance fighters, until France was liberated. The Maquis had fought long and hard against the Germans and the Malice, the forces of Vichy. There had been awful reprisals on Maquisards and the ordinary French people who had helped them. Whole towns had been destroyed, their inhabitants murdered in cold blood. Raf continued:

"The whole world seems to look on us as capitulators, afraid to fight, more concerned with saving Paris than in saving our honor by fighting, but believe me, we fought. These townspeople gave their lives for France. We had given so much, in lives and livelihoods, in the First World War, we had not recovered fully from that one, when the Germans attacked again. Both of these wars have ravaged French soil. The war has been in French backyards. I do not think that the Americans, or even the British, have had the war so close and personal. The British were bombed, cities destroyed, people made homeless, but they haven't had the enemy at their door, in their streets. We fought back the best way we knew how, and as best as we were able.

This war in Viet Nam was bound to be a failure. The world is changing, and people need to be free at last to control their own nations, and not be second-class citizens in their own homelands. I was against this war. I know Ho Chi Minh well. He is a nationalist. This is a war to reunite his country. America and Russia and China are seeing it as a potential battleground for their political ideologies. I dread to think of what comes next for the Indochinese peoples. Another Korea perhaps; their country, irrevocably pulled apart into different political factions by powers not their own? I sympathize with the Vietnamese, but I fought them to rescue my compatriots, who had made this last sacrifice of themselves for some notion now outdated. It is sad how many innocent lives pay the price for being caught on the cusp of change."

"I think we all need something new and progressive, but here we are, bogged down in struggles between Left and Right, which is the same old struggle between the classes in a new guise, and will no doubt go on and on, but hopefully not in perpetuity."

"I am something of a biologist. I see problems down the road of a more environmental nature. If we go on polluting lands, oceans and the air, and killing off other species, while we mindlessly over-populate, we shall have a much more serious battle on our hands between man and Nature. We use that atomic bomb, and it may well be the end of man and life on Earth, but I believe Nature always has an ace up her sleeve. We may be gone, but she'll have some hardy replacements to take our place. The earth has huge recuperative powers. We do not."

Nessa walked on, looking down and smiling to herself. She loved this man. He had something of 'Simon' about him with his light banter and easy charm, and he had the masculine presence and build of Drax, but there the resemblance ended. He was a man of words and actions. Yes, she loved this man. He was older than she by some thirteen years or so, but he was a man relevant to all ages, and he certainly didn't look his age, silver threads not withstanding. They only served to make him even more attractive. Nessa had found the love of her life at thirty-seven years of age.

Drax, in the meantime, had continued to flounder in the web of changes going on around him. It seemed as if America had shed the years of the New Deal, and responded to the insecurities of a changing world by back peddling, and strengthening its former oligarchy, run by laissez-faire capitalists and bankers. This would work well for most Americans, until the next, inevitable, crash. For rampant capitalism, like communism, was doomed to fail. Both ideologies carried within them, the seeds of their ultimate destruction. New, rapid developments in computer technology and application revealed these faults in present socio-economic theories. Alan Turing's invention and his ideas were being realized.

Drax went to Cuba to find his music, and he was successful. Cuba was preparing for a huge change. Havana was the playground of the rich and corrupt: the American Mafia held sway there; the CIA and FBI had clandestine operations going on there to monitor the socialist movements in Latin America and in Cuba itself; rich Americans had homes there, especially writers and other American ex-patriots, and Europeans flooded there, including their intelligence operatives and writers and ex-pats, especially from Germany. Havana was a hodge-podge of all kinds of intrigue and escapism, and, as usual, the people living outside the bigger cities, lived under deplorable conditions of poverty.

These diverse strains suited Drax's mood and his music. One evening, while he sat in the bar of his hotel in Havana, sipping a Cuba Libre, and trying to write down the notes that were in his head, the waft of some incredible perfume, jasmine, or hibiscus, something exotic and enticing, broke his concentration and created a somewhat sexual stirring in his loins. He looked around to see who had been responsible for such a sensation. She stood there with a much older man - her father possibly? She was dark-skinned, her black hair fell in a riot of curls down her back, almost to her waist. She was beautiful in a Velasquez painting sort of way, very Spanish, proud bearing, defiant flash to her black eyes, that defiance having a slight contradicting glimmer of seduction, so typical of her class and breeding. She was dressed in the height of fashion, in a diaphanous voile dress in pale pastel shades of blue and lavender, slight hint of pale yellow. She was very slender, and of medium height. Drax was definitely attracted to her, his body told him so.

The man and woman noticed him, although Drax sensed that she had noticed him as soon as she'd entered. They held a whispered conversation. Then the man, medium height, slender himself, thin tanned face with grey goatee, white panama hat on his grey hair, aristocratic look and bearing, pale grey suit, white leather shoes, ebony cane with golden dragon head, spoke,

"I hope that you will excuse this interruption. I can see that you are quite absorbed in your writing." He glanced down, and corrected himself, "I am sorry, your musical composition. My name is Senor Pascal Herrerro. Naturally I am giving you an abbreviated version. My full name, typical of Spanish names, goes on and on." His whole demeanor reflected old world charm, a time of grace and manners long passed. "May I introduce my daughter, Gia? We wondered if you were perchance, Drax Shaw?" Drax was taken aback. How could they know him? "Do not be alarmed. I am an acquaintance of your father's. I do not presume to say that I am his friend, but I hold him in very high regard, and certainly, from my point of view, I regard him as a very dear and trustworthy friend."

Drax felt as if his words had an undercurrent of meaning, but if they did, Drax had no idea what the man wanted of him. The man's kindly black eyes, in their folds of wrinkles, seemed to sense this, for he pulled back, as if reconsidering how he would proceed.

"I am very pleased to meet you Senor Herrerro and your beautiful daughter." Drax took her white-gloved hand and bent over it as if to kiss it. She raised her finely etched black brows in surprise, but softened the response with a smile. Drax suddenly felt seedy in his floral patterned tropical shirt and baggy slacks and canvas sandals. He knew his hair was an untidy mess of curls, tangled and greasy, as he had the habit of running his hand threw them as he worked. "My manners are terrible. Please excuse my appearance and my confusion. I was deeply absorbed in my work. I am afraid that is my only excuse." They laughed and dismissed his need to apologize.

"It is we, who should apologize for so thoughtlessly disturbing you," the man replied. "But I was so eager to make your acquaintance. Your father has sung your praises often. You have incredible talents, not only in composing music, but also as a brilliant and innovative architect and engineer."

"Please, after that compliment, I really must treat you to a drink." Drax said, smiling.

"No, I insist, let the pleasure of buying you a drink be ours."

They took their drinks over to a white wrought iron table with four similarly white wrought iron chairs set around it, all looking as finely made as filigree, yet strong enough to take the weight of the heaviest patrons. Dark green and lush palms surrounded them on three sides. They were in the far corner of the bar, well away from other customers. Large windows made up of separate square panes lined with black iron borders made up the corner in which they sat.

They talked of inconsequential things, Drax catching the enticing glances cast at him every now and again by Gia, to whom he smiled back seductively; or so he hoped. Then the conversation turned to much more serious topics:

"We are being watched, Mr. Shaw." Drax immediately tensed, all romantic feelings instantly evaporated.

"Who are you?" he snapped, fear clutched at his stomach, and he felt his Cuba Libre rise in his throat.

"My daughter and I have watched you working away here day after day, ever since you arrived. We have noticed that Batista's police have you under surveillance, as well as your own CIA. They are working together. Why would you arouse such interest?" Drax made as if to stand, but the woman gently put her hand on his. The man continued, "Please, Mr. Shaw, remain seated, and try to give the impression that we are having a casual conversation. I am a friend of your father's. After you had that secret session with the House Committee, I gather that the CIA approached you to work for them. You refused. You made it obvious that you were appalled by what you had done. They should have seen it as the act of a loyal American, and, at first, they did, but since then, you have worked in some politically sensitive regions of the world, eschewing all political affiliations, claiming to be apolitical."

Drax protested:

"I am apolitical. Look, Mr Herrerro, I am managing to lose myself in my music. I am recovering the fine touch I once had in playing the piano. This is an overwhelming relief. I want nothing to do with politics, business concerns or espionage of any kind. All that is over. I do not know why Batista's security police or the CIA are interested in me. They have no reason to watch me, and I am praying most fervently that doesn't change by my talking to you."

Mr Herrerro smoked his cigarillo, and narrowed his eyes as the smoke curled up around his head.

"Mr Shaw, have you ever heard of José Marti?"

"Do you mean the excellent man who wrote about independence for Cuba in the 1890's? He wanted democracy for Cuba. He wanted to avoid military rule and rule by corrupt dictators. He worked for the revolution in Cuba, hoping to free it from foreign control. He worked mainly from New York, didn't he? He died in battle, however, against the Spanish in…"

"1895," Gia supplied the answer. "A good man."

"A good man, indeed, but what has he got to do with me?"

"You must have noticed that certain elements in America have turned Havana into their sadistic playground of vice, narcotics and corrupt business practices. It is part of Cuba's charm that Americans and Europeans can come here to let their hair down, so to speak, in ways they wouldn't want made known at home. Now we have oilmen and real estate investors destroying Cuba's natural resources. It is time they left. We need a cleansing revolution. I would dearly like a bloodless coup like Marti, a democracy, but our younger revolutionaries favor a more Marxist approach. The rest of us would like a compromise, fair to all, but free from foreign control and foreign corruption. If people want to trade with us, do business with us, on an honest footing, free from any shady and downright evil connections, we should be more than happy. We are not America's bordello. We want to be a proud, upright, independent and democratic nation, such as Marti had intended. I admit that I like businessmen like your father, and I like some of the young Marxists, but I fear that in the latter case, there will be bloodshed. Batista and his American supporters will not give in without a fight, especially as socialism is anathema to the rich American oligarchy. This is a shame. I think a compromise could otherwise have been reached."

"It is more than a shame, father. It is a catastrophe! The catastrophe that faces all small nations caught between the self-serving super powers."

"Again, I ask you, what has this to do with me?"

"Come out of your hiding place from the world, Mr. Shaw and help your father help us. We live in New York, just as Marti once did, and we are fund-raisers for the coming revolution. Your father helps us. He has given me permission to talk with you about this while you are in Cuba."

There was a long moment of silence, as they watched Drax come to terms with this. Actually, what Drax was feeling, was a cleansing relief. The way to make amends for his stupid fear and misplaced patriotism lay before him. Something in his soul urged him to accept this challenge. He had a brief moment of anger towards his father for approaching him in this round about way, but then he realized that the time and place were perfect. He knew what his father and Kerr were involved in, helping to make America a democracy, and he wanted to be a part of it. He wanted Nessa to be proud of him, but then he looked at Gia, and maybe it wasn't Nessa he wanted to impress."

# SWAN SONGS

Paris: 1950's:

Raf Devos was a friend of the French Existentialist writers: Jean Paul Sartre, Simone de Beauvoir and Albert Camus. He introduced Nessa to them. Like many of these writers, Raf had not gone in for the formal conventions of marriage and sexual fidelity. He had taken the view that life was too short to load oneself down with personal baggage. He had lovers in almost every country he had visited in the course of his journalistic career. They were easy-come-easy-go relationships. He told Nessa that he had not been promiscuous. He had sexual relationships only with women of a more intellectual leaning, and he had avoided ties of a sexual nature with women who would be more clinging and expect more from him than an exchange of ideas and the odd night or two of more bodily passions. Nessa had laughed. He had laughed too.

"You see," he explained, "Intellectual stimulation is indelibly linked with sex for me. I do not like sex for its own sake, but when it comes after stimulating conversation and exciting ideas, then for me, sex is the culmination of the joy of sharing one's mind with a woman. Sharing one's body follows on quite naturally."

Raf and Nessa took holidays with Jeb and Loretta, and celebrated Christmas with them and all their friends in California. Jeb and Loretta stayed with them in Paris, much to Loretta's delight. She'd always been a Francophile at heart.

Christmas,1956, Raf and Nessa walked along the beach. The sea was rough, and the sea gulls and sandpipers stood in lines, shivering on the wet sand as they faced the high tossing waves.

"They look like they are debating with themselves whether to take on the challenges the sea and wind are giving them this day," laughed Raf.

"They are wise," replied Ness, "And of course desperate, they have to find food. Each day for them is a 'do or possibly die' day. Raf watched Nessa, as she strolled on, kicking up broken pieces of shells with the toe of her tennis shoes, her short blonde curls battered about. She raised a hand to shield her eyes from the airborne sand. The sand blew in his eyes as he caught up to her, and wrapped his arms around her.

"I do love you, Nessa Eiles," he shouted above the roar of the waves. "I love you very much."

Nessa hugged him back.

"I love you too, Raf Devos."

"Let's get married."

Nessa looked at him in surprise and laughed.

"Well, Raf Devos, of all the words I expected to come out of your mouth at this moment, those were the last ones I expected to hear."

"I can't do without you in my life on a permanent basis. I have found that, even though, I have met clever, beautiful women lately, who normally I would have bedded, I don't want to. I have a beautiful woman, whose mind challenges me, stimulates me as never before, and whose body excites me, stimulates me and satisfies me – no that isn't true, for I cannot get enough of you, Nessa. I want to share all the rest of my life with you. I am fifty two years old, and you are thirty nine. Am I, perhaps, too old for you?" He pulled his mouth down at the corners.

Nessa looked steadily into his wonderful blue eyes, now somewhat reddened by wind and sand,

"My answer is yes to your marriage proposal, Raf, and no, you are not too old for me. You love to be free to travel at a moment's notice, but I want a child."

"It will travel with us. What better education can a child have? We have so much to teach a child of life."

Jeb, Loretta and Steven were told at Christmas dinner that evening. They were thrilled.

Nessa and Raf were married on January 17th, 1957, and their son, Raoul Jeben Devos, was born November 29th of the same year, in Paris.

Drax Shaw married Gia Herrerro on Christmas day, 1957, at his parents' house on the Cape. Varvara and his grandparents, now well into their eighties, supplied the musical accompaniment, tears of joy running down their cheeks. Senor Herrerro and Carson were overjoyed, and made even more so, when Drax announced that he was going to join his father's business, and all that implied. Drax was going over to the 'good' side.

Gia had been married at a young age to a young revolutionary in Cuba, but he had been killed by Batista's forces. She had been expecting their baby, but, in her grief, she lost the child, and barely survived herself. The doctors told her that she could not have any more children. Drax had been fine with this.

On their wedding night, wrapped in each other's embrace, Gia snuggled sensually against him, her long black curls spread over his chest. She looked up at him and smiled seductively.

"I wish that I could give you a child, our child,"

Drax rolled over on her, and looking down into her liquid black eyes, he said throatily,

"Well then, let's give it a shot."

Martine, 'Marti', Varvara Elizabeth, named for José Marti and her two grandmothers, was born on September 19th, 1958.

Nessa and Raf traveled on his assignments together. They went to Africa, the Caribbean, Eastern European communist satellite countries and South America, and to all the newly independent nations on the cusp of change, including Indochina. They wrote articles and books together, showing the often-destructive influence of the Soviets and the Americans, and the corrupt and tyrannical leaders they put into power to serve their own ends. America opposed socialist leaders who would have brought great benefits to all their people, and given them a genuine democracy. Instead, America supported wealthy leaders, who opposed socialism in any form, and made only a small proportion of the population, usually their wealthy cronies, even richer and more powerful. This was, in almost all cases, detrimental to the livelihoods and freedoms of the rest of the population, and resulted in the pollution of their natural habitats and exploitation of their natural resources.

Nessa wrote an article that illustrated how the super powers had prevented any kind of progressive change throughout the remainder of the twentieth century, and had plunged smaller nations into debt and war, ruining their chances of establishing true democracies. The world seemed to have regressed into oligarchies, with an ever-widening gap between those with vast wealth and those struggling to make a living wage.

Nessa closed the article with her usual attack on value systems based on money.

"We need to replace the god Mammon with a social conscience. Value all life and seek satisfaction in less materialistic ways. We need to value compromise and cooperation. Utopian goals? Undoubtedly, but all things are possible. Evil goals are realized every day because they require the least effort. Why not Utopian goals that require more effort, but benefit all?"

Oh Nessa was lambasted by all and sundry for being a "Bleeding-heart Liberal", usually said with sneer and disdain, but she replied that she was proud of being so labeled, and found it infinitely better than being labeled as a selfish, greedy, hard-hearted fascist, with no conscience at all.

Manhattan, New York, March, 1970:
Drax and Gia mingled with the socially elite in the huge ballroom of the Grand Plaza hotel. They were attending a daytime luncheon and fund-raiser for UNICEF. The women had decided, unbeknownst to him, that Drax Shaw was the most desirable male there, and that was something, as there were many film and television personalities, as well as wealthy businessmen, bankers, academics and adventuresome journalist types present. Drax, dressed all in dark grey, with a black leather bomber jacket, did stand out, but he wasn't exactly the approachable type. Some women had tried the serious, intellectual gambit; some, the businesswoman gambit; some even tried the sexual flirtation tactic; all had failed miserably.

Drax was not in a talkative mood. He wanted to get back to the Cape, walk along the windswept beach with Gia, Marti running ahead of them with Cap, Cap wagging his big old fluffy tail, a wide dog smile on his face. Then he wanted to snuggle by the fire, Gia in his arms, Cap on the rug, chasing sticks through the waves in his dreams, and Marti upstairs, asleep among her sketches and books. Her paintings and drawings were very good for an eleven year old. Varvara had had a huge influence on the child.

Drax had spent the whole week talking business. He'd had enough. The music was backed up in his head, and he wanted time to write it all down, translate it into actuality. He wanted to play it for Gia, see her sitting there on the couch, her legs tucked under her, her long fingers stroking Cap's head, as she listened to him play. He could sense the keys under his fingertips, feel the warmth and security of the house nestled behind the dunes, while through the large bay window, he could watch the stormy seas pound the beach. He was playing the piano in his head. Drax snapped back to reality, and glanced self-consciously around him. Had he been moving his hands for real? No one seemed to be looking at him. They were absorbed in their chatter. Ah, someone had noticed him. Gia, who was surrounded by men of all ages, was looking at him, smiling sympathetically. These other gals didn't stand a chance. His smile told Gia so, as her moist dark eyes showed her love for him.

How lucky he was. He loved his wife and daughter. He thought fondly of how lovely his mother had been. His father and mother, and his wonderful grandparents, and Gia's father were all gone now. Her mother had died when Gia had been a child. Marti resembled her maternal grandmother, or so Gia's father had claimed. Elizabeth Glencannon had been the daughter of an Irish rancher and his Comanche-Mexican wife. Elizabeth had met Pascal Herrerro in New York, where she was working as a social worker, helping refugees from Cuba in the early 1900's. Gia had been their only child. She'd been born in 1919, when Elizabeth and Pascal had been in their forties. They had been too caught up in their revolutionary efforts to have children, but one night of careless passion, and Gia had been the result. They had loved her dearly. Gia didn't remember much about her mother. She had died from breast cancer when Gia was five years old, but she remembered her mother's love for her, and the fun they had together, and that she had been a big woman. Gia remembered her fondly. Elizabeth had been a large, happy woman, with masses of wiry ginger hair.

Gia had felt safe and warm in her embrace, and had loved her mother's soft lilting voice with its Irish and Mexican inflections. She remembered her mother telling her stories about her childhood adventures in New Mexico. She had imparted to Gia her love of life. Elizabeth had been the image of her father, but Pascal had said that her lovely warm brown eyes and her love for horses came from the Comanche in her. She loved to escape the cement canyons of the city to ride free and wild. Her red hair would fly free and untamed behind her. She rode without a saddle; she never liked her horses to be bridled and saddled."

Drax reflected on his young daughter's appearance. So far, she wasn't the beauty her mother was. Gia said that she had Elizabeth's large features, from the Irish side, but she had a darkish complexion, dark eyes, heavy brows for one so young. He had hoped that some of Varvara would have come through, especially the lavender eyes. The child and Varvara had been devoted to each other. Marti still cried for her grandmother, even though Varvara had died two years ago. Marti had been nine years old then. She certainly had Varvara's vivid imagination, and he loved the stories she made up, and the pictures she drew of beautiful fairy kingdoms. She had a rather fastidious side to her too, which reminded Drax of Carson. Well that wasn't so bad. He discovered that he was getting more and more like his father as he got older. Hadn't Gia said so the other day, when he'd taken her to task about filing her receipts?

He was jolted out of his reflections on family history, by some excitement at the entranceway. People had gathered in the foyer. He and Gia were left standing alone, a few feet apart, questioning looks on their faces. Gia joined him.

"Who has arrived – Jackie Onassis?"

"I have no idea. Shall we bother to find out?"

Selena Moss waved them over to join the crowd.

"You wait here, and I'll find out," Gia said.

Drax had stretched up to see better, and then he saw who had earned all that attention, for his eyes fell instantly upon her, and his senses drowned in the sight of her. Every fiber of his being remembered the passion, the feel of her, the excitement he always had felt on seeing her. She must be fifty-three. He was fifty-five. The facial features were more honed to fine angles. The incredible eyes were only marginally lined, and were softer, wiser, kinder. The hair was still golden and short, brushed off those incredible cheekbones. She was tall, and still very slender, and dressed in an expensive grey woolen skirt, grey roll-neck cashmere sweater, and a long black leather coat and high black leather boots. She looked more European somehow, not Miss California any longer. His eyes shifted reluctantly to the man at her side, with whom she exchanged soft glances and smiles; their eyes not leaving each other for more than a moment.

Drax's heart lurched. He felt a wave of jealousy and desperate longing surge through him. She should have been with him, at his side, looking at him like that, as she once had done. He felt tears start, but Gia was coming over to him, a lovely broad smile on her face. He quickly pulled himself together. He had to appear unfazed by Nessa's presence. Gia knew the whole story, and he bet she was coming over just to check on how he felt seeing his former love. Gia had noticed that he couldn't take his eyes from Nessa. Had it been only an instant ago that he couldn't stop looking at her? The smile had gone from her face, and she approached, an angry look in her dark eyes.

"I know, Gia, and I am fine. I have no feelings for Nessa."

"Are you absolutely sure?" she replied, screwing up her eyes, as if better to see the truth. He pulled her to him, and gave her a gentle shake.

"Of course. I didn't know you when I was involved with Nessa."

"And if you had known me then?"

Drax smiled suggestively and squeezed her thin waist,

"I'd have still wanted to ravish you and spend my life looking into your sexy black eyes. Why, my life with you is full of passion and excitement, as well as stimulating intellectually," he added, making an attempt to make his seductive smile, more serious. She hit him playfully.

"You better find me stimulating intellectually, or else."

"Or else, what?" he made to nuzzle her long graceful neck, but she moved away, laughing.

"No, Drax, not here. I have a reputation as a sophisticated woman of class to uphold."

"My love, you have more class and sophistication in your little finger than these women have in their entire being." She gave him a quick kiss on the tip of his nose.

"Her husband is the one the ladies are hurrying to see." She glanced up at him slyly. He met her sly glance, and pulled his mouth down in a slight sneer.

"You fancy him do you?"

Gia assumed a disdainful look of appraisal.

"He's not bad for his age. In fact, that makes him even more attractive. He has a really sexy wide grin, great teeth, fantastic blue eyes…Ah." She gave a mock shiver of sexual arousal. "Oh, Drax, I've got to admit to a deep attraction. Oh, he is the best the French have yet produced. I am not usually gullible to their charm, but this man, with his fabulous face, strong, yet classy physique, what I know about his adventurous life and courageous views, they all certainly produce a frisson of sexual interest." She stopped waxing erotic, and smiled up at him. He just stood there, looking at her with a smidgeon of disdain. She sobered, playfully. "Not my type of course."

"I am glad to hear it." He tried to kiss her on her neck again, but Selena came waltzing over, a sappy look on her face,

"Oh, Gia, isn't he gorgeous?" she gushed, hugging herself rapturously.

"She's not bad either," Drax said, in a tone of cold, calculating appraisal. Gia gave him a sharp, pointed look, he chose to smirk at.

"She is an old flame of my husband's."

"No, really?" Selena was like a Pointer sensing game.

Drax was less than amused, and he gave Gia a look of much tried patience. She repented. Drax never liked his personal life put out for public consumption. He, like his father before him, was a very private and reserved man. She had done it as a form of jealous revenge, to punish him for ever having loved another woman, but especially an incredible woman, like Nessa Devos. She gave him an apologetic glance, while leading Selena away, in an attempt to distract her. Selena kept looking back at Drax. She obviously wanted to know more, and would be a nuisance from now on. He hoped that Gia would drop her. He couldn't for the life of him think why she'd made friends with Selena in the first place. Drax sighed deeply. Blast the stupid woman, and blast Gia for being so silly! He took a fresh glass of champagne from a passing waiter, and he kept his eyes on anything but the people present. He didn't want to catch a glimpse of Nessa again. She had flooded his being, even while he was teasing Gia. He loved Gia, of course, he did. He wouldn't change his life for anything or anyone, except for that whole stupid episode over Rory. He'd change that in a heartbeat.

He knew Greg and Laura wrote to Rory and Syb, and had visited them in Leningrad, but they'd said they had been watched, and Rory's apartment, while very comfy and beautifully done out, was bugged. Rory and Syb had been cautious, and they'd been deeply moved by the visit, but the farewells had been difficult. Greg said, they'd just write in future. It was easier on them all.

Greg told him that Nessa and Raf visited Rory and Syb often. The Russians were more amenable to the French. Rory's socialist parents had visited often too. Rory's father, the socialist bishop, and Raf Devos had tried to get Rory's books published in Europe and Britain under a pseudonym, but to no avail. The public did not know Rory and Sybil Ellis-Rhys's true story. To family and friends, Rory and Syb were traveling the world. Rory's parents made up mail from them from all over the place to show relatives. Even the other Cambridge Spies who had fled to Moscow did not know what had happened to them, such was the agreement reached by Emil and Harold Macklin with the Americans and the Russians after Drax's betrayal.

Greg said that Rory had been allowed to write, so long as he wrote textbooks on ancient languages. These were published under a false Russian name, Yuri Elisanof. He was allowed to edit government papers, and he could write novels, but they were not published. Syb was allowed to teach math in schools, and she had written articles and books on mathematics. She actually enjoyed her work. She and Rory lived under the false names of Yuri and Sara Elisanof. Their families and Greg and Laura, Raf and Nessa wrote to them, using these assumed names. The world press never got so much as a hint of the deception. Rory and Syb did not write back. It had been their choice apparently, but everyone understood that it would be easier for them that way.

Drax finally looked up, and thankfully couldn't see Nessa anywhere. He caught a glimpse of Raf Devos, and he was impressive. He wore his sixty-six years well – too well, damn him! Wait a moment; people were stirring. Ah, they were leaving. He had to have one more look at her. There she was, emptying his mind of everything, but how she had looked when they'd made love.

"Drax!"

Damn, not now; he felt so desperately frustrated by the interruption, even if it were Gia.

"Drax, I think it is time we left. Marti will be waiting for us as it is. The teachers will be cross at having to stay with her until we come." Drax tried to find an excuse for stretching up to see over heads, but he knew he couldn't, Gia was watching him intently, as she pulled on her gloves. She put her arm through his, and before he knew it, they were outside on the rain-soaked sidewalk, waiting for their car, which was stuck in the long line of chauffer-driven limousines. The rain was coming down in earnest.

"God! Gia couldn't we have waited inside?"

She didn't answer. She was watching Nessa and Raf get into their chauffer-driven car. They were laughing. Nessa always had loved the rain. They looked very much in love. The car doors were closed, and their driver began to pull cautiously out into the busy traffic. Gia looked up at him.

"There she goes."

"Who?"

"Drax, please do not insult my intelligence."

"Why should I bother? You are doing a good job of it yourself."

Their car pulled up. Drax let Gia enter, while he walked around to the other side, and got in quickly, forcing himself not to look for Nessa's car in the traffic jam ahead.

Nessa and Raf snuggled in the back of the car. She let her eyes drift to the side mirror. There he was, about to get into the car with his beautiful Hispanic wife. She had seen them laughing together, their arms linked. He had nuzzled her neck. Nessa had felt a momentary heartache, but she'd tried to shrug it off, along with the almost instantaneous rush of images: of being locked in his arms, their bodies entwined, while snow storms raged outside; of rolling intimately together in the surf at twilight, and watching him stand there with her father, and remembering, wishing that he could be with her always, that they would have a wonderful life together, and then came the hurt of his rejection in China, his lack of concern when she had been in danger. She looked over at Raf, who was watching her, a look of concern on his incredible face. He squeezed her hand, inquiring if she were okay. She smiled and nodded. Yes, she was more than okay. She had Raf and Raoul, and she wouldn't change them for the world. How lucky could a gal get? She found it hard not to watch until he had disappeared from view, but Raf suddenly patted her shoulder, and she turned away.

"He is a very attractive man. Did you want to talk to him?"

Nessa shook her head by way of reply, and she laid her head on his shoulder. He ruffled her hair.

"I was curious to see how he'd aged. Raf, my darling, you have nothing to worry about, as all those women back there showed you. I was very proud."

Raf smiled, and kissed the top of her head.

"They only show me how very lucky I am to have you. I do, don't I?"

"You never need to doubt that, my love."

The coast above Santa Barbara: 1971:
Emil and Magda Franz had died within a year of each other in 1959. He had been eighty-eight years old, and Magda, eighty-six. Five years later, Marc Franz opened 'The Emil and Magda Franz Institute for Humanitarian Studies in Art, Music, Science, Medicine and Literature' in Hamburg, near the docks, and not far from Magda's old bookshop and art gallery, The Page & Canvas. Twelve years later, he opened a similar institute on the Santa Barbara coast, just above Emil and Magda's former home, where Marc and Tsai's eldest daughter now lived with her husband and infant daughter.

The Franz Institute was a beautiful building made of glass and natural rock, and was surrounded by trees and small arbors and gardens, where conference members could sit and talk, or find inspiration in silent contemplation. There were small lily covered lakes and ponds, in which beautifully colored koi swam lazily about. Small fountains provided water for the many birds. Bees, butterflies, dragonflies and hummingbirds darted from flower to flower, tree to tree.

The opening ceremony was to commemorate the anniversary of what would have been Emil's hundredth birthday.

"Who said there wasn't a paradise?" Nessa whispered to Raf. "This must be as close to Heaven as we can get here on Earth. It was how Emil wanted life to be."

A memorial service had been held in Hamburg back in 1964, when the Franz Institute there had been opened, but that had been strictly a German affair, the guests limited to local dignitaries, old friends from before the war and family. Ness and Raf had been on assignment in Algeria at the time, so she was glad of this second chance to honor Emil and Magda, along with all their other American friends.

Nessa, Laura, Greg, Sigi, Ben and Cat were in attendance – all Emil's former agents, with the exception of Syb, Rory, Kerr, Biff and 'Nika' Chatsle. Kerr and Biff were in Viet Nam, on secret missions. Sigi had given up on Kerr years ago. She had left movies too, refusing to grow old on screen in pathetic bit parts, or playing aging dowagers in television specials, as Bette Davis, Jane Wyman, Barbara Stanwyck, Lorna Trevelayan and Mandy were doing. Fiona and Alisyn were acting in on and off Broadway productions, and both had been awarded every stage-acting accolade there was. They were considered the grand dames of American theater. Sigi had gone into real estate with her son and daughter, whose father had been jettisoned a long time ago. She opened her own conference center in the Rocky Mountains of Colorado, where she had re-created the intellectual café society of Vienna, Bucharest and Budapest. It was a sort of elegant 'think tank', where ideas could be exchanged by people who were considered to be the best and most innovative in their fields of endeavor. She named it after her brilliant parents, 'The Max and Sonya Andrus Society for Intellectual Exchange'.

The older parental generation was represented at the Commeration too, by Jeb and Loretta and Steven. Jeb and Loretta were in their late seventies, bordering on eighty, and Steven had just turned eighty. Esperanza and the Franzs' maid, Marisol, had died; Esperanza, five years ago and Marisol just recently. Loretta still missed Esperanza dreadfully. Many of Jeb's old friends and partners had died, leaving their land to their sons, who carried on the cooperative. Jeb had retired, but he and Loretta stayed on in their house in the Sierra Madres. Their orchards were looked after by Esperanza's nephew, Juan, and his family. Jeb would leave the house and land to them when he died. Loretta and Jeb had decided that, if one outlived the other, he or she would take up Raf and Nessa's kind invitation to live with them.

Greg's Uncle Harold had died in a car crash, shortly after Syb and Rory had left for Russia. Greg, Laura and Emil had suspected that his 'fatal accident' had been arranged, but by whom: his adversaries in MI5 and MI6, or by the vengeful element in the CIA, or all of them? Nessa had been stunned when Raf had voiced similar concerns, when she had told him about her work for Emil and Harold during the war.

Raf had worked with them frequently, both during the war and after. He knew of Biff's undercover work for the 'good' CIA, spying on the warmongers. He knew of Rudy Von Silvren and 'Simon', and had worked with them during the war, and he had known of Nika Chatsle and Ben Robie's work, and of Kerr Toddy's work in Indochina.

"We, in the French Intelligence Service, are trying to protect Kerr's and Biff's backs. These are dangerous times throughout the world."

Nessa had been surprised. She did not know that Raf still worked with French Intelligence. He assured her that he did not, but he had them keep him up to date on Biff's and Kerr's welfare. They knew that Nika Chatsle could look after herself more effectively than they could.

"Are you a Red Dragon?"

Raf had laughed.

"No. I exert influence through my freelance journalism, and, therefore, I cannot be a Dragon. Neither can you, Ness, for the same reason."

Nessa was looking forward to seeing Laura, Greg, Ben and Cat. She had written to Cat, begging her to attend the American opening too, even though she had been part of the private German ceremony. Cat had written that of course she would be there. Ben had been hoping he'd see Kerr and Biff, but they were too deeply involved in Viet Nam. Biff's son Andy, also with the 'good' CIA, was in Viet Nam too.

"Will Nika Chatsle be coming?" Nessa asked Cat. She was so keen to see this amazing woman.

"I also was keen to meet her," Cat replied. Ben worked closely with her in the Maquis, so I am a little jealous of her, but she will not be here. I asked Marc, and he said that Mrs.Chatsle had not known Emil and Magda very well. She had worked with Emil briefly in New York before he had placed her and Ben within the OSS, to keep an eye on things."

"John McDonnell, my daughter Rhian's fiancé, is Andrew Chatsle's good friend, and he told us that Andrew is in Viet Nam. John would be there too, but he was called up for a medical exam at the American air base near Cambridge, and fortunately, he was 4F. He has flat feet, allergies and gold fillings, but a lovely lad." Cat and Nessa chuckled together.

"Thank God for flat feet," Nessa replied.

"He is very upset about it all. He hates the war, thinks it is unjustified, but he has friends, like Andrew, involved in it, and he wants to do his bit."

"Tell him, he is very lucky. He doesn't have to die, and more importantly, he doesn't have to kill innocent people fighting for their independence."

Cat nodded in agreement. Both women knew what they were talking about.

"Do you know that Rudy von Silvren and Lev Tashvin are in their eighties now? That whole exciting generation is passing. My parents and Johannes are in their eighties. I am trying to get them to write their memoirs for my daughters, Rhian and Dominque," Cat whispered, just as Marc stepped up to the podium to begin the ceremony. Nessa managed one last piece of information on another one of the guests.

"The man over there, with the lady in the large grey hat with a black rose, he is Professor Alex Tanner. He worked with Emil during the war. He is in his seventies, but he looks older. He drinks pretty heavily."

"He looks as if he does. Poor soul, another victim of the war, I expect."

After the ceremony, Cat, Ben, Nessa, Raf, Greg and Laura made a tour of the galleries and libraries that made up the Institute. Cat told them about the old bookshop cum art gallery her mother, Magda and Veronique Gustafsen, Johannes first wife, had run as a sort of soup kitchen during the war, and after the first horrible war. Cat had grown up in that bookshop.

"It was called The Page & Canvas. I loved it. It was a special place…" Cat drifted away, as if some painful thought had come to her. Nessa asked if the place had been destroyed in the firestorm of 1943. Cat shook her head.

"It was damaged, but we re-built it. It is still going, and Magda and Emil, the Gustafsens and my parents renovated the buildings next to it into apartment houses for the homeless, and for refugees and immigrants, but The Page & Canvas is still a bookshop and art gallery. It is still magical."

"You seemed sad there for a moment. I thought that maybe it had gone."

Cat sighed and shook her head.

Just before they exited the building, Nessa gasped in surprise, for there on the wall was a photograph of 'Simon', but not in SS uniform. He wore a casual shirt and tie and tweed sports jacket. His one hand was raised, holding a pipe near his mouth, as if he had just removed it to smile.

Laura noticed her reaction:

"Wow, what a handsome guy! He looks like a film star, an English film star, classy, blond and fine featured, but he also looks so friendly and kind. He has kind eyes."

"Oh, Laura, he was stunning, and so charming and droll. I worked with him on that mission I went on in Germany, to check up on their development of an atom bomb. His code name was 'Simon'."

Cat rounded the corner to the exit and she froze, a startled look on her face, tears welling up in her eyes.

"Cat, did you know 'Simon' too?" Cat looked as if she were struggling to hold back the tears.

"All these memories are getting to me, I guess. Yes, I worked with 'Simon' in our anti-Nazi resistance work, rescuing folks from the clutches of the Nazis. He was very brave and daring."

"He was very attractive, as that photograph shows, but he wasn't the slightest bit interested in me," Nessa laughed, trying to make light of the situation, but she thought that maybe 'Simon' hadn't felt that way about Cat, nor she about him.

Cat just smiled, and shook her head. Nessa and Laura exchanged a quick questioning glance as Cat moved on out into the sunshine, and into Ben's waiting arms. Nessa glanced up at 'Simon' one more time before leaving, and his face was cast in shadow by the tall feathery evergreens outside. The kind, smiling eyes seemed suddenly, momentarily, sad.

"It says here that his name was Max von Alt, and that he was an unsung hero. They have the name 'Simon' underneath in parentheses." Laura added. Nessa grabbed her arm and led her out. "I think there's a story there," Laura said, nodding suggestively in Cat's direction.

"I am sure there is, but let it go."

Paddington Station, London, Spring, 1991:
Nessa, Laura and Greg waited under the big clock in the main concourse, as the express from Heathrow pulled, sleekly and elegantly, alongside its platform. Pigeons strutted about underfoot, amazingly managing to avoid being trodden on by passengers hastily evacuating their trains, or rushing to catch the next one.

"Thank god, it is a lovely day out there," sighed Greg. "The blue sky and puffy white clouds, the trees in new leaf and the myriads of daffodils will provide a fitting welcome. The daffodils made him think of Rory and how they would have been an especially touching welcome for him; being the emblem of Wales, along with the leek. God only knows, they had all had sad losses: Jeb and Loretta, Steven, and last year, Raf. He'd been eighty-six, and had died of a coronary. He and Ness had been to a concert, and were on their way home. It had been an awful shock for Ness, for them all. Raf had seemed so fit and active. They had only just returned from a trip to Berlin to see how east and west were merging now that the Berlin wall had been down for a year. Nessa was still pondering Raf's last words. He had a look of terror on his face, as he'd clutched at her coat sleeve. He had seemed desperate to tell her something.

"Not a heart…" but as he'd closed his wonderful blue eyes, he'd given up and managed to say the word, "Love." Nessa had been too devastated to think about it at the time.

When Gorbachev lifted all restrictions, Rory was all set to return home to Wales. He had written to them, saying how eager he was for them to be together again. He had so many ideas he wanted to share, and he wanted to catch up on what they had been doing. Ness and Raf had sent him copies of their works, and Greg had sent sketches. It had been wonderful to be able to fully communicate again. Rory had not contacted Drax, although Drax had written to him.

The world at large still was not aware of Rory's and Syb's presence in Russia. There had been eager inquiries when Rory's stories were published in America and Europe under his own name. Many of their old university friends, friends from Bletchley days and the navy were writing to the publishers to get Rory and Syb's current address. Rory's books were well received. There was talk of a Nobel Prize for literature. Then Rory had a massive coronary and died.

The Russians regretted that, as no one ever knew of Rory's presence in Russia, they could not honor him as they had honored Kim Philby, one of the Cambridge spies, who had openly been exposed in the world press, and had defected to Russia. The British and American secret services couldn't honor him openly either, just as they hadn't been able to honor Biff Chatsle's bravery as an undercover agent, spying on the cabal of warmongers. He had died in a 'car accident' in the early seventies. Someone in the CIA had betrayed Biff. Raf had learned, through his sources, that Nika and Andy Chatsle were keeping a low profile, but together with Kerr Toddy and other reliable friends in the CIA, they were planning their revenge.

The crowds cleared, and there she was, carrying a large case, and striding along the way she always had done. Tears came to their eyes, and sobs of joy filled their throats and hearts to see her, to have Syb home at last. They began to laugh through their tears. Greg waved enthusiastically. She had a wide smile too, through her tears, and she began to run, despite the case. They pushed their way through the throng of passengers to run to her. They clashed in a foursome hug, laughing and crying and kissing, each taking turns to hold her face in their hands, and tell her with their eyes and their embraces, for words just stuck in their throats, how wonderful it was to have her there in front of them after all these years. Syb was sobbing and laughing and shaking her head, until the sadness, the irony of it all took over, and she sobbed for real, her shoulders heaving with emotion. It hurt so much. It was so unfair. She crumpled into their arms. They led her to a side bench, away from the crowd, not that anyone noticed them. The crowds were too caught up in their own haste to get to where they had to be.

"It is too, too cruel," Syb cried through her tears and runny nose. Nessa gave her some tissues. They sighed and commiserated with her, tears running down their faces. "Every step of the way, I worried there would be some snafu, that would mean I'd have to go back. I couldn't quite believe it, when there I was, in that wonderful plane, flying over the English Channel, the surf breaking on the shores of home. We descended through the clouds, and then suddenly, there below, were the green fields, the villages, the busy roads. Oh God, please let him have been with me, and not just in that bloody box. The sheep with their newborn lambs, the cows and horses, the old country homes, and then London, all these scenes were too, too much. Do you know that our plane flew right up the Thames? We passed the Houses of Parliament and dear old Big Ben and over Buckingham Palace and the parks, their gardens full of spring flowers, and, of course, millions of daffodils, raising their brave little golden trumpet heads, as if to herald our return. Oh, I am sorry. I always got silly when I returned home during the war. I just love it all so very much."

"Oh Syb, we understand. It must have been something. You haven't been home for forty years or so."

Syb straightened up, and took a deep breath:

"And I came home with Rory," her face crumpled into tears again. They hung their heads.

Finally, they got her calmed down enough to leave with them, to go to a flat they had rented in Westbourne Terrace, near Paddington Station.

That night, while a gentle spring rain ran down the French windows that opened onto a narrow balcony, they sat in their pajamas, leaning against comfortable big cushions on deep, cozy sofas, mugs of coffee, laced with rum, in their hands. The air was redolent of the fish and chips they'd had for dinner at Syb's request, complete with salt and vinegar, and wrapped in newspaper. Syb had devoured them with relish, and wiping her mouth afterwards, she'd crumpled up the greasy newspaper, and positively collapsed in delight.

"Oh, that was marvelous! I haven't enjoyed such a meal for so long! Oh God! Rory would have loved it."

They collected Rory's coffin from the customs shed the next day. They had hired a hearse from a funeral home in Merthyr Tydfil. It had been driven from Wales to Heathrow the day before. They followed it in a car they had rented, and the sad little cortege headed west in the pouring rain to the Welsh mining valleys. Syb had Greg overtake the hearse, and stop the Welsh side of the Severn Estuary that formed the border between Wales and England. They stood in the rain, and watched Rory cross the border. Nessa and Laura stood a few feet behind Sybil, tears streaming down their faces. Syb stood alone at the side of the road, clutching a bouquet of daffodils. She looked so forlorn, so tragic, yet she straightened and held her head high as Rory passed, and she blew him a kiss. Greg saluted. Laura and Nessa bowed their heads in tribute.

The minister prayed in Welsh, and the Ddraig Goch, the Welsh Red Dragon flag, was removed from the coffin, folded and given to Syb. Rory's coffin was lowered into the soil. They threw in handfuls of earth. Syb rested the daffodils near the gaping hole. The men filled in the grave, while they retired to the minister's home nearby for lunch. After lunch, they returned to the filled in grave, and Syb placed the daffodils on it. Another Welsh warrior had been brought home to rest, and, miracle of miracles, the sun broke through the heavy grey rain clouds, to bathe the grave and its small group of mourners in a golden light. They raised their hands in a loving farewell, and smiled through their tears. Syb, with a look of joyous wonder on her face, whispered into the sun,

"God speed, my love."

They spent the next few days reminiscing and catching up on more recent news.

"Raoul is married to a fellow doctor. They work for 'Doctors Without Borders'. They are out in Central Africa, helping the poor souls there. Francoise wrote to say that she is pregnant, so I hope they come to their senses and come home soon. They will live in my apartment in Paris. I have bought a lovely little home on the coast, just above Pismo Beach. It is on a promontory overlooking the sea, in a small glade surrounded by trees. I love it. You all must come and stay. We can sit out on the patio and watch the sun set over the sea, while we sip our cocktails."

"Sounds lovely Ness, and Syb, Laura and I will take you up on your kind offer, and you and Syb must visit us. We live in a cozy log cabin in a wood a few miles south of Vancouver. I have my studio out in the wood, and Laura and I spend our days wallowing in the natural beauty around us."

"I gather your parents left you their country estate, Syb."

Syb nodded:

"It has been in the care of the solicitors, lawyers, as you Yanks say, and accountants in my absence. I didn't give them the okay to sell, as I knew that somehow, sometime, Rory and I would be allowed to return home. It is too large for me, so I shall sell, and buy a cottage on the Gower in South Wales. Rory always loved going there before the war. I intend to visit you all often, and you must visit me."

Before they went their separate ways, Greg asked Syb how she felt about Drax.

"He has a townhouse in the Beacon Hill area of Boston, and the old family home on the Cape. He is seventy-six, and a widower. Gia died a year ago. He is bereft. He kept on working. He told me that the economic situation still bears watching. There are a lot of shenanigans going on, but then, when haven't there been? He tries to keep his investments and businesses on an honest track. He, along with some other wealthy guys, founded an eco-conservation and wildlife trust, and they are funding research on safe, effective ways to clean up the pollution from fossil fuels, nuclear waste and other toxic chemicals. They want to extend the wilderness areas to protect animals, so that they have the freedom to roam safely and unmolested over larger distances, and are not confined to national parks. Needless to say, they do not support hunting by humans, but support efforts to bring back non-human predators, and let them and their prey reach a healthy balance. Drax has found solace, after Gia's death, in being out in the wilderness, working with animals. He was also instrumental in having the American government apologize to the people of the Aleutians. They suffered horribly during the war. They were evacuated to less than desirable quarters on the Alaskan mainland, and our forces ruined their homes, some of our lads taking or destroying some of their dearly cherished possessions in their absence.

Drax has composed some beautiful pieces of music. His daughter, Martine, has helped him record his works, and she's got them out there, so that the public can appreciate his genius at last."

"How old is his daughter?" Syb asked, not meeting Greg's eyes.

"Thirty-three or four. She is an academic; a musical historian, and teaches at Harvard and Wellesley. Her husband is a physicist, quite brilliant. He is into nanotechnology at MIT, and gives seminars at Cal Tech in the summer months. Martine has inherited her father's musical ability, but she won't play publicly. She is an active fund-raiser for Drax's causes, and serves on the board of this wildlife protection consortium. She is a handsome woman..."

"Greg means that she is not a beauty," Laura interrupted.

"Well, that's not fair, Laura. She has rather broad features, very dark heavy eyebrows, dark eyes, but those looks are coming into fashion again. She is tall and quite slender. In any case, her husband adores her. They have three young daughters, and Drax can't stop singing the praises of all of them. He is very close to his daughter. She will take over his business concerns one day. He has prepared her well."

"Have you been in contact with Drax, Ness?"

Nessa shook her head:

"No, I don't need to."

"Neither do I," said Syb. Laura and Greg exchanged looks of well-at-least- we-tried.

Nessa's Cottage, north of Pismo Beach, California, Spring, 2005: The two elderly women sat in wicker chairs, plaid blankets wrapped around their legs, creamy-white woolen Aran sweaters pulled up to their chins. The sun was warm, but the sea breeze had a chill to it. They had sunglasses on to more safely watch the sun begin its descent into the purple-green waters.

"You see that big wall of cloud forming out there?"

Syb nodded.

"That will descend on us soon, covering us in thick moist mist, and you'll hear the old ancient lighthouse on the next promontory sound its eerie warnings."

"Nice that it is still there. They all have radar and sonar now, and computer maps to show them where the dangers are. Tell me about this young woman again, Ness."

"Her thesis was based on my political writings and on my screenplays. She knew about my early life, my intelligence work during the war, my involvement in leftist, liberal movements with Raf. Laura didn't tell her about you and Rory, but as Rory is now a world renowned author, she did say that she and Greg had met you both before the war, and that was all. Laura didn't tell her about Drax and me either, but the girl did ask about the friendship she knew Greg and Laura had with Drax Shaw, the philanthropist businessman and brilliant composer. She was interested in their involvement with environmental and wildlife concerns. She actually quizzed Laura on the work we did during the war. She had found out about Laura's work with Stephenson and Canadian Intelligence, and she knew that I had been in Naval Intelligence and had been to Bletchley, knew Turing and had worked on the Manhattan Project."

Syb grimaced and pursed her lips.

"They drilled the necessity of keeping quiet about our work at Bletchley into us so well, on pain of death, as I recall, that I find I cannot speak coherently about it. I had to bury it deep in my brain while I was in Russia. That was forty, and more, years of burying information so deeply in my brain, that I cannot easily retrieve it."

"That applies to Laura and me too. They have Bletchley on display for the public now. I often wonder how Turing would feel, if he could come back today, and see how far his ideas on computers have come. They were horrid to him, you know, after the war. He was arrested for improper homosexual advances to some young man, who had set him up. They forced him to take female hormones. The effects were so awful that he took poison and died. What a tragic end for such a brilliant man!"

"I detest the fucking establishment," Syb growled. "We need a whole new, progressive, enlightened way of doing things. We hoped for that after the war – the end of an unfair class system, but capitalists and communists put an end to that, and left us with the same old same-old."

"Worse than that – these fundamental religions saw their opportunity to rush in and fill the vacuum when the communists fell. America liked that. Religions oppose communism and distract the people from working for their rights."

Syb nodded her head in sad agreement. Nessa got up and collected their glasses.

"The others should be here soon. They should have had a clear sunny day for the drive down Highway One from San Francisco. I hope the mist didn't settle in there early."

"Is she writing about your Hollywood days?"

"Yep. Gosh, Syb, they've all gone. Fiona and Lorna died in the mid-nineties. They were in their late eighties. They died alone, no families. Sigi died in 2001, in her eighties, but she had family around her. Mandy died in 2003. She was eighty-three. She had a daughter from one brief marriage, and they were close. Alisyn died in the arms of her young lover in 1999, just before the new millennium. She was seventy-nine, so she missed reaching eighty."

"How old was the young lover?"

"I am not sure. In his forties, I think, but he loved her dearly, and has gone to great lengths to publish photos of her life, her movies and plays, and to remind people how very brave she was, taking on McCarthy and his bullies. We need to be reminded of her taking on the establishment, and how incredibly beautiful she was."

"God, Ness! You are handing that girl a whale of a story on a plate! What do you think of her?"

Nessa sat down again. She bit her lower lip, an anxious look on her face.

"Ness, what is it?"

"A man came to see me the other day. He had worked for Emil. He had been one of the communist lads Simon had hidden within the SS. He had seen Simon, Kurt, Danny and Marthe uncovered as spies and killed brutally before the Allies could liberate them. He escaped to Hamburg to tell Emil's friends there what had happened. They suggested that he could still be useful to the communists by staying in the SS. Obviously the SS hadn't tumbled to Addi, that's his name, being a communist spy in their ranks, as he hadn't been arrested at Flossenberg with Simon and the others. Emil's spymaster, Rudy von Silvren, suspected that the Americans would recruit former SS into their ranks, so they could help in the fight against the communists. Unknown to the Americans, the Soviets had spies, like Addi, already in the SS, so when America took these guys into the OSS, later the CIA, Stalin's spies came in with them. Addi told me that after Emil died, he had worked with Kerr Toddy, Biff Chatsle and Nika, as well as with Rudy and Raf. Addi was part of the good guy set up within the CIA…"

Syb interrupted her,

"And he was a Red Dragon, not a communist, Ness, as were Rudy, Rory and I."

"I'd guessed that." Ness gave Syb a big hug. "Addi said that Biff had penetrated some Zurt Enterprise thing, armaments dealers, military suppliers, oilmen, a whole cabal of evil, with guys inside our intelligence services and media, but he'd been betrayed and killed back in the early seventies. His son was in the CIA by then, and he worked with Kerr and Addi, but he went missing in Viet Nam. He'd been rescued by Dragons, but when his father was murdered, he was also exposed and could not return to the States. This cabal knew that his father had told him everything. Kerr was murdered, then Nika, in what appeared to be accidents. Andy Chatsle and the other good guys in the CIA helped expose a senator in the pay of this cabal, and brought down one branch of their evil influence, but others remained. Do you remember the Caventry Scandal?" Syb nodded. "Well the son of that family detested them so much, that he helped bring an end to the Caventrys and their sick ways. He joined the good guys, and changed his name to Felspar.

Addi went on to tell me that Raf and Rory had been murdered. I told him that I had suspected as much, as Raf had been desperate to try and tell me that he hadn't had an heart attack."

Syb hung her head, tears cascaded down her wrinkled cheeks.

"I knew that too. Our Russian friends, Dragons, warned us to be careful, but Rory was too ecstatic to be going home, and we were so busy reveling in our new-found freedom and Russia's to take precautions. We were tired of it all. We had to live like that for over forty years. We wanted to be free. When Rory was killed, our Dragon friends got me out to …safety?" Syb looked up at Ness in alarm.

Nessa shook her head.

"Not yet, Syb, I am afraid. Addi and Charles Felspar and the good guys have been hampered in trying to find the traitor in their ranks, who had betrayed Biff and Andy. Charles was killed for helping to bring down the Caventry branch of this Zurt Enterprises thing. Addi has remained undetected all these years. Now he has retired. The assassinations of all his friends, the good guys, made him decide that he had to warn me. He risked his cover and his life to visit me. He knew that Biff's son has information that could topple the whole Cabal. The bad guys suspect that the rest of Emil's little band may know this information too. They were going to let us grow old and die off, but there are indications that actions against them are underway, most probably fueled by us. They are right. Drax and Martine and others are instigating this clean up and are powerful enough to do it without alerting the public at large. Things will improve, and the people will never guess how or why. It may take a few years yet, but change is in the air, and it will come from the younger generation and wealthy people with a more progressive social conscience, like Drax and his daughter. Addi decided to forgo retirement and work with Drax."

Syb grinned:

"Dragons never retire. Thank God! Not entirely the young though, eh? Drax and Laura, you and me and Addi, we're no spring chickens. We are well into our eighties."

"And as dangerous as ever to this cabal."

"You bet. We can go out fighting to the last for a change for the better."

"Drax is back in the fold then?"

"He told Laura he is carrying on the fight for Greg and Rory."

"Nice of him."

Nessa nudged Syb's shoulder.

"Come on, let's mend fences."

Syb stood up.

"So, who is the traitor?"

"Addi and Kerr had their suspicions over the years, but no tangible proof. They had worked out a code. If either of them were in trouble, they would somehow try to mark the killer's identity on a list of suspects they kept with them always. Kerr managed to do this. He had a visit from an old colleague in the CIA, now retired, as was Kerr. Before the man killed him, Kerr had time to write down a number on his phone pad. Addi searched through Kerr's study after his death. He saw the number on the pad, just before the CIA collected all Kerr's papers and files. The number four was the person they had suspected all along. Alex Tanner had retired several years before, and was well on in years. He died from natural causes resulting from his alcoholism, wouldn't you know!"

"So, it was Alex Tanner. Then who are they sending for us?"

The mist had descended just as Gilly Toms and Laura arrived, Gilly driving carefully down the track to Nessa's cottage. They greeted one another with hugs and kisses. Ness asked after Maudey and Catsby. Laura replied that Wilby was looking after them. He adored them, and they loved staying with him. He spoiled them so.

Once settled after a light, but delicious dinner, with cocktails, Gilly began her research for her novel. This was to be recollections of a more personal nature that Gilly would write as a work of fiction. The factual stuff was in the process of being written up for Gilly's next magnum opus on women at war.

"I don't know why you ladies don't write your own memoirs."

"We're too old to tackle the potholes in our memory lanes," Syb said in her usual disdainful drawl. The others concurred. They were widows now, in their late eighties.

"We can't be bothered to look up the actual dates of events. We just like re-running the movie in our memories for as long as those memories hold out, and the reels are running down, the pictures getting fuzzier, and the sound track slowing to a long drawn out moan with each passing day," laughed Laura.

"You have described only the fun adventures. You must have had moments of panic, terror, doubt and sadness."

"We don't remember them," snapped Syb.

They talked until dawn, had a cup of coffee, and then they went for a walk along the beach. Gilly watched them cavort about in the wet sand, running away from breaking waves that lapped gently at their old, blue-veined feet. She dipped her toes in the sea, and watched the waves ebb and flow, and thought of the years that must have come and gone for them.

Nessa, Syb and Laura stopped larking about, and linked arms, as the waves ebbed and flowed around them. They thought back to that December of 1941, when they had stood just like this, only wrapped in the arms of the young men they had loved. They had been about to go off to war. Had it been sixty-four years ago? It seemed so fresh in their minds, the love and longing still so real in their hearts.

Syb glanced up at Gilly Toms, who had climbed up on a rock a little farther down the beach from them, the rising sun behind her, so that Syb had to raise her hand and screw up her eyes to see her more clearly, and even then she could not quite make her out.

"Where does Gilly come from?" she whispered.

Laura and Nessa followed Syb's eyes and squinted up at Gilly.

"She comes from a very wealthy family, who made their wealth from real estate in the early 1900s in Southern California," Nessa whispered back. They came originally from Wisconsin and Texas, I think. They own lots of land in the San Fernando Valley, acquired about the time of the Owens Valley scheme that hurt my family and so many other innocent families, and made so many of our ruthless profiteers so wealthy and powerful."

"So this is who they sent?" Syb whispered, the contempt evident in her voice.

"'Fraid so, but it is all taken care of, so don't worry."

"I feel so confused. I still can't forgive Drax for what he did to us. His father must have known the truth behind it all."

"Drax only learned of that after it was too late, but he has made up for it and then some since. He has built up a formidable opposition to these Profiteers, and will bring them down."

"You also knew of this, Ness?" Syb asked, turning from Laura to Ness.

"Not until Laura filled me in on Drax's efforts at Christmas, and like you, Syb, I had conflicting emotions about it all, but I was awed by all the good Drax and his daughter have managed to achieve, and…." Nessa's voice trailed off as she noticed that the other two had frozen, their eyes riveted on Gilly, who was pointing a gun, fitted with a silencer, at them.

Nessa squeezed their arms gently.

"I love you, guys."

There was a popping sound. They had closed their eyes in expectation of the shots, concerned about one another, who would be first, but then they realized that they were alive. They turned in amazement, and saw that Gilly was being led up the beach by two young women. Black vans had come screeching up the track, scattering sand and gravel into the air. Men and women in dark glasses and suits were spilling out of the vans, guns raised. Then they suddenly lifted their arms, dropping their weapons, as other men and women emerged out of the trees and had them surrounded. Nessa, Laura and Syb scrambled up the bank to join them, laughing gaily with incredible relief. They watched, smiles on their old wrinkled faces as the men and women, Gilly, one of them, were driven away by their captors. A young man approached them:

"Chalk up another one for us. These guys have had their day, but ever onwards, there are still others with whom we have to deal. Good morning, ladies." He saluted them, his eyes softening with respect and admiration for all these old ladies had achieved to make this a better world. They had been in great danger. It could have backfired on them, yet here they were, hugging and laughing."

"Diolch yn fawr." Nessa said, hearing his Welsh accent. "Thank you so very much."

"We thank you, ladies. That took a lot of courage, but then that is nothing new for you three. Are you all settled up and ready to leave?" They nodded.

"Come on then, let's be off to the Mountain."

⸻

Rockport, Massachusetts, Autumn, 2005:
The little white wooden art gallery on the corner of the main street was holding an end of season exhibit of Magda Franz's paintings of the North Sea coast of Germany. It was a mellow late afternoon, and the sunflowers still bloomed in the white fenced gallery garden.

The two elderly ladies, who manned the desk, stopped their fussing to listen to the strains of the beautiful nocturne the old gentleman played on the grand piano. He had been their only visitor that day. The polished wooden floors of the gallery, and the white walls on which Magda's paintings hung, reflected the hazy golden rays of the setting sun. The music seemed an excellent accompaniment for those pastel seascapes. A woman entered. They recognized her as the younger woman, who had left the old gentleman there while she went off to do some errand or other. They had come before, usually at the season's change. The elderly ladies exchanged smiles with her. She had short dark, graying hair, in a pageboy style. She had broad features, and a lovely smile. She wore a rather voluminous rust brown coat over her beige suit, and she had a beige woolen scarf stylishly arranged around her neck. She went through to the gallery. The man had given them a rather magical experience that they would not forget for a long time. The ethereal airs he had played exquisitely, right out of memory, requiring no sheets of music. He had stopped playing, once he'd heard the gallery door open, and he stood and retrieved his walking stick. He was still a very smart-looking man; tall, broad shouldered, wearing an expensive cashmere driving coat over a brown tweed suit. He had a dark brown woolen scarf around his neck, but his balding head was bare, the remaining hair white. The old ladies smiled as the couple left, no words were exchanged, that would have made the experience too real, and the old ladies so wanted the magic to remain. In their minds, they wondered if she were his daughter, or much younger wife. She was very solicitous of him either way. She offered him her arm to lean on, and he took it, despite having a walking stick. He had given an inquiring glance at the woman as they had left, and she had smiled warmly and given his arm a squeeze. It seemed as if her loving response had lifted a weight off his shoulders, for he straightened and smiled happily into the setting sun. The old ladies remained silent, watching the couple disappear into the purple and scarlet twilight. Eventually one of them asked the other if she knew the name of the beautiful ethereal piece he had played. The other shook her head sadly.

"Who are they, I wonder?"

He sat in the passenger seat, while she drove along the coast road. His mind was far away in time and place:

1941:
It was dawn, the sea whispered and the breeze disturbed the drapes. He looked back at her watching him, her long slender golden brown form lying on the bed, inviting him to go back and make passionate love to her. She must have guessed his thoughts, for her turquoise blue eyes moistened, and her pale pink lips parted in a seductive smile. Her short blonde hair curled around her beautiful face.

"You are into the music," she whispered. "What are you composing?
"You!"

※

A short man, curly brown hair, twinkling blue eyes, ran down the steep rain-drenched street, lined by tall narrow houses that seemed to lean against one another. He carried a music case. The rain ran into his eyes from his soaking hair. He brushed his hair back with his bare hand. He had closed up the school after the choir practice, and he now struggled with the key to open the door to his travel agency. He disappeared inside for a few moments, and then returned, re-locked the glass door, on which was written the name Draig Goch Travels (Red Dragon Travels), and under the name: 'Eco-Tourism, visits to world conservation sites, sustainable energy tours, wildlife conservation programs world-wide, geological tours, lectures on cosmology, visits to Indigenous peoples to learn their culture, languages, beliefs and cures and a trip back in time to ancient world sites.'

The man got into a large white minibus, and headed off into the stormy night. The town gave way to fields that bordered a rocky coastline. At last, he saw big floodlights that lit up a small airport set in a field. The man drove through the security checkpoint, with its armed guards, and collected three elderly ladies who had arrived on a small private jet from France.

They drove through the night along the wild coast, and then they headed inland, until at last, in the grey light of pre-dawn they saw the Mountain, where others awaited them.

※

With apologies to Lewis Carroll's Alice In Wonderland:
The time has come, the Dragon said, to believe in other things, in Nature's rights and Nature's might, and the good revelation brings.

# ACKNOWLEDGEMENTS

I am deeply indebted to all the authors listed in the bibliography. The history and politics of Southern California at the turn of the century and into the forties are expertly described in Carey McWilliams book. The war in the Aleutians and Alaska, is brilliantly described by Brian Garfield, and by contributors to Alaska At War: 1941-1945, and The Forgotten War: Volume Two, by Stan Cohen. The mysterious exchanges that occurred between the Soviets and the Americans on the ALSIB route are described by Alexander B. Dolitsky, one of the contributors in Alaska At War: 1941-1945, in his section: The Alaska-Siberia and Lend-Lease Program. I placed Rory there in a fictional exchange of top-secret data from the Manhattan Project. The experiences of American pilots shot down in Russian territory are recorded in The Forgotten War: Volume Two, in a chapter by John R. Smith, " 'Mission' to the Soviet Union." In this chapter, Mr Smith recalls his own experiences as an American pilot shot down over Russian territory during the war, and his account inspired the experiences Drax and his crew had in Russia. The recollections of the brave people who lived and fought in the Aleutians and Alaska to defend America, and to help the Russians win their war against the Germans, are a must read, as are the recollections of the Japanese who fought there. The Aleutian people suffered badly during their evacuation to safer areas, and the inhabitants of Attu were taken as prisoners to Japan, where they were forced to do back breaking work. Their homes were occupied by American forces on the Aleutians, and possessions they left behind were often stolen or vandalized. They received an apology from the American Government in the 1980's. The experiences of these brave people, and the bravery of the forces who fought under these impossible conditions should not pass into time, unacknowledged. I thank Mr. Garfield and all the contributors to Alaska At War: 1941-1945 and The Forgotten War: Volume Two for their very informative and inspirational accounts. These helped me in forming the historical background for Drax and Greg, and briefly, Rory, in my novel.

Colonel William Eareckson is a real hero, whose actions and brilliant ideas and bravery, as described in my story, are true enough, but his involvement with my characters is fictional. Brian Garfield gives Colonel Eareckson a more fitting tribute in his work of nonfiction.

The Cambridge Spies, Kim Philby, Guy Burgess and Donald McClean are real persons, but their involvement with my characters and my imaginary plots is the work of fiction.

Rory's accusations that the Cambridge spies unknowingly had allowed the establishment to clamp down on socialist, leftist and liberal movements by creating fear in the people of communist infiltration at all levels of their society, came from Dai Smith's excellent book on Aneurin Bevan and the socialist and labor movements in South Wales in the late forties and early fifties.

My story is a work of fiction. The characters' exploits are works of fiction, as are their involvement with real life historical figures. The German scientists, Durning and Schleidt, and Andrei Bronstein and his family are not based on real-life people. The cabal of warmongers, Emil and Harold's secret organizations, and the Red Dragon Society, as described in this book, are works of fiction, as are the Page & Canvas bookshop, the Café des Bons

Mots, the Emil and Magda Franz Institutes, Sigi's Max and Sonya Andrus Society for Intellectual Exchange, and Zurt Enterprises. My characters are works of fiction, and are not based on any real persons, living or dead. Any similarities to persons living or dead, or to any real organizations, are coincidental.

I want to thank my husband for his technical help, his wise suggestions, and for the daunting task of proof reading and correcting my grammatical and punctuation errors. Most of all, I am extremely grateful for his endless patience and loving support through all the years of our life together. I want to thank my daughters, my son-in-law and grandsons for their love and encouragement. To all my family and friends, human and non-human, I extend my sincerest gratitude for creative sustenance. I also thank everyone at CreateSpace and Amazon Kindle for their helpful services.

Any mistakes of any kind are mine, and mine alone.

Davies McGinnis

# ABOUT THE AUTHOR

Davies McGinnis received her doctorate in animal behavior at the University of Cambridge, England. She was a postdoctoral fellow at Stanford University, a visiting professor at the University of Massachusetts Harbor Campus, and a research associate at Harvard University and The Kennedy School of Government. She is a native of Wales, and now lives in New Mexico with her husband.

OTHER TITLES BY DAVIES MCGINNIS
Five Cats of Hamburg
The House on Kalalua.

# BIBLIOGRAPHY AND SUGGESTED READINGS

- Chandonnet, Fern (editor), 2008, <u>Alaska At War: 1941-1945, The Forgotten War Remembered,</u> University of Alaska Press, Fairbanks.
  Within this volume:
    - Chandonnet, Fern, "The Recapture of Attu."
    - Dolitsky, Alexander B., "The Alaska-Siberia and Lend-Lease Program."
    - Jacobs, William A., "American Strategy in the Asian and Pacific War."
    - Kasukabe, Karl Kaoru, "The Escape of the Japanese Garrison from Kiska."
    - Neeley, Alastair, "The First Special Service Force and Canadian Involvement at Kiska."
    - Nishijima, Teruo, "Recalling The Battle of Attu."
- Cohen, Stan, 1993, <u>The Forgotten War, Volume Two: A Pictorial History of World War II in Alaska and Northwestern Canada</u>. Pictorial Histories Publishing Company, Missoula, Montana.
  Within this volume:
    - Smith, John R., " 'Mission' to the Soviet Union."

- Garfield, Brian, 1995, <u>The Thousand-Mile War: World War II in Alaska and The Aleutians</u>. University of Alaska Press, Classic Reprint Series, No. 4.
- Goff, Richard, 2004, <u>Cuba: A New History</u>. Yale University Press, New Haven and London.
- Hinde, Robert A. and Watson, Helene E. (eds), 1995<u>, War – A Cruel Necessity? The Bases of Institutionalized Violence</u>. Tauris Academic Studies, I. B. Tauris Publishers, London and New York.
- Hinde, Robert and Rotblat, Joseph, 2003, <u>War No More: Eliminating Conflict in the Nuclear Age,</u> Pluto Press, London and Sterling, Virginia.
- Hinde, Robert A., 2011, <u>Changing How We Live: Society from the Bottom Up</u>, Spokesman, The Russel Press, Ltd., Nottingham, England
- Hodges, Andrew, 2012, <u>Alan Turing: The Enigma</u>. The Century Edition. Princeton University Press, Princeton and Oxford.
- Kelley, Cynthia C. (editor), 2007, <u>The Manhattan Project: The Birth of the Atomic Bomb in the words of its Creators, Eyewitnesses and Historians</u>. Atomic Heritage Foundation, published by Black Dog & Levanthal Publishers, Inc. Distributed by Workman Publishing Company.
Within this volume:
    - Herken, Gregg, "Enormoz Espionage"
    - Holloway, David; Albright, Jacob and Kinstel, Marcia, "Jump Start for the Soviets."
    - Rhodes, Richard, "From France to The Black Forest: Seeking Atomic Scientists."

- McKay, Sinclair, 2011, <u>The Secret Life of Bletchley Park, The WWII Codebreaking Centre And The Men And Women Who Worked There</u>. Arum Press Ltd.
- McWilliams, Carey, 2010, <u>Southern California: An Island on the Land</u>. Gibbs Smith Publisher, Peregrine Smith Books, Salt Lake City.
- Navasky, Victor S., 2003, <u>Naming Names</u>. Hill and Wang: A Division of Farrar, Straus and Giroux, New York.
- Philby, Kim, 2002, <u>My Silent War: The Autobiography of A Spy</u>. The Modern Library, New York.
- Smith, Dai, 1994, <u>Aneurin Bevan and the World of South Wales</u>. Dinefwr Press, Llandybie, Dyfed. First published in 1993, Cardiff, University of Wales Press.

Made in the USA
Charleston, SC
13 January 2017